NOT PRESENT *or* FUTURE...

SHEL EUGENE COX

ISBN 978-1-63525-019-0 (paperback)
ISBN 978-1-63525-020-6 (digital)

Copyright © 2017 by Shel Eugene Cox

All rights reserved. No part of this publication may be reproduced, distributed, or transmitted in any form or by any means, including photocopying, recording, or other electronic or mechanical methods without the prior written permission of the publisher. For permission requests, solicit the publisher via the address below.

Christian Faith Publishing, Inc.
832 Park Avenue
Meadville, PA 16335
www.christianfaithpublishing.com

Printed in the United States of America

PROLOGUE

"All you want to do is start crap, Natalie!! I'm so tired of it!!"

The environment exploded from the confrontation in the master bedroom. It was so loud that the noise vibrated its way through the halls. There was nothing different about this night; nothing out of the ordinary. However, lately, it didn't take much to set off either of the two bedroom inhabitants. For some reason, on this night, the stage appeared to be set and the mood created the atmosphere conducive for an emotional perfect storm.

And that is exactly where the kids found themselves: right in the middle of a tornadic environment of tears, shouting, and blame.

Unable to escape the drama, Leesha went inside Ben Jr.'s room and picked him up from his crib. As she exited the room, carrying her baby brother in her arms, she quietly ran past T. J.'s room and opened the door, finding him hiding under his covers.

"Come, on, T.J.," she whispered, trying not to make any more sounds than necessary.

T. J. climbed out of bed slowly, hesitating with every sound coming from the master bedroom just down the hall.

"It's okay, T. J.," Leesha continued. "Come on with me. Hurry."

T. J. grabbed Leesha's other hand, leading her to her room, and Leesha shut the door, quietly, behind her. She placed Ben Jr. in her bed and pulled the blanket over him as T. J. climbed in from the other side. Leesha slowly crawled into bed next to Ben Jr. and put her arm over them, both.

The boys stared up at the ceiling where Leesha had little yellow stars painted on a dark background. All around her walls were telltale signs of her coming of age. Lady Jaguar paraphernalia filled the walls, only shadowed by pictures of her favorite soccer player, Alex Morgan. The other side of her room displayed evidence of her love for Christian music. She had posters representing everything from Lacrae to Toby Mac, Mandisa to Jamie Grace. Her N.O.A.H. soccer uniform hung up on the closet with her soccer gear placed uniformly right below it.

This would be a treat for the boys. Any other time, Leesha's room would be considered undiscovered territory. But tonight was a little different. Leesha could see the concern in her brothers' eyes. One would think that, with her parents' turbulent relationship, the boys might be used to it by now.

"It's okay," Leesha comforted them. "Everything's going to be okay."

Barely fifteen, Leesha was tired of feeling like she had to be strong in these trying times. She was tired of dodging the bullets of fury from ricocheting from her parents' volatile relationship with each other, and feeling like she had to keep the boys out of the same line of fire. Unfortunately, this event was typical of most emotional storms in that she and her brothers simply had to ride it out.

"I'm sick and tired of you, Natalie," came the voice of their Father; deep, angry, and supercharged with emotion.

"I'm sick of you too, Benjamin!"

Their mother could dish it out as much as she took it.

"I just don't understand why you can't fight for me, Benjamin! Why do I feel like I have to do our marriage alone?"

"Alone? You think you are alone? You have *no* idea what it is like to be alone, Natalie! And why should I fight for you? Being married to you has been the most lonely and depressing aspect of my life!"

"Oh really, Benjamin, you really think you know loneliness? Where were you while I was here raising your kids...taking care of them all by myself while you were out playing 'Marine'??"

"It's the Marines that took care of us, Natalie! It's the Marines that feeds us, provide for us, and gave us this house...everything we have! Why can't you just be happy that I take care of you?"

NOT PRESENT OR FUTURE...

"You mean you take care of your Marines? I hate the Marines, Benjamin! I hate what it has done to you! I hate what the war has done to you!"

"Yeah, and you know what I hate, Natalie? I hate what you have done to me!"

"Benjamin, please stop..."

"I hate what you have done to me since we have been married!"

"Benjamin, please...stop!"

"I hate that all you do is complain; about me, about the Marines..."

Natalie couldn't hold it in any longer. She wept bitterly.

"Most of all, Natalie, I hate..."

Natalie looked up at Benjamin with pain and suffering in her eyes, dreading any further insult.

"What, Benjamin? What do you hate about me?"

"EVERYTHING!!"

Back in Leesha's room, Leesha climbed out of the bed and crawled over to the wall. She grabbed her headphones and put them on her head, turning on her music as loud as she could. She began to rock back and forth while on the floor, fighting to hold the tears in. Her brothers were still in her bed, both with eyes wide open. Leesha put her hands over her headphones in an attempt to completely drown out the noise from down the hall.

As the embattled couple expended just about all of their energy, the noises subsided, a little. Natalie was so emotionally spent that she practically collapsed on the bed and slid to the floor.

"I'm done, Benjamin. God help me, I'm done."

"I can't stand you, Natalie! I am so sick of being married to you! I wish I had never met you! I wish I could just go back and start over!"

Natalie was overcome with suffering and pain; stricken with guilt, shame, anger...just about every negative emotion that God had no intention for His most-prized creation to possess.

"Then leave, Benjamin! Get out, please?"

Benjamin grabbed a blanket from the closet and walked out of the room, slamming the bedroom door behind him. He walked downstairs to the living room and collapsed on the couch. Benjamin refused to leave, but he was not sleeping anywhere near Natalie, tonight.

Natalie sat on the floor, unable to move…unable to breath.

"I'm done," she prayed. "Lord, I am done. I want another chance somewhere else. I don't want this anymore. Give me another chance…somewhere else."

Leesha could not hear anything but her music. She had no idea that the fighting was over. As she still had her headphones on, music as loud as it could go, she was oblivious to everything. In her attempt to escape the quarrelsome noise, she found herself in deep contemplation about God's presence during this time.

I don't understand any of this, God! I'm so confused and conflicted! Are you, really, the 'God' my parents raised me to believe in? Are You the 'God' they raised me to love? If You really acted like fathers do, are You a 'God' that I could love? Are you a 'God' that I could pray to? To talk to? To trust? Will you even listen to me? Do you know that I am here??

Leesha looked up at her mirror, just to her left, and saw the piece of paper with her favorite Bible verse on it. She reached up to grab it, pulling the tape from the mirror that was used to hold the paper in place. She held it to her heart in desperation, hoping beyond all her confusion that she could cling to the words written on this piece of paper just like she did for so many other Bible verses. This one was critical, though, as she had no choice but to face her current life struggles, which seem to overwhelm her all too often. The more the thoughts and memories of her parents' quarrels filled her soul, the harder she squeezed the paper to her chest. In her doubt, she wanted to have hope, as she felt that she had no other reason to believe.

"God, if You are there, and if You can hear me, please help us? I can't take it anymore, God. Please help us? Please, God? Please?"

With that, she spoke the words that would somehow, some way, bring her hope and remind her who would, inevitably, take hold of the situation and work it as only He could. Through her pain, confusion and tears, she prayed the words that would bring her comfort once again; the words from Romans Chapter 8.

"For I am convinced that neither death, nor life, nor angels, nor principalities; not present, nor future, nor powers, nor height, nor depth, nor any other creature will be able to separate us from the love of God which is in Christ Jesus our Lord."

CHAPTER 1

Caught in a realm of half-awake and half-asleep, Natalie's soul was heavy. She found herself trying to break the feelings of despair and depression that held her spirit captive. She struggled to open her eyes, swollen in tears, to get a grip on her morning bearings. In the midst of her struggle, she could hear the words cast from the previous night, haunting her as the many hurtful and destructive conversations she had with her husband during the course of their marriage.

This moment was no different.

As she clinched her pillow, more tears flowing down her face, she heard Benjamin's words, once again, as he lashed out at her:

"I can't stand you, Natalie! I am so sick of being married to you! I wish I had never met you! I wish I could just go back and start over!"

After what seemed to be an eternity of pain shooting through her soul, she managed to pray a few words in her spiritual and mental anguish.

"God, please help me? Please, please just help me through this day?"

Natalie wrestled with the thought of simply having to get up. She then realized that there was no sound in the house. No running of little feet, no voices of little children in the hallway, and no audial evidence of sibling rivalry.

There was nothing.

Normally, she would not have minded, as she welcomed the calm atmosphere. But for some reason, the silence was a bit eerie. There was a different feeling about her surroundings that she couldn't wrap her mind around. She struggled to get her eyes opened, and for just a second, she wondered why her room seemed so abnormally dark. It had been a long night, no doubt, and surely it must be morning. She finally opened her eyes enough to see her room.

Only, she wasn't in her room.

What in the world??

Natalie became disoriented. She rolled over and noticed a clock on a night stand.

Only it wasn't her clock. 8:15.

It's 8:15?

Her thoughts raced.

Is it 8:15 in the morning?

She looked around her room, still trying to grasp the darkness with her eyes. The sun was up, it appeared, but it looked as if the light was blocked by heavy curtains in the windows.

What is going on here?

Bllllp!

Natalie jumped, startled as the phone rang.

That was not my phone. What is that??

She didn't know exactly what that sound was, but it sounded like a phone. She looked over at a cordless phone, on the nightstand, and picked it up, pushing the 'on' button and raising it to her ears.

"Natalie? Natalie, is that you?"

"Hello," Natalie replied. "Who is this?"

"Natalie, this is Shannon. Where are you? Mr. Sherman has his meeting in just over ten minutes, and he doesn't have his notes."

"I'm sorry…who is this?"

Natalie was still trying to collect her thoughts about who this was and what she was talking about.

"Natalie, this is Shannon from work. You aren't drunk are you?"

What? Drunk?

"Natalie, Mr. Sherman needed you to get him his notes. You were supposed to deliver them to him this morning. Look, if you are sick…"

"I'm sorry," Natalie interrupted. "But I don't know what you are talking about."

NOT PRESENT OR FUTURE...

Then it hit her. Shannon was the name of the secretary from the office at the company that Natalie had interned with fifteen years ago, just before she married Benjamin.

"Uh, um, I'm sorry. I am going to have to call you back."

"Natalie...wait...Mr. Sherman's notes..."

Click.

Natalie hung up the phone and sat up in her bed.

That was totally weird, she thought, still trying to wake up.

"Benjamin?" she called, as she looked around for her husband. She got up out of the bed and saw familiar surroundings, but she was not in her room. She saw, what appeared to be, her old studio apartment in Abilene, Texas.

"What am I doing here," she gasped. "This is a dream. It must be a dream."

Natalie sat on the bed, trying to catch her breath and to get a grip on this experience. She looked around the apartment and noticed that everything was exactly the way it was when she lived there.

But she wasn't living there.

What the heck was going on??

Bllllp!

Again, the phone rang, and Natalie answered it.

"Natalie, this is the one Saturday that you needed to be here. Where are you? You told us yesterday that you could work this morning for Mr. Sherman's meeting."

"Um, uh, I'm sorry, Shannon, but you are just going to have to do this one without me."

Natalie started laughing as she finished her answer. In fact, she was a bit disrespectful. But as far as Natalie was concerned, this was just another dream.

"Fine! Just tell me where the notes are and I can try to get them to Mr. Sherman before it's too late!"

"I'm sorry; I guess I just don't know where they are located."

Shannon paused in absolute disbelief.

"Natalie, what has gotten into you? You aren't like this."

"Well, I don't know what to tell ya."

At that moment, Shannon just assumed that Natalie was drunk. The 'Natalie' that she knew did not act like this. The Natalie that she knew was very dedicated to her duties, however miniscule they might be.

"Natalie, I am very disappointed with you. The Bakersfield project was very important to Mr. Sherman."

Shannon paused, trying not to lose control of her temper.

"I've got to let you go, Natalie. There's a call on the other line and it is probably Mr. Sherman."

Shannon hung up the phone, leaving Natalie sitting there listening to the tone. Natalie recalled a Bakersfield project that she worked on, just before left the organization, but she didn't have much to do with it. As she thought more about it, she remembered that she left the company -when she left Abilene- to move in with her mother in preparation for the wedding.

Sooo, why am I here now, getting phone calls about a project I have nothing to do with? UGH! Who cares!! Clearly this is a dream, and I'm going back to sleep.

"Ben? Ben, you awake?"

Benjamin was half asleep when he realized there was a teenage kid practically in his face; a kid that he was not familiar with.

"Ben, you—"

"What the…"

Ben interrupted the kid as he struggled to wake up, rubbing his eyes and looking around.

Where the hell am I? Who the hell are these people?? Did I spend the night somewhere? What in the world?

"Ben, can I still get a ride home?"

"Uhhh…"

Ben was stuck. Just before he could answer anything else, another voice came from the stairwell.

"That was a fun night, brother."

NOT PRESENT OR FUTURE...

Ben looked at the person as he finished climbing the stairs, holding a box of doughnuts in his hands.

Raymond? Raymond Caldwell?? What the heck happened to him? He's...younger.

Benjamin shook his head and squeezed his eyes, as if to try to wake up. He looked around, recognizing the place, but still unsure what was he doing there.

Okay, this is a joke! Either that or I am still asleep.

He backed up and caught the wall.

"Are you okay," Raymond asked.

"Um, yeah. Uh, where's Natalie and the kids?"

"Natalie? You mean, the girl you were engaged to?"

Benjamin looked up at Raymond with a very puzzled look on his face.

"Well, I'm not sure where Natalie is," Raymond continued. "But the kids are all here, except for Josh and Tyler. They left already because Josh had to work."

"Josh and Tyler?"

Benjamin's mind was rolling as he was trying to remember who these two boys were.

"Yeah. Josh Spangley and Tyler Mathews."

What? Josh played baseball for the Cincinnati Reds, and Tyler was married and worked at Whirlpool!

"Hey, man, are you okay," Raymond asked.

"Um..."

Benjamin paused while scratching his head.

"Yeah, I guess I just need a minute."

"Can I still get a ride home," asked the kid who woke him up.

Benjamin looked bewildered. Noting Benjamin's reaction, Raymond responded quickly to the boy.

"Yeah, Chance, I'll give you a ride home. I've got to head to the church anyway to drop off that game equipment."

He pointed at a ditty bag full of sports gear. Benjamin was in shock.

Chance? Chance...Dunbar? O.K., now this is getting really weird.

Benjamin looked around to see the living room in the house that he rented before he and Natalie got married. He still could not grasp what was doing there, now. He walked around the living room and soon found himself in the bathroom. He froze when he looked into the mirror.

What the freakin' heck???

His thoughts were racing. It was him, but he was just a tad bit younger.

O.K. Clearly, I am dreaming.

Benjamin walked out of the bathroom and noticed a couple of boys playing on the Nintendo; the Nintendo that he used to own. He then walked downstairs, looking around, and through the door that took him outside into the screened-in porch. The sun was up, and it was a beautiful September morning in Northeastern Oklahoma.

Benjamin exited the porch and turned around, staring at the house. Behind him, there was a little lake that was perfectly stationed right by the house. It was the lake that he had several youth group parties at, with kids swimming and having fun. He had many memories of it, and as serene as this experience was, Benjamin still could not wrap his mind around the fact that he is there, now, instead of at home.

As Benjamin tried to get a grasp on his current situation, Raymond approached him from behind.

"Dude, are you all right? You're kinda freakin' me out here."

"Man, to be honest, I'm not sure." Benjamin replied.

"Is everything better between you and Natalie? How did she take it when you called off the engagement?"

"What??"

Called off the engagement?? What is he talking about??

"Um, yeah. Wasn't it just the other night that you told me that you broke it off with Natalie?"

Benjamin looked puzzled again, and his reaction didn't escape Raymond's attention.

"Did you guys get back together? Has she been calling you or something?"

NOT PRESENT OR FUTURE...

Benjamin was still in a state of, well, something...but he didn't know what. He couldn't figure it out. He was awake enough to know that he wasn't dreaming; and he wasn't dead, as far as he knew. But he had no idea how to explain this bit of information.

"I don't know, Raymond. Um, well, I guess, I..."

Benjamin paused.

"Well, I am gonna run this little man home," Raymond interrupted, figuring he would move on from the subject of Natalie.

"I'll call ya when I have tomorrow's lesson planned, if you are still up to teaching?"

Teaching? Lesson plan? Say something, Ben...say something!

His mind was still trying to wrap itself around this situation.

"Um, sure. I'm up for it."

"K, brother. I'll call ya later."

"Okay, I'll...I guess I'll be here," Benjamin responded.

"Come on, you little knucklehead," Raymond taunted Chance, picking on him as they walked off. They always seemed to enjoy picking on each other...back then!

Okay, Benjamin thought. *What happened? What is the last thing I remember?*

He searched his mind for his last memory. It was of Natalie and the bad fight they had the night before. He ran through it in his mind. They were arguing, which turned to blaming, then yelling. Then...

Benjamin straightened up, recalling the nasty verbal onslaught that the two were engaged in just before he went downstairs and to the couch. Then he recalled the last thing he said to Natalie.

"I can't stand you, Natalie! I am so sick of being married to you! I wish I had never met you! I wish I could just go back and start over!"

Benjamin left Natalie lying on the bed in tears as he stomped downstairs, into the living room, where he slumped onto the couch.

That is exactly what happened.

In fact, he could still feel the anger, emotion, and the loathing he felt for her...

But he was not there. He was here. And she was not here.

How? How is this possible??

Benjamin looked around at the neighborhood surrounding his home. Not sure what to think or what to do at that moment, he walked back into the house, up the stairs, and into the living room where the two boys were still playing Nintendo.

"Hey, Ben, my mom is going to come by and pick us up in about an hour. Is it okay if we keep playing this game until then?"

"Sure," Benjamin replied. He didn't know what else to say, and he could not remember either of the boys' names.

"Hey, uh, I've got a headache, and I am gonna go back to my room and lay down."

"Okay. We'll just walk out in an hour and wait for my mom. Thanks for letting us stay."

"Um, you're welcome."

Benjamin walked into his bedroom. He shut the door, looked around, and sat on the bed. He had to look around again and again to make sure he was actually in this room. He rattled his mind, thinking over and over what he was doing there. Considering the fight he had with Natalie, he just kept shaking his head. His mind could not process this experience at all.

Benjamin fell back into bed and shut his eyes. The only thing he could figure regarding this experience was that it was all a dream, and when he woke up from it, he was going to pack his stuff and leave Natalie.

But for now, he thought, *I gotta wake up.*

CHAPTER 2

Natalie tossed and turned, unable to fall asleep.

You gotta get up, Natalie! You gotta get up!

She opened her eyes and rolled over, looking at the clock on the nightstand. 11:23.

Okay. This is really crazy. 11:23? And that is still not my clock. Where am I?

Trying to wrap her head around this current state of being, she managed to stay in bed long enough to pass the time away, at the least. But there was another issue: her stomach started growling, as she was hungry.

Natalie ignored her stomach -at least for the moment- and just figured that she should keep trying to go back to sleep. Not that this momentary lapse of reason was not a welcomed calm in the storm of hostilities with her husband, however brief it might be. She still struggled with the emotions from her fight with him the night before.

Natalie rolled over in her bed, covering her eyes from the brightness of the sun shining through the window. Somehow, she managed to doze off. She wasn't in too deep when she heard the phone ring again.

Blllip!

Natalie refused to answer it, trying to go back to sleep.

Blllip!

The phone kept ringing.

Ugh!

Natalie was getting frustrated. She reached over to grab the phone.

"Hello," she answered, almost forcefully.

"Well, good morning, sleepyhead!"

What? That voice!

"Who is this," Natalie responded as she sat up in her bed. She felt as if her heart stopped.

"Who do you think this is?"

It was an older lady with the most beautifully familiar tone.

"Honey, have you been drinking, because I didn't think you did that."

Natalie was in complete shock. She could not believe her ears. She tried to say it, but it wouldn't come out.

"Natalie, are you there?"

"Momma," Natalie answered, trying hard to fight back tears. "Momma, is that you?"

"Well, of course, silly! Who else would it be?"

Natalie started hyperventilating as she fell off the bed, and to the floor, dropping the phone in front of her. She quickly picked the phone back up and held it so tight to her ears that she hit the 'Off' button by accident.

"No, wait…Momma?"

Natalie looked at the phone and kept calling for her mother, seeing if she was still on the other end.

There was no answer.

Natalie frantically studied the phone, trying to dial the last number that she had of her mother, before she passed away. She dialed it, only to hear the usual rejection tone.

"We're sorry, but the number you called is not a working number. Please hang up the phone and try again."

"No, Momma," Natalie cried out.

What in the world is this? A dream? Was this some sick joke? I know my mother's voice, but…

Natalie dialed the phone again and heard the same tone. She dropped the phone and scooted back into the nightstand, still hyperventilating. She put her hands in her face as if to try to get her grip on reality.

Calm down, Natalie! Just breathe, and calm down!

NOT PRESENT OR FUTURE...

Natalie started shaking uncontrollably. She just sat there, looking throughout the apartment, still perplexed at what she woke up to. So many emotions controlled her mental state at that moment: the bad fight with Benjamin the night before; his wish to not have anything else to do with her; the fact that their children witnessed their horrible display of a domestic dispute; and her waking up here this morning. And now, hearing her mother's voice.

The phone rang. Natalie looked at it, shaking her head. She did not know what to think, but she quickly realized that, real or not, she was going to talk to her mother again. She crawled over to the phone, hit the answer button, and put the phone to her ear.

"Hello?"

"Hey, it's me. I guess we were playing phone tag trying to call each other back."

Natalie broke down crying. It was her mother, whom she had missed so terribly.

"Natalie, honey, are you okay?"

Natalie couldn't answer.

How is this possible?? You died two years ago!! How am I hearing your voice??

"Natalie, what's wrong?"

Natalie held the phone just as tight as she had earlier, still crying.

"Natalie..."

"Mom, please, just don't hang up? Please?"

This time Natalie was crying, uncontrollably.

"Just don't hang up, Mom."

"Honey, I'm coming to see you. I'm coming right now!"

"No, Mom! Don't hang up the phone, please??"

Natalie was still shaking. She slowed her emotions enough to quit sobbing.

"Natalie, tell me what happened. You sound like you are having a nervous breakdown."

"Just don't hang up the phone, please?"

Natalie was still trying to pull herself together.

There was an eerie silence on the phone. Natalie's mother was trying to figure out what was wrong with her daughter, and Natalie just didn't know what to say. The silence quickly broke with Natalie's mother, who was trying hard to control her own emotions, as she spoke as calmly as she could.

"Do you want to come home?"

"Home?"

"Yes. Do you have enough money to come see me? It shouldn't take much gas."

Natalie sat there, continuously trying to pull herself together. This was all so very surreal.

Am I really talking to my mother? Can I really see her again?

None of this made any sense to Natalie, and it sure wasn't getting any more logical. But it didn't matter. Natalie knew, somehow, that she wasn't dreaming. This was real. It didn't make any sense, but it didn't have to.

"Mom, I need to see you, but…"

Natalie could not remember where her mother lived. It wasn't like her mother moved a lot, but Natalie couldn't think of anything at this moment.

Think, Natalie…think!

"Why don't you come see me, Natalie? Maybe you can bring Carmella with you."

"Carmella?"

Carmella? What brought her up??

"Sure, bring her along. I just love seeing the both of you, together, having fun. You are just like two peas in a pod."

Carmella? I have not seen Carmella in so long.

After Natalie married Benjamin, they moved to Tulsa and Carmella moved to Dallas to start her career. They kept in touch and tried to maintain their friendship, but the distance got in the way. During college, however, Carmella lived nearby in Abilene, right where she was when Natalie left her.

Well, at least that is what had happened.

"Okay, Mom, I'll try to call her and—"

"No need," Natalie's mother interrupted. "I called her when you were trying to call me, but I didn't want to tell you, yet. She should be on her way to see you. I asked her if she would be interested in bringing you to see me if I gave her gas money."

"Okay, Mom. Regardless, I am coming. I just need you right now."

Natalie seemed to be in a much poised state, but a minute of awkward silence must have transpired before Natalie's mother spoke again.

"Natalie, honey, I have to ask you. Is this about Ben?"

Benjamin? Why would she bring him up right now?

"I know that you loved him, honey, and I am so sorry that you two broke off your engagement. I've been praying for you that God would help you through this."

"What?" Natalie responded. "What do you mean?"

"You and Benjamin. Is this because of him?"

Benjamin and I broke off our engagement? What in the world is she talking about?

"Um, Mom..."

Natalie paused. She honestly didn't know what to say, as she was even more confused now.

First, Benjamin and I have a terrible fight. He slammed the door as he left the room, leaving me in tears. Then I wake up in my old college apartment with no idea of how I got here, not to mention the fact that I look way younger, as evidence from my reflection from my vanity mirror. Now I am talking to my mother, who had passed away two years ago! Lord, what is going on, here???

"Mom, I don't know what to say about Ben. I guess you could say lately, everything has been about Ben. But right now, I am just so happy to talk to you; happy that I can come see you."

Natalie wiped another tear from her eye.

"Well, come on then, Natalie. I'll be here with your favorite soup waiting just for you!"

Natalie smiled as she felt warm inside. Her mother could always make her feel that way.

Oh Lord, please let this be real?

Knock. Knock. Knock.

Natalie looked up at the door, stood up off the floor, and went to look out of the window.

"Mom, hold on. Someone is here."

"It's probably Carmella. I sent her over there." her mother replied.

Natalie opened the window, and there, standing at the door, was the most radiant, charismatic girl she ever knew.

"Hey, girl," Carmella shouted, looking at Natalie through the window. Natalie dropped the phone as she lost her breath. She ran over to the door, opened it up, and hugged Carmella.

"Carmella, it's you!!"

Natalie held Carmella tight, trying to wipe more tears from her eyes.

"What's up, girl??"

Carmella knew something must be going on, as she struggled to breathe from Natalie's embrace. Natalie's mother was still on the phone, but she didn't say anything as she could hear both of them in the background. Natalie let go of Carmella and backed up enough to give her some space.

Carmella was a sight for sore eyes. Natalie felt surprised and relieved at the same time. Carmella was young and vibrant, just how she was back in college.

"I hear we are taking a trip, girl!"

Natalie giggled, then realized her mother was still on the phone.

"Oh my gosh; Mom!"

Natalie ran back into the apartment to pick up her phone, as Carmella followed behind her.

"Mom, I am so sorry I dropped the phone."

"It's okay. Just drive on up here, and we can talk."

"Okay, we are coming!"

Natalie suddenly had a burst of energy. She caught herself staring at Carmella, still in disbelief. She couldn't believe where she was at, who she was with, and what she was about to do. She kept trying to hold back the tears.

I am going to see her mother again! My God, I can't believe it!!

NOT PRESENT OR FUTURE...

Natalie rushed around her apartment, in confusion, as if she was not sure of what she needed.

"Hey, girl, slow down. Everything's O.K."

"I'm sorry, Carmella. I am just so excited. I don't know what to do."

"Well, first off, take a breath."

Carmella's voice was peaceful and encouraging. Natalie just stood there and inhaled, quietly.

"That's right, girl. Now where's your purse?"

Natalie walked over and looked by her bed, where she found her purse, sitting beside it. She picked it up, opened it, and looked inside it as if she were searching for gold.

"Do you have everything you need in it—keys, wallet, money..."

"Yes, I got all of it," Natalie responded.

Again, she inhaled quietly and stood there for a moment, trying to soak in the reality. When she opened her eyes, Carmella was at the door, waiting to leave. Natalie thought of one last thing to say.

"Carmella, thank you so much for going with me. I've felt like I really missed you, and as weird as it may seem...I am just glad we get to hang out."

Then Natalie realized that she really hadn't asked Carmella if she wanted to take this drive.

"Are you sure you want to come? Am I taking you from anything, or, do you want me to drive?"

"Girl, let's go! Your mom is waiting, and so is that food!"

"Okay. Let's go!"

Natalie checked around the apartment to make sure the lights were all out and nothing was left on when the phone rang again.

"Oh, hey, it might be Mom. Just a sec."

Natalie reached for the phone as Carmella stepped outside to start the car.

"Hello?"

"What are you doin', girl? Why ain't you been home when I call you?"

"I'm sorry; who is this?"

"Who do you think it is?"

The deep male voice projected from the other end of the line didn't give Natalie a comfortable feeling. She knew that voice, as it was all too eerily familiar. She was trying to pinpoint it, but it still didn't register in her mind.

"Um, well, uh, I have to…"

"It's Darnell!"

Natalie froze. She was stuck in fear.

Darnell?? Darnell Harris?? Why is he calling me?

Natalie tried to understand why she received this phone call. Trying to remember, it hit her that Darnell was a guy she dated briefly before she started communicating with Benjamin.

Carmella came into the house to see what the wait was, and she noticed the look on Natalie's face, along with her changed demeanor.

"Natalie," Carmella whispered. "What's wrong? Who is it?"

"Girl, did you *hear* me??"

Carmella froze. The voice was loud enough on the phone that she could hear it while she was standing over by the door.

"Natalie, that's not Ben, is it?"

Natalie pushed the off button, hanging up the phone.

"We gotta get outta here," Natalie responded, as they walked out of the apartment.

Natalie locked the door and practically ran to Carmella's car. She opened the door, got in, shut the door, buckled up, and then had the brief courage to look around to see who might be out there. Natalie looked over to see a car that looked just like her old one. Then she looked at the outside of the apartment and throughout the whole complex.

The coast was clear.

Natalie sighed, deeply. She still didn't understand any of this. Her mind was racing.

Benjamin. Fight. Kids. Emotions. Mom. Carmella. Darnell. Ugh!!

Carmella put the car in reverse, backed up, and they drove off. They reached the drive leading out of the parking lot, then onto the main road heading to Amarillo.

"Who was that on the phone?" Carmella asked.

NOT PRESENT OR FUTURE...

Natalie was still trying to catch her breath from her response to the call.

"It was Darnell."

"What? Darnell? You broke it off with him when you started dating Benjamin. He shouldn't be calling you anymore."

Natalie honestly did not know what was going on. Things were not adding up. She began to think about the current date and how things were transpiring, now, versus how they had with Benjamin. But for now she just had to catch her breath.

"You didn't call Darnell after Benjamin broke up with you, did you?"

There it is again. Another statement of Benjamin breaking up with me.

"No...no, I didn't," Natalie responded, seemingly unsure about her answer.

"That 'Darnell-guy' seems very dangerous."

"Yeah, especially since he assaulted that girl, the one you told me about a while back," Natalie responded. "I am not sure how he got out of jail."

"What?? When did this happen? That...that I told you about?"

Natalie looked right at Carmella, again, trying to figure out the mood of the conversation. Carmella looked confused. Then it hit Natalie. Maybe that hasn't happened...yet. Just another thing that seemed a little weird about today.

After Natalie moved in with her mother in Amarillo, following Benjamin's proposal, Darnell became angry and got into some trouble. He got together with a couple of other guys, got drunk, vandalized property, and assaulted some girl. It happened on a night that the area saw bad storms, and the police had a difficult time initially responding to the 911 call because they were out responding to storm-related emergencies. Natalie remembers this because...

Because...

Carmella told her about it after it happened.

At least, that was before this.

"Um..."

Natalie's mind was racing to come up with something. Carmella obviously had not told her that yet.

"You know what," Natalie sighed. "Maybe I was wrong. Maybe I am thinking of something else. I'm sorry. Please forgive me. I don't know where my mind has been lately."

"It's okay, girl. But I am seriously beginning to worry about you."

"Let's just get to Mom's house, and get some of that food."

Natalie was finally able to relax, but she was still a little perplexed.

"Carmella, what day is it?"

"Uh, Saturday."

Saturday. Okay, that's a start. It was kind of hot outside, so…

"Date?" Natalie asked without sounding too out of touch with current reality.

"It's the twenty-third…of September," Carmella joked.

September 23. From the way things happened, today, it's gotta be the year 2000. Okay, this is weird. But at least I have a starting point.

Natalie was still tired. She just put her head back on the headrest and dozed off. Carmella didn't mind, as she noticed how tired Natalie was. She just said a prayer for Natalie that God would continue watching out for her. Carmella didn't know what was going on, but she was glad to be in Natalie's company. Carmella put on her Christian gospel music and drove on.

CHAPTER 3

"Daddy? Daddy, where are you?"

"Leesha," Ben answered. "Leesha, I am right here!"

Benjamin stood in his house, looking around and trying to find His daughter.

"Daddy, I can't find you!"

"Leesha, I am here. Where are you?"

Benjamin started running, only he didn't feel like he was moving very fast. He ran through the house, trying to find Leesha. He ran upstairs, checked all the rooms, in the closets, and under the beds.

Nothing.

"Daddy!"

The screams were getting louder and louder, and Benjamin became more frustrated with every scream. Her voice was everywhere. The further he ran, the more intense the screams became. Frustrated, Benjamin ran out of the house and continued calling for Leesha.

"Leesha! Leesha, where are you??"

Benjamin ran around the house, but saw nothing. He happened to look over at the lake and noticed some splashing by the dock. He ran as fast as he could toward the dock, noticing that the splashing intensified as if someone was in the water, flailing around. He came upon the dock and dove into the water.

Brrrrng.

Benjamin jolted awake. He was covered in sweat, and his breathing was heavy. He had difficulty grasping where he was.

Brrrrng.

Coming to his senses, he was awake enough to realize that nothing had changed from this morning. He was still in his bedroom of his old rent house.

Okay, this is just weird.

Brrrrng.

Benjamin could hear the phone, but the ring tone was different. He got up out of his bed and walked toward the ringing.

Brrrrng.

Approaching the sounds, he saw the cordless phone sitting on the charger.

Haven't seen that in a while.

He picked up the phone and hit the 'On' button.

"Hello?"

"Hey, Ben, it's Raymond."

"Oh, hey, Raymond. What's going on?"

"Hey, brother, I am just calling to check in on you; just seeing how you are doing."

"Um, I guess I am okay."

Benjamin had a difficult time trying to figure out how to respond.

"Okay," Raymond replied. "Well, hey, we are having some of the youth over for some pizza. Would you like to come over?"

"You mean...tonight?"

"Yeah! Why don't you come on over."

"Okay. Just let me get up and around."

"Up and around? Are you still sleeping? It's nearly 5:30."

Benjamin looked over at the clock. It was late in the afternoon. He had been asleep all day.

"Yeah, I guess I was still asleep," Benjamin joked.

"Well, the kids are ready to take you down. Hurry on over. If it is still light out, we'll play some ball."

"All right. I'll be over soon."

"Cool! See ya soon!"

"Hey, wait," Benjamin responded, trying to get Raymond's attention before he hung up.

"Yeah?"

NOT PRESENT OR FUTURE...

"Um."

Benjamin was stuck. He could not immediately remember where Raymond lived. He tried to recall the way to get to Raymond's house, but decided in the last second that he could figure it out.

"Never mind, Ray. I'll be right over."

Benjamin hung up the phone and looked around. The house was quiet and empty. He walked over to the couch and sat down, holding his face in his hands; no doubt still trying to figure all this out. He was younger, still living in his old rent house, still working with the youth at the church, and apparently, he had broken off the engagement with Natalie.

Could this be possible? Am I really here?

Benjamin stood up and walked around the living area. His rent house was set up like a Barbie-doll-style home. It was a cute little house, originally designed to be a place for fun and socialization. The upstairs had a kitchen combined with the living room, and a bedroom at the far end. Downstairs was the washer and dryer, along with another bathroom and bedroom. Between the bathroom and the bedroom was a large coat closet.

As Benjamin walked down the stairs, still looking around, he opened up the closet door and recognized the Marine Corps and Tulsa county jail uniforms. He had forgotten about the jail uniforms; how they were black and white. It wasn't the sheriff who operated the jail, but some for-profit institution that Benjamin couldn't have cared less for. Pulling out the jail uniforms, he tried one on, in total disbelief of how skinny he was.

Wow! I can't believe I can still fit into these things.

He finished looking through the house and then went back upstairs. He still did not know what to think about this experience. He wasn't dreaming; he knew that much. In deep contemplation, he remembered the fight he had with Natalie, and the last words he said to her about wanting to 'do things over.'

I don't know why this is happening, but I guess I'll run with it.

As Benjamin prepared to leave, he couldn't help but to think about the comment that Raymond made regarding Natalie and the engagement ending. The only two things that Benjamin knew –so far- were that he woke up here this morning, and, for whatever reason, he was still here. Considering the fact that he told Natalie that he was sick of her and he wanted another chance at life, without her, he took this experience as a temporary blessing.

Well, if I am getting another chance at this I'd better take it; if that's what this is.

Benjamin grabbed his keys, walked downstairs, locked the door to the house, got in his pick-up, and drove off for Raymond's house.

"Natalie...Natalie? Hey, girl, time to wake up."

Natalie jumped in her seat and looked around, trying to get her bearings. She had to take a second to come to her senses.

"Natalie, are you okay? Man, you were sound asleep."

Natalie finally realized that, again, she was not dreaming. She looked over at Carmella and smiled.

"I'm awake, girl," Natalie responded as she stretched. "Oh, man, how long have I been asleep?"

"You were out of it just before we hit Anson."

"I'm so sorry, Carmella."

"It's okay. Hey, look, we are coming up on Clarendon. We have just about an hour to go. Do you need to stop?"

Natalie looked around at the beautiful Texas landscape. Canyons here, mesquite there — she loved the Texas panhandle.

"I could use a stop," Natalie replied. "I think I have some money here; I'll buy some snacks."

Natalie began looking through her purse.

"Okay. We'll stop at the first convenience store we find."

"We won't get a whole lot to snack on, on the count of Momma's famous soup."

"I heard that, girl!"

They made a quick stop at a local convenience store and hit the road just as quickly. Road 287 seemed to get longer the closer they got to Amarillo. Natalie was becoming more anxious.

NOT PRESENT OR FUTURE...

Oh, Lord, what am I going to do when I see mom? What will I say? I still can't believe this! Is this real??

Natalie's mind was racing as she continued to grasp the reality of the situation.

"So how are ya feelin', girl?" Carmella asked.

Natalie did not know how to answer that. She knew that she could trust Carmella, but how would Carmella even attempt to comprehend what Natalie was experiencing? She remembered how much she cherished Carmella while she lived in Abilene, and it was becoming more clear why she cherished her, now.

"I am feeling okay, I guess. Just really stressed out, lately."

Carmella kept driving and wanted to continue the conversation, but she didn't know what to say. Natalie had to find her own comfort zone.

"Carmella, today has been so surreal in many ways. I wish I could explain it, but all I can say is…I'm very glad to see you. I guess I have been so busy, and if I have been, then I am very sorry."

"It's okay, girl. We have both been busy. And I know that it has been hard on you since Benjamin broke up with you."

Carmella looked at Natalie directly.

"Did he ever tell you why he called off the engagement?"

Natalie didn't know how to answer that. After further consideration of Carmella's question, Natalie said the only thing she could say: the truth.

"To be quite honest with you, Carmella, it still feels very…new, and quite unexpected."

"Well, I still can't imagine it. I really just wanted to be sure you were okay. That's why I came over as quickly as I could –after your mom called me- to get you and take you to your mom's."

"And I absolutely thank you for that," Natalie responded with a smile.

Carmella didn't speak for about a minute. She just continued driving, with a look of serious contemplation on her face. Natalie just enjoyed the moment. Then the silence broke.

"Did you love him, Natalie? Did you love Benjamin?"

Natalie thought about that.

Of course I loved Benjamin. I loved him very much. I may not have liked him...maybe even loathed him, but...

"Yes, I did," Natalie replied.

"Do you still love him?"

Now that was the million dollar question, especially now. Natalie didn't know how to answer that, and quite frankly, she wanted to change the subject. Talking about Benjamin meant thinking about the children.

And there were no children, not here. Not now.

This was very overwhelming for Natalie, and just when she thought about how she would try and change the subject, she looked up and realized that they were getting close to Claude.

"Hey, it's Claude! We are almost there!"

Carmella sensed that Natalie tried to avoid that last question, but she didn't care. She joined in the excitement with Natalie, and the two just continued laughing and talking about girl stuff, something that they just loved to do.

As Highway 287 turned into Interstate Highway 40, they entered the Amarillo city limits. They were only on Highway 40 for about six minutes when they turned off the highway and on the main road, leading to her mother's neighborhood. Every corner turned, every traffic light crossed was one step closer to her mother's house. As they turned down the final street, Natalie became emotional and she struggled to control it. Carmella pulled the car into her mother's driveway and put the car in park.

"We are here, girl!"

Natalie sat in the seat, breathing...praying...anticipating.

There she was.

A figure opened the front door as Natalie got out of the car. She began to cry as she walked briskly up to her mother and wrapped her arms around her. Her mother held her, and though she did not know what was wrong with Natalie, she always knew how to make it better. Carmella came up behind them, smiled at their embrace, and walked into the house.

Natalie did not let go of her mother. She just cried. If it were just the Natalie of old —or in this case, young— she might not have been this emotional. But this Natalie was every bit torn, hurt, broken, grieving, depressed, and crushed in her spirit. All the anger, emotions, feelings, love, guilt, shame, hatred, desire, and emotional need came out in those moments. She let it all out in her mother's arms. That was one of the reasons that Natalie's faith in God was so solid: God loved her through her mother, and Natalie knew it.

CHAPTER 4

Benjamin drove down the road, still trying to recall Raymond's address. From what he could remember, Raymond and his family left the church about five years ago to take his first position, as an associate minister, at a church in Grand Prairie, Texas.

But that was another time. Benjamin had to remember where he was —or better yet, when he was— right now. He looked down at the clock in his pick-up. 6:00.

Okay. I really don't want to do this, but…

Benjamin was in a trance of some sort, no doubt, still trying to cling to reality. But as much as he was confused about his current situation, he was also curious. He couldn't help but to think about how things changed around the Tulsa area, and for some weird reason, he would have a chance to see it again before it had. If there is one way to determine that he was not crazy, he would drive through the town to try to determine what was different, and what had not yet changed.

At least that is how he figured it.

His rental house was about five miles west of Owasso. The road between was narrow and desolate, with the occasional house, here and there, along the way. Benjamin would definitely look for things that sparked his memory. Realistically, Benjamin had not driven down this road in a long time, so even if something were dramatically different, he wouldn't know it. For the time being, this is how he attempted to cope with this experience.

There was still the matter of the location of Raymond's house. Benjamin went over it in his mind. He had been there many times, before, in the past, for sponsor meetings and youth parties. Again, that was a long time ago.

Fifteen years to be exact.

Wait a minute; what's the date?

Benjamin guessed the year -based on the comments Raymond made about Benjamin breaking off the relationship with Natalie- but he had no idea of the exact date.

As he pulled into Owasso, still on 86th Street North, he decided that he would stop at the first convenience store he could find. He saw the old high school football field on the left side of the road, which sat right next to the elementary school. He passed Main Street, then a couple of restaurants, some residential areas, and then Highway 169. He continued under the overpass and saw a Shell gas station on the right. He pulled into the parking lot and walked into the store, where he saw a girl working over the register.

"Could you please tell me what the date is today, Ma'am?"

"Um, sure," the attendant replied, checking her calendar. "It's the twenty-third."

The twenty-third...of what?

Just as Benjamin looked around the store, the attendant pointed to the calendar, showing the month of September.

Okay, At least I know that.

"Thank you, Ma'am," he responded as he headed toward the door.

"Uh, do you need anything else, Sir?"

Benjamin was almost caught be her flirtatious demeanor.

"No, thank you, Ma'am," he replied as he exited the store.

Benjamin got back into his pick-up, drove out of the parking lot, and continued heading east on 86th Street. He thought that, by driving around, something would trigger his memory about the location of Raymond's house. He passed the church, then the little privately-owned convenience store behind the church, and toward the high-school. He found himself becoming frustrated when it finally hit him:

Raymond and his wife bought a house in the neighborhood behind the original Walmart.

He quickly turned his pick-up around and drove to the road that would take him to Raymond's home. As Benjamin pulled into the driveway of Raymond's house, he slowly began to remember more details about Raymond's home: the youth sponsor meetings, social gatherings, and youth parties. He even snickered as he saw the lamppost that he toilet-papered —with the help of the kids, of course— quite some years back.

Man, those were fun times.

Benjamin got out of his pick-up, walked up to the door and rang the doorbell. It didn't take two seconds before Raymond threw opened the door.

"Hey, brother! Come on in! We were just about to eat."

"Thanks," Benjamin responded. "I was gettin' kind of hungry."

They both walked into the kitchen area, and Benjamin saw Chelsea standing around the table visiting with a couple of other people from the church.

"All righty," Raymond began. "Now that Ben is here, let's pray."

Raymond led the prayer, and for the first time in a while, Benjamin felt somewhat at ease. He just listened as Raymond blessed the food.

"All right now, dig in!"

Benjamin went to sit down in the living room without taking any pizza. It wasn't that he wasn't hungry, but this had been a very interesting day, and he just wanted to sit for a minute to collect his thoughts. There was no doubt that waking up in his old bed, in his old room, in his old house, with no Natalie and no kids, was beyond comprehension. He continued to struggle with, what he perceived, was an altered sense of reality.

After about a minute alone on the couch, Raymond came in with a plate of pizza in one hand and a Sunkist in the other.

"Nothing better than a pizza and a Sunkist, ain't that right, brother?"

"Absolutely," Benjamin joked.

"You gonna get some?"

"Oh, yeah; I will. I'm just sittin' for a minute, collecting my thoughts. It's been a really weird day."

NOT PRESENT OR FUTURE...

"Yeah, I couldn't help but notice that you seemed to be a bit out of sorts earlier."

Raymond leaned in toward Benjamin to keep his next question discreet.

"Dude, seriously, is everything okay?"

"Um, I think so. I'm just kind of taking everything in right now."

"Care to share?"

Benjamin sighed, while thinking about how to respond. Before he could, Raymond came back with another question.

"Benjamin, whatever you are going through, is it about Natalie?"

"What do you mean?"

"Well, if you don't mind, it just seemed a little weird that you both were engaged, and you called it off, quickly. You never really shared why. You just did it. I was wanting to ask you about it, but didn't want to pry. I mean, I know you loved her, but..."

Benjamin was stuck. Quite honestly, he still had no idea what Raymond was talking about. He really had to think about this. He knew what month and date it was, and he knew that the current date was after he proposed to Natalie.

When did we get engaged? When did I propose to her?

Benjamin leaned forward and rubbed his temples with his fingers.

Okay, we went out to dinner at Chile's on 71st Street South, right next to the Woodland Hills Mall. Before that, I bought her a Precious Moments proposal figurine, which I had on me. We came back to the church for a youth function, and while she was distracted in conversation by some of the youth group girls, I got down on my knees and proposed to her in front of the youth group. I gave the figurine to Natalie, along with the engagement ring. Come on, man; what was the date?

Then he remembered. It was August 2.

And it is currently Saturday, September 23. Okay, so somewhere, in between, I, apparently, broke off the engagement with Natalie. Ugh! This is crazy!

"Well," Raymond continued, "you know we are here for ya. I definitely don't want to see you hurt, but if your decision was the right one, it is better you made it before you got married."

"Um, yeah, I guess you're right, Raymond."

That was enough talk about Natalie. The more he thought about her the more confused he became. It was time to change the subject.

"So tell me how things have been going, Raymond. Oh, did the boys have a good time last night?"

"Well, things have been going pretty good, brother…and the boys had an absolute blast at your house last night. In fact, just to give you a heads up, they are already planning their next party at your house!"

Benjamin laughed.

"Well, if they had that much of a good time, then I will have to invite all of them over again."

Raymond lightened up the mood a little bit, and they both started to talk about the kids as some more of the guests came into the living room. Benjamin got up, went to grab some pizza and a soda, and continued visiting with the rest of the group.

Natalie sat at the table with her mother and Carmella. She could not touch the stew that her mother made for her. Unable to eat, she just stared at her mother, studying her features, listening to her voice, and taking in every moment. For the first time in a while, Natalie started to feel a peace in her heart. Her emotions had been in overdrive for so long that it seemed like everything built up only to come to a resounding halt right in her mother's kitchen. It was very weird emotion for Natalie.

"Aren't you going to eat, honey?"

Natalie smiled so brightly that the mere sight of her expression caught the immediate attention of both her mother and Carmella. Natalie, oblivious to anything but the company she was in, didn't seem to care.

"Yes, Mom," Natalie snickered. "Yes, I am. I am just soaking in the moment."

Natalie looked at her mother and took a breath as if she was going to continue speaking but exhaled without saying a word. She just smiled in contentment as she picked up her spoon and began eating the stew.

"So let's get down to the nitty-gritty," her mother continued. "What is going on with you?"

Natalie looked up only to see both of them anxiously awaiting a response.

"Natalie, I want to be careful when I ask this, but…you aren't…"

"Oh no, Mom," Natalie interrupted. "I'm not pregnant."

Natalie caught that question just before it came out. Her mother's expression gave her focus away very quickly. Natalie might have been offended by that question as, normally, it would have bothered her. But she quickly remembered that her emotions haven't necessarily been normal, lately.

"Mom, I just needed to see you. I…"

Natalie paused, trying to figure out how to say what she wanted to. Talking to her mother had always been very easy for her, but how does she explain what has happened to her over the last twenty-four hours?

"I just really needed to see you. It really has been a very bad past couple of weeks, and I just needed my 'mother time.'"

"M…hm."

With that response, Natalie could see that her mother was not convinced with that answer. She knew that her mother wanted more information, but Natalie was just happy to be in her presence again. Her contentment must have been visible as the three of them looked at each other and started giggling. When they were all together, that is what they did, and it always made Natalie feel good. But for Natalie, it had been such a long time ago since they last did that.

Lord, if only they knew the truth…

"So what are we going to do tonight," Carmella asked, brightening the mood. "There is a new movie coming out tonight called

'Remember the Titans'. It's got Denzel Washington in it, and I wanna see it!"

"Oh, yeah, that is a good movie," Natalie replied.

"What do you mean, that's a good movie? It just came out tonight. How did you see it before now?"

Crap!! I did it, again!

Natalie tried to come up with a way to answer this question. This time, she definitely had the attention at the table.

"I meant that I have read reviews of it, and yes, I am sure it will be a good movie. I mean…it's got Denzel in it!"

"Mmm-hm," the other two responded, almost simultaneously.

Natalie kept quiet, hoping they would fall for her response. Natalie's mother looked over at Carmella.

"Well, let's go!"

Carmella looked at her watch.

"Well, it's 7:48; might have missed an earlier movie. Maybe we can see if there is a late showing."

"Let me get my purse," Natalie's mother responded, getting up from her chair and taking her bowl over to the sink. "It's been a while since I have been to a movie. You two should come see me more often."

"You can be sure that I will, Mom!"

Natalie smiled at the thought of going anywhere with her crazy companions tonight. She was so stuck in the moment that she did not think about Benjamin, the kids, the night before…any of it. She was a bit preoccupied, and she loved it. For the first time in a long time, she felt complete; almost unbroken. She couldn't explain it, but she didn't care.

Should I feel guilty about this? Realistically, it is not like I can do anything about my current situation. Why go nuts over something that can't be helped?

"All righty, let's go," her mother stated as she grabbed the keys to her car and headed to the door.

"Am I parked behind you," Carmella asked. "Do I need to move my car?"

"Mmm…no, I think we can make it, Dear."

NOT PRESENT OR FUTURE...

They all three got into the car and took off for the movie. Natalie sat in the front seat with her mother, enjoying the conversation the three of them were having. She was completely engulfed in her mother's presence, and she thought of nothing else but her.

Thank you, Jesus, for one more chance with my mother.

CHAPTER 5

As Benjamin finished his pizza, he sat back in the couch and enjoyed the company. He had always loved how much he felt accepted when he was with Raymond. Raymond, whose skin was as white as the driven snow, could have cared less about Benjamin's skin color. He lived and breathed the act of loving people, regardless of their race, gender, or cultural upbringing. None of that mattered to Raymond.

His youth group was just as diverse as the love in his heart. He had kids from every color, social status, educational surroundings — all brought into one heart with one mission: to bring Christ to all of them. Raymond was the real deal. He was far from perfect, but his minor flaws could easily be overshadowed by his Christ-like life and demeanor. His wife loved him. His children loved him. His youth group loved him. Benjamin always believed that God truly blessed Raymond with an incredible ministry, and he remembered how glad he was when Raymond brought him into the youth program as a sponsor.

"Did you get enough pizza," Raymond asked.

"Oh, absolutely! I am stuffed."

Chelsey came into the living room with another box of pizza about the same time as Benjamin answered Raymond's question.

"Well, we had some more leftover," she offered. "We had a couple of folks who weren't able to make it tonight."

"I know," Raymond sighed, almost communicating disappointment.

"Who didn't make it," Benjamin asked.

"Well, we invited William over tonight, and I was hoping he could have made it."

William? William Weatherly? Is that who he is referring to?

That response from Raymond got Benjamin's attention.

"I have been trying to witness to William," Raymond continued. "He's going through a lot right now."

"Yeah, I know William."

"I thought you did. I knew that you were talking to him, and I definitely appreciate that. He needs all the prayers and support he can get right now."

I wonder how much stuff Raymond actually knows about William.

Benjamin had to go back in his mind and try to remember the interactions that he had, with William, when they first met. Benjamin was able to recall the time where he and Natalie invited William and Julie to a marriage conference. It was at that conference that he and Natalie were able to witness to William and Julie. It was when William told Benjamin about his struggles with feelings of homosexuality.

But that was then.

"What has William been up to lately," Benjamin asked.

"I am not sure. I have tried to call him several times, and up until about a week ago, he returned them favorably. But lately…"

Raymond sighed as Benjamin listened.

"Chelsey and I were going to try to invite him to the marriage conference coming up next week as I think he would have enjoyed it."

"Marriage conference?"

"Yeah, we've discussed before, you and I. We thought that you and Natalie were going to go until you told us that you guys broke off your engagement."

Yes, of course! That's it!

Benjamin was finally able to put two and two together. It was the same marriage conference that he thought of earlier. And then he realized…

That was then.

Again.

"Well, I will keep trying to talk with him," Benjamin continued. "I remember; I mean, I have been able to talk with William in the past. I'll try again."

He caught himself in midsentence describing a situation as if it had happened years earlier. Which, in Benjamin's case, it had.

"All right. That sounds good, Ben."

Raymond seemed fairly content with Benjamin's statement.

"Hey, what time will you be at the church in the morning? I might have you help me set up for class."

"Um, well, what time do you need me?"

It seemed that Benjamin was caught trying to recall many things in this time. Trying to remember what time Sunday school started was no different.

"How about 9:00. We can set up the video projector and be sure we are both on the same page about the lesson plans."

"Okay. I'll be there."

Benjamin got up and grabbed his keys. He was glad for the company, but he had an urge to go driving around a bit. He looked at the clock, and it was about 8:45.

"I'm gonna head out so I can get some rest for tomorrow. I really appreciate the pizza and the invite."

"You are welcome," Chelsey replied. "Please come back any time. Maybe we can get the other youth sponsor girls, and we can tackle you guys in some card games."

Benjamin shook Raymond's hand and walked out to his pick-up truck. As he backed out of the driveway, he waved to Raymond, who was looking at him through the window, and he drove away.

Benjamin reached 86th Street North but sat at the stop sign for a second. He really did not know where to go, at this moment. He could go back to his house, but it was lonely, as the house was empty. He could drive around just to refresh his memory about the city of Owasso, or maybe even take a drive up to North Tulsa. At this point, though, nothing really appealed to him. He just sat there, praying.

"Lord, what is going on here? I can't get my head around this."

He couldn't help but to think about Natalie and the kids. The fights and arguments, that he and Natalie had in the past, seemed so trivial now. This 'experience' hadn't necessarily overshadowed the pain and anger he had been feeling about his wife over the past couple of years, but it sure challenged his own understanding enough to get his attention. The simple fact was he had no idea what was going on. It didn't make any sense to him, but he needed to figure out how to press on.

That is always how Benjamin dealt with any type of change or adversity: everything has a logical reason for it, so deal with it and press on. And that was another issue that caused so much conflict between him and Natalie.

Now, however, especially from what he had been learning lately, Natalie wasn't going to be an issue any more.

But the kids, what about them? They aren't here.

When thinking about the children, Benjamin struggled with their memories. He loved his children. He had an incredible relationship with Leesha, at least he had one until about the previous year. Tension built up between the two, and Benjamin could never figure out why. He had watched his little girl grow to become a beautiful young lady, and he was so very proud of her. But they had their issues, especially lately.

T. J. was Benjamin's buddy, as he was just a spitting image of Benjamin in every way. Benjamin was just as crazy about T. J. as he was about Leesha. Benjamin was most content with his children, and for a while there, everything seemed perfect for Benjamin and Natalie. They had decent jobs, a daughter and a son, and when Ben Jr. came along, he was just an added bonus to their family. The three children completed Natalie and Benjamin, and that was the one thing Benjamin will never be able to forget.

Could that be a problem for me?

Deep in thought, he never noticed a car coming up behind him, wanting to turn right. The car honked, and Benjamin snapped back to reality and realized he had to make a decision of where to go. It would be a difficult one for him, but for now, he would turn right, and head west.

When the movie was over, Natalie, her mother, and Carmella exited the theater and walked to the car.

"That was an incredible movie," Natalie's mother stated.

"Yes, it was," Carmella agreed. "It was good, and I just love me some Denzel Washington!"

The three of them laughed. Natalie didn't say much more as she had seen the movie many times. She did not want to make any comments that she might have to try to explain later.

"Who's up for ice cream," Natalie asked cheerfully, trying to change the subject. She looked at her mother as if to try to catch cues from her facial expressions.

"I don't mind running by somewhere to get some ice cream if you would like to, honey. We would have to go somewhere that is still open; maybe like run through McDonald's drive-through or something."

"That's okay with me, as long as it is not too late for you, Mom."

"No, it's not too late, just as long as I get enough rest for church tomorrow."

Church? That's right. Today is Saturday.

Natalie totally forgot what day it was.

"Are you ladies coming to church with me tomorrow?"

"Of course, Mom. We can run through McDonald's and grab some ice cream, go home, put on our p.j.'s, and then hit the sack. What do you think, Carmella?"

"That sounds good to me, girl!"

"That is, of course, unless you girls stay up late watching movies," Natalie's mother continued.

Both Natalie and Carmella laughed as they approached the car. Carmella looked over at Natalie's mother with a curious expression in her face.

"You know, Ma'am, I have known Natalie for, what, a couple of years now, and I have spent so much time with you…and I don't even know your name."

Natalie and her mother just looked at Carmella with puzzled faces.

"I've just always called you 'Ma'am'," Carmella finished.

That made both Natalie and her mother laugh, and her mother almost dropped her keys while trying to unlock the car door.

"It's Florance, dear. My name is Florance."

They all got into the car, still laughing and carrying on with each other, and left the parking lot. They talked about everything they could think of: what their best memories of each other were, going to school at Abilene Christian, how Natalie met Carmella, and, of course, their favorite subject: Florance's past. Natalie and Carmella loved to hear Florance talk about her childhood. It wasn't until they got to the discussion of the future that Natalie seemed to snap back to reality.

"Now what will your plans be now, Natalie?"

Florance knew her daughter well enough to know that, regardless of what kind of good time the girls had tonight, there was a different 'Natalie' this morning. Florance wanted to talk about what it was that got Natalie so emotional, and she had a feeling it had something to do with Benjamin.

"I don't know, Momma. I'm not sure, yet."

Again, in a time where it seemed like everyone knew more about her personal life than she did, she had no other response.

"Would you try and stick around Abilene; maybe try to find a full-time gig where you are now," Carmella asked.

"That is a thought."

Natalie didn't say much more than that. She had really been enjoying the atmosphere of her mother and Carmella, and this snap-back-to-reality didn't come with much welcome. Natalie was still in a weird state of euphoria. She really didn't want to have to think about anything but being with her mother. But deep inside, she knew what was coming. If this was, in fact, not a dream, she dreaded what was coming.

"You know I would love to have you stay around Abilene for a while," Carmella continued. "There are lots of cute Air Force guys that hang around the base."

"Ugh, no way. I have had my share of military men, and I am just not even thinking about seeing anyone right now."

Both Carmella and Florance snapped their heads at Natalie's direction, each possessing a very puzzling look as Natalie's response seemed overemotional. Natalie did not care. She knew that Carmella's statement was all in fun, but even if Natalie could have controlled her gruff response, she was not sure she would have wanted to.

"Well, okay," Carmella responded, cautiously. "Hey, look, we are at McDonalds."

They drove through the drive-through, ordered some shakes, and headed back to Florance's house. They were not but a mile away from their destination when Natalie felt some sense of guilt at her response to Carmella, earlier. She didn't know how to approach the reality of what she was feeling or, for that matter, what she was experiencing. But Natalie did not want to leave it with her emotions getting the best of her.

As they pulled into the driveway, Natalie, sitting in her seat and holding her shake, sighed heavily in anticipation about what she wanted to say. As Florance put the car in 'park', Natalie started to speak.

"Carmella, I am sorry about the way I snapped at you. And Mom, if I puzzled you, I am sorry as well."

Natalie did the best she could not to get too emotional. Both Florance and Carmella just looked at her with compassion in their hearts as Natalie continued to talk.

"Right now, the only thing that makes any sense is you two. I know I have shared a little bit with both of you, and I can't imagine what you both have been thinking of my emotional state today, but I have no way of expressing how I am feeling or what I am thinking."

Natalie paused, wanting to be sure she communicated herself, appropriately.

"All I can ask from both of you is to please just be there for me right now. I need both of you, and I am so grateful that both of you are there for me."

As she finished her statement, Natalie began crying. Florance and Carmella continued to comfort Natalie the best they could. They gave Natalie a few minutes to cry, and when she felt she was done, they got out of the car and went into the house. For Florance,

NOT PRESENT OR FUTURE...

it was a long day; worrying about her daughter, worrying about her on her trip, and the emotions that Natalie brought with her when she got to the house. Florance was ready to call it a night.

"Well, ladies, I am hittin' the sack."

She walked up to Natalie and put her arms around her, squeezing Natalie tight.

"I love you, Natalie. You have been such a wonderful blessing to me, and I pray the God will look after you and continue to show you where He wants you."

Natalie just held onto her mother. She took in every moment of her mother's embrace.

"I am sorry about Benjamin," Florance continued. "I liked him. He seems to be such a good man, and I hoped he would make you happy. But no matter what happens, I will always be here for you."

Natalie tried to hold back the tears at her mother's declaration. Natalie knew the truth, and the thought of the truth proved too much for her. So Natalie didn't think. She just held her mother.

"I love you, Mom!"

"I love you too, child," Florance responded as she let go of Natalie and went to bed.

Natalie turned and went into the living room where Carmella had turned on the TV and sat down beside Carmella on the couch.

"Hey, you!"

"Hey, you, yourself, girl," Carmella replied jokingly, but with some reservation.

"What's on TV?"

"Not much. Looks like some college football highlights, some news… a few shows…"

Carmella paused as she was scanning the channels. She then looked down at a box full of VHS tapes.

"I'll watch a movie with you, if you can find one you want to watch."

Carmella just wanted to talk to Natalie, but figured that talking was done for the day.

"Sure," Natalie responded. "Not sure how late I can make it without falling asleep, but we can throw something in to watch."

Carmella went through the box of VHS tapes and saw some of Florance's favorites: Titanic, Godzilla, The Lion King, and Independence Day. Natalie's mother was quite the diverse movie collector.

"How about 'Independence Day'," Carmella asked. "I like this one. It's got Will Smith in it!"

"Okay, put it in."

Carmella put the movie in the VHS player, and started playing it. Natalie just shook her head, teasingly, with a smile on her face. She recalled why Carmella loved this movie.

"What," Carmella asked, expecting some sort of tormenting remark from Natalie.

"You and your 'Will Smith'!"

They both laughed. As the movie played, Natalie began to feel anxious and jittery. There was no denying what she already knew. There were no kids. There was no Leesha to come climb into bed with her to talk; no T. J. to come get his kisses; no Ben Jr. to tuck into bed.

Natalie's concerns were spot on. For now, at least, they were just thoughts.

What will happen when I wake up tomorrow?

Natalie looked over through the living room window and saw the moon. As weird as it was, all she could think about was Benjamin. She loved him, hated him, admired him, and despised him...all at the same time. Given her current situation, as hard as it was to swallow, she might think it wouldn't matter, but these feelings were still there. Whatever this was; whatever reason this was happening, it was going to be difficult for Natalie.

But for now she was in the last place she expected. And for now that was all right with her.

CHAPTER 6

After Benjamin arrived home, he went upstairs into the living area and sat down on the couch.

Man, this room is dark!

He could see only enough to make out where the couch was in the living room. His house was dark and very quiet. As he sat on the couch, he tried to remember where the light switches were. He glanced over by the kitchen and noticed a red light blinking. He stood up and walked over to the source of the blinking light, looking down at it and realizing it was his answering machine. He saw just enough light to illuminate the 'Play' button, and he hit it. As the machine started playing, it lit the room up enough for him to notice a light switch by the kitchen door. Benjamin walked over to the switch and turned it on.

Illumination!

The light wasn't very strong, but it was enough for Benjamin to see the switch to the living room ceiling fan also attached to a light, and he walked over to turn it on, as his answering machine played the first message:

"Message 1: 'Sgt. Jones, this is Lance Corporal McDaniels. We have a funeral at Floral Haven Funeral home on Monday if you are interested. I am so sorry that I am calling you this late, but I checked the faxes today, and a funeral request came in late. I am just now able to call you. Please let me know as soon as you can if you can make it. Showtime is 11:00 a.m. I believe you have my number, so just call me when you can to confirm. Thanks for the consideration and have a great weekend!' Beep."

Sgt. Jones?? I can barely remember being 'Sgt. Jones'.

Benjamin's instinct was to question why they would get his rank wrong, until he conveniently remembered that he was experiencing the time warp of confusion.

Benjamin loved working Funeral Honor Details. He hadn't worked one in so long he almost forgot how to participate. Luckily, he remembered where Floral Haven Funeral Home was, and he could just get caught up on the specifics before the service.

What he did not remember was Lance Corporal McDaniel's number.

"Message 2: 'Senior Jones, this is Captain Hoffman. Hey, is there any way you could make it in tonight? We had five people call in sick, and we could really use your help. Please call me here at the jail as soon as you get this message so I can confirm.' Beep. There are no more messages."

Oh Crap! The jail? Do I really still work there??

Other than seeing the jail uniform in his closet, Benjamin completely forgot that he worked there, and he certainly wasn't prepared to go in tonight.

UGH! I hated working at the jail. I hated everything about it.

Thinking back to when he and Natalie started getting serious in their relationship, Benjamin recalled how sick he got when he worked at the jail. He thought about how the stress of his employment there affected his marriage with Natalie, especially in the beginning. It was a major cause of problems for both of them, and at that time, Benjamin became very unhappy. About three months after they got married, Benjamin quit the jail, went to work for QuikTrip, and went to college on his GI Bill.

But, again, that was then.

Regardless of how he felt about the jail, Benjamin would find the number and respond to Captain Hoffman. Because of his experiences at the jail, Benjamin tried very hard to forget about working there, but he did remember that he really respected Captain Hoffman, who cared about the detention officers.

But for now, Benjamin needed to find the number that he had for Lance Corporal McDaniels. If there was one thing that Benjamin really enjoyed about being a reservist, it was conducting Funeral Honor Details for the reserve center, no matter how long it had been since his last participation.

Benjamin searched the table that the answering machine sat on. He saw many numbers, but not the one he needed. He then searched through a set of drawers under the table. He opened the top drawer, where there was a list of phone numbers written on a piece of paper.

Okay…number…number…number…ah, there it is!"

He dialed it instantly, and the phone no more started to ring when Benjamin looked around for a clock. Realizing that it must be late, he almost questioned his decision to return Lance Corporal McDaniels's call. Benjamin glanced back at the answering machine when he saw a desk clock. It was 11:12.

Man, it's late!

And just then, someone answered the phone on the other end.

"Hello?"

"Lance Corporal McDaniels?"

"Yes?"

"This is Major Jones, just returning your call."

"Major…Jones?"

Oh crap!

"I am so sorry; it's Sgt. Jones. I am so sorry to bother you, and I really hope I did not wake you, but…"

"Oh, you didn't wake me, Sgt. Jones," she interrupted. "We aren't in bed, yet. So did you get my message?"

"Yes, I did…and I want it. I will be there thirty minutes prior, unless you need me to come by the center first."

"You don't need to come by the center, first. I'll be meeting you at Floral Haven. I'll have the 'I&I' and Corporal Bates with me."

"The 'I&I' will be with you?"

"Yes, the deceased was a retired Lieutenant Colonel, so Major Thorpe will be presenting the flag. We just need you to fold it."

"Okay. I'll be there."

"Great, we will see you there. Have a great weekend, Sarge."

Lance Corporal McDaniels hung up as Benjamin turned the phone off.

Okay, now I have to call the jail.

Benjamin started looking for the number when the phone rang. He answered it, immediately, as he hadn't put it back on the charger.

"Hello?"

"Hey, Senior Jones, this is Captain Hoffman."

"Hey, Captain, I just got your message, and I was just about to call you back."

"Can you come in tonight, Senior? I'm sorry to ask you this, and I know it's your night off, but…"

"Yes, I can, and I'll be in as soon as I get my uniform on."

"Great, man! Thank you so much for this. Please hurry, and I am sorry but I have to put you in a pod tonight."

"Um, okay, I should be there soon," Benjamin replied.

He hadn't worked in a jail pod in so long, but…

"Thanks, Buddy, see ya soon."

Benjamin hung up the phone, went downstairs to grab is jail uniform, and quickly put it on. He locked the door, ran to his pick-up, got in, turned it on, and left for the jail.

On his way there, he recalled that he had to help prepare for Sunday school that next morning, but quickly realized there was nothing he could do about that.

Maybe when I get off work, I can call Raymond and tell him that I can't make it, after all.

Benjamin would have to deal with that, later. For now, he had to remember how to be a detention officer, once again. It was a tough job in many ways; definitely tougher than Benjamin ever imagined.

He drove down Highway 75 right into Tulsa. As he came upon the downtown streets, leading to the jail, he became a little nervous. The idea of being locked up in a pod with a bunch of inmates wasn't a pleasant one. It wasn't because he was afraid, but he just hadn't done it in so long that he had to remember how to do the job. His anxiety level rose as he pulled into the parking lot at the jail and got out of the car. He just stood there, staring at the facility.

Why do I still work here?

He sighed heavily and walked in the doors. He came upon the control center, and as the control center officers saw him, they unlocked the main entrance doors for Benjamin to go through. He went through the corridor and into the main hallway, leading toward the control desk where Captain Hoffman was waiting for him.

"Man, thank you so much for coming in."

"No problem. Where do you need me?"

Captain Hoffman sighed, almost in disappointment.

"I need you in Pod 3, tonight."

"Pod 3; okay," Benjamin responded. He started walking toward the pod when Captain Hoffman called for him.

"Senior Jones, look, I need you to understand something. Pod 3 has had many issues over the last two nights. This is one of the reasons that I needed you, tonight. Some violent folks were arrested, and they are assigned to that pod. Right now there are two officers in there. We almost had to call in the SORT Team because it got so rough. But most of the inmates are in bed now. Just keep your eyes open, and be careful."

"Okay. I will."

Captain Hoffman handed Benjamin an inmate roster before Benjamin took off for the pod. The pod doors opened up, and he went inside. He saw one officer at the control desk and one making rounds up on the second deck. As they saw Benjamin, they both gave him his turnover. They were sure to include the heavy activity that occurred in that pod the last few nights.

As they left the pod, Benjamin looked around to see many faces staring at him through cell windows. He said a prayer, then proceeded on with his roster check. He started up the stairs to the second deck and went to every cell door, checking inmate armbands. Some inmates gave him a hard time, but for the most part, his inmate count went generally uneventful.

As he came down the stairs, he looked over at a cell door that flew open with an inmate barging out of the cell. Just when Benjamin was about to order the inmate back into the cell, another door from the other side of the pod flung open, and two other inmates exited that cell swiftly. Before Benjamin knew it, the inmates charged each other. Benjamin grabbed his radio and called for help.

"This is Senior Jones, and I need assistance in Pod 3!"

After the call on the radio, Benjamin ordered all three inmates back to their cells. About that time, inmates from all over the pod started banging on their cell doors and creating chaotic noises. The fight was on between the inmate from the first cell and the two from the second. Benjamin knew he had to do something as the two inmates were intensifying their assault on the other one.

"This is Senior Jones! I need assistance in Pod 3 now!"

The fight was getting bloody, and Benjamin realized that he had to act in order to stop the violence.

"You two, get off him and get back to your cells now!"

"Screw you, Uncle Tom," one of them yelled back at Benjamin.

"Oh, I know you did not just call me that!"

Benjamin ran up to the fight and quickly disabled one of the attacking inmates, throwing him on the ground and placing handcuffs on him. Leaving the cuffed inmate lying on the ground, Benjamin leaped for the other inmate, who had all but beaten the third inmate into a bloody mess. Benjamin went to grab the inmate to subdue him when the inmate turned on him, attacking him ferociously. Benjamin did his best to protect himself as the inmate went to grab his radio. Benjamin struggled with the strength of this inmate, who kept trying to overpower him. The other inmates in the pod intensified their verbal chaos, yelling and banging on the doors as much as they could, trying to encourage the inmate who was attacking Benjamin. The inmate successfully grabbed Benjamin's radio and threw it to the ground, smashing it into several pieces.

"Call for help now, pig!"

The inmate who had been initially cuffed managed to roll over onto his knees, stand back up, and proceeded to kick the target of their violent show. Benjamin was losing control of the pod, and he knew it. As he continued to wrestle with the second inmate, he began to feel like he was going to lose control of himself. The inmate attacking him brought his fist up against Benjamin in an uppercut, but Benjamin maneuvered out of the way and responded with a quick punch and jab into the inmate's throat, causing the inmate to grab it. The inmate, then, fell to the ground on his knees, and Benjamin ran back over to the cuffed inmate, kicking the one bleeding on the ground. Benjamin grabbed him, swinging him over his hip, and sending him to the floor, landing on his stomach with a hard crash. The inmate groaned in pain, as Benjamin grabbed his second set of cuffs, went back over to the inmate holding his throat, forced him on the ground, and cuffed him quickly. Benjamin looked up to see one inmate bleeding on the ground, another lying on his stomach with cuffs on, and the third at his grips, also with cuffs on, still struggling to breathe.

Benjamin quickly ran to the pod operations desk and hit the 'Contact Control Center' button. He looked around as some of the inmates were trying to pick their way through the cell doors while others continued banging and yelling. Finally, the pod doors opened up and Captain Hoffman came in with two other detention officers, followed by a nurse.

"Get these guys to medical now," Captain Hoffman yelled while pointing at the two cuffed inmates. He looked over at the inmate who had been severely beaten.

"And we are going to need a gurney."

Captain Hoffman looked over at Benjamin.

"You had better go to medical with them, Senior Jones. These guys will stay behind to finish the count and put the pod down for the night."

Benjamin didn't argue. As another nurse came into the pod with the gurney, the nurse, Benjamin, and Captain Hoffman loaded the inmate into the gurney. Then Benjamin escorted the inmate and the nurse to medical. Upon his arrival, Benjamin was handed a medical report to fill out but his hands were shaking so bad that he had to calm himself before he could start writing. He went into an unoccupied room within the medical ward and started filling out his report. Just as he started, he heard the main door open, followed by the sound of a familiar voice.

"Where is Senior C.O. Jones?"

"He is in that room," responded a voice of one of the nurses.

Benjamin heard footsteps walk up to the door of his room, and in walked Chief Beckett.

"How are you doin', Senior?"

"A little shakin' up, but I am okay."

"I am glad. Listen, we need to talk."

Chief Beckett looked over his shoulder to ensure nobody was listening in on their conversation.

"I just saw the recording of the incident, and some of your actions could very well be deemed as inappropriate."

"What? What do you mean?"

"The video shows your use of force to be too aggressive."

"Too aggressive?? Are you freakin' kidding me?"

Benjamin was floored.

"Look, Ben, don't make this harder than what it already is. You know that the inmates are going to take this to a higher level. I just think that…"

"They were beating the crap out of the other inmate," Benjamin interrupted, forcefully.

"Look, I know what they were doing, but you should have waited for help."

"I called for help, Sir! I called for help twice and got no answer!!"

"Ben, you need to calm down! You are not making this any easier for yourself."

"I can't believe what I am hearing! This is ridiculous! I mean, what was I supposed to do? Leave those inmates to beat that other dude to death?"

"Benjamin, I have one inmate who has a crushed larynx and another who claims his ribs are broken from you throwing him on the ground. Once more, we have all this on video. Now I know you were trying to help the other inmate, but this is not going to be good for us…or you."

Benjamin sat there, shaking his head in disbelief.

"So what happens now, Chief?"

"I have to send you home and file a report. You will most likely be put on leave without pay until the warden can sort this out."

"All right," Benjamin responded as he got up. "I'm leaving."

"Hey, I still need your report, Senior Jones."

"If I still have my job, I'll gladly bring it to you."

NOT PRESENT OR FUTURE...

Benjamin walked out of the medical ward. He continued to the main hall leading to the exit and passed by the main control desk where he saw Captain Hoffman filling out his report. Benjamin said nothing as he kept on going, proceeding to the exiting hallway. As Benjamin came to the final control doors leading out of the facility, he hit the button for the control room officers to let him through.

"Senior Jones, Chief needs to talk to you."

"Open these doors," Benjamin pressed.

"Senior, we can't until—"

"Open these doors, now!!"

The control room officers looked at each other as one of them hit the button, removing the locks to the doors. Benjamin went through the doors, out through the main entrance, into the parking lot, and got in his pick-up. He sat there, trying to make sense of what just happened, and wishing he would have just not come to the jail at all. He started his pick-up and left the parking lot, heading home. He could not help but to think about the insanity of what just transpired.

None of this is happening the way it should be. None of it!

CHAPTER 7

Natalie opened her eyes, slowly, as the sun came through the bedroom window. She lay there for a second before initially realizing that she was is in different surroundings than she was used to. She quickly sat up, looking around to get her bearings.

This looks a little familiar. Ugh, I gotta wake up!

As she rubbed her eyes, she stood up out of the bed and walked over to the door when the aroma of bacon hit her. She closed her eyes and took a deep breath through her nose, savoring every characteristic of the aroma, and exhaled very contently, instantly realizing where she was.

Oh, Lord, I am really here!!

There was no misunderstanding that smell. She opened her eyes and opened the bedroom door. She walked down the hallway and into the living room where she could see Carmella and Florance sitting around the kitchen table, drinking coffee and laughing at each other.

"Well, good morning, sleepyhead. Perfect timing."

Florance greeted Natalie with a big smile, as Natalie walked over to her and gave her a hug. She had to try holding back a few tears.

"Good morning, Momma."

Carmella just sat there, watching the two embrace and enjoying Natalie's demeanor. It made Carmella's heart warm to see Natalie in such peace, especially after the previous day. Natalie let go of her mother and sat down at the table next to Carmella.

"How about some biscuits and gravy, bacon, eggs, and hash browns?"

NOT PRESENT OR FUTURE...

Carmella and Natalie looked at each other with eager anticipation as Florance placed their individual plates in front of them.

"Dig in!"

Natalie all but scarfed down her breakfast. With all of the drama lately, she had not had much of an appetite. Her mother's cooking was one way to cure that.

"Once you girls get done, go ahead and get dressed and we will head off to church."

Natalie was so content with the meal she didn't realize that her mother was already wearing her favorite church dress. As she finished her breakfast, she drank her orange juice, got up from the chair, and kissed her mom on the cheek. After thanking her mother for breakfast, Natalie placed her plate in the sink, and went back to her bedroom to get dressed. As Natalie shut the bedroom door, it hit her:

Oh man! I didn't bring anything to change into!

She started looking around the room and rummaged through the closet. She found an older, pretty dress and pulled it up to herself, inspecting it in front of the mirror.

This is pretty, but will it fit?

She stood there for a brief second, trying to figure out how the dress got in that closet. It wasn't big enough to fit her mother, and Natalie hadn't recognized it. She quickly undressed and pulled the dress over her head, sliding it on. She looked at herself in the mirror again.

It looks okay. A little tight in the back, but…

She turned to reach the zipper in the back. With no problems, she was able to zip up the dress, and realized that the dress fit perfectly.

Now about some churchy shoes…

Natalie left the bedroom and walked back into the living room where Carmella had just finished her breakfast.

"Momma, may I borrow a pair of shoes? I didn't bring any for church. I need some for this dress I found…"

"Oh, look at you," Florance interrupted. She had Natalie's attention as she looked over her dress.

"Is it okay, Momma? I found it in my closet, and though I am not familiar with it…"

"I bought that for you some time ago, honey. I was hoping it would fit. Turn around and let me see it."

Natalie spun around slowly, showing Florance all sides of the dress.

"Mmm, girl, look at you," Carmella teased. "Gonna have to fight off those choir boys!"

Natalie giggled at Carmella while twirling in her dress, allowing Florance to continue inspecting it.

"Yes, dear, I sure do have a pair of shoes that will fit that dress. Come on and get them."

Florance turned toward her room, but paused just before she lost sight of Carmella.

"What about you, Carmella? What are you wearing?"

"Guilty," Carmella replied. "I didn't bring a dress either."

"Well, you might as well come on too, dear. I think I got something for ya."

Carmella jumped up from her seat, put her plate and glass into the sink, and followed Florance into her bedroom with eager anticipation. Florance always had beautiful dresses, and if there was one in her closet for Carmella, she felt destined to wear it.

After about twenty minutes of looking, trying on dresses, and comparing shoes, all three emerged from the house ready for church, looking quite content with their individual attire choices.

Natalie looked over at Carmella, who was beaming like the sun in the beautiful dress and shoes that Florance picked out for her. They all three got in the car and took off for church.

As they approached the church parking lot, Florance pulled into her favorite parking spot and the three exited the car. It was no doubt, from the looks that all three women were getting, they would be a hot topic of discussion, especially from the men. They all walked into the church, trying to maneuver around the cadre of people making their ways to their seats. A few of Florance's friends stopped her for a chat, which seemed to turn into a lengthy discussion. Florance loved to talk, as evidence by her chattiness with whomever chose to stop her, and Natalie had to pry her away from her group of friends.

NOT PRESENT OR FUTURE...

As they took their seats in the pews, the service started with worship and hymns, which was one of Natalie's favorite moments during church service. The music filled her soul as she praised God with all her heart. Hands in the air, Natalie sang and prayed, drinking in the atmosphere, and thanking God for her time with her mother. She still found herself questioning the reality of her current situation. For that matter, Natalie still had a hard time believing anything that was happening to her at that moment.

Natalie brought her hands down and opened her eyes. Instinctively, as her hand touched the back of the pew in front of her, she immediately reached for Benjamin's hand before she realized he was not there. She had to come to her senses, but for some reason, it was difficult to do so. She looked down at her right hand and realized that Leesha was not there either.

"Lord, please…"

Natalie began to pray before she realized she could not finish her prayer. She didn't know what else to say.

Calm yourself, Natalie. You are here with your mother. It's going to be okay.

She snapped back to the reality, determined to focus on with what was happening at that moment. She had her mother back, and nothing was going to change that.

As worship ended, the preacher took the podium and the service began. Natalie suppressed her emotions and ignored her memories. If this was a chance at a new life, however it came about, she was going to take it.

Now, I have to figure out what to do with my 'new' life.

Looking over at Carmella and Florance, it was all clear to Natalie that she would have to do just that.

At least that is what she thought.

put his feet on the floor. Lowering his head in his hands, and covering his eyes, he had a hard time gathering his thoughts due to the pain.

"Natalie," he called instinctively with the intent on asking for some medicine.

He managed to get his eyes to open enough for him to realize that he was in the same room where he was the day before, and Natalie was nowhere in sight. Benjamin stood up out of bed and stumbled into the bathroom. He looked on the sink for some type of painkiller, and stumbled around the drawers below the sink where he found a bottle of Motrin.

"Oh, thank you, Lord!"

He opened the bottle and grabbed four tablets, shoveling them into his mouth. He reached down and grabbed a swig of water from the faucet. As his eyes focused a bit more, Benjamin then stumbled his way back to his bed and fell into it. He rolled over just enough to try to locate his clock.

8:23.

Okay, I can still make it to church. But first, I have to get rid of this headache.

As he lay there thinking about what happened just a couple of hours earlier, he desperately tried to capture the scene in his mind.

Was it a dream as well?

His head was pounding so severely that he felt nauseous, and he didn't want to move. It was enough for him just to be able to think.

I just have to ease my breathing. Just breathe slowly.

While lying there in his bed, waiting for the medicine to kick in, Benjamin dozed off, falling asleep just enough to escape the pain in his head. His eyes opened, slowly and he looked back at the clock.

9:01

Crap! I gotta get up.

Benjamin sat up, realizing that the medicine must be working as he did not feel the deep, throbbing pain in his head any longer. He got up, took a quick shower, then went to his closet to try and find some church clothes. He glanced at that clock again and, realizing he was going to be late, decided to try and call Raymond, thinking he could catch Raymond before he left for church.

Benjamin looked over at his list of numbers on a paper calendar located beneath his phone. He read through the numbers, allowing himself to become familiarized with each one, again. He knew that Raymond's number was there, and he kept looking around on the paper until he found it. It was then that he noticed one particular number that he hadn't seen in a while.

Florance Barnes. Florance?? Natalie's mother?

Benjamin looked at it closely and noticed Natalie's number right below it, scratched out but revealing enough to where he could still make it out. He took his glance off those numbers to regain his focus on his original search.

There it is!

As Benjamin picked up the phone and dialed the number, it answered after two rings.

"Hello?"

"Hey, Chelsey, this is Benjamin. I know that Raymond must be at the church but could you please tell him that I am really running late this morning? I had to go into work last night and..."

"Sure, I'll tell him," she interrupted. "I am just now leaving the house."

"Oh, thank you. Please tell him I am hurrying."

"Okay; we'll see you there," she responded as she hung up the phone.

After looking through his clothes, Benjamin found a decent shirt and a pair of pants that he thought were good enough for church. After putting on his shoes, he scurried out to his pick-up and took off. He pulled into the church parking lot and walked into the church, where he met Brian at the door conducting his normal pre-sermon greetings.

"Benjamin, what's happening, brother?? It's good to see you!"

"Good morning, Brian. Have you seen Raymond? I am running a little late today and..."

Benjamin paused as he started looking around.

"He's right over there," Brian replied, pointing toward the sanctuary.

"Thanks, Brian," Benjamin responded as he walked over to Raymond.

Raymond was gathering kids from the sanctuary and corralling them to the youth room as Benjamin approached him.

"Ray, did you get my message?"

"I sure did, brother. No worries. Chelsey said you had to work last night."

"Yeah, they called me in at the last minute and, well…it was just a bad night."

"Well, how 'bout you tell me all about it over lunch?"

"Sounds good," Benjamin replied as they both walked toward the youth room. Raymond handed Benjamin a stack of papers.

"Here is your lesson for the junior higher's, if you still want to teach it."

Ben took the lesson plan and looked over it quickly.

"I would have had this to you well before now, but we just got crazy this week."

"No problem," Benjamin responded. Then it hit him. He totally forgot his Bible.

"Oh, crap! I gotta grab a Bible."

"There are some in the youth room," Raymond replied.

"Great! Thanks, Raymond!"

Benjamin and Raymond entered the youth room, and just before Raymond could give his instructions, a group of boys approached them, both.

"Benjamin, what's up??"

It seemed like the entire youth room of eighty plus kids lit up as Benjamin and Raymond walked through the doors. In a matter of seconds, Benjamin was surrounded by all the boys, giving him high fives, wanting to hang around him, and most importantly, wanting to schedule another fun night at his place. Raymond just laughed. He loved to watch Benjamin with the kids. The kids loved having Benjamin as a youth sponsor, and Raymond knew it.

"Okay, okay, okay," Raymond started, trying to get the kids' attention. "All junior higher's go with Benjamin and the rest stay with me."

NOT PRESENT OR FUTURE...

"WHAT??"

About twenty-five boys simultaneously responded in a comical protest.

"Yes, that's right, all you high schoolers are stuck with me today," Raymond teased.

"Hey, Benjamin, will you be here tonight?"

"Uh, yes, I...believe so," Benjamin replied, hesitantly, as he took the junior-higher's in the other room to conduct his lesson.

"All right, we will see you tonight," came shouts of admiration from some of the high school boys in the group.

Benjamin gave Raymond the usual thumbs up, communicating that he had the junior-higher's under control. He then took his kids in the other room and began his lesson.

Following the lesson, which was generally lively and rambunctious -as the junior higher's tended to be- Benjamin joined Raymond and Chelsey for the church service. Benjamin was very tired, and it showed in his demeanor, but he did the best he could to stay awake through the service. As it ended, Raymond and Chelsey got up and started toward the pre-school to get their children. Raymond looked back at Benjamin, and noticing that he hadn't moved, Raymond became concerned about him.

"Hey, brother, you doin' okay?"

"Yeah, I am just very tired. Like I said, last night was a very long night."

Benjamin was tired, and he was still fighting a bit of a headache. At this moment, all he really wanted to do was go to bed. He wasn't sure what was wrong, but for some reason, he started breathing heavily. His demeanor seemed to change, and he didn't want to go to lunch. He didn't want company. He didn't want anything.

"Hey, Raymond, would you mind if I took a rain check on that lunch? I think I am going to go home and get some rest."

"Yeah, sure, brother, go home. If you need to cancel for tonight, don't worry; just let me know."

Benjamin stood up and walked toward the exit door. Raymond watched Benjamin as he left, and he said a prayer for Benjamin.

Raymond knew there was something not right with him. Benjamin was acting very peculiar, and it was beginning to concern Raymond.

"Do you think he will be okay," Chelsey asked Raymond.

"I think so. I am gonna have to get with him, later, to see what's going on with him."

As Benjamin approached his pick-up, he pulled his keys from his pocket and dropped them onto the ground. His hands started shaking, uncontrollably.

No, not again; not here.

Benjamin tried to overcome this shaking sensation –along with his breathing- and picked up his keys. He unlocked the door, opened it, and sat in his pick-up as quickly as he could, shutting the door behind him. With every second, his breathing became even more intense.

I've got to get a grip! Why am I going through this, here?

Benjamin experienced this before, especially the past few years. Natalie had noticed these symptoms when he came back from Afghanistan, but when she brought them up, Benjamin would always shrug it off and state that he just had to work through it. Over the course of a few years, though, his symptoms just worsened.

But I'm not the same as I was. I am here, in this time, now. This doesn't make any sense!

As he sat there trying to control his breathing, he began to pray.

"Lord, whatever is going on with me, please help me?"

Almost immediately, his breathing began to ease, but his mind continued to run. Benjamin began to think about Natalie and the kids. To him, they were just as real as if they were sitting right in front of him.

But they aren't real! Right? Ugh!

Benjamin struggled with the thoughts of his family. He didn't want to think about anything at that moment. He just wanted to leave. He felt like he wanted to run; to escape, just like he had felt many times before.

But escape from what? There was nothing to escape from.

He opened his eyes, turned on the pick-up and started the drive home. When he arrived at his home, he went into the house, straight to his bedroom, and sat on his bed. All he could do was breathe. He looked at his hands, which had stopped shaking. For whatever reason, he felt so overwhelmed and very exhausted. He kicked off his shoes, leaned back into his bed, and fell asleep.

Carmella and Natalie pulled into the apartment complex at 9:54. Natalie was tired, but she had a very restful weekend despite the emotional ride. Carmella pulled up in front of Natalie's apartment and Natalie exited the car.

"Thank you for everything you did for me this weekend, Carmella. I am so thankful you were there for me."

"No problem, girl! I will be checking on you tomorrow. Let me know how it goes. I am hoping that they keep you."

"I am not sure why they would, honestly. I'll see you, later, girl!"

Natalie closed the car door and went to her apartment. As she went to unlock her door, she looked back at Carmella as Carmella drove off, waving. Natalie went inside her apartment, shut and locked the door behind her, then sat on her bed.

Man, what a weekend!

Natalie looked over to her answering machine and saw that she had fourteen messages.

What the heck? Fourteen messages??

She reached over to push the 'Play' button on the machine.

"Message 1: 'Hey, girl, where are you at? You need to call me.' Beep. End of new message."

From the sound of it, Natalie figured it was Darnell, but she was not going to call him back. She had to tell him to move on, somehow.

"Message 2: 'Hey, I am tired of calling you! You best call me back.' Beep. End of new message."

Oh no! These better not be all from him.

Messages 3, 4, 5…on and on…were from Darnell, and definitely not what Natalie needed to hear. While the messages kept playing, Natalie stood up and started getting ready for bed. She went into the bathroom to brush her teeth when she heard a different voice on the machine.

"… 'take care of this so we don't have this happening any more. Please give me a call if you need to discuss this further.' Beep. End of new message."

Natalie looked over at the machine from the bathroom. She quickly dropped her toothbrush, rinsed her mouth, and ran over to the answering machine, drying her face with a towel. As she got to the answering machine, she replayed that message.

"Message 11: 'Ms. Barnes, this is the apartment manager. We are getting complaints that someone keeps banging on your door, looking for you. One of the other tenants even stated that this person threatened them. I might ask that you please take care of this so we don't have this happening any more. Please give me a call if you need to discuss this further.' Beep. End of new message."

What is he doing?? This guy's crazy!!

She would go talk to the apartment manager in the morning to apologize for the disturbances. But for now, she sat back down on the bed to finish listening to the messages, afraid of what she might hear next. Messages 11, 12, and 13 were all from Darnell. Just listening to them made Natalie feel completely nauseous. It was all she could do to listen to the final message.

She stood up to end the messages, and as she put her finger on the button, she paused for a second to see if it was Darnell's voice.

"Message 14: 'Natalie, honey, it's Mom. I just wanted to tell you that I love you. I had a very good time with you and Carmella this weekend, not to mention that Denzel is always good lookin' in his movies. Please give me a call when you get home. I will be praying for you. Please remember that I am always here for you.' Beep. End of new messages."

Natalie soaked in the joy of hearing her mother's voice on the machine. She still felt blessed that she actually got to see her mother again; to spend time with her, to hold her. It was all she could do to leave her mother to come back to Abilene, and she probably would not have done so if Carmella did not have to come back. In reality,

Natalie did have to make some decisions now that, apparently, she was not with Benjamin any more.

Any more. Any more?

That thought, for some reason, made her feel lonely. How would she cope with all this? It wasn't just waking up here, now. It was also the fact that she had three children; children who were no longer in her life and, from the looks of things, weren't going to be.

Natalie, you can't think about this now. You just can't. You can't handle this.

Before allowing herself to become any more emotional, Natalie picked up the phone and called her mother. She could not explain much at the present moment, but for some reason, she could talk to her mother. Right now, that seemed to be enough.

CHAPTER 8

Benjamin got up early and got ready for the funeral honor detail. His uniform was immaculate; pressed and blemish free. Benjamin enjoyed every opportunity he had to put on his uniform. It was something that he had to consider heavily before he left active duty.

Benjamin wanted to leave for the funeral, early enough, to run by the reserve center before the funeral at Floral Haven. Normally, he would have just gone and worked the service but he was curious as to how things looked at the center.

In 2011, all the military personnel left the old facility -which the Navy leased from the city of Broken Arrow- and moved to a larger, newer facility located down the road. Though the new facility was very nice, Benjamin enjoyed the fact that this one was easier to locate and quicker to get to.

Benjamin grabbed his cap, inspected his uniform one last time, and left. He pulled into the reserve center and walked into the Marine Corps side. He looked around to see who was behind the counter.

"Hey, Sgt. Jones, how are you?"

It was Lance Corporal McDaniels, who had seen Benjamin from the side office.

"Hey, how are you doing, Lance Corporal? It's been a while," Benjamin responded as he walked up to shake her hand.

"Ummm, if a week is a while, then…"

Crap! I did it again, Benjamin thought.

"You're right. Sorry 'bout that. Been a crazy week, I guess."

And that was putting it lightly.

NOT PRESENT OR FUTURE...

"Aren't you…a little early, Sarge," Lance Corporal McDaniels asked, looking at her watch. "I didn't realize you were coming here before going to the funeral."

"Oh, uh, I…I just needed to get some stuff done."

Benjamin had to come up with something that made sense, quick.

"I was looking into, maybe, getting some admin work done."

"Oh, does it have to do with your commissioning package? Were we able to get you squared away for your OU paperwork?"

OU paperwork?

Benjamin thought about how to answer that question.

"Uh, yes, yes, you were. Thank you so much for that!"

Benjamin went along with her questions in the hopes that she knew what she was talking about. After all, he did go to the University of Oklahoma, but, from his perspective, that was a while ago. Things are just a bit different now.

"Major Thorpe would have endorsed your letter once if you were in your senior year, but he's leaving soon. But there are still things we can help you do to prepare."

"Major Thorpe," Benjamin inquired.

"Yes, the 'I&I,'" she responded, smiling as if she was trying to figure him out.

Benjamin looked confused. He had to try and remember Major Thorpe. Major Shimshi was the last Instructor and Inspector that Benjamin remembered.

"When is Major Thorpe leaving," Benjamin asked.

"Uh, his change-of-command ceremony is next week. I thought you were participating in that."

"Um, I am."

Benjamin just about got caught, again. He really needed to shut up, but he had to dig out of this hole.

"Could you remind me again the time of the ceremony? I want to be sure I am here on time."

"Here…"

Lance Corporal McDaniels walked over to her desk and picked up a pamphlet.

"Here is a copy of the event schedule."

Lance Corporal McDaniels handed Benjamin a schedule with the date, time, and his position in the event.

"Thank you! I'll be there!"

She saved him. Otherwise, he would have had no idea about this ceremony.

"Um, who is replacing Major Thorpe?"

"Major Robert Shimshi."

Okay, now I remember!

Benjamin was getting back on track of things. In the past, Benjamin didn't really do much at the reserve center until just after Major Thorpe left, which explained why he wasn't familiar with him, now.

"So as far as my college paperwork, did you need anything else from me?"

"Oh no, Sgt. Jones, we have everything we need. Just enroll in your classes and be sure you submit your grades to us. You have to maintain a 'C' average or better to continue receiving your GI Bill benefits."

"Okay. Thanks for the help!"

About that time Major Thorpe came around the corner wearing his dress uniform.

"Are you ready to go, Sergeant," he asked Benjamin.

"Yes, Sir!"

Lance Corporal McDaniels walked up to Major Thorpe and handed him a binder.

"Here is the paperwork for the funeral, Sir, and Corporal Bates is pulling the duty van around now to pick you both up."

"Thank you, Lance Corporal McDaniels. Oh, and did you send out the message regarding 'CTT volunteer' orders?"

"Yes, Sir! I sent them out this morning and will put them in the plan-of-the-month for the drill weekend."

"Thank you, Lance Corporal."

Major looked back over at Benjamin.

"You ready?"

"Yes, Sir," Benjamin responded.

NOT PRESENT OR FUTURE...

They both walked out of the building and toward the van. Major Thorpe had Benjamin's attention, as Benjamin was curious about the 'CTT volunteer' orders that Major Thorpe referred to. But he also thought that Lance Corporal McDaniels was scheduled to join them for the funeral honor detail.

"Isn't Lance Corporal McDaniels coming with us," Benjamin asked.

"No. It turns out we just need the three of us for this one."

They both continued walking toward the van. Benjamin got in the back and Major Thorpe climbed into the passenger's side. As Benjamin looked over at Major Thorpe, he decided to inquire about the comment regarding the 'CTT volunteer' orders.

"Major, what were you referring to when you asked Lance Corporal McDaniels if she sent out the message on the 'CTT volunteer' orders?"

"It's Counterterrorism Training. The Marines are looking for some trainees and instructors to take a set of year-long orders, to Camp Pendleton, to help train Marines for a more dangerously perceived terror threat that we might face in the future."

"Okay," Benjamin responded. He tried to remember how he had missed hearing about that when he and Natalie were dating each other. Maybe it was better he didn't know about it. His military career was difficult for her as it was. If he had to leave her in the beginning of their relationship, it never would have worked.

Not that any of it made a difference now, anyway.

"If you are ever interested in the opportunity, just let Lance Corporal McDaniels know, and she will get you set up with orders."

Benjamin didn't know how to answer that. He had gone through so much being a Marine that, quite honestly, he felt he needed a break. But...

"Thank you, Sir! I will."

"I wish I could go," responded Private Sissler, as he drove. "I mean, I like being here, but sometimes I feel like I am missing the action."

I can assure you, Benjamin thought, while considering all the conflict he has been through in Iraq. *You are not missing a thing.*

They pulled up to the funeral home and went inside to get their show-time. After they met with the funeral director, they all sat in back and watched the service. About an hour later, they took their positions: Private Sissler playing the hymn on the bugle as Benjamin and Major Thorpe folded the flag. As Benjamin completed his fold, he saluted the flag and marched to the back of the auditorium as Major Thorpe presented the flag to the family of the deceased veteran.

Benjamin really loved this part of being a Marine. He loved the opportunity to serve the families of those fallen Marines by participating in these Funeral Honor Details. It always gave him a sense of pride, and he took every event seriously. Since he also got paid to participate in them, he would look to make himself more available for each Funeral Honor Detail that the reserve center needed help with. Considering what was happening at the jail, and the fact that he had no idea how this whole excessive-use-of-force thing was going to play out, it looked like he might be available to help the reserve center more often.

As the funeral ended, the three of them got into the van and headed back to the reserve center. When they pulled up into the center parking lot, Benjamin asked Major Thorpe if he needed any help carrying anything in.

"Nope. We got it. If you have more time to do funeral honor details, just let Lance Corporal McDaniels know."

"Yes, Sir! Have a good day, Sir!"

"You too, Sargent!"

Benjamin got in his pick-up and drove off. As he headed home from the reserve center, he thought about the direction that he needed to focus on taking in his life. It looked like getting his degree at OU was still an option, and though in his mind he had no desire to do all the schoolwork again, he didn't think that he had much choice, given his current situation. The orders sounded interesting, but Benjamin had too much of what was about to come, already. In reality, he was still trying to deal with this experience he was having, and though it was crazy, he would have to take it one day at a time.

At least until he could come up with a new life plan.

CHAPTER 9

Beep. Beep. Beep. Beep. Beep. Beep.

Natalie's alarm sounded, and she reached over to shut it off. She opened her eyes and tried to get her morning bearings.

Okay. I am still in my apartment. I guess this is not a dream.

She got up quickly and started getting dressed for work. She was determined to go into the Arger Corporation and apologize for her actions. At this point she had no idea how she was going to explain what happened or if they were going to even listen to her.

Honestly, why should they listen to me? From a professional standpoint, my actions were so inappropriate. This is so crazy!

The Bakersfield Project was a huge deal for both the Arger Corporation and the Tramsen Corporation, and Natalie's absence from the meeting probably screwed things up.

I have no idea how I will explain this, but I have to try.

She went through her dresses, picked the one she was going to wear, put it on, and grabbed her best pair of shoes. Putting on makeup quickly, she rushed over to her purse to make sure she had her keys and her wallet. When she finished with her makeup, she grabbed her purse and was walking to the door when…

Blllp.

Natalie turned her head toward the phone, immediately looking for the caller ID and realizing there wasn't one.

Crap!

She kept forgetting that these weren't the iPhones she was used to, displaying the number on the phone when she received a call. Hesitantly, she answered it.

"Hello?"

"Hey, girl, just wanted to say good luck today!"

"Oh, Carmella, it's you. Thank you!"

"Well, of course it's me, silly. Who else would it be?"

"Uhhh…"

"Never mind, don't tell me," Carmella joked. "Just go get your job back. Can't have you runnin' away back to Amarillo now, can we?"

Natalie laughed.

"I just wanted to wish you good luck, girl, and let you know I love ya and am prayin' for ya."

"Thank you, Carmella. I will call you as soon as I get back."

"Okay, girl! I'll be looking for it. See ya."

"See ya!"

Natalie hung up the phone, nearly giggling at Carmella's response when Natalie realized it was her on the phone.

Who else would it be calling me? I'd rather not think about it.

At that moment, Natalie remembered that she had to go by the office and apologize about Darnell. She practically stumbled out of her apartment in her heals, and walked over to her car. She got in to start it up, realizing that she did not lock her apartment door. She got back out of her car, went to lock the door, and went back to her car. She put her keys in the ignition to start her car, but the engine was very weak, turning over.

Oh no! Please don't do this??

She sat there for a second and hoped that she could get the car started.

"Lord, please let this thing start?"

She turned the key again and, with a sigh of relief, the car started. She drove around to the apartment complex front office, put the car in park, and went inside the office, leaving the car running as to not take a chance in it not starting again. As she walked into the office, she noticed the manager sitting at a desk with his eyes glued to his computer screen.

"How can I help you," he asked without even the slightest move of his head.

"I'm Natalie Jones from Apartment 17."

He quickly turned his head to see her standing there as she continued.

"I just wanted to come and speak to you…"

"Oh, yeah, so you're the one," he interrupted.

"Excuse me??"

"You're the one we keep getting complaints about some dude banging on your door."

"Yes, that's me. I just wanted to apologize about this. I don't know why he is doing this."

She was a bit offended by his demeanor, but she tried to maintain her poise.

"What? Is he your boyfriend or something?"

"No!"

"Well, we have been getting complaints, so either you get him to quit, or we will call the police on him."

"That's fine; do what you need to do."

"We can't keep having disruptions like this in our complex," he continued.

"I understand, Sir. I will take care of it."

He walked up to a white dry-erase board showing drawings of each apartment room with the names of its current occupants.

"Did you say your name was Natalie 'Jones'…because it says 'Barnes' right here," he stated, pointing at her apartment lot on the board.

Oh no! I did it again. Quick, Natalie, say something!!

"Did I say Jones? I don't recall that."

"Yes, you did. You said Natalie 'Jones'. You know you should let us know when you get married or change your name. We have to keep our records updated."

He was becoming testy, and Natalie did not feel comfortable with it. She opened her purse, pulled out her driver's license, and showed it to him.

"My name is 'Natalie Barnes'. I don't know what you heard, but here it is on my driver's license."

At this point she was borderline irate, and she was about to let him know it.

"Okay, okay," he responded. "Don't get upset."

Clearly he could see that he set her off. Natalie turned around, put her license back in her purse, and exited the office. She got into her car and left to head toward the Arger Corporation. She had to calm herself down a bit while she was driving. Thinking about her encounter with the complex manager, she tried to figure out why he acted that way.

Was I being rude? Did I come across as too abrupt? Either way, it certainly did not explain his unprofessionalism. What a jerk!

As she continued to her office, she went from feeling frustrated to feeling nervous. She simply had no idea how her boss was going to handle the situation with her, and she was very concerned. As she pulled into the Arger Corporation parking lot, she parked her car and turned it off. She sat there for a second, praying and trying to calm her nerves. She got out of the car and went inside the office where she saw Shannon sitting behind the desk.

"Hi, Shannon. I was just wondering if I could talk to Mr. Sherman. Does he have a minute?"

Shannon hesitated, but she was willing to check to see if Mr. Sherman would be willing to see her.

"Natalie, I will go let him know you are here, but I have to let you know: we lost the account."

Natalie would probably be extremely disappointed if only she understood what her role was. She vaguely remembered the Bakersfield Project. It was a big account that Arger Corporation was trying to land, but she really was not involved in the process. She was hoping —and praying— that this was not the same account that she recalled.

"I wish I could tell you what happened, Shannon. I am so sorry."

"I am afraid you are going to have to tell Mr. Sherman that. I wish that will be enough."

Natalie sat down on a chair as Shannon went to inform Mr. Sherman of Natalie's visit. She wished, so hard, that she knew what she was supposed to do. It would have made it easier to feel guilty for something that she actually knew that she messed up.

"Natalie, go on in. He's waiting."

Natalie stood up and walked to the door. She looked into the office and noticed Mr. Sherman facing away from her and writing something down on his table behind his seat. Natalie knocked on the door, gently.

"Come in, Natalie."

Natalie came and sat down on one of the two chairs in front of his desk.

"Sir, I am so sorry. I have no excuse. I don't know what happened. I…"

Natalie froze as he turned his chair to face her.

"Natalie, I can't tell you how disappointed I am in you. What bothers me the most about this is that you worked so hard on this project right alongside of me. I can't fathom why you would blow the meeting like you did."

Natalie lowered her head, trying to think of anything to say.

"I would ask you why you weren't there, but all that is irrelevant right now.

Natalie could tell that he was very disappointed. From what she remembered of him, she really enjoyed working for him. In fact, if it weren't for her marriage to Benjamin, she would have stayed to work for Mr. Sherman.

"Sir, I have no right to ask this, but please, please let me stay. I know that I made a mistake, and I know what that account meant to this organization. I love working here. I love being here. I really, truly cannot tell you what happened. But if you give me another chance, I can assure you I will be the administrative professional that you need."

Mr. Sherman trusted Natalie and knew that she was sincere, but that made this issue even more difficult. He did not have a choice.

"Natalie, I really appreciate your enthusiasm for this organization. But I am afraid that my hands are tied. I have to let you go."

"I understand," Natalie replied, still feeling so weird about all this.

Mr. Sherman picked up an envelope and handed it to her over his desk.

"Natalie, this is your final paycheck. I just want to thank you for the good work that you did for me while you were here."

She stood up from her seat and took the envelope.

"Thank you, Sir. I...I appreciate it!"

She held the envelope in her hands, unable to move. She felt so guilty.

"I am truly sorry, Sir," she stated as she turned to leave the office. His response made her pause and turn around.

"Natalie, if you a need reference, please send them to me. As far as anyone needs to know, this never happened. I will never tell anyone why you left. You really did a great job for me while you are here, and I know you will succeed wherever you are."

"Thank you, Mr. Sherman. I really appreciate that."

Natalie turned and walked out of the office. She stopped by Shannon's desk to say good-bye to her, and left. Natalie then walked to her car. She stood at her car door, going over in her mind about this situation and how it turned out. She could not grasp what her responsibility was in this crucial meeting that she missed.

She just had to know.

Natalie walked back into the building and went straight to Shannon's desk.

"Shannon, I know that this sounds crazy, but I need to ask you something."

Shannon gave Natalie her attention. Natalie shook her head in disbelief at what she was about to ask.

"What was it that I was supposed to do for Mr. Sherman on Saturday? What was I supposed to bring to this meeting?"

Shannon looked perplexed, but answered Natalie's question, anyway.

"Natalie, you had all the charts and financial information for our account submission. You had the investment numbers, the papers...you had everything. You were going to go to the meeting to set everything up and have all the notes ready for Mr. Sherman."

Shannon paused to catch her breath.

NOT PRESENT OR FUTURE...

"I mean...you even said you would bring coffee and donuts." Natalie looked frazzled.

Man, I really wish I could have known to be there.

"What was worse: Mr. Sherman was completely embarrassed."

That hit Natalie hard. She had to leave. This was getting to be too much for her.

"I understand, Shannon. Thank you for telling me that."

As Natalie turned to walk away, Shannon caught her just as she approached the door.

"Natalie, I have to ask you a question. What happened? I mean, this is not like you. I know that Mr. Sherman doesn't care, but I have never seen him like this before. It almost sounded like you were drunk on the phone. What happened? Why did you blow this off??"

Natalie sighed, thinking about how to respond.

If only you knew, Shannon.

Natalie honestly didn't know what to say. She stood at the door, wanting to walk out of it so she could just get away, but stood frozen solid. Then she received a small type of reprieve.

"Natalie, was this about...Benjamin?"

Natalie thought as she turned her head toward Shannon, giving her a perplexed look.

What? What did she know about Benjamin?

It didn't matter. Benjamin would become a small scapegoat for Natalie, if only, at least, for the moment. Natalie shut the door and came back inside to talk to Shannon. She honestly did not think that her relationship with Shannon was anything more than that of an acquaintance. However, Natalie felt like she owed someone an explanation. It might as well be Shannon.

"Benjamin and I were engaged, but I honestly don't know what happened between us. I was dealing with some really rough stuff on Saturday. As crazy as it sounds, I just can't give any more explanation than that."

Natalie talked with Shannon for a little bit, trying to explain her situation. At the least, Shannon seemed to understand, and it made Natalie feel a little better. As Natalie finished up, she looked at her watch.

"Well, I'd better go. Thanks for listening."

"You're welcome, Natalie. I hope that things work out for you, and I am really sorry about losing you."

"Me too," Natalie replied. Then she thought about something that Shannon said before and decided to inquire about it.

"Shannon, where is the stuff that was supposed to be presented for this meeting?"

"From what I know, you had all of it—all the charts, grafts, notes, PowerPoint presentations…everything."

"Okay," Natalie responded, trying to figure out where all that stuff might be. "Do you need them back?"

"No. It's kind of irrelevant now."

"Okay. Well, if you need anything, please let me know. I'll see ya around."

"Okay, take care," Shannon responded as Natalie walked out the door.

As Natalie walked toward her car, she wondered where the charts, graphs, notes, and all the other stuff might be. She didn't recall seeing it in her apartment. When she got to her car, she opened up her trunk to see a box with several charts and poster boards.

"There they are!"

She picked up a printed-out PowerPoint packet, and started reading it, turning from page to page, becoming more and more interested with every paragraph. This account would have created jobs. It would have exploded the business, and it really would have been good for Natalie.

This could have been the start of a great career for me!! Oh man!!

After reading through the presentation, she looked over the notes and studied the charts and graphs. She was absolutely intrigued; not so much on the information she saw but the fact that she had anything to do with the preparation in the first place. From what she could gather, based on the notes, she was the one who researched all the information and background from the Tramsen organization.

Considering this, she tried to recall anything that she could from when she worked at Arger before she and Ben got engaged.

Tramsen was another oil-type company, and the CEO was Jonathan Quartermain. She actually had met him at a luncheon that she went to with her boss, just before she left Arger, to marry Benjamin. She could not remember much about Mr. Quartermain, but she did remember his soft-spoken, lighthearted personality. When thinking about all of this, she came to the crazy realization that she had done so much work in this process and it was all going to waste.

Natalie sat there for a minute and thought about this account. She shook her head, wondering how she could fix this. After a few minutes of consideration, she decided to do something crazy; something the old 'Natalie' would never do: she was going to Tramsen. She put the charts, graphs, notes, and presentations back in the box, shut the trunk, and got in her car, starting it up. She drove out of the parking lot and onto the main roadway, before she realized that she forgot where this place was.

"Okay, Natalie, think! Where is this place?"

She was trying to remember where Tramsen Oil Company operated from. She knew she had been there before, but that was so long ago. Natalie turned down another street before it hit her:

Tramsen office was located on State Highway 84, just south of Saddle Creek Road.

They had just built the building when Natalie started running her errands between there and Arger in the past.

And that is where she was going.

Natalie got to the parking lot of Tramsen, parked her car, opened up her trunk, grabbed the box full of stuff, and went inside to the main secretary's desk.

"Hi, I'm Natalie Jones, I mean, 'Barnes'. I was wondering if I may be able to talk to Mr. Quartermain."

"Who are you with?"

"I am with the Arger Corporation."

The secretary looked up at Natalie, and then stood up from her chair.

"Just one moment."

The secretary she went through a door just to the side of her desk. Natalie was a little nervous, but she had to try something. She realized quickly, while she was reading through the program, that Arger was not the only organization that could benefit from this project. The secretary came back through the door and held it open for Natalie.

"Mr. Quartermain is right through here. Just go to the double glass doors. He is waiting for you."

"Thank you," Natalie responded as she walked through the door, carrying the box of materials. As Natalie came to the glass doors, the secretary came up behind her and held one of the doors open.

"Thank you," Natalie responded, again.

Natalie entered Mr. Quartermain's office, and Mr. Quartermain was sitting at a table with two other men. Natalie froze for a second when she realized that Mr. Quartermain was not alone.

"I am so sorry," Natalie said as all three men looked her way. "Sir, I did not realize you were in a meeting."

"Oh, don't worry about it, darlin'; come on in," Mr. Quartermain responded as he got up to shake her hand. He had that southern charm with his strong Texas accent.

"What did you say your name was?"

"Sir, my name is Natalie Barnes, and I worked at the Arger Corporation."

That seemed to catch the attention of the other two men still sitting at the table.

"Sir, I have to explain something to you, and I am requesting just a few minutes of your time."

"O…kay," Mr. Quartermain responded, obviously hesitating.

Natalie took a deep breath and prayed silently.

Lord, be with me. Tell me what to say to fix this.

"Sir, I was supposed to have this presentation set up for your meeting with my boss, Mr. Sherman, on Saturday. However, due to a family emergency, I was not able to make it."

That's a lie, sort of, but I don't really know what else to say.

"I came by here asking you to please take a look at this material that we prepared for the meeting," she continued, looking down at the box.

NOT PRESENT OR FUTURE...

All three men were stunned. Neither of them looked like they knew what to say. They just looked at each other, obviously perplexed. Mr. Quartermain seemed shaky in his response.

"Well, this is a bit unorthodox, uh, Ms. Barnes, and I am just not very comfortable with this. Where is your boss? I can't believe he would allow a meeting of this magnitude take place like this... without his presence."

"He doesn't know I am here, Mr. Quartermain. In fact, I need to tell you that I was let go today because of this."

Natalie paused, but just before Mr. Quartermain could respond, she continued.

"However, I worked on this project. I researched for it. I studied the actions. I analyzed the data, and I presented the analysis."

All the men appeared to be captivated as Natalie continued.

"Sir, I do not want the results of my actions to determine the potentially successful relationship between two very competent organizations. All I am asking is that you take a look at this material."

Mr. Quartermain looked intently at the box.

"Darlin', why is this so important to you? If you were let go from Arger, what is in this for you? I don't necessarily see you getting your job back," he joked.

"Because this joint venture will create jobs in Abilene and elsewhere in Texas," Natalie responded.

Again, that seemed to get the attention of all three men. She had them captivated, and she kept going.

"This project is good for Abilene. It is good for your company... and for Arger. And whether I work there or not, I don't want to see this potential go to waste."

Natalie backed away from the box.

"Again, Mr. Quartermain, all I am asking is that you take a look."

Looking at the other two men at the table, Natalie concluded her presentation.

"Thank you all for your time. I can see myself out."

"Now, wait, uh, did you say your name was 'Natalie Barnes'?"

"Yes, Sir. It's nice to see you, again, Mr. Quartermain. I only wish it could have been under better circumstances."

"I tell you what, Natalie. I will take a look at this and see what we can see."

"Thank you, Sir."

Natalie walked to the door when she turned, facing the group.

"You gentlemen have a good day."

"You too," Mr. Quartermain responded.

Natalie exited the office and proceeded to the parking lot. She sat in her car for a second, and prayed.

"Well, Lord, not that I expect anything to happen from this, but at least I tried."

Natalie started her car and drove home, expecting that moment to be the last that she would ever see of either of the two companies. But she felt comfortable that she did what she could to help her old boss and, hopefully, that would be enough.

CHAPTER 10

Benjamin tossed and turned, caught between wanting to go back to sleep and trying not to. His nightmares just kept coming, and they were getting more and more intense. Over the past couple of months, his dreams were so insidious that there were a couple of times that he would have sworn that he was not alone; that there was someone -or something- with him. On many occasions, he tried to explain his dreams to Natalie, and though it was not her intention to downgrade his horrible sleeping experiences, she always passed them off as some type of PTSD symptom. That reaction from her only compounded Benjamin's frustrations.

But again, that was before all…this. Considering this experience, and where he was, now, Benjamin still kept asking the same question:

If what I am going through, right now, was real, then why am I having these dreams and memories as if this 'other' life took place?

Overwhelmed with this thought, he really had to find a way to deal with that since it was apparent that this experience was anything but a dream. Trying to wake up, Benjamin rolled over and looked at the clock.

5:59. Okay, I have to get up and head to the jail to find out what is going on.

This whole thing of not knowing was really disturbing Benjamin. He got up, showered, and put on his jail uniform. He sat down at his table, realizing how hungry he was. He stood up and looked through the refrigerator, which contained a gallon of milk and some other cold items. He checked his cabinets and found some cereal.

Well, at least I can have that.

As he sat back down, he looked over and noticed his Bible. He realized that, with all the things that had been going on with Natalie, especially the past six months or so, he could not remember the last time he actually prayed.

Perhaps it is time now, he thought.

He picked up his Bible and started reading. He moved through the Bible, going from book to book, page to page, taking in each verse is if he had, somehow, found gold. He came upon Psalm 18:1-3, one of his favorite verses. He read it loudly, over and over.

"I love you, Oh Lord, my strength. The Lord is my Rock, my fortress and my deliverer; my God, my Rock in whom I trust. He is my shield and the horn of my salvation, my stronghold. I will call upon the Lord who is worthy to be praised, so shall I be saved from my enemies."

Benjamin did not know why, but he felt that this verse meant more to him than ever at this moment. He put his Bible down and prayed. When he finished, he grabbed his keys, headed down the stairs, and out the door. He got in his pick-up and drove to the jail, stopping by a local QuikTrip to grab some coffee. The time was 8:09, and Benjamin hoped that Chief Beckett would be in.

As Benjamin pulled into the jail parking lot, he said another quick prayer and went inside. He went upstairs and walked directly to Chief Beckett's office. Benjamin peeked in and noticed Chief Beckett on the phone. As Benjamin did not want to disturb him, he waited outside until Chief Beckett finished his phone call. Benjamin's presence must have stirred Chief Beckett as he concluded his phone call, quickly.

"Senior Jones, come on in."

Benjamin walked into the office and sat down in a chair in front of Chief Beckett's desk.

"Look, I don't know how to say this, Senior, but a lot of trouble is coming from the incident that happened Saturday night."

"Okay," Benjamin replied, curious as to where this conversation was going to go.

"The family of the victim filed a lawsuit against the jail, citing that we did not do enough to protect their son."

"But I tried; I called for help! I radioed for assistance…and I didn't get any!"

"I know you did, Senior. But that isn't all."

Chief Beckett repositioned himself behind the desk as to get more comfortable.

"The other two inmates who started the fight are filing charges against you for excessive use of force."

"Seriously?? They're filing charges against me??"

"Look, I am just letting you know what is coming down the pipes. The DA is determining whether to file charges against you for excessive use of force."

"Chief, you know this is ridiculous. I mean, this is stupid."

"I'm sorry about this, Benjamin, but you can't come back to work unless this gets cleared up. We will have a review board to determine if you can even still work here."

"Are you serious?? Really? I mean, Chief, you saw the evidence. It's on the tape…everything!"

"Yes, it is," Chief Beckett continued. "Even what you did to them."

Benjamin sat there in disbelief. He could not understand this at all.

Is this really happening to me? Could I really be facing charges? What would happen then? A trial? A judgment? What would I lose? This crap is not worth it!! Why did I ever work here???

Benjamin stood up and started for the door.

"Benjamin, sit down. I am not done!"

Benjamin froze where he stood. Chief Beckett's demand clearly rubbed Benjamin the wrong way. He turned around, grabbed his badge, took it off his shirt, and placed it on the desk in front of Chief Beckett.

"I'm done, Chief! I'm not waiting around to see what happens next. This isn't worth it. You know where to find me."

"Benjamin, look, this isn't what we want," Chief Beckett responded, realizing the seriousness of Benjamin's response. "Let's just see where this goes."

"I don't care where this goes! I don't want to do this anymore."

Benjamin left the facility and drove back home. He needed some time to think; some time to figure things out. Based on recent events, he needed to find a new job. But for now, he just needed to pray that he would not wind up in jail.

Is this real, he thought. *This can't be! This is not the life I remembered.*

Natalie was dressed and ready to go. She thanked Theodore and Phyllis for letting her stay over. As Carmella left for work, Natalie went out, and started submitting resumes and filling out applications. She went from place to place, using a newspaper ad containing local jobs that she highlighted the night before. She even went to the Diamondback Golf Club -Theodore's favorite place- to apply for an administrative position that they were advertising for. She had high hopes that today was going to be a good day for job hunting.

After spending all morning filling out applications, she started getting tired. She forgot how exhausting job-searching was, and she was about done for the day. She decided to go surprise Carmella by taking her some Taco Bueno for lunch. Carmella worked at a local department store, not too far from where she lived. Carmella loved working there for all the discounts she received when buying clothes, and Natalie remembered when Carmella would take her shopping just to use her employee discounts.

Natalie seemed to make it a habit to go by and 'torment' Carmella while she was at work. She would relocate clothes to different places, hide Carmella's price guns, and other stuff to make Carmella's day a little more surreal. It was all in fun, and Carmella enjoyed it, just as long as she never got into trouble.

After they finished eating, Natalie left the store and continued her job search. Her time spent with Carmella provided her just a little more motivation to keep searching. She went from place to place, saying a prayer before each application she submitted, before moving onto the next. When she was done, she drove back to her apartment. The afternoon spent job-searching seemed to be longer than the morning, and she was clearly exhausted. She looked forward to getting inside and calling her mother, as she was eager to hear her mother's voice.

As Natalie exited her car and started walking up the sidewalk to her apartment, she heard another car come screeching around the corner and quickly pulling up next to hers. She turned and looked to see a man getting out of the car and heading straight for her. It didn't take her long to figure out who he was.

Oh my God! Darnell!!

Natalie could not believe it. She froze where she stood as Darnell walked right up to her and started yelling at her.

"You don't get to tell me when we are done! Only I get to do that!"

"Darnell, you need to leave now," Natalie responded as her heart started to race. She felt very uncomfortable with his intimidating approach. Darnell just stood there, staring at her, with an angry look on his face.

"Darnell, I do not want to see you anymore," Natalie continued. "You need to move on!"

He just stood there, refusing to move, and only showing his anger. Natalie went from being intimidated to getting angry, herself.

"Darnell, I am going inside and I want you to leave. Please don't call me anymore??"

With that, she turned and went to her door, unlocking it and walked in. She turned to look back at him and saw him still standing there.

"Good-bye, Darnell."

Natalie shut the door behind her. She stood there, trying to hold back the tears and calm her breathing. After a few minutes she sat down on her bed, trying to calm herself down even more. She reached over, picked up her phone, and called Carmella, telling her everything that had just happened with Darnell.

"Girl, I am so proud of you! I can't imagine how hard that must have been to face him and tell him that."

"Oh, you have no idea," Natalie responded. "I am just glad to get it over with."

"Do you want to come over?"

"No, I'm okay. I am going to call my mother and hit the sack."

"Okay. You just keep me informed about your job-searching and let me know if you need anything."

"Okay, girl! I will see ya later! Have a good night."

"You too," Carmella responded, and they both hung up.

Natalie dialed her mother's number, and they talked. Natalie was on the phone for a while, enjoying the time spent talking with her mother. She told her mother about her day and everything that happened with Darnell. Natalie received the same encouragement from her mother as she did from Carmella. It was comforting, and it helped her sleep that night.

Over the next few days, Natalie kept filling out applications and submitting resumes. She received a few phone calls for interviews, but nothing panned out. She spent time with Carmella and looked forward to the weekend to get back to Amarillo to see her mother.

Natalie seemed to be getting used to how things were moving in her life. But in the midst of the job-searching and time spent with her best friend, Natalie was subjected to a slow, daily struggle of missing the voices of laughter, pitter-patter of little feet, and the hugs of her children. Though she tried to move on with this life, she could not forget the memories she had with her children. She even found herself thinking about Benjamin, as she wondered, on occasion, how he was doing.

Most of all, she was stuck with the same question that she had been asking for the past week: why did they break off the engagement? It didn't make sense. She pondered the thought, over and over, and though she could not understand it, Natalie came to the only conclusion she could: she had to know why she and Benjamin ended their relationship.

CHAPTER 11

"Daddy? Daddy, where are you?"

Benjamin looked around the room. He heard Leesha's voice but couldn't see her.

"Daddy, where are you?"

"Leesha, I'm here! I'm right here! I can't find you!"

"Daddy? Daddy??"

Her screams became worse. Benjamin looked around and tried to find Leesha. He tried to run but was met with a force that just kept him from moving. Finally, he saw her. She was standing with her back toward him as he ran toward her. Then he woke up, shaking, sweating, and breathing so heavily that he had to sit up and try to calm himself down. He looked over at the clock.

5:39. Ugh! It's too early to get up, but I am not about to try to go back to sleep!

The previous couple of days had been long. Benjamin was able to participate in a Funeral Honor Detail on Wednesday, but the rest of the time was spent job searching. Benjamin remembered his job at QuikTrip in the past and decided to apply there, again. He was simply waiting for an interview.

He was still stressed about the possible decision from the district attorney to file charges against him for the excessive force claims. Waiting for that decision; the 'not knowing', was killing him, and he really wanted an answer. He still could not believe the predicament that he was in.

He decided to get up and take a shower. He stumbled around to find his dirty clothes so he could wash them. He didn't feel like doing anything else, so maybe some housework was enough to get him moving around. He gathered all his dirty clothes and threw them by the washer. After he got out of the shower, he went upstairs to grab a bowl of cereal. He didn't know why; he would probably just waste it by letting it sit there. The past few days he wasted several bowls of cereal. He would pour the cereal, then the milk, and when he sat down to eat, he found himself zoning out to the point to where he completely forgot he prepared his own breakfast.

This time has to be different. I've gotta make some changes.

After he poured the milk in his cereal, he sat down at the table. As he was about to take a bite, the phone rang.

"Hello?"

"Benjamin, its Chelsey."

"Hey, Chelsey, what's up?"

Benjamin could tell that she was a little emotional, and he tried to remain cordial as he was trying to figure out why he was getting a call from Chelsey this early in the morning.

"Benjamin, I don't know how to say this, but Brian and Ray have been at the hospital since two this morning."

She paused as she began to cry.

"Chelsey, what happened?"

"William Weatherly committed suicide late last night."

With that, she couldn't hold it in.

"Oh my God," Benjamin replied. "Not William."

"Raymond wanted me to let you know," Chelsey continued as she tried to regain her composure.

Benjamin did not know what to say. He was caught in shock.

William was Paige's father. He was Julie's husband. He was…my good friend. William was my witness.

Was.

Benjamin couldn't say a word. He didn't know what to say if he could have.

"Chelsey, uh, I, uh, I gotta go. Thank you for telling me."

"Benjamin, they are at St. Francis hospital, if you want to go see them."

Click.

NOT PRESENT OR FUTURE...

Benjamin hung up the phone. He felt sick. He felt hollow. He felt...ashamed. He was so caught up in his own world the last couple of days that he completely forgot about trying to contact William. Now it was too late.

Benjamin sat back down at the table, watching the sun rise over the lake. It was beautiful, peaceful...graceful even. Everything was quiet.

Everything was quiet, except Benjamin's soul.

He got up from the table, completely ignoring his bowl of cereal sitting there getting soggy, and went back to into his bedroom. He knelt down by his bed to pray. He felt stuck. He was kneeling for what seemed to be a long time, but nothing came out of his mouth. Nothing came into his mind. After about two minutes, he finally gave up.

Lord, I don't know what to pray for. I am so sorry. I feel like I failed You...again.

He sat up on his bed and leaned back against the pillow, completely shrouded in sorrow and guilt. He was just about to doze off when the phone rang, again. Benjamin looked up toward the bedroom door, realizing he left his phone on the table by the charger. He got up slowly, walked out of his room and picked up the phone.

"Hello," Benjamin answered, expecting this to be another call about William.

"Benjamin, its Chief Beckett. Do you have a minute?"

"Chief Beckett, um, I'm sorry, Chief, but this really isn't, I mean, I..."

Benjamin paused.

"Hey, look, I didn't mean to bother you. I just wanted to let you know that, from what we understand, the district attorney is not filing charges against you. You don't have to worry about that any more. I just wanted to let you know that."

Benjamin was still thinking about William. Honestly, he really didn't care about anything that Chief Beckett had to say at that moment.

"Uh, thank you, Chief."

"So how are you doing, Ben?"

Click.

Benjamin hung up on Chief Beckett and went back to bed. He decided that he was not going to answer the phone any more for a while. Too tired to stay awake but too exhausted to sleep, he just gave in to his emotional state. He simply didn't move.

Natalie tossed and turned in her bed. Still out of it, she could hear the sound of a baby crying in the background. Her mind told her it was Ben Jr.

"Honey, could you get Ben Jr., please?"

Her request was instinctive, as she was more asleep than awake. She kept hearing crying, and at this moment realized that, for some reason, Benjamin must not be home.

"Leesha, honey, could you get Ben Jr.?"

The cries softened, but Natalie could still hear them. Thinking she had to wake up and go get Ben Jr. herself, she opened her eyes, finally completely awake. She looked around to find herself still in her apartment. She sat up, shaking her head, trying to figure out what she was hearing. Again, there was crying, but it sounded like it was coming from outside her apartment. Natalie sighed. Turning her body out of the bed and putting her feet on the floor, she sat there, putting both of her hands over her face. She looked up and around her apartment. The deafening silence was too much for her. She looked over at the clock.

9:13.

She looked at her answering machine as if she were expecting a message.

Nothing.

The last couple of days had been busy but, for the most part, unproductive. She went on a few interviews and received a few more phone calls from potential employers, but nothing panned out, so far. She tried to keep her head up and her focus clear. After all, it was Friday and she was going to drive to Amarillo -just as fast as she could- to see her mother.

That is, if her car would make it.

Then there was the issue of her bank account. Natalie was afraid to look in it. She was very grateful for the money that Mr. Sherman paid her, but she wasn't sure how long it would last her. As much as she feared looking into her account, she had to know what she had to work with for the remainder of the month.

But for now…

Natalie needed to call Benjamin. After thinking about him all week, it was clear that she was not going to get any real closure about him without talking to him. She rummaged through her drawer, looking for Benjamin's number. She knew she had it, and she needed to find it. After looking through the drawer next to her bed, she got up and searched the dresser.

She found nothing.

She looked by her mirror, and again: nothing. She looked on her countertops, by the sink, inside her closet. Still: nothing.

She started to wonder what could have happened to his number.

Did I throw it out after the engagement was called off?

She sat back down on her bed, thinking about Benjamin. She really wanted to call him but began to realize that may not be probable at this moment. She bent down to pick up her house shoes when she noticed a piece of paper lying under the bed, near her nightstand. She knelt down, picked it up and turned it over to see what was on it.

Benjamin's number! There it is! I found it!

Her heart stopped for a second. She slowly sat back on the bed, contemplating her next move. She looked at the phone, then back at the piece of paper. She wanted to call him, but now that she found his number, she was scared to do so. After about ten minutes of consideration, she finally decided that she really just needed to hear his voice. For some reason, at that moment, that would be enough.

She picked up her phone and dialed his number, taking a deep breath in as the phone began to ring. It rang and rang. Suddenly, his voice came over the phone but Natalie could tell it was an answering machine.

"'This is Benjamin. Please leave a message.' Beep."

Natalie sat there for a second, unsure of what to say. Then, her mouth just opened.

"Benjamin, this is Natalie. I just wanted to see how you were doing. I guess it has been a while since we spoke. I hope you are okay. Would you…I mean…I was wondering if you would call me."

She paused, briefly, to catch her bearings.

"Okay, I hope to talk to you soon. Bye, Benjamin."

She hung up. Her heart raced a little bit, and though she was glad the answering machine answered the call, she really wanted to hear his voice.

At least I tried. Now, about that crazy friend of mine…

Natalie picked up the phone, again, and called Carmella at her job.

"Hey, girl, it's me."

"What's up, girl," Carmella responded as she was folding a display shirt.

"I am going to head up to Amarillo to see Mom. I just wanted to let you know, and to thank you, again, for being there for me this week."

"Girl, you are welcome! Hey, will your car make it to your mom's?"

"I hope so. I'm headed there either way. I think it will be okay. Once I get it started it should be fine."

"Okay, girl! You be safe! You know I would go with you if I did not have to work."

"I know, Carmella. I will call you later, okay?"

"Okay! See ya later."

They both hung up, and Natalie began packing her stuff for the trip to Amarillo. It did not take her long as she quickly threw some clothes in a small suitcase. She decided against calling the bank to check her account and thought it would be better to just pull some money from an ATM. She grabbed her purse, along with her suitcase, walked out of her apartment door, locking it behind her. She walked to her car, loaded it up, and got in. She said a prayer, and started her car. Though it sounded a little weak, it started up and she was ecstatic.

"Thank you, Lord! Please be with me on the road."

She left the parking lot, and on to Amarillo she went.

CHAPTER 12

Natalie managed to make it to her mother's house. Filling her car up before she left Abilene, so she didn't have to stop along the way, she pulled into her mother's driveway with just a little less than one-eighth of gas in her tank.

"Thank you, Lord," Natalie prayed as she put her car in park.

She got out of the car, and grabbed her purse and her suitcase. She walked up to the door of her mother's house where she found her mother waiting there with open arms.

"Hey, Natalie, welcome home! Come in; come on in."

"Hey, Mom," Natalie responded as she walked in and sat down on the couch, instantly feeling glad to be there. She was slowly getting used to the idea that her mother was back. It wasn't so surreal to her any more.

"Was it a long ride?"

"No, not really," Natalie responded. "I took the time on the road to do some thinking."

"So what's going on?"

"Well, I have not found a job yet. I thought I might hear something by today, but…"

Natalie paused. She wouldn't be home to get the call if she had.

"Haven't heard from Darnell anymore," Natalie continued.

"Well, that is good, honey. It's a good thing. You need to move on from him."

"I thought I had, Momma. He seems to be having a hard time about it, though. He scared me when I told him to stop calling me."

"Well, maybe now he will get the hint."

"And, well, I've just been job searching," Natalie continued. "That's about it."

"Have you heard from Benjamin at all?"

Natalie looked at her mother, inquisitively.

"Well, as a matter of fact, I actually called him this morning. I just wanted to talk to him and see how he was doing."

"What did he say?"

"He didn't answer. His answering machine picked up, and I just left a message."

"Well, at least you tried."

"Yeah, I did. I was nervous. I wanted him to answer but was glad that he actually didn't," Natalie responded, sitting back into the couch and getting comfortable, enjoying her mother's presence.

Natalie and Florance continued their conversation, and Natalie soaked in the moment as she remembered how she loved talking to her mother about everything. Natalie didn't remember anything else since she came into her mother's house. After a while, Natalie and Florance realized it was getting a little late, and they both were getting hungry. As they were discussing what to do for dinner, Florance popped out a question that caught Natalie off guard.

"Are you going to try to call Benjamin again?"

Natalie looked at her mother, nearly surprised at her question.

"I'm not sure. I don't even know if I have his number with me."

"I still have it."

"You have it? How do you have his number, Momma?"

"Natalie, how many times did you call him from my home? You brought him home to see me on several occasions. I have his number written on the wall by my phone."

Florance pointed at the wall by her phone.

"Oh. I forgot that was there."

"Mmm-hm," Florance teased. "How about that?"

Natalie giggled.

"Well," Florance continued, "how about it? Are you going to try again?"

Natalie sighed. She wanted to call him. She wanted to hear his voice. Most importantly, she wanted to know 'why'? Why did they

NOT PRESENT OR FUTURE...

break off the engagement? What happened? Why was she here, now, instead of where she should be: with her children and her husband in a different time?

Not that she expected him to know that answer, but...

"Okay," Natalie responded as she got up to get the phone.

"No need for that, honey. I've got the phone right here."

Florance held up the phone for Natalie to get it.

"Great! Now all I need is..."

Florance held up a piece of paper with Benjamin's number on it, interrupting Natalie's statement.

"I thought you said it was up on your wall with your other numbers, MOM!"

"It is. But I thought I'd just make this easy for you."

Natalie was curious.

Why is this so important to my mother? I have to know.

"Why do you think I should call him, *Mother*?"

"Because I think you need to know."

"Know what, exactly?"

"I think you know what," Florance responded, smiling. "I can see it in you. You really love him, but maybe you don't realize it yet."

Mom, if only you knew the truth.

"What I am surprised about," Florance continued, "is that you don't know why you two are no longer engaged?"

Well, again, that is the million-dollar question.

Natalie didn't have an answer. She just looked away. Regardless, Natalie wasn't going to challenge her mother, no matter how she actually felt about Benjamin. Natalie looked over at the clock.

7:13.

Florance got up to make dinner. The two talked so much over the past couple of hours that they totally lost track of time. Natalie walked out to the back porch, which was screened in and protected from the local flying elements. She could smell the dusty air of the Texas Panhandle, some of the things that usually made her allergies go berserk. She sat down on one of the porch chairs, looking out at the beautiful Texas sunset, trying to talk herself out of making this call. But she couldn't help it. She realized that she left her apartment so fast she would not know if he called her back until Sunday night when she returned. She needed to try.

Ugh! Okay, Natalie, let's do this!

She said a prayer, dialed the number, and braced herself, emotionally.

Benjamin finally got up. He knew it was late in the afternoon, but he didn't care. He let the day get away from him, but decided that he just didn't want to be around anyone.

He could not get his mind off of William. Being so caught up in his own state of being, he completely forgot about others that he might have influenced, except for some of the kids, of course. While he was resting, he couldn't escape the constant nagging of his inside voice, which consistently seemed to harass him.

"Wake up, Marine!"

He heard it more and more, especially lately. The voice of his previous commanding officers and senior enlisted supervisors, that once motivated and encouraged him, rang through his ears, over and over. It was usually at times that he needed to pay attention and focus on the critical issues in his job or his life. He had a bad habit of worrying so much about himself and paying little attention to others.

This time, though…

Benjamin looked around the house. It was still quiet and lonely. It was a deafening silence; loathsome and heavy. He had a hard time getting used to it. He looked at the clock.

7:21

Benjamin really needed to call Raymond. He felt bad about hanging up on Chelsey. He needed to apologize to her. He went over to the phone, looked over to the answering machine, and noticed that he had a couple of messages. Benjamin hit the 'Play' button.

"You have four messages. Message 1: 'Hey, Benjamin, this is Ray. Um, I'm just checking on you, buddy. I hope you are doing okay. Give me a call, okay, and we can talk. Call me later.' Beep."

NOT PRESENT OR FUTURE...

Benjamin expected that. He would call him as soon as this was over.

"Message 2: 'Benjamin this is Brian. Hey, buddy, I am sorry about William. I have been talking to Ray, and he told me that he called you. I am just checking on you. I'll give you a call later.' Beep."

Benjamin didn't expect that, but was glad for the call.

"Message 3: 'Benjamin, its Natalie. I just called to see how you are doing. I hope that you are doing okay. I...I guess I will talk to you later.' Beep."

Benjamin was startled. Natalie had tried to call him. He didn't know how to react to her message. He almost felt a sense of relief from hearing from her.

But that feeling was short lived.

"Message 4: 'Benjamin, why haven't you called me? I am tired of waiting on you. If you can't find the time to call your mother, then just why do I even care enough to call you?' Beep. End of new messages."

Benjamin could have done without that last message. The relationship that Benjamin had with his mother left much to be desired. It was a very complicated one, and the sound of his mother's voice ruined whatever enjoyment he might have had from hearing Natalie's message. Just as he turned to walk back into the bedroom, the phone rang. He turned and looked at it, sighing as if he did not wish to be disturbed. He walked over to pick up the phone.

"Hello?"

"Benjamin? Hey, it's Natalie."

Benjamin was silent. Even though he just heard her voice, he didn't know what to say.

"Benjamin, are you there?"

"Yeah, I'm here. How are you doing?"

Natalie started shaking as she was very nervous about this call. This was the first time she had heard his voice in a week, and it sounded much younger.

"I am doing okay," she responded. "I just wanted to call you and see how you were doing."

"Things are going good," Benjamin responded, acting like he was busy. He didn't say any more than necessary, and Natalie caught that.

"How's school going?"

"Ben, I graduated in June," Natalie giggled. "I am done with school."

"Oh yeah, right."

"Okay," she continued, not sure of what else to say. She tried to think about what else she could talk about, but nothing came to her mind.

"Well, I got a lot going on, Natalie. I am glad you are doing okay."

"Um, okay," she responded. To Natalie, Benjamin seemed like he was trying to shorten the conversation.

"You take care of yourself, Natalie. It was good to hear from you."

"You too," Natalie responded, trying not to get emotional.

Benjamin hung up, and Natalie held the phone in her hands thinking about Benjamin.

You too. Benjamin.

CHAPTER 13

Benjamin sat in one of the pews in the back. He hardly felt like being at church. The weekend he was looking forward to either went too quickly for him to enjoy, or was plagued by nightmares casting his own guilt and memories. Either way, Benjamin was not sure about this life; this…new experience. He needed to be at church because he knew it would lift his spirit a little bit, though he could just as easily stayed in bed. William's funeral would be held on Tuesday at one of the local funeral homes. It would take everything Benjamin had for him to go and pay his condolences to William's family and say 'goodbye' to William. It was all still so very surreal, even to the point to where Benjamin kept questioning this existence.

This should never have happened, Benjamin thought, thinking of the relationship that his family had with William's family.

The memories of William, Julie, Paige, and their youngest son, Matthew, all seemed like a lie. Benjamin and William were good friends, and both of them enjoyed watching their daughters grow up together. They coached soccer together; they fished together; they spent time together. When Benjamin and Natalie moved to Quantico, Virginia, so Benjamin could fulfill active-duty orders, William and Julie came to see them on several occasions. When Benjamin deployed, Natalie leaned on William and Julie.

That was how it was.

It just didn't make sense, and it didn't seem real to Benjamin. He just couldn't figure out what happened. As Benjamin was deep in thought about William, Brian came to a high point in his sermon.

"I want you all to consider this scenario. Jesus is on the cross with one thief on one side and one on the other. Let's take a look at the Book of Luke, chapter 23:39. It says, 'One of the criminals hung there hurled insults at Him, saying, "Aren't You the Messiah? Save yourself…and us!" But the other criminal rebuked him. "Don't you fear God," he said, "since you are under the same sentence? We are punished justly for we are getting what our deeds deserve. But this man has done nothing wrong." Then he looked at Jesus and said, "Jesus, remember me…when you go to Your kingdom."'"

Brian paused.

"Now I want to stop right there and consider the magnitude of what is transpiring here. There are two criminals hanging alongside of Jesus. I do not believe that this was by chance or some type of coincidence. One of the criminals insulted him, and the other did the only thing that, at that moment, he could think of doing."

Brian had the full attention of the church, and even Benjamin could not help but look up and listen intently.

"Realizing his sin; realizing the life that he chose to lead, faced with the decisions he made in his life…the other criminal knew that he was finished. He knew that he would die, and he knew that he would be judged according to his acts. The Bible doesn't say whether or not Jesus met this person previously, but somehow, this criminal knew that Jesus did nothing to deserve this treatment. How did he know it? We are not necessarily sure. But he knew it."

Brian paused, again, before he continued.

"And when he realized that his life was over, he came face-to-face with the author and giver of life: 'He who holds the keys to death and Hades.' Whether he realized that or not, he knew that Jesus had a kingdom. Considering all the things going on in the mind of this criminal, he had the audacity, the gall, to ask Jesus if Jesus would simply remember him when Jesus went to his kingdom."

Benjamin felt a sense of peace, even if temporarily, from his shame. He wanted to hear more.

"I want you all to think about that for a moment," Brian continued. "This criminal asked Jesus if he would simply 'remember' him. He knew that he could not possibly ask Jesus to save him, because he was a sinner. There was no way that an eternity in a beautiful heaven with a loving God was possible, so he asked Jesus to simply 'remember' him. And what if Jesus left it there? What benefit would that have done for the criminal to know that, even though he was on his way to eternal damnation without God, Jesus would occasionally remember him? What would the criminal have to gain?

But there is another issue here. The criminal, knowing his fate, showed faith in Christ. He recognized Jesus's majesty and His authority. How he knew that, again, we aren't quite sure how, but he did. And we aren't really sure why he asked Jesus to remember him. Was he afraid? Did he really believe that Jesus had a kingdom or was he just hoping beyond hope that this Jesus was everything he had heard up to that point, and just figured that he had nothing to lose by reaching out to Jesus? We don't know. But Jesus did know. And while in absolute pain, tortured by the soldiers, accused before the Sanhedrin…and even shunned by God the Father, Jesus did something amazing with his authority. First, Jesus showed absolute compassion and mercy to the criminal on the cross next to him. And second, Jesus showed His absolute authority to the people by allowing Himself to remain on the cross to die for their sins, while still maintaining the power and authority to promise eternal life to a lowly sinner who was paying the due penalty for their actions. What magnificent grace and power Jesus displayed by his everlasting love for us!"

The whole auditorium was silent. You could hear a pin drop.

"All this from a single request for a memory."

Benjamin's heart sank, and he became emotional. He considered the magnitude of his sins and the choices he made in his life. At that moment he also thought about the mistakes he made while married to Natalie, and those he made while raisin his children. Benjamin became overwhelmed with guilt. He tuned out the rest of the service. At the altar call, he just stood up and counted the seconds until service was over. As Benjamin walked out of the pew, he headed toward the doors, trying to avoid any talkers. As he walked through the auditorium doors into the main church hallway, he saw Chelsey talking to another parent. Benjamin needed to apologize to her for the way he acted on the phone, so he waited patiently, but out of view of Chelsey, until she was done talking. As she turned to head toward the nursery, she heard Benjamin behind her.

"Chelsey," Benjamin called as Chelsey turned around.

"Hey, Benjamin."

"I just wanted to apologize for hanging up on you when you called me. I am sorry. I was completely taken off guard when you told me that. I…I have no excuses. Please forgive me."

Chelsey smiled as she went to give Benjamin a hug.

"No need to apologize, Benjamin. How are you doing?"

"I think I am okay; just been resting a lot. I have really been tired lately."

"I completely understand, Ben. Have you talked to Ray yet?"

"No. I saw him this morning before Sunday school but wasn't able to catch him. I'll catch him tonight."

"Okay," Chelsey responded. "You be careful, and we will see you later."

"Okay, Chelsey. See ya later."

Benjamin left the church and drove home. For whatever reason, he felt completely exhausted. He wanted to go to bed, but was afraid to sleep. He had nightmare after nightmare just about every night. Waking up in the middle of the night, soaking in sweat, was becoming a normal experience. He knew that it affected him; such as in this case. It was all he could do to stay awake in church service and on the road. When he got home, he went straight into the house, into his bedroom, and collapsed in his bed. Once again, he was oblivious to the world around him. He had a funeral honors detail scheduled the next day in Locust Grove, and as far as he was concerned, he wasn't getting up until then.

That is, if he could stand the nightmares.

CHAPTER 14

Natalie opened her eyes, trying to convince herself to get up. She was still tired as she got in late the night before from visiting with her mother. It was a great weekend—shopping, movies, talking, worshiping, reminiscing—all with her mother. Since Natalie had some time to really think about things lately, she seriously began considering moving to Amarillo and living with her mother. Especially since...

Benjamin.

What a weird phone call that was. Natalie couldn't help but to think about him over the weekend, and though she enjoyed her time with Florance, Florance suspected that Natalie's mind wandered, occasionally, throughout the weekend. No doubt it was about Benjamin. One would think that things should be becoming clearer to Natalie: she and Benjamin were not engaged. She had her mother again. She lost her job at Arger. Honestly, other than Carmella, Natalie had no reason to stay in Abilene as she was done with school. Her life was right in front of her, and the possibilities were endless.

So why am I feeling so...off?

She could not grasp it. The reality was that she was missing her children. It was getting harder, every day. So Natalie wakes up and finds herself here, now...but that doesn't change her previous experiences. Natalie carried everything with her: her memories, emotions, feelings... everything. Natalie could recall, in detail, the pain and joy of childbirth. She could recall Leesha's smile, T. J.'s activeness and Ben Jr.'s facial expressions. She could recall the emotional growth of them all—the tears, the laughter, the nights of reading before bed. Natalie thought about the busy schedules of running her children here and there, from T-ball to soccer and from the babysitters to Bible study.

Natalie carried all of it.

But there are no children. Where are my children??

Before all of that, it was Benjamin. The wedding, the ring, his touch, the passion, the love, his promotions, his failures.

The Marines.

Ugh!! The damnable, horrible, patriotic, honorable Marines!

That was Benjamin's mistress, if there ever was one, and Natalie hated it. It always seemed like he worked harder at being a Marine than at being a husband. It took an emotional toll on Natalie, and how she hated it!

Oh, how Natalie hated it!!

The joy when Benjamin got his commission to the tears when he left for deployment.

The joy they all felt when he would come home to the fear and frustration of Ben's personality, afterward.

The love, the hate, the feelings, the fights...all of it! Natalie dreamed about it at night and dealt with the plague of memories all day. One would think that this should be getting better. But it wasn't. It was still all there. Her phone call to him just made it worse.

Ugh! Why did my mother press so much?

Natalie sighed. The most significant question that she had about all this was: where is God? Why is He allowing this to happen? It was like she was caught up in some weird 'Family Man' movie of some sort. As far as she knew nothing like this happened to other people. There is no such thing as time travelling. So in reality, why did this happen?

Man, I am really going crazy thinking about all this!

Perhaps she was going crazy. Just the thought of all this exhausted her. As she contemplated getting up and doing anything to start her day, she rolled over to check the clock.

9:34.

It was really time for her to get up. Being Monday, she thought she would go job searching, again, and maybe see what Carmella

NOT PRESENT OR FUTURE...

was up to after work. The job-searching was key, here. If she was not careful, the bills would pile up fast.

As she rolled out of bed, the phone rang. She reached over to her nightstand and answered the phone.

"Hello?"

"Natalie, Sherman here."

Mr. Sherman? What does he want? Oh, no!! Did he find out what I did?

Though she was caught off guard from his call, she thought it comical how he always identified himself as 'Sherman' when he addressed himself.

"Yes, Sir," Natalie replied, more curious than comical.

"I hope I am not bothering you. Do you have a minute?"

"Yes, Sir."

"I just had a very interesting conversation with Jonathan Quartermain."

Oh no! He knows! He is going to be mad at me!

"Are you familiar with him?"

"Yes, Sir," she replied, feeling like she was being tested.

"He and I discussed the day you, apparently, went to visit him. Is that true? Did you go and see him the day I let you go?"

Natalie gulped. She knew she was in trouble.

"Yes, Sir."

"So what motivated you to go to him after you left here?"

"Mr. Sherman, I did not go ask him for a job, if that is what you are wondering."

"No, I know that. But you took him all the material of the project. That was…very risky. Do you mind if I ask why you did that?"

Natalie's heart started racing. She needed to own up to this.

"Sir, it was because of me and my actions that we did not get that account. It was because of me that the two organizations did not come to a collaborative relationship. It was because of me that jobs were not created…and that you did not get the account that you worked so hard for."

Natalie paused to catch her bearings.

"Sir, I went there, not because I wanted a job, nor was I trying to keep mine with you. I knew I messed up. I went there because I believe in the project. I believe in creating jobs. That project was so vital to both of the corporations, and I truly just did not want to see all of that go to waste because of me. I was no longer working with Arger anymore, so I figured…what the heck."

"Is that right?"

"Yes, Sir!"

"Because you know that your actions could have caused more damage than good. Taking our project to them without direct representation from our organization could have been very detrimental."

Natalie sighed, waiting for the hammer to drop. She couldn't resist responding.

"Mr. Sherman, you have to believe that I would never do anything to hurt Arger. I didn't take that project to Mr. Quartermain to try to hurt you. I wanted to, in some way, make up for what I did. I really do care about the organization, Sir."

"Natalie, I believe that…and that is why I called you. We have worked out a very good deal with Tramsen."

"I'm sorry; what???"

Natalie was stunned by what she just heard, and she almost dropped the phone.

"That's right, Natalie. They really liked our proposition. Mr. Quartermain agreed with all of our points, and we have developed, collectively, a business partnership which includes three accounts."

"Three?? You got three accounts??"

"That's right, Natalie! I couldn't believe it myself!"

Mr. Sherman started laughing.

"Sir, I am so happy for you and Arger. Thank you for telling me about this."

"Well, Natalie, that isn't all. We need an account representative for these accounts. One account is manageable for my office but not three. I need a full-time representative to manage these accounts and act as the program manager."

Mr. Sherman paused.

"Didn't you just graduate from Abilene Christian?"

"Uh, yes, Sir," she replied.

"Well, how about it, Natalie? You want the job?"

"Sir, I don't know what to say! I...I..."

Natalie couldn't believe it. She started shaking, trying to gather her thoughts before she continued.

"But, Sir, as much as I would love to take this, what about..."

"Don't worry about that, Natalie. What you did was brave... and unorthodox...and incredible! Mr. Quartermain really appreciated your position when you came to him. And when he realized that you weren't trying to get anything from him or hurt us on the process, he saw that you had loyalty. That means a lot in this business, Natalie. Mr. Quartermain wants you to work for us working with him on these accounts."

"Sir, I...I don't know what to say."

Natalie was in tears. She couldn't believe it.

"Well, based on what I just told you, I was hoping you would say yes."

"Yes," she responded quickly as she stood up. "Yes, I will, Sir! Thank you so much!"

"Great! We will need to rehire you so we have to go through the admin stuff. Oh, and you are getting paid at a higher rate."

"Really?"

Natalie noticed a comical change in his voice.

"Now you haven't gone out and done drugs or anything, have you?"

"No...no, Sir," Natalie giggled.

"Wonderful! Then you should have no problems with the drug test. You are hired! Come by the office next Friday, if you can, to get you back into the system and conduct the drug test. Then you should be good to go to start on Monday. Is that okay?"

"Um, yes, Sir."

"Great! I will have Shannon call you with the details. And Natalie..."

"Yes, Sir?"

"Good job! I am glad to have you back."

"Thank you, Sir."

"Have a good day, Natalie."

"You too, Sir."

Natalie pushed the 'Off' button on her phone.

What the heck just happened?? Oh my gosh! What just happened?? This is so unbelievable! I just got the opportunity of a lifetime!

She jumped up on her bed, jumping around and trying to contain her excitement. As she jumped off of the bed she reached for her phone.

"I gotta call Benjamin!"

She grabbed her phone and dialed Benjamin's cell number before she realized her current reality. Dialing the number that she knew, from 'then', the phone started ringing when it hit her.

He doesn't have a cell phone. He's not going to answer this.

She hung up the phone just as it was on its' fourth ring. Natalie was excited, and her immediate instinct was to tell Benjamin about it the job. As she sat there, realizing her reality, she caught her breath and suppressed her emotions. She sat on the bed thinking that she had this great news, and she wanted to share it with someone. Naturally, her mother and Carmella would be the ones she would contact immediately.

Why did I think about Benjamin?

She shook her head again at any thought of him. She then dialed her mother's number and told her about the job. She would call Carmella later, but now she let herself soak in this moment.

Benjamin returned from his funeral duty in somewhat better spirits. He was learning more and more about the opportunities that the Marines were offering to those who accepted orders to Camp Pendleton. Those orders were becoming more attractive by the minute.

He also felt better, physically, than he had in a while. He got some good, much-needed rest over the weekend, and he was going to need it. William's funeral was in an hour. Gratefully, Benjamin was able to get back from Locust Grove in time to make it to William's funeral. Since he decided to wear his uniform to William's funeral, Benjamin was already dressed for the occasion. As Benjamin went into the house and up the stairs, he walked over to the answering machine to see if he had any messages. He pushed the 'Play' button as he saw that he had three messages.

"You have three new messages. Message 1: 'Benjamin, its Chief Beckett. I need you to give me a call. I need to talk to you. I wanted to tell you that you are about to be served with papers. The two inmates that filed charges against you are now suing you for excessive use of force. Please give me a call when you get a chance.'"

Really?? This is just not going to go away.

"Message 2: 'Benjamin, its Raymond. I just wanted to check in with you and make sure you are doing okay. We will see you this evening at the funeral. Please call if you need anything. God bless.'"

Benjamin was good to go to the funeral, but he wasn't sure if he was emotionally ready for it.

"Message 3: 'Benjamin, this is Perry Blacksmith from the jail. I need you to call me. We need to discuss this issue regarding the lawsuit filed against you. Please call me as soon as you get this message.' End of new messages."

Benjamin wasn't even going to call the jail. He was not in the mood to mess with that nonsense. He grabbed his keys and headed out the door. He loathed the idea of going to this funeral, as he knew that seeing William, in that state, was going to be difficult. As he got to his pick-up he got in and went to turn on the engine when his right hand started shaking.

Oh no! Not now!

He was really getting tired of these symptoms, and this was just not the right time for this 'shaking' fit. As he sat in the pick-up, he tried to control his breathing: inhaling and exhaling as calmly as he could. As his mind focused on the moment, he got caught up in William's memory, which is exactly what he did not want to happen. He thought about how his daughter and William's daughter grew up together.

Speaking of that, where is Julie? I have not seen anything of her since, well, since I woke up in his old house.

Most significantly, he wanted to know about Paige.

Benjamin did not get any of this, and it was too much for him to handle. Then the reality hit him: there was no Leesha, and he didn't even know anything about whether or not he would ever see Paige.

"Lord, what happened," Benjamin prayed. "Why is this happening? This is not the way it was supposed to go. I know better, Lord."

Was that a bold statement? In reality, what do I really know? Oh Lord, why was this all happening??

Benjamin found himself asking this question just about every day. At first, when he thought he was getting a second chance, he didn't protest much. Now, it just seemed more like a life he didn't want than a life that he thought he desired.

After sitting in his pick-up for about five minutes, his shaking fit slowed. He was able to start his pick-up, and he headed to the funeral home in Owasso. As he pulled into the parking lot, he saw William's parents standing just outside the funeral home. Benjamin sighed, opened the pick-up door, and got out. As he walked up to the funeral home entrance, William's mother saw him and approached him to give him a hug.

"Thank you for being here, Benjamin."

"Yes, Ma'am," Benjamin replied. "I am so sorry."

Benjamin choked up as he released his hug from William's mother and entered the funeral home. He walked into the auditorium and sat in the back. Up in the front of the auditorium, near the casket, stood Brian and Raymond. Raymond just looked at William, shaking his head, and appearing to be trying not to become emotional. Benjamin felt alone. He wanted to go talk to Raymond. He wanted to see William. He wanted to do anything…but be there.

Brian looked up and saw Benjamin sitting at the back pew, and walked back to talk to him. Brian sat down next to Benjamin and put his hand on Benjamin's shoulder.

"How are you doing, brother?"

"I guess I am okay," Benjamin replied.

"Benjamin, I know it has been a wild week. Just let me know if you need anything."

"I will, Brian. Thank you."

Brian got up and proceeded to the front to begin the service. Benjamin looked around and noticed that he did not see Julie. He wondered who else knew about the relationship that William had with Julie, and, her pregnancy. He guessed it didn't matter, at that point, but it didn't make Benjamin feel any less concerned for Julie.

As Brian began speaking, Benjamin found himself fading away in his thoughts and memories. Benjamin was so lost in thought that he did not realize that Brian was done with his eulogy until about two minutes after he concluded it. Benjamin got up from the pew and walked out of the funeral home. Getting into his pick-up, he wasted no time getting it started, and driving home.

Once Benjamin got to the house, he sat in his car for about an hour, just thinking and reminiscing. He had so many questions, and had no idea where to go to get them answered. The reality of the William's death really hit him, hard.

Why did William take his own life? People had tried to help William. He knew better!!

This was just really difficult for Benjamin. What was worse, Benjamin struggled with his faith for so long -while experiencing marital problems with Natalie- that he was really trying to figure out God's Will in all this. God was never easy to figure out, and like that of so many other people, that only made Benjamin's faith more challenged.

"Jesus," Benjamin prayed. "Where are You? I need you. I know that I have not been what I needed to be for You, and I am sorry. I feel so guilty about William…and…"

With that, Benjamin became emotional. The sleepless nights, the nightmares, the jail, Natalie and the kids, or the lack, thereof… and now this experience—it was all too much for him to handle. As Benjamin collected himself emotionally, he got out of his pick-up and went into the house. He hung up his uniform and showered. He then sat down at his table and looked around. Once again, his house was quiet. Benjamin did not want to do anything. He didn't want to watch TV, play videogames…nothing. Benjamin just sat there. For reasons he did not understand, he continued to feel stuck, and he had no idea where to go from here.

CHAPTER 15

"I don't know, Mom; I can't figure it out. My first instinct was to call Benjamin and tell him about the job. I don't know why. I wish I could just move on from him…but I can't."

"Well, maybe you should go see him."

"Mom, I'm not going to, I mean…"

Natalie stalled, frankly surprised at her mother's response.

"Natalie, honey, you have a problem. You talk about your frustrations with this man constantly, and—"

"I know, Mom," Natalie interrupted. "He makes me so furious!"

Florance was wondering where this built-up frustration was coming from. From her perspective, Natalie and Benjamin weren't engaged that long. Florance sighed loud enough that Natalie could hear it on the other end of the line.

"Okay, Mom," Natalie continued as if she could read her mother's mind over the phone. "I…I just want my life back."

"Back from what, exactly?"

Natalie didn't know how to answer that. She didn't know what she really wanted.

"I don't know. I guess I should be excited about this opportunity with Arger, and I should be happy…and I am."

"But?"

Natalie had to face it. She loved Benjamin. This reality, this experience —or whatever she was going through— didn't change the way she felt, even considering their big fight.

"But I just have to know, and I don't think I am going to get anything from him over the phone, so…"

"So go see him! You don't have to go back to work until Monday, right?"

"Oh, wait; I have to get my drug test and do my administrative paperwork for hiring."

"Do you think they would let you do all that on Monday?"

"Probably; at this point, they might."

"Well…then go see Benjamin."

Natalie sighed, this time loud enough for Florance to hear it.

"I really think I should, Mom."

"We can even see if you can stay with your Aunt Wanda in Sapulpa."

"That's right," Natalie responded. "I almost forgot about Aunt Wanda."

"I'll even go with you if you want me to. We can go together, and I will stay with your Aunt Wanda while you go see Benjamin."

"If he even wants to see me?"

"Well, there is only one road for you to take if you want to move on, Natalie. And I am afraid it leads right through Tulsa."

"You're right, Momma."

"We can even bring your crazy girlfriend if you want to on this trip," Florance joked. "I'm sure Aunt Wanda would love her."

"Everybody loves Carmella," Natalie laughed.

Natalie thought for a second while Florance was on the other end listening for more.

"I guess I will call Benjamin and see if he will be willing to see me. Maybe we can meet for lunch or dinner…or something."

"Give him a call and I will call Aunt Wanda and ask if it is okay that we come stay with her. Whether he sees you or not, we can just take a trip. Would you like to try to go tomorrow or Friday?"

"Well, let me ask Carmella if she can come with us, and we will go from there."

"Okay, I love you, Natalie! Good luck with Benjamin. Let me know what he says."

"Thanks, Mom. I love you too."

Natalie hung up the phone and reached for Carmella's work number. She quickly dialed it, hoping to catch Carmella at work.

NOT PRESENT OR FUTURE...

"Hello?"

"Is Carmella available?"

"Speaking, girl!"

Carmella was her cheery self, as usual.

"Hey, didn't mean to bother you, but I wanted to ask you a question."

"Shoot," Carmella replied.

"What is your schedule tomorrow through the weekend?"

"Well, let me look at my schedule. Why; what's going on?"

"Mom and I are going to Tulsa -either tomorrow or Friday- and we are going to stay with my Aunt Wanda over the weekend."

"Tulsa, huh? Wait, are you gonna try and see—"

"Yes," Natalie interrupted, comically. "Yes, I am."

"Mmm-hm!"

Natalie caught Carmella's comical response.

"Carmella, I have to see him. I have to know. I am so caught with this nonsense in my head right now and, well..."

Natalie paused.

"Well...what?"

"Well, I need to be sure that I am ready to move on with my life. But right now I can't get him out of my mind. I think this will help."

Carmella sat with a weird, but not too uncomfortable, silence.

"Well, then...what are we waiting for?"

"Wait, what??"

"I just checked with my supervisor, and I can take Saturday off. That was the only day I had to work over the next four days."

"Really," Natalie asked. "You can go??"

"I'll be packed and ready!"

"That's wonderful!! Hey, we have to swing up to Amarillo and pick up Mom."

"That's no problem! When are we leaving?"

"Well, what time do you get off tonight?"

"I get off at five."

"Would you like to drive up to Amarillo tonight, and we stay the night with Mom, then leave tomorrow for Tulsa?"

"Sounds good to me, girl! I just have to get home, pack up, and have my stuff ready. Will your car make it?"

"I think so," Natalie replied.

"Okay, then pick me up…what, about 5:30?"

"I'll be there! And Carmella, here is, yet, another time you have been there for me. Thank you for that, and for understanding."

"Girl, you are welcome! Let's go have some fun!"

"Okay! I will see you at 5:30."

"See ya!"

As Natalie hung up the phone, she felt a little relieved that Carmella was able to go on her trek to Tulsa. Having Carmella and Florance in the car for the six-hour trip to Tulsa would be interesting, to say the least, and the three of them would have a blast. Natalie was excited. But that excitement soon simmered when she realized she had to call Benjamin. Natalie sat on the bed, reached over for his number, and held on to the phone, praying.

"Lord, I don't know what I am doing, or why. But I feel like I need to do this. Whatever happens, please be with me."

Natalie dialed the number and waited.

"I don't want to hear about any more of this," Benjamin exclaimed as he was talking to Warden Blacksmith.

"If they are going to sue me, then what can I do?"

"Benjamin, you will need to get a lawyer. These inmates are not going away, and their families are coming after us. We have washed our hands of this. I am afraid that you are on your own."

Benjamin felt sick.

Oh, God, I am so sick of the jail!!

"Isn't it enough that I no longer work there?"

"Like I said, Benjamin, you need to get a lawyer. I am sorry we have to part like this. Please let us know if you need anything."

Click.

Benjamin hung up. He had had enough.

Oh, Lord, I have to get away from here!!

NOT PRESENT OR FUTURE...

As he sat on his bed, disgusted from the conversation that he just had with Warden Blacksmith, he tried to collect his thoughts. He was still tired, as he seemed to feel overly exhausted, lately. He knew that it was not healthy, and he knew that he had to do something. But it just seemed like he had no energy, no drive, and no desire.

I cannot believe I have to continue dealing with that stupid jail!

"God," he prayed, "why is this happening to me?"

As he sat on his bed, contemplating whether or not to go to sleep, the phone rang. Benjamin was not in any mood to talk to anyone, but reluctantly, he answered the phone.

"Hello?"

"Benjamin, its Natalie."

"Natalie? Hey, what's going on?"

Benjamin caught his breath, as he was surprised to hear her voice.

"I was just wondering how you were doing."

"Ummm, I'm okay," Benjamin responded swiftly, leaving no hint that he was in any way interested in talking to Natalie.

"Benjamin, I am coming to Tulsa and I want to know if you would like to meet with me. Maybe we could have lunch or something."

"You are coming here?"

"Yes."

"Um, why?"

"I wanted to know if you would be willing to see me. I wanted to see you and see how you are doing."

"You wanted to see me?"

"Yes, Benjamin. I just want to see you and see how you are doing. Is that okay?"

Benjamin didn't know how to feel about seeing Natalie. He didn't know if it was because he didn't want to see her or if it was because he almost felt ashamed to do so. Regardless, he had thought of her a few times, so he relented.

"Sure. When?"

"I am driving up there tomorrow. How about Friday or Saturday? We could meet for lunch in Owasso…say at Mazzios, or maybe the Golden Corral?"

"Sure, we can meet at the Golden Corral."

"Okay," she replied, somewhat relieved. "Are you doing okay?"

That was a loaded question. Benjamin didn't know what answer to give. He really wanted to conclude this conversation, and he really had no desire to see her. But…

"Yeah, things are going great," he responded, hesitantly.

"Okay," she replied, picking up the hint. "I'll call you when I get to Sapulpa so we can set a time."

"Okay. I'll see you later."

"Bye, Benjamin."

Click.

Benjamin hung up, wasting no time to get off the phone.

Natalie is coming to see me? Why? The relationship is over. What does she want?

It's not like Benjamin didn't have any time to think about things lately, so minus the dreams he had been having, Natalie really wasn't on his mind. Once he got used to being here, Natalie began to fade from his focus.

This really is not a good time for her to come see me. I'm ready to move on from her. Aren't I?

After thinking about it for a couple of minutes, Benjamin just considered this a moment of closure for Natalie. Maybe this is what she needed. After all, Benjamin had no recollection of their supposed 'break up', so he just decided to go along with the ride.

Benjamin shifted his thought back to the fact that he had two more funeral honor details to cover over the next two days, and he would spend some time at the reserve center researching the opportunities for reservists in Camp Pendleton. He also had to get a lawyer, which was not going to be fun. He was going to need some more money. As disgusted as he felt about the situation at the jail, he tried to maintain whatever spirit he had at the moment. Natalie's phone call was a brief reprieve from the reality of his current situation.

Maybe seeing Natalie is not going to be such a bad thing after all.

CHAPTER 16

Natalie pulled into the Golden Corral parking lot. She was so nervous that she tried to get her mind on something else, even if it was just temporarily. She tried to add a positive aspect to her anxiety.

At least we are meeting at a place that we both love to eat at.

Natalie, Carmella, and Florance had arrived at Natalie's aunt's house on Thursday night. They all had a great time, spending time together shopping, and enjoying Tulsa. Natalie was nervous about seeing Benjamin, and the other three helped keep her mind off of Benjamin until the lunch meeting. Overall, so far, this weekend was a great trip. Monday would be even better as Natalie would begin her new job at Arger.

Natalie was still on an emotional high from her conversation with Mr. Sherman. She still could not believe what happened, there. But as awesome as that opportunity was going to be for Natalie, she couldn't help but to think that she still wanted to move to Amarillo. Having her mother back was an incredible blessing for Natalie, and she found herself wanting to be closer to Florance, naturally. This next few weeks might be interesting, but…

Natalie snapped out of it quickly when she saw Ben pull up in his old pick-up truck.

It's not so old. I forgot how nice it was back then, or now, or… whatever.

Benjamin parked and sat in his pick-up for a couple of seconds. He was totally unsure about how this meeting was going to go. He got out of the pick-up and walked up to Natalie. The closer he got to her, the more nervous he became. Neither of them realized that they were both going through the same thing, which made it hard on both of them from their own perspectives. Natalie could do nothing but stare at Benjamin as he approached her, and her heart jumped.

Handsome! So handsome!! Lord, look at him!!!

After all of this time, she did not know what to say. She watched is eyes and his mood. She had been so nervous about this as she had no idea how he'd act.

"Hey," Natalie gulped.

"Hey, Natalie."

Benjamin replied, but barely. All he could do was just stare at her. He had forgotten how beautiful she was. For a moment, he almost let his emotions get away with him before quickly snapping back to reality.

"Have you been doing okay, Benjamin?"

"Yeah. I guess I just can't believe that you took the drive up here."

"Why not?"

"Because I wasn't sure how you took things."

Took things? How I 'took things'?

Natalie wasn't sure how to respond to that. She chose not to as she could clearly see how nervous Benjamin was.

"Hey," Benjamin continued. "Would you like to grab something to eat while we are here?"

"Sure."

Natalie went from being nervous to being really nervous. There he was: the man who would become her husband. The man she loved, then despised, then loathed, then hated.

But…

She was so conflicted. She had completely fallen out of love with him, slowly, over the last couple of years. But, even through all that, this man was still the father of her children.

And now…

After they went through the pay line, they picked a table and grabbed their food. They both sat down and Benjamin instinctively reached for Natalie's hand to pray, but caught himself and withdrew his hand from holding hers.

"Um, sorry about that."

Natalie studied him. Something wasn't quite right, not quite… Benjamin. Of course, he was younger. But she knew Benjamin just as much now as she did then. However, instead of focusing on what wasn't right, she pushed her hand out to his.

"It's okay, Benjamin. You can pray."

"Okay," Benjamin replied, cautiously and gently taking her hand.

WOW!! Breathe, Natalie!! Just breathe!!

As soon as he touched her hand, Natalie flinched, almost reactively, and could hardly catch her breath. She gulped and did her best to control her breathing, which seemed to hasten with every second.

"Are…are you okay, Natalie?"

Natalie shook her head affirmatively, but swiftly, followed by a dainty smile.

Benjamin returned a smile, which to Natalie, made it even worse.

Pray, dang it, just pray, Natalie thought. *Please pray! Hurry!!*

Her heart kept racing, and she felt as if she were going to explode. Benjamin knelt his head, as did Natalie, and he blessed the food. To Natalie, it was a beautiful prayer, for some reason. It didn't matter what he actually said. In fact, Natalie had no idea what came out of his mouth. She was still trying to control herself.

"Amen," they both said, simultaneously.

He let go of her hand and withdrew his hands behind the table to his lap so he could get a grip on himself. He looked up on the table to see where he put his fork. Natalie smiled a little, then grabbed her fork and joined him.

"How are things at the jail?"

"Uh, they are okay," he responded. He didn't feel comfortable with divulging too much information about the jail, so he changed the subject, quickly.

"I have been spending some extra time at the reserve center. In fact, I've been working more funeral honor details."

"Really?"

"Yeah, I forgot how much I loved working there with the Marines."

What? You forgot? You forgot... what? You worked with the Marines at the reserve center up until the time you received your commission. You travelled to Fort Worth every weekend to work with another unit.

Natalie couldn't resist. She was confused at his last statement.

"What do you mean, 'you forgot how much you loved working there', Benjamin?"

"Oh, I, um…"

Benjamin took another bite of his food while trying to think about what to say. Natalie didn't flinch. He kept her gaze.

"I took some time away a while back, and I just got back into it. I still enjoy the reserve thing."

Natalie's mind was racing. She tried to remember his commitment to the Marines when they got back in touch with each other, before they started dating again. Then it hit her:

You didn't take time off. You worked for them as much as you could, just like you are doing now.

His statement bothered here, but she didn't say anything. She actually found herself enjoying this meal with Benjamin and didn't want to ruin it. But there was still something about his demeanor that she could not put her finger on.

"How about you? How is it going with work? I bet it's nice now that you graduated school and all."

Natalie thought very hard about how to respond to that. Benjamin was there when she graduated school. He went to the ceremony.

"Well, it has been interesting. I have been trying to do some soul-searching about what to do now that school is over. And it looks like I am getting a promotion at work."

"Really?"

"Yeah," she responded. "It's been pretty wild lately."

Benjamin smiled, as if he felt foolish.

"Yeah, I guess you have been busy, haven't you, Natalie?"

Natalie couldn't take it anymore, so she decided to make things interesting.

"Benjamin, do you mind if I ask you a question?"

"Yes; anything, darling."

Darling? Did he just call me 'darling'?

Natalie's eyes closed in a pause.

Control yourself, Natalie! Don't blow this!!

She took a deep breath and opened her eyes. Benjamin had that look about him; that look he gave when he was trying not to show himself.

Natalie was getting suspicious.

"What happened…I mean, with us?"

"With us?"

"Yeah, I mean, why did we break off the engagement, Benjamin?"

Benjamin froze.

"Um," he responded, unable to come up with an answer.

"You broke off the engagement with me, right, Benjamin?"

She wanted to ask the question, but not in an accusatory manner. Benjamin sat there, unable to respond. He simply did not know what to say. Natalie could tell that his mind was moving a million miles a minute.

"Benjamin, I'm not angry with you."

She leaned over and touched his hand. He looked up at her. He still didn't have an answer.

There should be an answer, Benjamin. There must have been a reason for you to break it off. There just must have been a reason.

There must have been something.

Anything.

Unless you don't know why you broke it off.

She saw it. Or at least she thought she did.

"Benjamin," she continued, as she put her fork down on the table. "I really want to know."

"I guess, maybe…I just wasn't ready…"

You weren't ready?? No, that is not a good answer! That's not good enough! I know you, Benjamin! You don't give answers like that!

She decided to press a little further.

"Did something happen? Did I do something wrong?"

He still didn't answer.

"Benjamin…"

"No, we're not talking about this anymore," he interrupted.

There you are! That's the 'Benjamin' I know.

"I'm sorry, Benjamin," she replied as she picked up her fork to continue eating. She was trying not to get emotional as this was, obviously, becoming a tense situation. Benjamin thought for a second. He could end this once and for all.

"Do you really not know, Natalie?"

Natalie looked up, stunned.

"No, Benjamin, I don't. I mean, we were engaged, and then we weren't. I mean…I…"

She paused, but Benjamin didn't say a word. Natalie was getting frustrated. She was done with being careful.

"Benjamin, what do you remember?"

"What do you mean?"

"What do you remember…about us?"

Why did she just ask me that??

She had Benjamin's full attention. Emotions and feelings of anger and discomfort were building up inside him. He felt like she was cornering him, like she had done so many times in the past. He started breathing, heavily.

"Benjamin, please? I just want to know—"

"You want to know why I broke it off, Natalie? It was because I was tired of the fighting and the bickering and stuff."

The look he gave her was a look of anger. She had seen that look before, but not when they were engaged.

Why is he so angry? Did we fight while we were engaged?

She couldn't remember any fights. Then she looked, deeper, into him: there was a lot of anger in his eyes. She was even more convinced that, even though this was the younger Benjamin, he knew something more than what that 'younger' Benjamin should know.

He must know something. This doesn't make any sense to me!

Somehow, he knew. It was like they were both taken away from their 'old' lives and brought back here for some reason.

"Benjamin, I am sorry. I don't remember any fights while we were still engaged. I mean, we weren't really engaged that long."

NOT PRESENT OR FUTURE...

She paused for a second. Benjamin looked as if he was calming down a bit as Natalie sat there, eating. She hadn't planned on spending a lot of time with Benjamin, originally, when she scheduled this meeting with him. But now that she was here, something made her want to stay.

"I don't know what is happening," Natalie continued. "But I just wanted to see you and make sure you were okay."

Benjamin sat there for about a minute while Natalie studied him. He was trying to determine how to respond to her.

"I'm okay, Natalie. I am just real busy doing my own thing right now."

For some reason, Natalie's heart began to hurt again. She was held captive by her own expectations.

This wasn't the way this was supposed to go. Right?

Benjamin noticed her demeanor, and tried to change the subject.

"So are you staying with your 'auntie' in Sapulpa?"

"Yes, Ben, I am," she replied, as she began playing with her purse.

"Well, that's good. As for me, other than working, I really haven't been doing much outside of helping out at the church."

"Okay. You working with the kids?"

"Yeah," he responded with a smile. "They seem to keep me busy."

"I'll bet Leesha would have loved to see that," Natalie responded, instinctively.

Benjamin responded with a quick smile, but soon realized what Natalie just said. Natalie slipped subconsciously. She realized it at the same time he did. Benjamin just looked at her as she looked at him.

"I have to go, Natalie."

Benjamin stood up, pushed in his chair, and walked off.

"Wait," Natalie responded as she grabbed her purse.

Benjamin walked out of the Golden Corral, quickly, as she followed.

"Benjamin, wait!"

He kept walking; speeding up, the closer he got to his pick-up. She kept following him, trying to keep up with his pace. He was just about to the pick-up when Natalie lost it.

"Benjamin, stop!!!"

He turned and looked at her with a fierce glaze, but she didn't care. She walked up to him as he stood there, staring at her. Trying to avoid any irrational response, Natalie became emotional.

"Benjamin, what is happening here?"

"What do you mean, Natalie? What do you want?"

"Benjamin, why are you so angry? Why did you call off our engagement? Why won't you talk to me?"

Natalie couldn't take it anymore, and she didn't care. She was going to find out something. He didn't answer her. He just looked away from her. His response only fueled her resolve.

"Benjamin, what do you remember? Do you remember… Leesha? Do you know who I am talking about when I say her name?"

His body language gave it away.

You do know! Somehow, you know about Leesha. But how?

"Benjamin, please tell me what is going on?"

"I don't know what is going on!!"

"Do you know who I am talking about; about Leesha?"

Benjamin said nothing. He just stood there, refusing to look at her. He was focused enough not to answer her.

"Benjamin, I don't think I'm crazy, but I can't help but believe that you and I aren't meant to be here."

Benjamin turned and looked at her, in shock.

Did she just say that? Did she really just say that?

"Benjamin, I think about and dream about…"

She just about gave up and started crying. Ben turned is eyes away from her. He could not look at her, any more. She got herself together enough to finish the sentence.

"I think about a little girl and two little boys."

Benjamin closed his eyes, trying not to become emotional, himself. She knew as well. They both did. He didn't know what to do. He was so confused. All he wanted to do was leave.

I don't need this. I don't want to hear this.

"Natalie, I have to go. I…"

He did not know what else to say. He got in his truck, started it up, and drove away, leaving Natalie in the parking lot.

I don't believe this, she thought. *I cannot believe any of it. Benjamin knows about the kids!*

Natalie thought that he was acting weird, but now she knew for sure. She just shook her head in total confusion.

How is this possible? What happened to us? Why is he acting this way? Why is this happening, God??

Natalie walked over to her car, trying not to cause any more attention than she already had. She got in, turned on the car, and sat there, thinking about what happened. She thought about his reactions, and tried to make sense of them.

If he did remember the kids, why didn't he acknowledge them? If he did remember them, why would he choose a path to take that would ensure they never existed? Was that his choice?

Was that…my choice?

Struggling with her thoughts, Natalie drove to back to Sapulpa to get Carmella and Florance. It was a long drive, but Natalie knew she had to get both of them home. They were going to leave as soon as Natalie arrived at her aunt's house so that they could take Florance home and proceed to Abilene. Natalie was tired enough, after this emotional meeting with Benjamin, that she felt she needed to stay the night with Florance and drive home on Sunday.

Emotionally, Natalie didn't know how to feel. She just didn't understand any of it. She couldn't figure out Benjamin's actions. The reality was that she went to see him for some type of closure -at least that is what she told herself- but she was no closer to her satisfaction than before she came to Tulsa. She wanted to move forward in her life, and she hoped this would help her do it. Right now, she didn't know how she was going to do it, but she was going to do it, nonetheless.

CHAPTER 17

As Benjamin drove out of the church parking lot, he headed towards Turley to visit his mother. He wasn't looking forward to this visit, but he thought he would just entertain her for about an hour or so. He kept thinking about the sermon and everything that Brian preached about, today.

He also thought about how difficult it was for him to fall asleep the previous night. The dreams were becoming more vicious, it seemed, with each passing night. They seemed to evolve around conflict and fighting…shooting and explosions. Benjamin was having more experiences of waking up in the middle of the night, causing him to check his doors and windows, and ensuring that his house was secure. He was getting to the point to where he was afraid of falling asleep. Natalie had suggested, on many occasions, that he should talk to someone about his experiences during deployment. Stubbornly, he had fought against that idea for so long.

Maybe there is more to this than I can handle. Lord, please help me deal with this.

Benjamin was so conflicted. He felt terrible about how he treated Natalie at the Golden Corral. He lied to her, and he knew it. He knew it, and it ate at him. What was worse was that she knew it, too. He can't lie to her, and he knew that. It didn't matter, though. All he wanted to do was start over and live a new life, but the prospect of doing so seemed a lot harder than he originally imagined. He caught himself thinking about Natalie and the kids more and more, every day.

But why think about the kids? They aren't real, and…

NOT PRESENT OR FUTURE...

He swallowed hard at the rest of this thought:
They're not gonna be.

As he pulled into Turley, he turned down the street leading to his mother's house. He started getting anxious as he loathed the idea of going any further. He pulled into the driveway and put the car in park. He sat there in deep anxiety.

Just get in, spend some time with her, and leave.

Benjamin got out of the car and walked to the front door to see his mother standing there waiting for him.

"Hi, Mom."

"Hi, yourself," she responded, hatefully. "It's about time you came by to see me."

He opened the screen door and entered the house as his mother walked into the living room. Her demeanor spoke volumes, and she was already getting on his nerves.

"So what have you been up to? No doubt hangin' around that church in Owasso, I take it."

"I've been busy, Mom," Benjamin replied, trying to avoid the trap. "I've been working and doing more stuff with the Marines. In fact, I'm thinking of taking orders again."

"Again?? You just got done with them. Is this part of you trying to become some type of officer or something?"

"Yes, Momma, I would still like to become an officer in the Marines. But that might be a while."

"Don't know what you want with those military folks any way."

"Momma, I love the Marines. It has been good for me. I have made a lot of friends and—"

"You have friends here," she interrupted. "You have Ricky and the others. I don't know why you keep leaving them."

"Momma, I didn't leave Ricky...or you. I just went to better my life, that's all. I..."

He paused in frustration, but tried not to lose his temper.

"I just wanted more for myself."

'Wanted'? You 'wanted' more? Be careful, Benjamin! Don't let her get you!

"Oh, so, what: we aren't good enough for you?"

"Okay, Momma. Please stop."

She was persistent. It was no comfort to Benjamin realizing that she hadn't even started, yet.

"Since you have been going to that church, you have been acting like you are better than everyone else."

"Now, Momma, that's enough!"

This is why I did not want to come over! This is why I've always had a strained relationship with my mother.

This is one of the reasons that Natalie and I fought…a lot.

"Well, I can't complain too much," she continued. "At least you wouldn't be working in that jail with all them racist cops."

"Oh, that's it!"

Benjamin couldn't take it anymore. He got up and went to kiss his mother on the forehead.

"Where are you going?"

"I gotta go, Mom."

"Go on then!! Go hang out with all your 'cracker' friends; the ones you left us for."

"Momma, what is your problem? What's the matter with you??"

Benjamin turned back to look at her, awaiting her response.

"What's the matter with you, Benjamin?? I'm tired of you leaving us all the time for your 'friends', as you call them!"

"Who are you talking about, Momma? What 'friends' are you referring to?"

"I'm talking about your friends at your church, and your 'Marines'! Those 'friends'!"

"What's wrong with the church and the Marines, Mama?"

"I'm surprised you don't know, son! Look at you; goin' to a white church, joining the white man's military, then working in a jail with racist pigs. That's not how I raised you!"

"No, Mom! You raised me to hate people; to blame people for things that they did not do. You taught me that if they didn't look like me, then they are the 'enemy'!"

Benjamin lost control, but at this point, he didn't care.

"What's the difference, Mom? What's the difference between us and the other 'racists', as you call them?"

"Because they hurt us, and they treated us like slaves, and they had slaves!"

"Mom, I don't know anyone who hurt you! I don't know anyone who owned a slave!!"

Benjamin backed up to get a grip on himself before he made his last statement.

"And I don't know anyone who is more full of hatred than you are!"

His mother looked at him with total shock. She could not believe the way he was talking to her. Benjamin was tired of her hateful rhetoric. One thing is for certain: it wasn't just the past few years all built up inside him. He was carrying the emotions, anger, frustrations, and hurt that his mother had caused him all his life, even during the course of his marriage. What was worse was he defended her to Natalie.

"I can't do this with you any more, Mom," Benjamin grimaced. "I can't live or think like that anymore. I know that there are racist people out there, but there are also wonderful people, and many of them are people that I love."

His mother just sat on the couch staring at him in anger as he continued.

"You always complain about all those white people that had slaves, but have you ever considered the many white people that died to free those slaves? That died to help end racism? That died to help make the changes that needed to be made?"

Benjamin lowered his head in exhaustion. That is how his mother made him feel. Just as he was about to turn toward the door, his mother answered him.

"I don't care about those people, Son."

"Well, then, that's your problem," he responded as he opened the door to leave.

"I'll bet this has to do with that Natalie-girl, doesn't it, Benjamin? I didn't like her then, and I still don't! Can't believe you are even thinking about marrying her."

"YEAH, AND YOU DIDN'T LIKE MY KIDS, EITHER!!!"

Benjamin froze for a second at that statement, really trying hard not to respond, any further, in anger. The look on his mother's face gave it away. She was stunned. He sighed, deeply, as he knew he slipped up.

"What are you talking about, Son? What 'kids'?"

"It doesn't matter, Mom. I'm leaving."

Benjamin opened the door and left. As he walked to his pick-up, he realized that his mother did not know that they broke off the engagement. She was still in shock about his statement, but he didn't care. He was so tired of his mother's attitude.

He remembered when he brought Natalie home to meet her for the first time, and the time he brought her home to announce their engagement. Neither time was met with pleasantries. His mother hated Natalie, and Benjamin never understood why. She never wanted anything to do with Natalie after they got married, either.

Benjamin's children always felt awkward around her, too, which triggered his comment regarding them. What was worse was that Benjamin knew of his mother's detrimental attitude towards Natalie and the kids but, for whatever reason, he allowed his mother to become a thorn in the side of his marriage, and Natalie really despised him for it.

Sitting in the car, trying to control his demeanor from his eventful visit with his mother, he realized his own fault in how he allowed his mother to be such a controlling factor in his marriage… and in his life.

"I'm so sorry, Natalie," he sighed, softly.

If only you could hear me; if only you could hear my apology.

Benjamin remembered that, from past experiences spending time with his mother, she had the uncanny ability to alter his mood. He hated how his mother made him feel. Her words were powerful and persuasive. What made it worse was that she was such a negative person, all the time. Her bitterness wasn't necessarily unwarranted. She had several terrible experiences as a child. Living in Alabama in the 60's and 70's, it was a difficult time for her, as it was for many African-Americans living in the south. She got through it with God; at least that is what Benjamin understood. But for some reason, through time, she just changed. She had so much hatred in her heart that it caused her to not trust anyone that did not have the same skin color that she did. She began to blame people for the mistakes she made in her life. She took no responsibility for the choices that she made while raising Benjamin, and in many cases, her actions caused a significant rift in their relationship.

This bitterness had a significant effect on Benjamin. He struggled with it as well. It wasn't to say that Benjamin did not have his own experiences with prejudice and racism -which only compounded his confusion- but he also had people in his life who loved him, regardless of what he looked like. He did not understand it. He had a hard time accepting it. And when he was approached with it, he made the assumption that many others made: it was all a lie.

Until he found Jesus.

Benjamin knew about God. His mother shared God with him. But her bitterness ran so deep that she began to show more anger than love. That bitterness had such an effect on Benjamin that he grew up believing that all white people were inherently racist, and there was nothing they could do about it. There were many times that he didn't want to believe that, but he couldn't overcome what he was taught.

Until he found Jesus.

His mother moved around from place to place, living a nomadic life. She dragged Benjamin along with him, and when he would challenge her decision to keep moving, she would just pull her weapons of guilt-trips and Bible-thumping, claiming that if God 'commanded' Benjamin to honor his mother, he'd better do it. Benjamin despised that about her. He began to question everything that he thought about religion, and thought that God was just something that someone used against him when they wanted something.

Until he found Jesus.

When Benjamin and his mother moved to Amarillo, he found himself, once again, trying to fit in at a new school. This time, though, he met some kids who went to church and invited Benjamin to a church youth activity.

That is when he met Natalie.

They dated for a little bit, as Benjamin was just two years ahead of Natalie. Then, out of nowhere, his mother moved Benjamin to Tulsa where Benjamin transferred to Booker T. Washington High School. Neither Benjamin nor Natalie wanted a long distance relationship, but they kept in touch. While in Washington High School, Benjamin played football, basketball, and ran track. One night, after a football game against the Owasso Rams, several players from both teams got together and prayed, just following the conclusion of the game. Benjamin joined them, and after the prayer, one of the Owasso players invited Benjamin and his prayerful teammates to an evening youth function at the Owasso First Christian Church.

And that is when he found Jesus.

Benjamin started going to the church in Owasso, but his choice to do so was met with adversity from his mother. He had a very hard time understanding her position on his attending that church, considering that he was learning about God, learning about living for God, and learning about what God wanted for his life. Needless to say, that church was a thorn in the side of the relationship between Benjamin and his mother. And he hated that.

Benjamin considered all of this as he drove home from his mother's house. He was going to lead a small-group tonight, but after that confrontation with his mother, he did not feel like doing so. When he got home, he went into his house and collapsed on his couch. He was very frustrated, and his energy was drained. This time was just like all the other times after he left his mother's house, and he knew better than to go over there in the first place. He just stretched out on the couch and dozed off.

Brrng.

Benjamin sighed, looked over at the phone, but refused to move.

Brrng.

Benjamin looked at the phone again, and this time, decided to get up to answer it.

"Hello?"

"Hey, Benjamin, it's Brian. What are you up to?"

"Brian?"

"Yeah, Brian, from the church."

NOT PRESENT OR FUTURE...

"Oh, Brian; I'm sorry about that," Benjamin replied. "What's going on?"

"I was wondering if you would be willing to leave early enough to come by and get me, and give me a ride to the church tonight. My car is acting up, and I have to get it looked at."

"Um…I wasn't sure if I was going to evening service, tonight."

"Oh, I'm sorry. Raymond said you were scheduled to lead a small-group tonight."

"Um…"

Benjamin really didn't feel like doing anything, but he respected Brian, and loved his sermons. He didn't feel right not helping Brian out.

"I'll be there, Brian. What time?"

"Oh, Benjamin, if you weren't coming tonight, you don't have to make a special trip."

"No, it's okay. Just tell me what time to be there."

"Could you be here about 3:30?"

"Yeah, I'll be there," Benjamin answered. "See ya then."

Benjamin hung up the phone and collapsed on the couch to take a nap. He shut his eyes, and time seemed to pass quickly as he woke up and noticed that the time was 3:13. He jumped up, quickly, put on his shoes, grabbed his keys, and headed out the door. He drove, quickly, as he was running a bit late, and found himself pulling into Brian's driveway at 3:32, just as Brian came out of the house. Brian walked to Benjamin's pick-up and waved to Janet as he got in.

"I'm sorry I'm late, Brian."

"Nonsense, brother! You are right on time. And as we all know," Brian continued jokingly, "Marines are never late."

"You got that right, brother!"

"So how have you been?"

"Mmm, I guess okay," Benjamin replied.

Right away, Brian could tell that something was wrong. Benjamin looked like he had been raked across the coals.

"Are you sure? You just look like you have had a rough day."

Benjamin was feeling very negative, most likely due to the visit he had with his mother. He was still drained, and had a hard time pulling out of the funk he was in.

"Brian, can I ask you something?"

"Shoot!"

"Do I fit in at your church?"

"What? What are you talking about?"

Brian was stunned at the question.

"Brian, I'm serious. I don't see a whole lot of black people at your church."

Brian was shocked. He did not know how to respond. He prayed that God would give him an answer as he clearly had no answer for this.

"Benjamin, where is this coming from? Did something happen in the church? Did someone say anything to you; something that made you feel you were not welcome?"

Benjamin knew that the answer was 'no', but he didn't want to admit it. Brian began to feel like Benjamin wanted him to say the wrong thing, and he felt like he was caught between a rock and a hard place.

'Brian's' church, Brian thought. *I hope I have never given the impression that it was 'my' church. First, Benjamin had been going to that church since before he joined the Marines.*

Second...

"Benjamin, let's make something very clear here. It is not 'my' church. It is God's church, not mine. I am only the minister."

Benjamin didn't change his demeanor, and Brian noticed it.

"Benjamin, we don't discriminate at the church. Christ died that all might be saved. His Word is for all of us."

Brian looked over at Benjamin and continued. "Seriously, Benjamin, did something happen at the church?"

"No, it's cool. I don't want to talk about it."

"Benjamin, really, I need to know. I need to know where this coming from."

Benjamin looked frustrated, but Brian insisted.

NOT PRESENT OR FUTURE...

"It just seems like God blesses some and not others. Sometimes God seems like a white God, like Christianity is a white man's religion."

"Benjamin, I can assure you that God is not a 'white' God, and that Christianity is not a 'white man's' religion. Remember, Benjamin, Jesus was a Jew. We don't know what he looked like, and I seriously doubt that God cares about the color of our skin. When we stand before God on the Day of Judgment, the last thing He will care about is our skin color."

Brian sighed. He was still shocked, but concerned, about Benjamin's inquiries.

"Benjamin, are you sure you are okay?"

"Yeah, I'm fine."

Brian really wanted to know where this was coming from, but they arrived at the church, and Brian had to prepare for Sunday evening service. He opened the door and looked back at Benjamin.

"Hey, Benjamin, look...I want to finish this conversation, okay?"

"Okay," Benjamin replied. "Look, it really ain't no big deal."

Brian shut the door and left the pick-up even more concerned than when he was inside it. He prayed for Benjamin and hoped that nothing happened in the church to cause Benjamin to question it, or those that came to worship in it. Benjamin sat in the pick-up. He really was not in the mood to work with the kids that evening. Though he knew it was wrong, he put the pick-up in 'drive', and went home. All he wanted to do, at that moment, was just be alone.

It was late. Natalie and Carmella pulled into Natalie's apartment complex, exhausted. Natalie was very glad that Carmella was willing to take her car as Natalie's car was just about on its last leg. Natalie was even more thankful that her mother was willing to take her car to Tulsa, and though Natalie enjoyed the travelling company, her feelings were bittersweet, considering that she thought it was a wasted trip. In fact, she felt really bad that they made the drive at all.

If it wasn't for Natalie's aunt being so cool, Natalie really would have felt guilty about it.

Well, as far as I am concerned, it's all over. I can move forward.

So she thought.

As Natalie got out of the car, she grabbed her bag, pulled her keys out, and walked up to her apartment door. She found a note taped to the door with her name on it. Natalie took the note and tried to read it in the dimness of her porch light.

Ms. Barnes, please contact the front desk at your earliest convenience.

"Great! What now?"

She opened the door, waved at Carmella, and went inside, shutting the door behind her. As she put her purse down on the bed, she looked around the apartment and began to feel very uncomfortable. There were different things in her apartment that seemed out of place. Scanning around her apartment, she couldn't breathe.

Oh my God! Somebody has been in here!!

Whoever was in her apartment didn't try very hard to hide their intrusion. Natalie went to her door to ensure it was locked, and she checked every window. There was no back door to the apartment and no evidence of tampering in the windows. She had no idea how anyone could get in there.

Natalie did not feel safe. She grabbed her phone and called Carmella's house.

"Hello," came a deep male voice on the other end.

"Hello, Mr. Theodore?"

"Yes?"

"Sir, it's Natalie. I am so sorry I am calling so late. Has Carmella made it back yet?"

"Um, not yet. What's going on?"

Natalie began to shake.

"Mr. Theodore…somebody broke into my apartment while we were gone."

Natalie paused as her shaking become uncontrollable.

"Natalie, honey, are you okay?"

NOT PRESENT OR FUTURE...

"Yes, I am okay. I just wanted to ask Carmella if it is okay if I stay with you guys tonight. I promise I will get up quickly because I start my new job, tomorrow."

"Absolutely! You are welcome here any time."

"Thank you so much! I'll come right over."

"Okay, we'll tell Carmella, who...looked like she just pulled up."

"Thank you so much, Mr. Theodore. I really appreciate it!"

Natalie hung up the phone, grabbed her bag and put her night items in it. She reached over and grabbed her purse and practically ran for the door. She looked through her peephole to see if anyone was there. She continued to shake, as she was overcome with fear, but she knew she had to get to her car. Natalie sighed. It was pitch black outside. As if that wasn't enough, there was no guarantee that the car would even start.

"Lord," Natalie prayed, "please let my car start."

Natalie took another deep breath, opened the door, shut it behind her, ensuring that she locked it, and ran to her car. She unlocked the car, got in, and locked it back up, looking around to ensure nobody was around. She put the keys in the car and prayed, once more. She turned the key and the car started.

"Thank you, Jesus!!!"

She left the parking lot as quickly as she could and drove straight to Carmella's house. When she got there, she got out of the car, grabbed her stuff, and ran up to Carmella's front door. Just as she went to knock on the door, Carmella opened it.

"Are you okay? What happened?"

"Somebody broke into my apartment. My stuff was scattered everywhere. I called your house immediately and...and...I'm so sorry I woke your dad."

Natalie was still shaken up. She tried to calm her herself down.

"Natalie, it's okay. You're okay now. Just calm down and breathe. I'll get you some warm tea."

"Thank you, Carmella. Hey, shouldn't you be going to bed? Don't you have to work tomorrow?"

"Actually, I close tomorrow night, so I don't have to be at work until Noon. You are the one who needs to rest. You've got a big day tomorrow."

Natalie sat down on the couch and tried to collect her thoughts. After about a minute, Carmella brought Natalie a coffee cup full of warm tea.

"Wow! That was quick!"

"I just warmed up tea in the microwave," Carmella responded. "Now take some of this and try to relax."

Natalie took a sip of the tea, put the cup down, and fell back into the couch. Carmella went into her bedroom and changed into her pajamas. As she came back into the living room, Natalie was lying on the couch, completely motionless. Carmella grabbed a blanket and covered Natalie with it. As she walked toward her bedroom, Carmella looked back at Natalie and prayed for her.

"Lord, please be with Natalie? Please help her, and keep her safe?"

CHAPTER 18

"Here's your new office, Natalie. I hope you like it."

Mr. Sherman led Natalie to a corner office with a beautiful view.

"Now please don't forget to get your drug screening done so we can conclude your hiring process."

"I will...I mean, I won't, Sir. And thank you so much for allowing me to do this today. I am so sorry that I had to leave last week. I do appreciate you letting me do take that time to go home."

"No problem. I hope that everything is okay."

"I believe so," responded Natalie as she was looking through her new desk.

"Great! Go ahead and get unpacked, and get settled in. We have a meeting with Mr. Quartermain tomorrow, and I want to try to get you plugged in as soon as you can. He is very excited to get this thing moving."

"Yes, Sir. I am too," Natalie replied as Mr. Sherman left her office.

There she was, sitting in her office, in her brand-new position, facing the world as she always longed to. Even before she became a mother, Natalie had desires of fulfilling a wonderful career, somewhere, and now she had her chance. She sat down in her chair and looked around her office. Empty walls, empty shelves...an empty trashcan. Natalie could not help but to think that, regardless of this blessing she received from Mr. Sherman and the Arger Corporation, she felt just as empty, inside. She thought about Benjamin, still not knowing how to feel about her time in

Tulsa. Hopefully, it would become the closure she was looking for. But for now...

She just felt absolutely incomplete.

She took a deep breath and straightened up her demeanor, trying to focus on the moment.

Come on, Natalie! Look at what you have done. You should be so proud of yourself!

Natalie must have been caught in a trance as she didn't hear the IT worker trying to get her attention.

"I'm sorry, Sir. I guess I wasn't paying attention."

She looked over to see an older man in working coveralls approaching her to shake her hand.

"Good morning, Ma'am, I'm Phillip from 'IT'. I am here to set up your computer system, fax, and phone."

"Oh, okay," Natalie replied. "I am so sorry. I guess I got caught up on the position."

"It must be very exciting for you, Ma'am. We look forward to working with you!"

"Thank you," Natalie responded as she noticed his bag of tools. "Do I need to get out of your way so you can set up?"

"I will need to get behind the desk and over by your chair, just to make sure of the validation of the electronic set-up."

"Okay, that's fine. I have to leave anyway to go do my drug screening. Thank you for getting all of this set up!"

"You are welcome, Ma'am! I should be done with all of his in about an hour or two."

"Okay," Natalie replied, as she grabbed her purse. She turned to leave the office when she noticed that Phillip was wearing earphones.

"Listening to music?"

"Oh, uh, yes," he replied. "I'm sorry. Is it too loud?"

"Oh no. I was just making an observation."

"It's 'Michael W. Smith'. I love his music."

"I do, too," Natalie replied. "Which album are you listening to?"

"I 2 Eye."

"Really?"

"Yeah, I'm listening to 'Leesha' right now."

Natalie froze, and her heart jumped.

"'Leesha'? That's what you're listening to?"

"Yeah, it's a beautiful song. Have you heard it before?"

"Oh, yes! I named my daughter…uh…"

She paused, as she caught herself.

"I mean, I…"

"You have a daughter named Leesha, and you named her after this song? That is so cool! Most people haven't heard this song. It wasn't, necessarily, one of Michael W. Smith's most popular ones."

"Oh, really," Natalie responded, really unsure of what to say now.

"Well, here."

Phillip took off his earphones and handed them to Natalie. She put one of them in her ear and started listening. It was 'Leesha', and Natalie's heart sank.

"Um…"

Natalie pulled the earphones from her ears, grabbed her purse, and began to leave.

"Thank you, Phillip," she whispered as she left, wiping a tear from her eye. Walking by Shannon's desk, Natalie tried to regain her composure.

"Shannon, I have to leave to go get my drug screening. I should be back over lunch. Do you need anything?"

"No, thank you. Thanks for asking, though."

Natalie walked out of the building, completely feeling overwhelmed. She was unsure about everything. She found herself so confused, and almost afraid.

But why am I afraid? What is wrong with me? Was it the song?

Is this job happening too fast?

Is this job, this life, this…whatever this is…is this what I really want??

Natalie felt so alone, and she couldn't shake the feeling. She got in her car and went to the lab to get her drug screening done. Thankfully, she was in and out of the lab, quickly. She got in her car and started thinking about what she wanted to do for lunch. She had no desire for anything. Nothing appealed to her.

Oh, Lord, what is wrong with me??

At that moment, she realized that she needed to talk to her mother. After starting her car, she drove to her apartment. When she arrived at her apartment complex, she looked around, quickly, just to be sure that Darnell was not anywhere in sight. Natalie got out of her car, went to her apartment door, unlocked it, and went inside, locking it immediately. She was certainly getting tired of the continuous phone calls and tormenting periods of harassment.

This is ridiculous!! Why do I feel like a prisoner in my own apartment?

Catching herself for a moment, she picked up the phone and dialed her mother's number.

"Hello?"

"Hi, Mom, it's me."

"Hey, you! Shouldn't you be at work?"

"I was, Mom, but I just wanted to call you and talk to you for a bit while I am on lunch."

"So how's it going on your first day at your new, exciting job?"

"It's okay."

Natalie really didn't know how to answer that. She was almost afraid to tell her mother how she was thinking. Florance caught it. She could read her daughter like a book.

"Natalie, what's going on, honey? Are you okay?"

"Well, Mom, this is a very exciting day for me. I mean, I just got this new, wonderful opportunity. I have a new office and a great boss. I am even working on this incredible project that anyone in my position would want."

Natalie paused.

"But...," Florance responded, waiting for Natalie to continue. Natalie broke, emotionally. She began to cry, and she couldn't control it.

"Mom, what is wrong with me? I don't know what to do."

Florance was always good at calming her daughter. She was an incredible mother who always knew how to help Natalie. It was why her death was so difficult for Natalie, when it happened. Maybe it was one of the reasons that Natalie found herself clinging to Florance,

NOT PRESENT OR FUTURE...

recently. But Florance couldn't figure out Natalie's emotional state. She just figured it had something to do with her strained relationship with Benjamin. Florance was a little more concerned, this time, as they just spent the previous weekend laughing and visiting in the car during their trip to Tulsa. She was determined to find out what was going on with her daughter.

"So talk to me, Natalie. Is it Benjamin?"

"I don't know what it is," Natalie responded, trying to calm herself. "All I want to do is be with you, Mom. I just feel like, like…"

Natalie lost it, again, trying to find a way to control herself. Florance just listened, patiently. When Natalie was able to get control of her emotions, she finally said what she wanted to say.

"Mom, I want to move up there to Amarillo to be closer to you. I don't know much right now, but that is what I do know."

"Okay," Florance responded, still listening intently.

"I can find a job -and a place to live- in Amarillo. I have been feeling like this for a while, Mom, but I didn't know what to do about it, honestly."

By this time Natalie was able to gain her composure.

"Natalie, are you sure that this is what you want? I mean, I would love to have you closer, and you can even live with me until you get on your feet, but I just want you to be sure that this is what you want."

Natalie thought about it. There was only one response she could give at this moment.

"Yes, Mom. I want to be closer to you in Amarillo. I can't explain it, but that is what I want. I know that Carmella is here, but I think she would understand. Besides, we won't stop being friends just because I move away."

"And my question about Benjamin," Florance inquired.

"Look, Mom, I am not going to lie to you and say he doesn't bother me. But after this past weekend I might have to accept that the relationship with him is going nowhere."

That statement was very difficult for Natalie to make, and the thought of that crushed her heart. Natalie had few moments in her life where she physically felt pain from her emotional woes, and this was one of those times.

"Mom, please? I have made my decision. Can I just move back to Amarillo?"

"You know you are welcome here any time, honey. You are my daughter, and I love you…and I want to see you happy. I tell you what, give it just this week. See what happens at work. On Friday, if you have still made your decision to move back, then I will tell you to come on home. How's that? I just want to be sure that this is what you want."

What I want is to be with you, Mom! Aside from that, nothing else matters.

Natalie took a deep breath.

"Okay, Mom. I'll try. I'll give it to the end of the week. Thank you for, at least, letting me have the option."

"You are welcome, child. I do look forward to hearing about this new job."

"Well, it is exciting, and Mr. Sherman has been very sweet about all of this. He didn't even ask me for the money back that he gave me when he let me go. I almost feel guilty about that."

"Well, maybe you should bring that up to him."

"Maybe I will," Natalie responded.

"Natalie, do you have enough to cover your apartment for the rest of the month?"

"I have this apartment until the end of the month, so regardless of what happens, I am okay. On my off-time, I will just take it slow and spend as much time with Carmella as I can. She would love that."

"Okay, that sounds good to me. Whatever you decide, just know that I love you."

"I love you too, Mom."

Natalie said 'good-bye' to her mother and grabbed her purse to leave. Her heart felt warm and comfortable, following that conversation. Natalie believed, for the first time in a while, that she would be okay. There were some decisions that she had to make, but such was life, and her mother would be a part of it, once again.

NOT PRESENT OR FUTURE...

"Thank you, Lord! I don't know what I did to have my mother back, so thank you."

Just as Natalie was about to walk out the door, the phone rang. She shut the door and turned back to answer the phone.

"Hello?"

"Natalie?"

It was a deep male voice at the other end of the phone.

"Yes," she answered.

"Natalie, it's Benjamin. I...I just wanted to see if you made it back okay."

"Benjamin," Natalie responded, half in shock.

Benjamin? Really? Now? You're calling me, now??

"Yeah, I didn't mean to bother you, but—"

"But what," Natalie interrupted. "But...what??"

"Natalie, I am sorry about the way I acted at the Golden Corral, I just had to leave."

"You just had to...leave??"

Benjamin could hear the frustration in her voice.

"Natalie, I didn't call to—"

"Then why did you call, Benjamin," Natalie interrupted, again. Benjamin fell silent. He could feel her frustration over the phone. Normally, Natalie would have tried to contain herself, but at that moment, she didn't care.

"Natalie, I'm sorry about how I acted."

"Benjamin, why did you call me?"

"To say that I am sorry, Natalie."

Benjamin was becoming frustrated, himself. Natalie could sense it, but she didn't care. She sighed and gathered her bearings.

"Benjamin, what are you doing? I came to Tulsa to see you. I just wanted to talk to you, and you pushed me away. Why do you always push me away?"

Natalie became emotional, and got caught up in the moment.

Wait a minute, Benjamin thought. *Always push her away? We weren't engaged that long.*

"I don't always push you away, Natalie! What...what are you talking about?"

By this time, they were combining frustrations between both of the lives they had. Natalie might have thought that she needed to be careful, but she was convinced that Benjamin wasn't completely ignorant about this 'experience'. They both sat silent on the phone until Natalie spoke up.

"Benjamin, I can't do this right now. I have to go. You had your chance to talk to me when I came up there."

"Yeah, okay," Benjamin replied, clearly disappointed. Natalie was caught. She couldn't hang up. One voice in her head told her to do that, but her heart told her not to. She didn't think she wanted this call to end like this.

"Benjamin, are you okay?"

"Yeah, I…I…"

Benjamin lost his self, emotionally, for a second. Natalie could hear it, but she didn't know how to respond. She didn't know if she even cared. But she couldn't help but to hang on to the phone.

"I just wanted to say that I was sorry, Natalie. I don't know what happened. I don't have an answer as to why we called off the marriage. I just don't have any answers."

That was something, and it was enough to keep Natalie's attention, if even for a minute.

"Thank you, Benjamin. Thank you for telling me that."

Benjamin cleared his throat. He wanted to apologize to her about him choosing his mother over her all those years, but it seemed a bit irrelevant at that moment.

"Well, you take care, Natalie. I hope you are doing okay."

"I am, Benjamin, and you take care as well."

Natalie was about to hang up the phone. Her heart was raging inside of her and her emotions were going crazy.

What are you doing, Natalie? Don't hang up with him! The kids! What about the kids? What about our relationship? What about…

"Bye, Natalie."

"Good-bye, Ben."

She hung up the phone, feeling more confused and empty than she was before. She just felt like there was a giant hole in her soul.

Just take a breath, Natalie. Just breathe, and get back to work.

Natalie stood back up off the bed, her purse still strapped to her shoulder, and walked to the door. As she opened the door, Darnell was standing on the porch.

Natalie froze.

"'Sup, girl?"

"Darnell?"

"Yeah, it's me. We need to talk."

"Well, I can't. I have to go to work, and you need to leave."

Natalie stepped out of the apartment and locked her door.

"I ain't goin' anywhere, girl!"

"Well, you can't stay here and I have to go to work."

She started walking to her car as Darnell followed her.

"What do you mean 'I can't stay here'?"

Natalie reached her car door, and she turned and looked at Darnell.

"Darnell, we are through. We are done. Do not bother me anymore. Do not come by to see me. You need to stay away from me!"

Natalie was trying to overcome her fear, but this was getting hard.

"Is that how it is?"

"Yes," Natalie replied, commandingly.

"So whatchu got: another guy out there, or something?"

"I'm leaving. Good-bye, Darnell."

Natalie got into the car and put the keys into the ignition. Darnell tried to get into the car on the passenger's side, but the door was locked. Natalie was startled and rolled down the window.

"What are you doing?"

"I told you we need to talk."

"I have nothing to say to you, Darnell. Now leave me alone!"

Natalie backed the car up and sped out of the parking lot, leaving Darnell standing there. As she passed the parking lot exit onto the road, she tried to catch her breath and calm herself down.

That was scary! That man is crazy!! I can't do this!

When she came upon a red light, she tried to catch her breath. She didn't know what he did when she left, and she didn't care. She only hoped that he left, after she did, and would disappear for good.

Hopefully he got the message. Please, Lord, let him get the message??

Natalie noticed that it was getting close to one o'clock, so she went through the drive-through at Taco Bueno and picked up a couple of soft tacos and a sweet tea. She then went back to the Arger Corporation to check on the progress of her new office. As she drove, she couldn't help but to think about the call she received from Benjamin.

Why did he call me after treating me so badly? Did he really want to apologize to me? What was going on?

What direction should I take, now?

Ugh! Focus, Natalie! Let's take one thing at a time.

She grabbed her food and went into the building to her new office to eat and begin preparing for her meetings.

Benjamin just held on to the phone. Though he did not think he would resort in calling Natalie, for some reason he felt that he needed to hear her voice. Looking down at the piece of mail that he had just received, he shook his head in disbelief. It was a letter from a local attorney. The warden wasn't kidding: Benjamin was getting sued by the two inmates that he had to fight off to protect the other.

Lately, he felt like he was losing control of everything in his life. His visit with his mother certainly did not help things. Most significantly, he could not shake his thoughts of Natalie. The less he thought about Natalie, the more he missed her. The more he thought about Natalie, the more he felt undeserving of her. This emotion was even stronger when he thought of the kids.

There are no kids! Oh, Lord, there are no kids!"

Benjamin loathed that thought. His apparent decision to break off the engagement with Natalie was a serious gamble, and he knew it. The scenario was simple: get back with Natalie, marry her and have the children, or continue on with his life of desired happiness.

Yeah, the scenario is simple. The choice is much harder. So what is my real problem? Am I pursuing the life that I wanted without Natalie, or am I running from the chances of being an unfit husband and father? After all, if I don't try, then I can't fail.

That thought was making more sense to him every day. Many times throughout his fatherhood, Benjamin felt like a failure to his children. He tried to love them, tried to take care of them, tried to guide them, and tried to look after their best interests. Most significantly, he tried to love Natalie.

Then Benjamin considered all the things he did with the Marine Corps. He left Natalie, twice, leaving her with babies on both occasions. To say that his deployments were hard on her would be an incredible understatement, just like they were for every other Marine wife, or the wives of those deploying for any branch of the military. The Army, Navy, Air Force and Coast Guard were no different. It was a way of life for the spouse of a deployed veteran. Benjamin hated that.

He had a decision to make, but he had to get Natalie out of his head because she only clouded his mind. He had no job at the jail, and wouldn't go back if he had. He had no wife or children. In essence, he could see no real direction in his life. Most detrimentally, he had no idea of where to go, what to do, or, of what God wanted for his life.

Benjamin was heavily considering the orders to Camp Pendleton. At this moment, the only thing that made any sense was the Marine Corps. Benjamin also knew what was coming over the next year, and he thought he had the perfect opportunity to get ahead of it. He started thinking about the sermon that Brian preached, recently. It seemed like, for some reason, there was a lot of focus on being a Godly husband and a Godly father; something that Benjamin hadn't felt like he had been for so long. Taking these orders would mean being absent for a year or more, depending on how much he enjoyed what he was doing. Considering what was coming the following September, Benjamin figured that, even if he took these orders for just one year, he would be gone much longer.

At this moment, Benjamin was ready for that.

CHAPTER 19

"Burn, baby, burn!"

One of the Marines set the porch on fire. Inside the house, there were people moving around and trying to get out.

"Hey," Benjamin yelled. "There are people in there!!"

Benjamin ran to the door and tried to pry it open.

"It won't budge!"

The doorway was boarded up by thick boards all across the frame. The fire spread from the porch to the house, and people were screaming.

"Help us! We can't get out!"

Benjamin ran around to a window that was partially boarded. He ripped the boards off and looked inside.

"Hey! Come over here! I'll get you out!!"

Benjamin could see through the window just enough to determine how many people were in the room, as it quickly filled with smoke.

"Please help us!"

"Over here," Benjamin yelled, still trying to get their attention.

"Benjamin! Benjamin, is that you?"

That's Natalie's voice, Benjamin thought. *No! It can't be!*

"Benjamin, please help us!"

"Natalie, where are you?"

"Daddy? Daddy, where are you?"

Who is that... T. J.? Was that T. J.'s voice??

"Benjamin, we're getting hot in here. We can't breathe. Please help us!"

The fire continued to spread, and in an instant, it seemed to completely engulf the house. In a panic, Benjamin looked around, and saw people standing around.

Where were the other Marines? Why did they torch this house? Why was his family inside?

Benjamin ran from window to window trying to find a way to get to his family, and get them out of the house. All of the windows were boarded up. Benjamin ran back to the first window he came to and saw that the fire had spread to the inside of the house.

"Benjamin...Benjamin, please??"

Natalie's voice was faint, but the screams from the children were getting worse. Benjamin tried, again, to pry the boards off the window. Before he knew it, he was thrown from the house and landed on his back. When he looked up, he realized that he had been thrown about twenty feet. He looked around to try to figure out what happened, but he saw nothing. He started running back to the window when he noticed a person on the roof of the house.

"Hey," Benjamin yelled, frantically trying to get the person's attention.

As he walked toward the house, the person turned to look at Benjamin, and Benjamin froze. Whoever this person was made Benjamin feel nothing but fear. The look on his face was plain evil. Benjamin tried to look away, but couldn't. He kept hearing the screams from inside the house, but he could not move to help them.

He became overcome with absolute dread.

The 'thing' on the roof started smiling. It was horrid and insidious. Benjamin tried to look away. He tried to run.

He tried anything.

"God, help me," he began to scream.

That seemed to get the attention of the 'thing' on the roof as it turned into the most frightening being that Benjamin had ever seen.

"God, help me!"

Benjamin looked around. By now the house was engulfed in flames. He couldn't breathe, and he could no longer see the being on the house. He turned to run, but the being was standing right in front of him. Benjamin couldn't move. He felt like he was struck in his soul. He didn't know what else to do.

"Jesus!!"

The being jumped upon Benjamin, and Benjamin woke up in his bed. He was coughing and gagging, trying hard to catch his breath. His bed was wet as sweat covered his whole body. He felt nauseous, and jumped up, quickly, and ran to the bathroom, stumbling as he reached the bathroom door. He made it to the toilet, just in time, before he vomited.

"Oh my God! What is happening to me?"

After he vomited, he stumbled over to the sink where he turned on the water and splashed some on his face. His eyes were closed as he grabbed a hand towel hanging up on a hanger, by the mirror. When he opened his eyes, he was frightened by what appeared to be a ghostly face reflected in the mirror, showing from behind him on the glass shower door. Benjamin spun around quickly as fear shot through his soul, only to find no one there. He gasped for air, trying hard to take a breath, as he fell to the bathroom floor. He sat there, motionless, trying to gain some type of composure. He felt everything from the dream: fear, despair, loathing…pain. It was overwhelming and absolutely more than he could possibly bear. He was convinced that there was something in that dream with him.

After a couple of minutes, Benjamin was able to come to his feet and walk back to his bedroom. He looked at the clock.

7:56.

Benjamin wasted no time. His alarm was set to go off in four minutes, so he started getting dressed to go to the reserve center. He didn't even shower. He just wanted out of the house. He grabbed his keys and ran out the door, forgetting to lock it. Getting to his pick-up, he started it and drove off. Once he made it to the reserve center, he parked his pick-up, got out, and went straight into the office, where he saw Corporal Bates behind the counter.

"Hey, Sergeant," Corporal Bates greeted, looking up from a fax machine. "Is there a funeral today? I thought it was tomorrow?"

NOT PRESENT OR FUTURE...

"The funeral is tomorrow, Corporal. I am here to talk to someone about the opportunity in Camp Pendleton. Are the Marines still looking for reservists for this new counterterrorism project?"

"Yes. Are you interested?"

"I am. How soon can I leave?"

"Wow, you're in a hurry, huh?"

"Well, maybe," Benjamin responded. "What are the administrative requirements for this? Are there any specific prerequisites I need to be considered eligible for this duty?"

"No, but the Marines are looking for those who were on active duty, at one point. They aren't looking for non-prior service Marines, just yet. They need the experience."

"Well, that's me. So what do I need to do?"

"Let me grab your file. When was the last physical you had?"

"Um, I'm not sure. Pretty recently, if I remember correctly."

"Uh, oh, here it is," Corporal Bates responded as he located the medical documentation in Benjamin's file. "Your last physical was…May of this year, so that won't be an issue. Your in-processing information is all here from when you joined the reserves. All of your physicals were just a few months ago, so, you are still good."

"Great! What's next?"

"Well, we have some other admin stuff to take care of, and we will need to get your bank information for pay and…"

"Hey, Sarge!"

Benjamin turned to see Lance Corporal McDaniels walking into the office, inadvertently interrupting his conversation with Corporal Bates.

"Hey, Lance Corporal," Benjamin replied.

"Sergeant Jones wants to take those orders to Camp Pendleton," Corporal Bates responded as Lance Corporal McDaniels sat down at her desk.

"Really? Cool! They would be lucky to have you, Sarge! Let me pull up the orders requirements, and we'll get you going."

After about an hour of filling out paperwork, setting clearances and confirming billets, Benjamin was nearly ready to go. The only thing left was getting the approval letter from the new 'I&I',

Major Shimshi. Corporal Bates did not think that obtaining that approval from Major Shimshi would be a problem, but he was out of the reserve center for the day. Lance Corporal McDaniels was just about done wrapping up the administrative actions for Benjamin's orders.

"Okay, Sargent Jones. We got everything we needed. The billet was approved by Camp Pendleton. It looks like you are good to go from their end. All we need now is the approval letter from Major Shimshi, and we should have it tomorrow."

"Thank you, Lance Corporal. I guess I'm done, here. I am gonna head home and get start preparing."

"Roger that, Sarge," Corporal Bates replied as Benjamin walked out of the office. Heading out of the reserve center, he got in his pick-up and headed home, stopping only to get something to eat. Once he got home, he started going through his stuff. He forgot how much stuff he had, and it would take some time to go through.

Maybe Hope will let me keep renting the house while I'm gone until I can determine the level of commitment to these new orders. I'll ask her about it, tomorrow.

But for now, he had to prepare to be an enlisted Marine again. After a while of going through his things, and determining what to pack, he became tired and decided to watch some TV. He dozed in and out over the course of a few hours, and he finally fell asleep. He woke up, almost as quickly, to the sound of the phone ringing.

Brrrng.

Benjamin turned over in the couch, feeling groggy, but slowly waking up.

Brrrng.

He reached over and answered the phone, trying to wake up.

"Hello?"

"Hey, Ben, this is Raymond. Dude, did I wake you up?"

"No, no, I was just watching TV. I, uh…"

He looked at the clock. It was 9:42

"Okay. Hey, the reason that I called is because I wanted to know if you would be willing to help me out with the middle school, tomorrow. I am taking about twenty kids and a few parent to Northside

Christian Church for a night of middle-school worship. We do this every once in a while for our Wednesday night service."

"Okay," Ben replied, "Um…"

"I would never bother you, but of all the adults that are coming, I am the only guy. The rest are moms. If you would be willing to go with me tomorrow night, I would really appreciate it. I could use another male for all the rowdy boys we have."

"Yeah, I'll come with you. I'm sorry. I am just trying to wake up."

"Hey, no problem, brother! You are helping me out. I almost had to cancel, but I thought about you in the last minute."

"No problem. What time do I need to be ready?"

"We will leave at 5:30 and arrive about 6:20. The event starts at 6:30, and we will be done about 8:00. Usually, though, we stop at the Chik-filet on 71st Street, on the way back, for some ice cream and stuff. I'll pay for your ice cream."

"Cool! I'll be ready."

"Great! Thanks for doing this for me. By the way…"

Raymond paused for a second.

"There will be a little girl very excited that you are coming."

"Let me guess," Benjamin considered. "Samantha."

"You guessed it," Raymond replied, trying not to laugh.

"Okay, I'll see ya tomorrow, Raymond!"

"Okay, brother. See ya."

Benjamin hung up the phone and shook his head. He hadn't worked with middle-schoolers much, but Samantha was his buddy. She was just twelve years old, trying to find her way through middle-school, just like the rest of them. She and Benjamin met when she worked with Benjamin during Vacation Bible School, helping him serve snacks to the younger kids. She absolutely loved Benjamin, and he thought the world of her.

Benjamin looked up at the clock and decided to get up. He needed to continue working on his packing, and going through his belongings. He could not believe how exhaustive it was going through everything he had. He was already tired from the lack of sleep he had been experiencing, lately. Today was a very frustrating day, anyway, with the drama at the jail still tormenting him. He was so glad that Major Shimshi was going to approve his orders, and he just hoped that the lawsuit would not haunt him while he was gone.

Only time would tell. But either way, it looked like he was going to Camp Pendleton.

Natalie's first week was going very well. Her meetings were successful, and she definitely made Mr. Sherman grateful that he brought her back. Both he and Mr. Quartermain saw success in this project, and they both saw dollar signs. Natalie was only concerned about creating jobs, and she made her feelings known about it. Both Mr. Sherman and Mr. Quartermain assured Natalie, consistently, that creating more jobs was on the horizon. From the specifics of the project, Natalie knew that their promises were sound. If Natalie did choose to move to Amarillo, she could feel confident that she contributed to a great project. The more she thought about moving in with her mother, the more she loved the idea. She was glad, however, that her mother convinced her to stay on with the Arger Corporation a little while longer. Natalie was proud of the work she accomplished, and at the very least, she was building some much needed administrative experience.

In the evenings, Natalie just spent time at Carmella's house. She found that, the more time she spent with Carmella, the more she enjoyed it. Natalie thought about how her relationship with Carmella was impacted after Natalie married Benjamin. Natalie tried to stay in contact with Carmella after she and Benjamin married, but life just got in the way. Natalie enjoyed this aspect of her current 'experience'. Natalie also loved Carmella's parents. She really appreciated the fact that Carmella's mom and dad allowed Natalie to stay at their house during the week, amid her issues with Darnell.

Natalie became very concerned that Darnell would continue showing up at her apartment, and she hoped that her absence would encourage him to stay away. Natalie just needed some time, enough, to decide what she wanted to do about moving in with her mother.

Darnell was becoming a huge factor in her decision, even though she didn't want him to. As far as Natalie was concerned, her decision about moving was about her mother, as she was getting used to having her mother in her life, again. For whatever reason this was happening, Natalie wanted to take advantage of that time.

Natalie also found herself experiencing other feelings that she could not fathom. Of all of the memories and emotions that she carried with her regarding things that, technically, haven't happened yet, she could not get certain memories out of her head. As far as she was concerned, these were things that she would rather have forgotten: actions that caused her much shame and torment coming from her guilt. The worst of all was the affair she had just a few years before things really started getting bad with Benjamin. She could not understand why the memory of that haunted her so much. It was something that she was able to keep from Benjamin and, she was thankful, as she would do anything to go back to that night and change the events.

As if carrying all those memories and emotions weren't enough, Natalie had one other concern: she carried that shame and guilt, and it made her feel alone much of the time.

Benjamin went on one of his two-week training assignments, and just before he left, they both had a huge fight. Natalie found herself in wanting —wanting understanding from Benjamin; wanting Benjamin to fight for her; wanting Benjamin to show her that she meant more to him than the Marine Corps. She struggled with her bitterness for so long that it manifested itself into something so much more dangerous. One night, she went out in the town with some friends while leaving her children with a babysitter. These so-called friends started out as acquaintances that Natalie met online through a 'Military Souse Support Group'. The purpose of the group was for women to support each other as accountability partners while their husbands served on deployments. It sounded great from the beginning, until Natalie began communicating with a particular group of ladies that seemed to make it a sport to seek extramarital activities while their husbands were away. At first, when Natalie realized what they were up to, she chose to distance herself from the group.

But one particular day, while Benjamin was conducting his annual training, Natalie ran into one of the ladies at the store, who invited Natalie to a night out with the girls. It would have seemed innocent enough, but at that moment, Natalie did not care about innocence. Going out with the girls was Natalie's way of getting back to Benjamin, from her perspective. That is what her focus was. But the night proved to be more than captivating when a good-looking gentleman, who knew all the right things to say, enticed Natalie, and she had to lie her way out of a hotel room to relieve the babysitter three hours late. The next morning, Natalie received an email from one of the ladies that shot an arrow right through her spirit.

"Hey, there, you crazy thing, you! What a hot date that was last night! Take that to your church and tell all them goodie-two-shoes what a wild night you had. Bet you'd be the talk of the town!"

Natalie was beyond sick with guilt. At first, she felt absolutely betrayed by the ladies in that group. They knew she was a Christian, and from what she could tell, it seemed like they took pleasure in her moment of weakness. She prayed and prayed for God to forgive her. She prayed and prayed that she would not see any of those ladies again. She would not tell Benjamin about the encounter as she knew it would end her family. Natalie tried to forget it ever happened, and moved on. She nearly had a nervous breakdown when the gentlemen that she was with that night tried to contact her in interest of scheduling another 'engagement'. She would make it clear to him that there would be no more.

For days after that incident, Natalie would feel as if she were living in chains. She felt convicted at church. She felt enslaved by her guilt, and she could hardly look at her kids. When Benjamin returned home, instead of trying to love him more like she thought she would, her attitude toward him actually became worse. Natalie was stuck in a labyrinth of fear and anxiety. In time, Benjamin just considered her demeanor toward him as typical 'Natalie'. In reality, shame and guilt squeezed Natalie to the point of leaving her unable to breathe, most days.

Natalie would face this sin with God, alone. Nobody knew about it but Him, and that was hard enough for Natalie.

But considering where she was, now -or when- she was, that should not be an issue. She should not feel guilty about something that hadn't happened yet, resulting in defiling her marriage bed when, technically, she wasn't married. But she did feel guilty, and it was becoming worse every day. This was just one of the many emotions that Natalie would have to deal with. Still convinced that these would eventually go away, however, she pressed on to experience her second chance at this life.

That is what this was, right? It must be. It was a second chance. What else could it be? A new life with a new future and a chance to make some better decisions, or, a life without Benjamin, Leesha, T. J. and Ben Jr.

It looked like Natalie would just have to get used to having a second chance. However, to her, whatever this was she was going through just didn't feel like a second chance.

CHAPTER 20

Benjamin was absolutely sick. He could not believe the conversation that he just had with Major Shimshi.

My orders were on hold, and in danger of being cancelled?? What the…"

Benjamin grabbed his keys and his uniform cap. He got in his pick-up and headed to the reserve center. When he arrived, he walked into the office to see Lance Corporal McDaniels behind the counter.

"Good morning, Sgt. Jones! Private Sissler and Corporal Bates will be ready to go to the funeral in about ten minutes. They are squaring away their uniforms."

"Roger that," Benjamin sighed. "Could you please remind me where the funeral is?"

"It's in Tahlequah."

Lance Corporal McDaniels went to the door leading out of the office.

"Sgt. Jones, Major Shimshi wants to talk to you before you leave. Will you come with me?"

Benjamin followed Lance Corporal McDaniels to Major Shimshi's office, as she knocked on the office door.

"Sir, Sgt. Jones is here."

"Come on in," Major Shimshi signaled, quietly, as he was on the phone.

Benjamin sat down on a chair in front of the major's desk, and Lance Corporal McDaniels left to go back to the main office. Benjamin listened as Major Shimshi was talking on the phone.

"Yes, this is Major Robert Shimshi from the Navy and Marine Corps Reserve Center, Tulsa. I need to speak with Warden Blacksmith. Yes. Yes. I am the Inspector and Instructor for the Marines at the center. Thank you."

"Just one minute, Sgt. Jones," Major Shimshi whispered to Benjamin as he covered the mouth piece of the phone. He had Benjamin's full attention.

"Yes, good morning Mr. Blacksmith, this is Major Robert Shimshi, the 'I&I' at the reserve center. We spoke yesterday. I am going to be there about 1300 today, and I would like to meet with you then, if you have time. Yes. No, that won't be necessary, but I do want to see the recorded incident in its entirety, not just what the news is showing. Mr. Blacksmith, here's the issue: I have a set of orders here for Benjamin Jones, and right now, due to this lawsuit, I can't send him anywhere. The Marine Corps has authorized me to make the final decision on whether or not he goes, and I want to see all of the evidence of this circumstance so I can make a legitimate decision. Right now, potentially, his career is on the line…depending on where this goes. I would like to see the recording myself. Well, Mr. Blacksmith, that is a direction we could go. I could get a JAG lawyer for Benjamin Jones, and we could get the Marines involved, or we can just make this easy. All I want to do is view the recording. Thank you, I will be there at 1300. Have a good day."

Benjamin heard the conversation and was anxious to hear what Major Shimshi was planning.

"Well, Sgt. Jones, I am going to the jail to talk to the warden and to see the video of the incident, myself. I know that the news agencies aren't showing the whole thing, so I am going to watch it and use it for my consideration."

"Okay, Sir," Benjamin replied.

"Look, Sargent, I don't care for this anymore than you do, and I will try to figure out what I can, but the Marines is not going to be on board with sending you to Camp Pendleton for these orders while you have a pending lawsuit against you. The warden also said that the inmates you assaulted filed charges against you."

"Sir, I did not assault those stupid inmates. I protected another inmate from their assaults against him."

"I know, Sargent. But this case against you is troubling, not to mention that it appears to be politically motivated. I am going to go down to the jail to find out what I can for you. Go do your funeral, and I will contact you when I can."

"Yes, Sir," Benjamin replied. "Thank you for trying."

Benjamin stood up from the chair and, just before he made it to the office door, he turned around, curious.

"Sir, what did you mean when you said that you could get a JAG lawyer for me, and getting the Marines involved?"

"Oh, you caught that, did you? It was just smoke. I was trying to get him to do what I wanted him to do."

"Okay, Sir. Thank you for your help, regardless."

Benjamin left for the funeral. It would be an hour drive to Tahlequah, about two hours for the funeral and an hour back. He might not hear from Major Shimshi until the morning.

Man, I hate this!! I hate waiting like this!!

He was very grateful for Major Shimshi's help, but he was so disgruntled that this was even happening in the first place. If Benjamin hated the jail before, he really hated it, now. He couldn't be mad at the Marine Corps; their concern about this lawsuit was legitimate. From the perspective of Marine Corps leaders, Benjamin had been accused of excessive use of force against inmates he was supposed to protect. He lost his job, had charges filed against him, and finally, had a lawsuit filed against him. Not necessarily the baggage that the Marine Corps needed.

Okay. Let's just get through this day. Even still, I had better continue looking for a job.

The funeral in Tahlequah went like all the others did, and when it was over, Benjamin hurried back to the reserve center. It was a little late so Benjamin did not expect to see Major Shimshi at the center upon his return. As the three funeral honors participants pulled the van to the side of the center, Benjamin got out and grabbed his cap and keys. He turned to go to his pick-up when he noticed a red Ford Mustang pulling into the center.

Is that Major Shimshi?? It is! No way!!

As Major Shimshi parked his car, he got out and saw Benjamin walking toward him.

"Sgt. Jones, I was hoping I would catch you before you got home. I have some news for you that I know will make you happy."

"Sir?"

"I am approving your orders. You are not on hold any longer."

"Huh...I mean, Sir?"

Benjamin responded questioningly, clearly shocked and confused, but trying not to appear disrespectful in his response.

"I went to the jail to talk to the warden, and the moron wasn't even there."

"Really? Seriously??"

"Yeah, that's exactly what I thought. 'Really?' I mean, I went there to get the truth about what happened and some guy named 'Allister Becket' met with me."

"The Chief of Security? You met with the 'chief'?"

"I did. He showed me the video tape, and then I left. I figured that if the warden could not even take the time to meet with me, they obviously weren't worried about the lawsuit, and as far as I am concerned, neither will the Corps."

"Sir, I am so sorry. I can't believe the warden treated you like that. I mean, you went there to meet with him, right?"

"I did. But Sgt. Jones, never mind that. You are on your way to L. A. Are you still packed?"

"Yes, Sir, I am!"

Benjamin still could not believe what he was hearing.

"Well then, be ready. Make sure you are here, tomorrow and Friday, to finish the administrative requirements for the orders."

"Yes, Sir," Benjamin replied. "Oh, shoot!"

Benjamin looked at his watch. It was 4:46.

"You okay, Sargent?"

"Yes, Sir! I have a date with a bunch of kids!"

Benjamin ran to his pick-up, got in, started it up and left the reserve center. He had to be in Owasso by 5:30. He drove as quickly as he could to get to the church, and he was in such a hurry that he forgot that he was still in his uniform, and he did not have a change of clothes.

Crap!! I can't show up at the church like this!! If I hurry, maybe I can get home, change my clothes, then make it to the church.

But he would be cutting it close. He sped up and jumped on Highway 11 to Highway 75. He got to his house in no time. He ran in the house, tore off his uniform, threw on some shorts and a T-shirt, and ran back out to his pick-up. He drove down 86th Street North right to the church; just in time to see Raymond pulling the vans around to load. Benjamin parked his pick-up and walked over to Raymond.

"Hey, brother! I was praying you'd make it."

"I am sorry, Ray. I got here as quickly as I could."

"You doin' all right?"

Benjamin smiled.

"Yes, I am," he answered, shaking his head. "Yes…I…am."

Benjamin felt good for the first time in a while. He was very content, especially right now.

"Benjamin!!"

Benjamin turned to see a young girl running toward him, practically crashing into him as she gave him a big hug.

"Hey, Samantha! How are you?"

"I am good," Samantha rejoiced as she hugged his waist. "I am so glad you are coming with us, Ben!"

"I told you," Raymond teased, smirking at Benjamin. "I told you she would be excited."

"Yeah, she's my driving buddy," Benjamin replied as he tapped the cap that Samantha was wearing.

"All right, Benjamin! Let's get the kids in the vans."

Raymond, Benjamin and the middle-school mom's loaded the kids in the vans. Benjamin got into the driver's seat in one of the vans, and Samantha jumped in the passenger's side. They were ready to go worship in Broken Arrow for the night, and for the first time in a while, Benjamin was actually excited to be working with the kids.

NOT PRESENT OR FUTURE...

Natalie made her decision and she knew she had to tell Mr. Sherman about it. She felt so guilty that she was going to leave, but she felt now, more than ever, that she wanted to be with her mother. She sat at her desk, pulling together all the paperwork from her meetings. When she was done gathering all her paperwork, she picked up her phone and called Shannon.

"Shannon, it's Natalie. Is Mr. Sherman still in?"

"He sure is, Natalie."

"Thank you. I wanted to try to catch him before he left."

"Do you want me to see if he is available?"

"Please?"

Natalie hung up the phone only to pick it back up again almost as quickly as she hung it up.

"Natalie, he is there, and says to come on in."

"Thank you, Shannon."

Natalie got up from her desk and walked to Mr. Sherman's office, knocking on the door.

"Hey, you, come on in!"

"I was wondering if I could talk with you for a minute, Mr. Sherman.

She thought she would be nervous, but she wasn't. In fact, she was at peace. Natalie sat down at the chair in front of his desk and took a deep breath. Mr. Sherman gave her his full attention.

"Mr. Sherman, I wanted to say that these last couple of days have been so very incredible, and this opportunity has been more of a blessing than I could have ever imagined. I am so very thankful that you gave me this chance. But…"

Natalie hated this. But she knew she had to do it. For some reason, she just knew it was the right thing to do, and she was trying to convince herself to just say it. She still had Mr. Sherman's attention.

"Sir, I am moving in with my mother in Amarillo. I need to be with her. I am so sorry, and I do not want you to be disappointed. I know it is soon, Sir, but I am moving this weekend."

Mr. Sherman looked down, appearing disappointed. Natalie felt she owed him an explanation.

"Please understand, Sir, I had made the decision to move before you offered me this position, and I thought this would be enough for me to stay here, but I really want to be with my mother. I hope that you understand."

"Natalie, you are full of surprises, aren't you?"

He sighed as he was trying to figure out what to say.

"But, I understand. I am not quite sure what has happened the past couple of weeks, but what I do know is that you have been absolutely awesome the last week. I hate to lose you, again, but I understand when you say you want to be closer to your mother."

Mr. Sherman repositioned himself in his chair.

"I lost my mother a couple of years ago, and even though we knew it was coming, it was still very difficult for me."

Natalie looked up at him as he spoke, emotionally frozen solid at what at his comment. She knew exactly how he felt.

"So I do understand, Natalie. Do you need anything from me?"

"No, Sir," Natalie responded, completely surprised at his pleasant response to her news.

"In fact, I am not asking you for any money. Sir, you don't even have to pay me. You gave me so much when you let me go that I could not ask you for anything, more. You gave me an opportunity here to make a difference, lead this project, and create jobs. That is experience that I would never have had otherwise, and I can't thank you enough."

She stood up and looked across the desk.

"I'm the one who's losing here, Mr. Sherman. You have been the best boss anyone could ever ask for, and I will never forget it!"

As she got to the door, Natalie looked back at Mr. Sherman, who seemed to be writing something on a piece of paper.

"I'll have my stuff together on Friday. That will be my last day."

"Thank you for everything, Natalie. I mean that."

Natalie smiled and walked back to her office. She knew that she made the right choice, no matter how she felt about the Arger Corporation. She would miss it; that much was sure.

When Natalie got went back to her office, she grabbed her purse and went out to her car. She started it up, quite surprised that it still did so, and headed out of the parking lot. She was going to go to Carmella's house when she decided to head for her apartment. She had not been there since before the weekend, and she figured it was time to get back there and start packing. Since Natalie was moving in with her mother, she could get rid of a bunch of stuff; not that she had much stuff to begin with. She was still a bit afraid of being at her apartment by herself, but since it was still daylight out, she felt pretty safe.

When she arrived at the apartment complex, she parked her car and looked around. Even though it was light outside, Natalie was still a little paranoid. She sat in her car for about a minute, and when she felt comfortable enough to walk to her apartment, she got out of her car and stood in front of it, looking around. There was nothing. There were no people around, no busy-bodies coming and going from their apartments…nothing. Natalie felt completely safe. She walked to her apartment door, unlocked it, opened the door, and went inside. She stood there, looking at everything in her apartment and immediately began planning on what she was going to pack. She went to her phone, picked it up, and called her mom.

"Hello?"

"Hey, Mom, it's me. I just wanted to let you know that I did it. I told Mr. Sherman that my last day was Friday. Mom, I have made my decision: I want to come home."

"Natalie, that is wonderful! And I am very proud of you for thinking this through."

"Thanks, Mom. Thank you for all of your support and confidence in me."

"You're my daughter, and I love you! So what are you going to do for the time being?"

"Well, I am going to pack up everything, fast, and start bringing stuff home. I don't want to be here any longer than I have to be. The first of the month is right around the corner."

"Yes, it is," Florance responded jokingly. "So hurry up and get here!"

"All right, Mom, I am going to get packing. I am gonna call Carmella to see if she wants to come over to help me when she gets off work."

"You two stay out of trouble, you hear?"

"Yes, Mom, we will. Bye."

"Bye, honey."

Florance hung up just as Natalie did. Then Natalie called Carmella, almost immediately.

"Hey, you! What's going on?"

"Just workin', girl! What's up with you? Did you tell Mr. Sherman you were going to quit?"

"Yes, I did. It was hard, but I know he will be fine. I did what I wanted to do. I fixed my mistakes, and I am very glad that it didn't take long."

"No, it didn't, girl. You were climbing that ladder quick at the Arger Corporation!"

"Girl, you're crazy," Natalie responded, trying not to laugh. "Hey, are you coming over tonight after work…to help me pack? I'll buy pizza."

Natalie was all but teasing Carmella.

"So…come over to help you pack, or go home and watch movies all night. Hmmm, let me think."

Natalie was getting a dose of her own 'teasing' medicine.

"Okay, okay," Natalie responded. "We can watch movies here while we pack. And like I said, I'll buy pizza."

"Well, okay, I guess I have nothing else better to do."

"Oh, how did I ever get so lucky to have an awesome friend like you, Carmella?"

"Oh, I just captivated you with my awesomeness!"

Natalie couldn't hold it in. She just started laughing. She had to calm herself down before asking Carmella for a favor.

"So you're gonna come over tonight after work?"

"Yes, you are just too convincing for me, girl," Carmella replied.

"Okay, I'll see you tonight. What time will you be here so I can be sure to have the pizza ready?"

"I get off at 7:00, so I should be there about 7:15."

"Okay, girl, see ya then."

"Okay," Carmella responded as she hung up the phone.

NOT PRESENT OR FUTURE...

Natalie started separating things in her apartment. She walked over to the nightstand and pulled out her drawer to see a partial phone number on a piece of paper. She opened the paper to see Benjamin's phone number.

Really? Why am I finding this, again?

The more Natalie tried to forget about Benjamin, the more she found herself thinking about him, especially when she was alone.

Perhaps that was the reason she did not want to be alone.

She put the piece of paper back in her drawer and shut it. As Natalie began packing, she counted down the minutes until Carmella arrived. That was going to be the highlight of Natalie's night. As far as she was concerned, she was going to focus on enjoying her final few weeks with Carmella before moving to Amarillo.

CHAPTER 21

Benjamin and Raymond loaded the kids up in the vans after the worship service ended. It was a fun evening of songs, testimonies and worship, and the kids were pumped.

"Hey, Benjamin, what do you say we head to Chik-filet's?"

"I'll follow you, brother!"

They exited the church parking lot and headed out, straight down 71st Street to Chik-filet's. The kids were excited, as evidence of the noise level in each van. As they pulled into the parking lot, both Benjamin and Raymond parked their vans and prepared to corral the kids. Each mom got out, followed by their individual groups of kids. Raymond and Benjamin did a head count, and in they went. They ordered their ice cream, and each kid went into a designated section of the dining area.

Finally, Benjamin thought. *It's my turn.*

He looked at Raymond, shaking his head at the kids.

"It's a lot of work, isn't it, brother?"

"Wouldn't trade it for the world," Raymond replied.

"Would it be okay with you if I just got, like, a chocolate shake?"

"Ben, you can have whatever you want!"

They both ordered their ice cream and shake, then looked for a place to sit down. Raymond maneuvered his way through the gauntlet of kids and reached the back corner of the dining area. Benjamin looked over and noticed Samantha patting the seat next to her, communicating to him that she wanted him to sit next to her. He laughed as he walked over to grab a plastic spoon from the condiments section, then over to the table.

NOT PRESENT OR FUTURE...

"Well, scoot 'em over," Benjamin joked as the girls laughed at him.

It was a lively table. Benjamin and Samantha shared the side with their backs facing the door while Jennifer, Ashley, Abby, and Sharon squeezed into the booth across from them, picking at each other and scooting each other over, comically. As Benjamin sat at the table full of middle school girls, cutting up and eating ice cream, Jennifer, who was sitting on the end of the seat, froze in complete and obvious fear. It wasn't a millisecond from the time that Ben noticed her expression.

"EVERYBODY GET DOWN!"

The girls screamed as a man came through the door, pulling a sawed-off shotgun from the inside of his long overcoat. Acting in instinct, Benjamin jumped up out of the seat, grabbed the gun with his left hand, and punched the gunman in the face. Benjamin made quick hard jabs—face, face, throat, face, throat, face; a site one might see in a kung-fu movie. The gunman was shocked as he clearly was not ready for Benjamin's response to his hostile invasion, but in his courageous reaction, Benjamin failed to see another man coming right behind the first, pulling a pistol from his coat pocket. Benjamin kicked the first man in the knee, causing him to completely let go of the shotgun. Once released from the grip of the first gunman, Benjamin swung the gun around and smacked the other gunman in the head –hard- just after he came through the door. The second gunman fell to the ground, knocked out, cold, with a large bruise on the right side of his head. Almost immediately, Benjamin turned back around to see the first gunman get back up and charge him. Samantha saw the gunman jump at Benjamin, and she screamed as he grabbed the gun, trying to wrestle it from Benjamin's hands.

"BEN!!!"

This man was strong, and completely intent on his actions. It was all Benjamin could do to hold on to the gun. As far as Benjamin knew, this gun was loaded, and wrestling with a violent man over a loaded shotgun in a close environment with women and children was beyond dangerous.

I have to end this now!!

Benjamin said a quick prayer and, with all of his might, he pushed the gunman back outside of the door.

Benjamin quickly glanced at Raymond while he fought the gunman in the vestibule.

"Get everyone out of here!"

Women ran throughout the restaurant, grabbing their children and running to the other door, exiting the Chik-filet as quickly as they could. Raymond was right behind them, followed by the youth moms who ensured that all the kids were accounted for.

The gunman fought hard, and while yelling obscenities at Benjamin, he refused to give up his grip on the gun. The gunman kept trying to put his fingers in the trigger, but Benjamin kept his hand over the trigger guard, preventing the gunman from reaching it.

While the fight was on, Raymond was able to get all the kids out of the restaurant, and met the manager -with the employees- on the other side. People grabbed their phones and began dialing 911. Raymond was thankful that all his kids, and the rest of the families that were inside, appeared to be safe. They all started to scurry over to the next parking lot when Raymond was stopped in his tracks by a frantic yell from one of the youth moms.

"Where is Samantha???"

Raymond checked over all the kids and did not see Samantha. Quickly, while trying not to panic, Raymond walked back to the window of the Chik-filet and saw Samantha standing in the middle of the ordering aisle watching Benjamin.

"Samantha!"

Raymond ran back to the door that they originally exited from, where he saw Benjamin and the gunman still in the vestibule. From what Raymond could tell, Benjamin was getting fatigued from the fight. This guy was not giving up, and he seemed to possess abnormal strength for a man his size. Benjamin kept his edge over the gunman, fighting and maneuvering as best he could to keep the suspect from getting a dangerous foothold over him. Through the corner of his eye he saw Raymond run through the Chik-filet after Samantha, who was standing there in tears watching the fight…

And praying.

NOT PRESENT OR FUTURE...

The gunman looked over at Samantha, then back at Benjamin. The look on the gunman's face seemed to change.

"I'll get her," he hissed to Benjamin as Raymond grabbed Samantha, trying to move her outside. "I'll get her and there is nothing you can do about it."

Benjamin was overcome with fear.

Samantha refused to move.

Benjamin was almost out of strength. He had done everything to stop this man, but he could not overpower him.

The perpetrator tried to pull the shotgun away from Benjamin, continuously, as he was moving his way back inside. Benjamin's hands were sweaty, and he was losing his grip on the gun. He looked over at Samantha, who was looking back at him with fear in her eyes.

"God, help me," Benjamin prayed as he looked back at the gunman, who possessed an evil smirk on his face. As if a bolt of lightning shot through Benjamin's body, he got a burst of strength and he swore he could hear the voice of his former drill instructor, again, go through his mind.

"Wake up, Marine!"

Benjamin looked up at the gunman and peered deep into his eyes as if to communicate a warrior's promise.

"Not tonight!"

Benjamin resolved to defeat this gunman as he planted his feet and put on his 'war face'. Benjamin lashed out at the perpetrator, hitting him as hard as he could with his fists. The perpetrator kept getting knocked back, further, with every punch, each one harder than the one before.

"Ben?"

Samantha stood there, watching the duel, and refusing to go with Raymond. Benjamin did not stop. The gunman fell to the ground, and Benjamin continued his onslaught. He kept pounding and pounding. As the gunman lost his grip of the gun, Benjamin grabbed it and threw it back inside the restaurant as quickly as he could, then continued his assault on the gunman. He hit him and hit him, harder and harder. The gunman's face became red with blood very quickly, but Benjamin wasn't done.

"Ben??"

Benjamin kept going.

He was so oblivious to his surroundings that he couldn't hear anything, or anyone. It wasn't until the shout of a voice that screeched down his back that he finally regained himself.

"BEN STOP!!!"

Benjamin snapped back to reality. The gunman was on the ground, with blood all over his face, appearing completely unconscious. Benjamin looked up and to his right to see Samantha standing there, in tears, with Raymond holding her. It was Samantha who yelled at him to stop, and she had a horrid look on her face. Benjamin was breathing ferociously. He looked at his hands, which were shaking almost violently. He sat back and put his hands over his face. The dark truth about the reality of what happened overtook him.

He had lost it.

Benjamin was so overtaken by the whole situation that he was completely oblivious to the panic from the people inside the Chikfilet. He didn't notice people hitting the floor, covering their children, screaming and crying. He did exactly what his training taught him to do: to act, and act fast. Eliminate the threat. Kill…only if a life depends on it.

That is what Benjamin was trained to do.

But he lost control.

And…

He did it in front of Samantha.

Raymond took Samantha, who was still emotional, outside the other door as the police arrived. Benjamin was still sitting on the floor by the gunman, who was still unconscious. Two police officers, the first to arrive at the scene, pulled their firearms and demanded that Benjamin raise his hands, which he did without protest.

"That's not the bad guy," some of the people yelled. "He saved us!"

Still, as a precaution, the police told Benjamin to get on his belly with his hands stretched out. Benjamin, knowing the drill, complied, still breathing heavily. One of the officers holstered his sidearm, approached Benjamin, grabbed his hands, and pulled them back behind him to cuff him.

"Sir, this is only for yours and our protection."

NOT PRESENT OR FUTURE...

Benjamin knew they were only doing their job. He knew the routine. The officer helped Benjamin up, as more police cars arrived at the scene. Benjamin stood up with the officer's assistance as several other police officers entered the Chik-filet, from both sides of the building, to clear any other potential danger, and secure the area. Once away from the scene, Benjamin was escorted to a police car on the other side of the parking lot. Another officer searched Benjamin as he was asking Benjamin the basic questions: name, where he was from, and what he was doing there. After checking Benjamin's I.D. and receiving clarification from officers on the other side of the parking lot, the officer un-cuffed Benjamin, as Raymond approached him.

"Are you okay, brother?"

Benjamin was covered in blood from the gunman. He was still trying to calm down as another police officer came to inquire about the incident. Benjamin told him what happened, as best as he could remember it. After a while, it seemed the officers finished their questions and an ambulance pulled into the parking lot. Benjamin became concerned that there was a victim in all of the action, and fearing for the families of the kids in the restaurant.

"Officer, who is hurt?"

"The guy you beat down," the officer replied, nearly snickering.

About an hour passed, and parents started showing up to pick up their kids. Many of them were parents of the kids in the youth group, no doubt, and they were all very relieved for the safety of their children. Brian showed up to check on the youth group, and Raymond told him about the incident. When it was clear to do so, Brian and Raymond came over to Benjamin to check on him.

"Hey, Ben. You okay?"

"I...I think so, Brian."

"Everything's all right. They are all safe," Brian responded as Benjamin appeared to get emotional.

"Samantha saw everything, didn't she, Raymond?"

Both Brian and Raymond tried to think about how to respond.

"Benjamin, Samantha is safe tonight because of you," Brian responded.

The truth was the truth, but it didn't make Benjamin feel any better. In fact, he felt like, like…

A monster.

Benjamin could not get that look out of his mind; the look that Samantha had when he raised his head. He had seen that look before, only it was from his own wife and kids. He felt so terrible.

There was some activity coming from the restaurant. Benjamin, Raymond, and Brian looked up about that time to see the police escorting the second gunman out of the Chik-filet in handcuffs. Then they saw the ambulance leave the scene, followed by a police escort.

Raymond and Brian breathed a sigh of relief as Benjamin tried to calm his emotions. About that time, a man in a suit came up and talked to them.

"Mr. Jones," he inquired, looking at Benjamin.

"Yes, Sir?"

"I am Detective Scott Berry, and I just wanted to see how you are doing."

"I am okay, Sir."

"Mr. Jones, I want to convey my gratitude for what you did. I am going to try to explain this to you the best I can. But first, I have to ask you a question: why did you intervene when the gunman came through the door?"

That's a stupid question! I mean, I know that they have to ask, but…

"It was instinct. I saw the gun, and I reacted. I knew I had to stop those guys. They were dangerous."

"Well, you're right about that," Detective Berry replied. "Initial indications show that the gunman you fought was high on PCP. It is a wonder you were able to stop him at all."

Benjamin sighed, shaking his head.

"Listen, normally we tell people not to intervene with dangerous active-shooter situations, but all of the statements we collected supported your decision to act. And I have to tell you…it is a good thing you did."

Benjamin looked up. The detective had his attention.

NOT PRESENT OR FUTURE...

"These men were wanted for suspicion of assault and battery, rape, assault with a deadly weapon, robbery, and other violent violations. Texas authorities are looking for them as most of their chaos started there. They don't live in Oklahoma and have no reason to be here, so we are not sure why they are in Tulsa."

Brian, Raymond, and Benjamin looked at each other, stunned.

"The Broken Arrow police department received a call about two hours ago of two men in a car that fits the description of the one that the suspects used. It was loitering, suspiciously, at a McDonald's down the street. For whatever reason, they left the McDonald's parking lot and, to the best of our knowledge, drove here. By the time the B. A. police officer showed up at the McDonald's parking lot, they were gone."

The detective kept the attention of the three men as he continued.

"I guess their decision to tackle this Chik-filet was a bad one, but the real reason I am here is to tell you that these were very bad men. They have hurt people with no remorse. We suspect that, based on what they had in their possession -which was enough ammo to cause a large commotion- we believe that they intended on going on a killing spree."

He then looked over at Benjamin.

"Sir, what you did here tonight was incredible. I am not sure how you ended up here, but there are many, many people that will be glad you did."

Benjamin didn't feel like a hero. He acted like any Marine would in his situation. Normally, he would feel honored to do so. Tonight, however, just seemed different. Marines fight. They kill. They die. That is what Marines do.

That is what they are trained to do.

Benjamin did what he was trained to do. He protected lives. He fought terrorists; at least that is how he saw it. As far as he was concerned, two men with a history of violence showing up in a restaurant, while carrying guns with the intent to kill anyone, were terrorists. He eliminated the threat. He did, exactly, what any Marine would do.

So why was this so hard for him?

While considering all this, the detective continued on with his assessment.

"Sir, a few of the statements I received conveyed that you are a Marine. Is that correct?"

"Yes, Sir."

"Well, again, I am glad that you were here. I guess this goes to show what happens when bad guys mess with Marines."

Brian and Raymond smiled, almost snickering at that statement. Benjamin, however, didn't show any emotion. He thought about it, over and over, as he couldn't shake the guilt he felt from the look Samantha gave him. It wasn't what he did that bothered him. It was the fact that Samantha saw him at his most violent. She did not need to see that, even if his actions were to her protection. There was no way for Samantha so un-see what she saw.

"Well, Mr. Jones, as far as we are concerned, you are good to go. By the way, are you hurt at all? Do you need to go to the hospital?"

Benjamin looked at his hands, which were bruised up, scraped up, and there were some small blood splotches, but he ignored all the bruises.

"No, Sir, I am okay. I am just ready to go."

"Okay, Sir. You have a good night."

Detective Berry walked away to finish up his part of the investigation.

"Are you sure you are okay," Raymond asked Benjamin.

"Yeah, I am fine. Just ready to get home."

The three of them walked to the vans.

"We have to get these back to the church," Brian directed. "I'll take one if you do."

"Okay," Raymond replied, and then realized he only had keys to his van. "Benjamin, do you mind riding along?"

"No, I don't. Brian can have the other van."

Benjamin handed Brian the keys. Brian went to Janet, who drove him to the scene, and told her to meet him at the church as he would return with the van. Raymond went to open the van door, when he paused for a quick prayer. Brian saw him from the other side of the van and walked over to check on him. Raymond looked up and became emotional.

"I'm just taking a minute to thank God, Brian."

"Maybe we can thank Him together," Brian responded as Benjamin walked back around to join them. They all bowed their heads and prayed where they stood. Benjamin listened as they prayed. He didn't know what to pray. He didn't know because he felt guilty about that incident. He was angry at those gunmen who came to hurt all those people, and he wanted to let them know about it. He was still feeling hostile, even though the incident was over.

He had no pity. He felt no compassion.

He only felt anger.

As the other two prayed, Benjamin could not help but to try to calm his mind.

Lord, I am so sorry for the monster I have become. Maybe I need to leave. Maybe Natalie was right about me. Maybe I am not the man I need to be, for You. Maybe I'm not the father I need to be.

Maybe...just maybe.

Carmella and Natalie were getting tired. They had been working hard to pack Natalie's stuff for the move. Of course, the later it became, the more tired they were both becoming. Carmella had spent more time watching the latest 'Nash Bridges' show than packing, but Natalie didn't care. Natalie just enjoyed Carmella's company. It was about 11:30 p.m., and it was about time to call it a night, anyway.

Natalie wasn't going to go in to work until about 8:00 or 9:00, and Carmella didn't work until the evening, so neither of them were in a desperate hurry call it a night. As Natalie finished a box full of bathroom supplies, she put the box on the floor near the kitchen when the phone rang.

Blllp.

Natalie walked over to her phone and answered it, wondering who could be calling so late.

"It might be my parents," Carmella guessed, just as Natalie answered the phone.

"Hello?"

"What are you doin' girl?"

"Who is this?"

"Don't talk to me like that, girl! You know who this is."

"Darnell, why are you calling me?"

Carmella turned her eyes to Natalie in disbelief.

"Are you serious," she whispered to Natalie.

"I told you we aren't done until I say we are," Darnell commanded.

"Darnell, there is no other way to say this: leave me alone and do not call me ever again!"

Natalie hung up the phone in frustration.

"Unbelievable," Carmella fumed. "Just incredible! The guy's a freak!"

"He will be the one thing I won't miss," Natalie responded as she sat down on the bed.

Blllp.

"What," Carmella snapped. "This is getting ridiculous! I'm going to answer the phone."

"Don't, Carmella. Just…don't. Let the answering machine get it."

As the machine went through its normal spill, Natalie and Carmella stared at the answering machine, ready for the inevitable.

"Um, Natalie, It's Benjamin. I was just…I was just wondering if you were there."

"Benjamin??"

Natalie was in shock as she and Carmella looked at each other with complete surprise in both of their faces. Natalie didn't move.

"Girl, get that," Carmella protested.

"What am I going to say to him, Carmella??"

"Well, I guess I missed you. I just wanted to see how you were doing," Benjamin continued.

"Natalie, answer it! Do you not want to talk to Benjamin?"

"I…I don't…"

NOT PRESENT OR FUTURE...

"Well, take care of yourself, Natalie…"

"Natalie, answer the phone! You will regret it if you don't."

This time, Carmella was serious. Natalie rushed over to the phone at about the time it sounded like Benjamin was hanging up.

"Benjamin," Natalie answered, practically in a panic. "Benjamin, I'm here! Benjamin, are you…are you there?"

"Hey, Natalie. I'm here."

"Hi," Natalie replied, practically lighting up like the sun. At least, that's the way it looked to Carmella. Carmella started making flirty faces to Natalie, teasing and tormenting her. Natalie tried not to laugh.

"Natalie, I didn't mean to wake you. I…just—"

"You didn't wake me, I was, um…I was just packing some stuff."

Carmella got up, grabbed her purse, and headed for the door, still teasing Natalie on her way out. Natalie picked up her small bed pillow and threw it at Carmella.

"I'm just gonna go," Carmella joked, smiling as she walked out the door. "You, two, have a…good night."

"Bye," Natalie whispered back to Carmella as Carmella closed the door behind her.

"Natalie?"

"Ben, I'm here. I was just saying 'good-bye' to Carmella."

"Carmella? How is she doing?"

"Carmella is…Carmella. She is great. She has been such a good friend over the last couple of weeks."

Benjamin could only assume that Natalie meant that Carmella was good for her when the engagement was called off. He felt so guilty.

"That's good. I always thought that Carmella was awesome."

"Yeah, she is. So how are you doing?"

Benjamin sighed. He didn't know what to say. He knew he couldn't lie to her, but…

"I've been…okay."

"Just…okay?"

Natalie couldn't help but notice the uncertainty in his voice.

"Yeah, I guess so."

Benjamin wasn't going to divulge any information.

"Okay," she sighed.

Lord, he just called, and it seems like this conversation is already getting awkward. Besides, I'm still hurt from his actions at the Golden Corral.

"Natalie, I needed to talk to you. I know that you should be angry with me, and I won't take too much of your time."

"Okay."

He peaked her interest, but he froze. He didn't know how to say what he wanted to. They both stumbled over each other as they tried to talk.

"Benjamin, are you..."

"Natalie, I'm...I'm..."

He couldn't say it. Natalie was waiting patiently for him to finish. She didn't know if she didn't want to interrupt him, or if she really cared to begin with. Naturally, she was a bit confused. Could he be trying to apologize to her? Natalie was going to be patient. In some weird way, she was comfortable just hearing his voice.

Benjamin took a deep breath. He was trying to apologize to her but the words just could not come out.

"I'm just calling to see how you have been doing, Natalie."

Natalie was disappointed, but tried not to let it show.

"I'm okay, Benjamin, really."

She wasn't divulging much more information than that. In reality, when it came to Benjamin, she was a wreck.

"That's good," he responded.

"What have you been up to lately, Benjamin?"

"Nothing. Just hanging out and working."

"That's good. How's work going?"

Benjamin sighed. He didn't know what to say. He wasn't about to discuss the orders with Natalie on account of her past feelings toward the Marines.

"It's going okay, I guess."

He wasn't very loquacious, and Natalie felt a bit awkward at his quick responses.

"Benjamin, why did you call me?"

Benjamin could sense a touch of rudeness in her question, not that she didn't have the right to be that way. He wanted to talk to her, even if just to hear her voice, but the conversation was becoming more uncomfortable by the second. He so desperately wanted to apologize to her, but he couldn't.

"I wanted to talk to you, Natalie. I wanted to hear your voice."

"You wanted to hear my voice," she responded, but with less tension.

"Yes."

"Benjamin, I came to see you. I drove to Tulsa...to see you, and you ran out on me."

"I know," he replied, feeling guilty. "I'm sorry for running out on you like that."

What? Did he just apologize?

Natalie was confused, and caught up in her emotions. She was making changes in her life, and though she believed she cared for Benjamin -maybe even loved him- she couldn't take the emotional roller coaster.

"Benjamin, I need to ask you something. Do you love me?"

Well, that was unexpected. Of course, Benjamin loved Natalie; at least he believed he did. Now all he had to do was answer that question. That was the problem. Over the last couple of weeks, he felt like he couldn't be around people that he loved. Either they find out who he really is, or it just became too hard for him to receive love from someone else.

That had been the problem in his life for a long time.

"Benjamin, are you there?"

"Yes."

"Yes, you are there, or yes, you love me?"

"I'm here, Natalie."

Say it, Benjamin, just say it! Tell her the truth!

But...what is the truth??

He was so caught. What was worse is that he knew how he felt about her, but it didn't really matter.

I made my decision that I wasn't going through life with her, again. I am moving on.

Aren't I?
I don't want to be married to her...again.
Right?
Then why am I calling her? Was this a game? I needed to hear her voice, but why? I could have called anybody, but I called Natalie. Why?
What am I afraid of?
Facing the truth?
Why couldn't I say it? Would I hurt her again?
What about the kids?
That's easy. There are no kids.
But that's not easy. That's hard. I miss them!
But, wait, this isn't about the kids...is it?
Ugh!

Benjamin became more frustrated with every thought running through his head. He had to face Natalie's question in his own mind. No matter what happened before; no matter what they had been through, children and career aside, Benjamin came to the realization that he loved Natalie. That didn't change over the last couple of weeks. In fact...

"Benjamin, I'm waiting for an answer."

"Natalie, I..."

Benjamin froze again.

"I understand," Natalie interrupted, feeling like her heart was breaking again.

"No, Natalie, it's not like that."

"But the way you treated me at the Golden Corral; the things you said to me..."

"I know, Natalie, but..."

He could tell that she was becoming emotional.

"I know I hurt you. Uh, I..." He sighed.

Benjamin was not going to answer her question. Natalie was just about ready to hang up. This was it. She was ready to move on. But just before she did so she wanted to ask Benjamin one more question. It was hard for her, but she needed to know something; something that bugged her since their meeting at in Owasso.

"Benjamin, what do you think about?"

NOT PRESENT OR FUTURE...

"What do you mean?"

"I mean: what do you think about?"

That was an interesting question, albeit a bit easier to answer.

"I think about you, Natalie. I think about the future. I think about wanting to be a better man for God. I think about the kids I work with. I think about…many things."

"Do you know what I think about, Benjamin? I think about three children."

What? What is she referring to?

"Why do you think about three children, Natalie?"

"Never mind."

"Natalie, I want to know. Please tell me."

Is Natalie talking about the kids?

Benjamin suspected something at the Golden Corral, but he was too shallow to realize anything during their visit.

"I just think about three children, Benjamin. Do you think about children?"

"I do, Natalie."

"Okay," she replied as she wiped her tears from her face. "I think of a beautiful girl and two little boys."

Okay, Benjamin thought. *This is weird. Can it really be?*

And then it happened, something that Natalie let slip from under her breath, in a deep whisper, but Benjamin caught it.

"I miss them."

Benjamin's heart jumped. He didn't know how to respond, or what to say. This conversation had to end. It was getting to be too much for him.

"Natalie, I have to go. I have to get up early tomorrow."

"Okay."

Natalie didn't want to hang up but she couldn't stay on the phone with him any longer. Benjamin couldn't take it anymore. He tried to finish the conversation without seeming like he was rushing off the phone.

"I'll try to call you later, okay, Natalie?"

"Okay," she replied, feeling in her heart that he would never call again.

"Good-bye, Natalie."

"Good-bye, Benjamin."

Just as she went to push the 'Off' button on the phone, she raised the phone to her ear again quickly, trying to catch Benjamin before he hung up.

"Wait," she cried. "Benjamin, are you there?"

Beeep.

There was no one on the other end. The conversation was over. Natalie sat on the bed, crying heavily.

"God, I can't do this anymore. Please take this from me. I love him, but I can't do this anymore."

Natalie dropped to her knees by her bed.

"Father, why is this happening? What am I supposed to learn? Why am I here? I miss my children, but they don't exist. How can I miss someone that doesn't exist? I miss my husband, but he is not my husband. But I feel like he is still my husband! What is going on with him? What is going on…with me?

Oh God, please help me."

CHAPTER 22

Music was playing, people were dancing, and Natalie stood by the bar in a beautiful blue gown. She was looking around, trying to figure out how she got there, and she didn't recognize anyone she saw. She started walking toward the door when a very handsome man approached her. She didn't recognize him at first: tall, handsome and dressed in a tuxedo, meant only for an environment such as this. As he approached Natalie, he extended his hand to her.

"Dance with me."

Natalie could feel the weight of his stare. She knew who this was, and she became caught between temptation and conviction.

"Don't be afraid, Natalie, it's okay. We will dance the night away and have an evening to remember."

"I…I can't," Natalie responded as her heart raced the more he insisted. He moved in, closer, to her body, taking her hands and rubbing her arms. Every time he touched her hand, her shoulder, or her waist, she felt the flames of desire shoot through her.

She was so conflicted.

Natalie broke away from him and turned to walk away. As she got to the door, she felt someone grab her arm. She was turned around by the man, who pulled her close to him.

"Don't fight this, Natalie. It will be okay. We've done this before, remember?"

"No…no! I can't."

The man pulled her even closer to her and tried to kiss her. She fought him and was able to pull away from him, only to look over to the side and see three children standing there, in the hallway, looking at her. It was Leesha, T.J., and Ben Jr. The look on Leesha's face was of pure disgust.

"Mom, what are you doing??"

"Leesha," Natalie replied, surprised to see Leesha there and trying to figure out how she got there. "I'm not doing anything, honey."

Natalie walked toward Leesha to hug her, as she couldn't believe that Leesha, T. J. and Ben Jr. were standing right there.

"No, get away from me," Leesha yelled as Natalie approached her. "We know what we saw!"

Natalie stopped. She didn't know what to say. She became overwhelmed with guilt.

"Yeah, tell them, Natalie. Tell your children what you've done."

The tall, handsome man seemed to change his demeanor.

"What...what are you talking about," Natalie asked.

"Your children have seen you. They know what you did."

"No, no...I...get away from me!"

As she turned to look for the kids, they weren't there.

"Leesha! T. J.! Ben Jr.! Where are you?"

Natalie frantically looked around for the kids but couldn't find them. She ran to the door and tried to open it, but it was locked. Natalie turned back around to see the man standing there, smiling at her with a wicked smile.

"Where are my children?"

"You don't deserve them," he replied. "You made your choices, and they don't exist anymore."

"What?? No, no..."

Natalie couldn't respond, as she lost her breath. She had a feeling of complete sense of loathing and despair.

"I know what you did, Natalie. You don't deserve the children. You don't deserve Benjamin."

"What are you saying?"

"He doesn't love you."

"That's not true!"

"Of course, it is. You are not worthy of him."

"Please, leave me alone!"

Natalie felt like she was falling further and further in despair.

"You are not worthy of anyone, Natalie. You are a terrible wife."

"No, I'm not listening to this! Leave me alone."

Natalie tried to fight off the insults, but it was too much for her to handle. She fell to her knees and started to pray. But before she started, she heard a different voice talking to her and her entire being was overcome with fear.

"God, please…"

"God can't hear you, you adulteress!"

"NO!!"

Beep. Beep. Beep. Beep. Beep. Beep.

The alarm went off, and Natalie woke up, breathing heavily. She hit the button on her alarm and sat up, trying to control her breathing. She was trying to clear her mind, as she finally came to the realization that it was just a dream.

Or was it? It was so real!

Natalie felt like crying. She remembered praying the night before, crying out to God after her discussion with Benjamin.

I don't understand this! I prayed for You, Lord, to help me last night, and I had this crazy dream. Why?

Natalie sighed, and after she was able to catch her breath, she slowly got out of bed and made her way to the bathroom for her morning shower. She was so tired. That conversation she had last night with Benjamin took every little bit of emotional strength out of her.

I've got to pull myself together. I only have two days left, and I need to be at my best to ensure that the project is going to be left in good hands.

As Natalie finished getting ready for work, she grabbed her purse and keys, and headed out the door. On her way to work, she stopped by a Dunkin Donuts store to grab some coffee, which was very weird for her as she never drank it. She knew, however, that she was going to need some extra energy for the day. As she got to work, she parked her car, but sat in it for a few minutes trying to keep her mind on her work.

Lord, I can't wait to get back to Amarillo. Please just give me the strength to finish up these last few days?

Natalie knew that Mr. Sherman was going to be good to her, and that made these next two days easier to deal with. Natalie said another prayer and went inside to continue her turnover. It was a rough morning for Natalie; validating reports and correcting figures.

Maybe the rest of the day would be better. I just have to do this one more day!!

Benjamin tossed and turned all throughout the night. As the sun came up, he decided that he needed to get up and get around. Considering all that needed to be done, he could be in bed no longer. He got ready for the day; packing up a few more things, and prepping his uniform for the funeral honors detail he had later on in the afternoon. When it was time to leave, he walked over to his landlord's residence, which was on the same property, about a hundred feet away from the house he rented. He knocked on the door, checking his watch. She opened the door, holding a cup of coffee.

"Hey, Ben. How are you?"

"I've just about got it all packed, Miss Hope. I really appreciate you letting me keep the home. Are you sure it is okay?"

"Of course, Ben. I won't let anybody in there."

"Okay, thank you! I will send you a check every month for the rent."

"You're not leaving yet, are you?"

"Oh no. I just wanted to come over and see you before I head to the reserve center. I've got another funeral to work today. I will see you before I leave. It looks like I fly out on Monday, but today I will find out for sure."

"Okay, let me know if you need anything before you leave."

"Thanks, Hope! I will see you later."

Benjamin got in his pick-up and headed for the reserve center. When he arrived, he checked in at the front desk to get the destination, and the van keys.

"Hey, Sgt. Jones," Private Sissler greeted. "We will be ready in a few minutes. It's local today, Sergeant. So we are staying in Tulsa.

NOT PRESENT OR FUTURE...

However, there is one in Owasso, tomorrow, at Mowery Funeral home. It's yours if you want it. You can meet us there if you would like since you live out there. It could be your last one before you leave."

"Yeah, I'll take that one, Private. I don't plan on travelling anywhere over the next few days."

Benjamin grabbed the van binder and the keys. Then he remembered that he was going to check on the trip to Camp Pendleton.

"Hey, any word on my travel plans?"

"You should have your travel itinerary today," Lance Corporal McDaniels responded as she came around the corner. "We just about have your orders ready, Sarge."

"Thank you, Lance Corporal!"

"Also, Sgt. Jones," Lance Corporal McDaniels continued, "Major Shimshi wants to speak with you, if you have a moment."

"Sure."

Benjamin walked to Major Shimshi's office and knocked on the door.

"Good morning, Sir. Did you want to see me?"

Major Shimshi turned around from reading a report from behind his desk.

"You just like creating drama, don't you?"

"Sir?"

"You are all over the news, Sargent."

Major Shimshi pointed at the television on the wall, which was set to a local news station, covering the incident at Chik-filet, from the night before.

"I don't suppose you could tell me what happened," Major Shimshi inquired.

"Did the news mention my name specifically, Sir?"

"No. But from what I understand, you fight like a beast and you are the only person in this city who seems to enjoy getting into trouble."

Major Shimshi sat down at his desk and faced Benjamin.

"Seriously, are you okay, Sergeant?"

"I am, Sir. But to be quite honest, I am just ready to go. I am really looking forward to this new mission."

"Well, you are not wanted for anything, so there is no reason to delay. The staff assured me that you would have your itinerary, today."

"Thank you, Sir!"

"You may be getting a phone call or two. What you did last night was incredible, and people will want to recognize you for what you did; especially the Marines."

"Major, I don't want any recognition. I don't want anything. I would prefer if we could just move on. I just want to get to Camp Pendleton."

"Okay, Sargent. I'm trackin'."

He was curious as to why Benjamin wanted to go on these orders so quickly. Surely he couldn't be running from anything. Lately, he was the most 'dangerous' person in Tulsa. As they concluded their conversation, there was a knock at the door.

"Sgt. Jones, we are ready to go, only if you and the Major are done."

"Go ahead," Major Shimshi responded, releasing Benjamin. "I guess we are done here."

Benjamin got up from the chair and headed for the door.

"Oh, and Sgt. Jones," Major Shimshi continued.

"Yes, Sir?"

"Don't go taking on any biker gangs or invading any armies while you're out, okay?"

"Yes, Sir," Benjamin snickered.

Benjamin, Private Sissler, and Corporal Bates got into the van and left for the funeral. Being local, it wouldn't take long to get there. That was good for Benjamin, who just assumed to conclude all activities in Tulsa and get back to finishing the packing for his trip.

CHAPTER 23

"I know that I said that tomorrow would be my last day, Mr. Sherman. But trying to get my stuff together, and packing up my apartment is taking a bit longer than I would have hoped."

Natalie dreaded this conversation, but she really didn't want to come in to the office any more. She had already checked out, mentally, from the Arger Corporation. She knew she was moving on so, as far as she was concerned, there was no point in avoiding the inevitable.

"I kind of figured that, which is why I asked you to come in to see me."

Oh, great! I hope he didn't bring me in here to give me any more bad news.

Natalie didn't think she could handle any more drama. She just figured that all she had to do was make it through the day. Actually, she was so caught up in what she was going to tell Mr. Sherman about Friday that she almost forgot that it was Mr. Sherman who, initially, wanted to see her.

"Natalie, the reason that I wanted to see you today is to say how much I have appreciated you during the time you have been with me, especially the past two weeks. I am going to ask you to please forgive me for not telling you this the other day, but you did catch me at a loss with your resignation."

"Yes, Sir. I am sorry about that. You don't deserve that and… and…"

Natalie couldn't finish.

"And, I wanted to give you this," Mr. Sherman interrupted, while handing Natalie an envelope. "This is your final paycheck."

"Thank you, Mr. Sherman."

"And…this is your bonus check," Mr. Sherman continued, handing Natalie another envelope.

"My bonus check?? Sir, I…"

"Natalie, you deserve this. You saved a great project by your tenacity and courage. It took a lot of guts to go to Mr. Quartermain and do what you did, and I wanted to be sure that I recognized you for that."

Natalie was speechless. This was an incredible show of kindness.

"Sir, thank you so much," Natalie responded, trying to hold back the tears.

Your really aren't making this easy for me, Mr. Sherman.

"Just wait till you open it, Natalie."

"Sir, I am just grateful for what you have done for me. I can't thank you enough."

Natalie took the envelopes and held them close to her as she stood up to leave his office.

"One more thing, Natalie: if you need a reference in Amarillo, please use me. I believe, from speaking to Mr. Quartermain, that he would be a very good reference as well."

"Thank you, Sir! Thank you so much for everything. I most definitely will use you as a reference. And if you ever need anything from me, please let me know."

Mr. Sherman got up from his desk and walked around it to give Natalie a hug.

"Good-bye, Natalie. God bless you on your new adventures."

"Good-bye, Mr. Sherman. God bless you, too!"

Natalie left his office quickly, trying to avoid becoming any more emotional. She walked to her office and grabbed a box with her stuff in it. She started walking out, passing by Shannon's desk.

"Good-bye, Shannon. It has been wonderful working with you…again."

Shannon got up from her chair and came around her desk to give Natalie a hug.

NOT PRESENT OR FUTURE...

"Good-bye, Natalie. I will miss you!"

"I'll miss you too! Thank you for everything."

Natalie grabbed her box and left the office. She got to her car, put her box in the back seat, and sat in the driver's seat. She reached over to her purse to pull out the two envelopes that Mr. Sherman gave her. Her paycheck was a little more than what she suspected: $1,667.00. It was a gracious amount, and she still couldn't believe the salary that Mr. Sherman paid her. She put her paycheck back in the envelope and reached for her bonus check.

I wonder how much this is. Whatever it is, I am grateful that he thought of me!

As she opened her envelope in anticipation, she gasped.

"Five thousand dollars!! Five thousand dollars???"

Tears began to flow as her hands started shaking. She got out of her car and practically ran back into the office where she caught Shannon filing paperwork.

"Hey, Natalie, did you forget anything?"

"I need to see Mr. Sherman!"

"He just left; you just missed him."

Natalie froze, turning and looking at Shannon as if Shannon were giving Natalie a hard time. Natalie tried to control her emotions.

"Really?? He really did leave??"

"Are you okay?"

"I just need to talk to him about this bonus. I can't accept this."

"What? Your bonus?"

"Yeah, I just need to talk to him," Natalie continued, her voice breaking up as she was still in tears.

"Natalie, listen to me. Whatever it is: trust me, you've earned it. I have worked for Mr. Sherman for a long time, and I can tell you that he doesn't just give money away. If you received this blessing from him, take it. Like I said, you've earned it."

"Yeah, but..."

"But, it's yours, Natalie," Shannon interrupted. "Go and enjoy it."

Natalie stood there for a second, then then gave Shannon another hug.

"Thank you, Shannon! Thank you so much!"

Natalie found herself, again, in her car and trying to figure out what to do from there. Her instinct was to call Benjamin and share the news with him, but that wasn't happening. She decided to call her mother, instead.

This had turned out to be a great day, and Natalie had received a huge blessing, but she still felt empty inside. She started her car and drove back to her apartment, trying to shake this loathing feeling. Once she arrived, she walked in and immediately went for the phone to call her mother. Natalie could not understand why, but she just felt exhausted and defeated. The blessing she received from Mr. Sherman was incredible, and should have made Natalie feel better, but that was not the case.

In fact, she felt even more alone.

As she dialed her mother's number, she waited in anticipation to hear her mother's voice. As Florance picked up the phone, Natalie almost broke down.

"Mom, it's me."

It didn't matter what her mother said at that moment. Hearing her mother's voice was always calming, and for reasons she could not explain, Natalie needed it now, more than ever.

CHAPTER 24

Benjamin was thrilled. He had his orders and travel itinerary in his hands. He was even more excited to be almost home so he could continue going through his stuff, and determining what he was getting rid of. He had one more funeral honors detail to participate in, and then he could focus on his orders.

As he pulled up into the house, he parked his pick-up and went over to see Hope. Benjamin approached the porch and knocked on the door.

"Hey, Ben," Hope greeted as she opened the door.

"I didn't mean to bother you, Miss Hope, but I just wanted to give you a copy of my orders and my travel itinerary…just in case you needed them."

"Thanks, Benjamin. I'll put these with the contract. Also, I went ahead and drew up extended contract to cover the time you will be gone. If you get extended, we can talk about it then."

"Thank you, Ma'am! I will be at the house finishing up my packing and stuff. If you need anything else, just let me know."

"I will, Ben. See ya later."

She closed the door, and Benjamin practically ran to the rent house. He went inside, and while he was taking off his uniform, he noticed that he had two messages on the answering machine. Benjamin walked over to the answering machine and pressed the 'Play' button.

"You have two new messages. Message 1: 'So are you going to call me or what? You have gone a couple weeks without calling me or coming to see me!' Beep."

It was his mother. Benjamin would not be in any hurry to talk to her. He knew that he should call her, but...

"Message 2: 'Hey, Ben, it's Ray. Just wanted to see how things were going. I have not heard from you, today, and I just wanted to be sure that you are okay. Brian and I were talking about you, and, well, we just wanted to check in on you. Give me a call.' Beep. End of new messages."

Brian and Raymond? Oh, man! I haven't told them I'm leaving!

It wasn't that he didn't want to tell them, but from the beginning of the orders' process, it seemed like Benjamin was hitting a brick wall just trying to get the orders. And then he had another thought.

What do I do with my pick-up truck?

Benjamin couldn't take it with him, nor would he want to. It was a good little pick-up, it ran well, and most importantly, it was paid off. Regardless, Benjamin needed to do something with the pick-up. It was kind of short notice, though.

What do I do with it? Ugh! Can't think about that right now.

The pick-up issue would have to wait. Benjamin needed to tell Raymond and Brian that he was leaving on Monday. Considering that it was late afternoon on Friday, Benjamin had better call Raymond, quick. But Raymond might have to wait. For some reason, he felt that he needed to tell Brian first. Benjamin looked for Brian's number and dialed it on the phone.

"Hello," Janet answered.

"Miss Janet, this is Benjamin. Can I talk to Brian?"

"Absolutely, Ben! He's right here."

Janet handed Brian the phone, and all of a sudden, Benjamin started feeling a bit guilty.

"Hello?"

"Hey, Brian, it's Benjamin."

"Hey, Ben, how are you? How have you been feeling? We have been thinking about you."

"I'm okay. I was wondering if I can bother you for a minute."

"Absolutely, Ben. Shoot."

NOT PRESENT OR FUTURE...

"Brian, I have not told Raymond about this yet, but there is an opportunity in the Marine Corps that I am going to take, and I will be travelling to Camp Pendleton in a couple of days for a year-long set of orders."

"Really??"

"Yeah. I have been working on this for a couple of weeks, but I never said anything because I did not know if I could ever get the orders. I just got them today, and I fly out on Monday."

"Is that right?"

"Yes. I am going to call Raymond here in a minute, but I wanted to let you know first."

"Wow, Benjamin, this is rather...sudden."

Brian seemed like he was at a loss. Benjamin could hear it in Brian's voice.

"And you said you will be gone for a year?"

"Yeah. It's really a good opportunity, and to be quite honest with you, I am looking forward to the orders."

"Well, okay, Ben. I appreciate you telling me."

Benjamin sensed an awkward moment, and he was ready to get off the phone, but he did not want to seem rude to Brian. Just then, a thought came to Benjamin on what he could do with his pick-up.

"Brian, listen, can I ask you one more question?"

"Yeah, shoot."

"Do you know anyone who needs a pick-up? I don't want mine to sit around waiting for me, and I can't take it with me. I have no desire to make money from it. I have the title here, and I am willing to give it to anyone who needs it."

"Well, yeah, Benjamin. I'm sure we can find someone who can use it. If you would like to leave it with me I can be sure it is given to someone who needs it."

"Thanks, Brian. I appreciate it."

"Benjamin, this is fairly sudden. I mean, I know that you just got out of the Marine Corps. Are you sure you want to do this? A year is quite a while."

"Yeah, I'm sure, Brian. I like the orders and I think I could really contribute."

"Well, okay, then. Will you need anything else?"

"I could use a ride to the airport on Monday. Personally, I would like to be able to spend my last hour here with someone I trust; someone that I know will be praying for me while I am gone."

"You got it, brother! Anything."

"Thank you, Brian. I really appreciate it."

"You're welcome, brother. Will I see you on Sunday?"

"Don't see why not. I plan on being there."

"Okay, brother. Don't forget to call Raymond."

"I won't. Thanks for your help, Brian. I will talk to you later."

"Okay, Benjamin. I'll see you later."

They both hung up the phone, and Benjamin sat on the couch contemplating on whether or not he was going to call his mother. He tried to convince himself to call her, and then he tried to convince himself not to. He took a deep breath, said a quick prayer, and dialed his mother's number.

That was all it took.

Blllp.

Blllp.

The phone kept ringing, but Natalie was not answering it. Ever since last night, she was getting phone call after phone call. At first she answered, and no one would speak on the other end. Whoever it was, they were harassing her. Natalie just tried to ignore them, but ignoring the phone calls didn't make them go away. Carmella was closing the store tonight, so she would not be coming over. She only had to work a couple of hours the next day, and she kept bugging Natalie to go see a Christian motivational speaker after Carmella got off work. Natalie didn't feel like doing anything but getting out of Abilene.

Blllp.

"'Hi, this is Natalie. You know what to do.' Beep."

Nothing. There was someone there, but whoever it was just said nothing. Whoever it was calling her continued to harass Natalie, and she was tired of it. She got to the point to where she didn't want to pack, she didn't want to eat, and she didn't want to move.

Natalie was struggling, and she knew it. She wished that she could just teleport herself to her mother's house. If she did not have any more stuff in her apartment, she would leave that second. Natalie crawled in bed, just wanting to pass the time away. Perhaps she would feel better in the morning when Carmella came over. But right now…

Natalie grabbed the television remote control and started flipping through channels. She really didn't want to watch anything, but flipping through the channels was, at least, something. When she got bored flipping channels, she settled for the local news station. The weather was on, and there were signs of a major storm brewing over the next couple of days.

Yeah, Natalie thought. *There seems to be a major storm brewing, all right. It's in my soul.*

She felt so lost and alone that she began to pray.

"Lord, please be with me. Please be with me, and please, Lord, whatever is wrong with me, please take this cup from me?"

Natalie drifted off in prayer and fell asleep. She would not wake again until the morning.

CHAPTER 25

"Natalie, why don't you come with me tonight to see Dorothy Morris? I have an extra ticket."

Carmella saw that Natalie really needed some encouragement, as she waved the ticket in a teasing manner. Natalie looked away as if she wasn't interested, but Carmella pressed.

An 'extra ticket', Natalie thought. *She didn't have an extra ticket. She bought one, specifically, for me.*

"Come on, Natalie. Dorothy Morris is awesome! She is such a great speaker, and right now, you look like you need to hear what she has to say."

"Now what exactly would she say to me?"

Natalie cracked a smile as Carmella was dancing back and forth, round and round, with the ticket in her hand. Natalie couldn't help but laugh at Carmella's comic routine.

"A-ha! There's that smile. I knew I'd get you, girl!"

Natalie shook her head, but she kept her smile.

Oh why not? I mean, it's not like I have got something more pressing to do tonight. There is no more packing to do. The apartment is lonely. There are no kids, no husband, no house to take care of, and no dinner to make. Nothing.

That's been the problem.

Natalie needed to take a break. She had been packing since she got up that morning, and she could really use some time away from her apartment. Besides, a chance to hear Dorothy Morris was one not worth wasting.

NOT PRESENT OR FUTURE...

Dorothy Morris was known for her Christian speaking engagements. She was a little old African-American woman somewhere in her 60s, but she was spunky, and she had a knack for drilling her point right into the depths of your soul.

It might just be I need tonight, Natalie thought. *Wait, Dorothy Morris: didn't she pass away not too long ago?*

"Hey, didn't she pass away not too long ago or something?"

Then it hit her. She almost messed up again. She still caught herself in a perplexed state, on and off, but quickly snapped out of it. First it was her mother, and now this. It's not like Natalie hasn't just had the craziest experience so far with all of this do-it-over, time-travelling stuff.

"Died? Girl, what are you talking about? She ain't dead. We are gonna see her, tonight!"

"Well, why not?" Natalie replied. "I'll go."

Honestly, what would it hurt? Sure, let's go hear a woman who, technically, has been dead for the last couple of years.

Or had she?

It didn't matter. Natalie was going, and Carmella was sure to see it that way.

"I'll pick you up at five. Be ready. We have to get good seats!"

"Okay," Natalie responded as Carmella walked out of the apartment.

Just then, Natalie's phone rang. Carmella just happened to look back as she was out the door to see Natalie standing there, looking at the phone.

"Are you gonna get that?"

"Maybe later," Natalie responded, going to the sink.

"Let me guess: Darnell."

"Probably."

Natalie thought for a moment that maybe it could be Benjamin, but...

"Girl, you need to just stay away from him. He would just drag you down."

Carmella paused, following her comical response. She watched Natalie's lethargic demeanor. Her heart went out to Natalie, and she felt that she couldn't leave Natalie's apartment without saying something else.

"Natalie, I'm really sorry about Benjamin. I thought that your relationship was getting serious."

"Maybe it was getting too serious, Carmella."

At this point, Natalie was so confused about Benjamin. It wasn't like she could just cry over him a little, and move on. The feelings were there — the history, the passion, the children, the memories… the covenant. It was all there, and it was certainly not going to just fade away like some crush. As much as Natalie did or did not want to admit it, Benjamin was still her husband in so many ways, even if not by time.

"Okay, whatever, girl," Carmella responded, trying to make Natalie smile. "I'll be here at five. You have just one hour."

Carmella left, and Natalie began to get ready for the evening. In the process of her dressing and makeup, she called her mother. Of all the craziness going on in this time-travelling experience that she could not explain, having her mother back was a miracle. This conversation with her mother was just as pleasant as the rest of them until, of course, when her mother asked about Benjamin.

"When are you gonna see him again, Natalie? I like that man. I sure hoped that you two would have been able to work things out!"

Natalie did not know what to say. She really couldn't say anything. Just about the time Natalie was going to get into her spill about Benjamin, the doorbell rang.

"Natalie? You ready??"

It was Carmella, and was she ever so ready for a fun night!

"Oh my gosh! Mom, I have to go. I'm going with Carmella to see Dorothy Morris, tonight."

"Dorothy Morris? I just love Dorothy Morris! Go have fun and call me when it is over."

"I will, Mom. I will. I promise. I love you!"

"I love you too, Natalie."

Click.

Natalie took a breath and thanked God for her mother, yet again. Her prayer was interrupted by another knock at the door.

NOT PRESENT OR FUTURE...

"Natalie, let's go, girl!"

"Okay, I'm coming."

Carmella and Natalie jumped in the car and took off toward the convention center. They ran through the drive-through of Taco Bueno, and Carmella treated Natalie to some party burritos and cheesecake chimichangas. They finished eating just as Carmella pulled into the convention center parking lot, which was filling up quickly.

There were women everywhere; all trying to get into the convention center to hear the 'most delightful' Dorothy Morris. Carmella and Natalie made their way into the center hall and found their seats. After a couple of announcements, the wait was over. Dorothy took the stage, and the crowd erupted. Appearing before all the ladies -the frail, spunky woman that she was- she smiled bright and filled the auditorium with her spiritual light.

Dorothy spent most of the event encouraging the women and sharing Biblical passages. She was radiant, and every woman in that auditorium soaked up her comical kindness. Natalie enjoyed it, and she was so glad she went. Natalie began to feel a peace and she closed her eyes for a moment.

"Lord, speak to me. Please tell me what I need to hear in this time of confusion."

At that moment, something caught Natalie's attention. There was nothing happening out of the ordinary, as Dorothy was still speaking. Maybe it was the tone change, or even the topic. Regardless, Natalie was brought back to her senses as Dorothy continued speaking.

"Ladies," Dorothy insisted with a more intent focus. "I am going to tell you something, right now, that you all need to hear."

Dorothy paused as she looked around.

"Love your husbands."

That was it.

There was a silence in the auditorium as if the women were waiting in expectation of something more.

"Did you hear what I said, ladies? I told you to 'love your husbands.'"

There were some claps and some snickering. Some women just appeared to become uncomfortable, and even look away from Dorothy. Natalie was stuck. She could not look away as Dorothy continued.

"Let me tell you a story, ladies. A long time ago, when my husband was in the Army, we used to have, somewhat, of a hostile relationship. I was mad at him all the time. I was mad at him because the Army took him away from me. I was mad at him because of what the Army did to him while he was away from me. I was mad at him when he made mistakes; when he made mistakes as a father, and that was just the beginning of it."

Natalie still did not move. She felt this overwhelming feeling that, somehow, this was meant for her to hear.

"I was a bitter wife," Dorothy continued. "I blamed my husband for everything. I prayed that God would do something to that man. I prayed that God would fix him and make him into something else than what he was. I hated the man that my husband was, and I wanted a new husband. I was terrible to be around. I was so angry all the time at him, and I made life a living hell for him. And what was worse, my attitude made its way to my children."

Dorothy paused.

"Then something happened, ladies. God got a hold of me and shook my inner being to the point that I could not breathe. He told me to wake up. God said to me, 'Dorothy, who do you think you are, asking Me to fix your husband? Is there something wrong with him? What is your problem, Dorothy?'"

Again, silence in the auditorium, but tears were beginning to build, throughout.

"When I realized what I had become, I fell to the floor and I cried. I begged for God's forgiveness. I prayed for it. I desperately needed it. God straightened me out, and He opened my eyes to the reality of my husband's world, which is what I needed to see. You see, ladies, my husband already had a commanding officer. He didn't need another one!"

Cheers rose from the crowd.

"My husband joined the Army because he felt he was called to do so; called to serve his country. Here I was trying to take away his sense of honor to fulfill my pathetic sense of overbearing need. Now don't get me wrong, ladies. I still had my needs, as we all do, and I needed my husband. But what I failed to realize in all my self-loathing and self-pity was that my husband needed me, too. He needed a wife, a partner, a best friend, a lover, a mother of his children…"

Cheers turned to clapping, as many women stood to their feet, wiping the tears from their eyes.

"My husband needed me, and when he needed me the most, instead of loving him, I chastised him. I almost –almost- ruined my own marriage. He and I were that close to calling it quits…"

Dorothy paused.

"Until God got ahold of me. Then I realized that I was the problem, not my husband. And, ladies, let me tell you something. When God gets a hold of you, you can either shut up, straighten up and listen, or, you can decide to turn your own way."

More laughter, clapping, and cheers rose from the crowd.

"You see, ladies, my husband was not the problem. But because of my actions, he was turning into the problem. I chose my husband. Then I wanted him to be what I wanted him to be, the way I wanted him to be. That is not what I told God I would act like when we married."

Natalie's heart sank. She felt so much guilt. Then, she felt conflicted.

Should I feel guilty? I'm not even married.

Am I?

No ring. No proposal. My husband, or future husband, or whatever…he doesn't even want me.

"What does the Bible say about this? Let's look at Ephesians chapter 5."

Dorothy opened her Bible and began to read the verse.

"'Submit to one another out of reverence for Christ.'"

Dorothy closed her Bible.

"That's the first thing that the chapter said, ladies. 'Submit to one another out of reverence for Christ.' I should not have to explain what that means, but if you need help understanding it, then come see me when this is over."

More laughter and cheers filled the room.

"Now we get to the good part: 'Wives, submit yourselves to your own husbands as you do to the Lord. For the husband is the head of the wife as Christ is the head of the church, his body, of which He is the Savior. Now as the church submits to Christ, so also wives should submit to their husbands in everything.'"

Dorothy looked up.

"Now, ladies, what do you think that means?"

Silence filled the auditorium.

"God has commanded us to submit ourselves to our own husbands as we would the Lord. This verse says it, ladies. It says it right here."

Dorothy pointed to her Bible.

"Now I know that this is a very unpopular verse among the feminists in society today, but I am here to tell you that you won't be standing in front of the feminists on the Day of Judgment. You will be standing before your Holy Father in heaven: the One who told you to submit to your husbands."

Her words were met with the occasional 'Amen' and clapping.

"And we just think that we are so used and abused if we do it God's way that we should just revolt and run our husbands off. Shoot, for that matter, let us not get married at all."

More laughter and clapping.

"But God said in Genesis that it was not good that man should be alone. So what then should we conclude, ladies? Were we, in fact, created for man? Can we actually believe that? Should we believe it?"

She looked around the room at the all the faces. Some bewildered; others, intent.

"Well, I don't know about you all, but I was created for something special, and that something special gets to come home and get his lovin' every day after a hard day at work!"

That broke the silence. Laughter and clapping filled the auditorium, again.

"Let's continue because I just know that there are many of you in here that believe that you are getting the short end of the stick. We heard from God about what He expects from us, but what about what He expects from our husbands. Ladies, have you ever considered that?"

Heads were shaking and more shouts of 'Amen' filled the auditorium.

"'Husbands', and this is God speaking, not Dorothy. 'Husbands, love your wives, just as Christ loved the church and gave himself up for her to make her holy; cleansing her by the washing with water through the word, and to present her to himself as a radiant church, without stain or wrinkle or any other blemish, but holy and blameless.'"

Dorothy paused and looked up.

"Ladies, do you understand what that means? Your husband is to love you so much that he would die for you, cleanse you, and present you as radiant, without stain or wrinkle or any other blemish. Ladies, your husband presents you holy and blameless by his love for you. You, not the other way around. It is his responsibility to love you, care for you, and, by his love for you, present you without stain, wrinkle, or blemish. You are made 'holy and blameless,' in a sense, through him. The responsibility for this type of 'sanctification,' if you will, is on your husband. Now why don't you just let that sink in for a moment?"

More silence. Some women were crying. Some were deep in thought, but there was no doubt who had the floor.

"Let's continue: 'In this same way, husbands ought to love their wives as their own bodies. He who loves his wife loves himself. After all, no one ever hated their own body but they feed and care for their body, just as Christ does the church—for we are members of his body.'"

Dorothy glanced up and, taking ques from the crowd, she continued.

"And now the finale. 'For this reason a man will leave his father and mother and be united to his wife, and the two will become one flesh. This is a profound mystery. But I am talking about Christ and the church. However, each one of you also must love his wife as he loves himself and the wife must respect her husband.'"

Dorothy still had the attention from every woman in the auditorium, and Natalie was just as captivated. She felt like she couldn't move.

"There it is, ladies," Dorothy continued. "It's right there. Instructions for both husband and wife. But I want you do understand that the man has the hardest job. He must love you and take care of you and present you blameless. He must provide for you. He must lay down his life for you. He must 'sanctify' you and present you as without blemish. So with this type of responsibility, don't you believe that he deserves your respect, your admiration, your…your prayers?"

Clapping and cheers came with women standing on their feet, wiping tears from their eyes and waiting for more.

"Now I ask you this, ladies: who among you has failed to love your husbands and submit to him as your head of the household?"

Hands were raising up throughout the auditorium, including Natalie's. She was so caught up in her own emotion she just raised her hand without thinking about her current situation. It wasn't until she looked up when she noticed Carmella staring at her in disbelief that she came back to her senses. Natalie was speechless, not sure how she was going to explain this. But with tears in her eyes and her heart yearning for Benjamin, she did not care. Natalie then lowered her hand.

"Ladies, this verse we just read is so critical. This is one of the reasons why there is no such thing as homosexual marriage because a woman cannot 'sanctify' another woman and a man cannot 'sanctify' another man. First, it is impossible. Second, it would not be holy. Remember, ladies, the human marriage relationship reflects that of the relationship between Christ, as the groom, and the church, as the bride. It is not the other way around."

There seemed to be a small uncomfortable feeling in some of the women in the auditorium, but that did not stop Dorothy from speaking.

"Remember, ladies, God does not change. We change, but He does not. We can say things like, 'I have changed; my husband has changed…times are changing.' And that may be the case. We look for ways to justify our actions when we go against God's Word when it comes to our relationships. I am here to tell you that God never changes. He is the same yesterday, today, and tomorrow."

More clapping and 'Amens' filled the room.

"Now, ladies," Dorothy continued. "I know that there are some of you in here who are married to men who may be ungodly, abusive, difficult to live with, cheaters, or, above all else, just not good husbands. I can assure you that God knows this, too. God still loves you, and He wants you to have the most fulfilling marriage you can imagine."

More tear wiping and clapping from the crowd.

"Ladies, if you are finding yourself in a harmful relationship, no matter what the reason may be, I want you to come pray with me -up front- and all these women will pray for you. If you are lonely, or just need prayer, then come up here and let's go before our Father, together. Because the bottom line is, ladies: no marriage is perfect. But God created marriage as He created man and woman, so no marriage is perfect, but as it is, it is holy and flawless. But only God can make it that way."

As women from all over the room came down for prayer, Dorothy walked down to them and asked other women to lay hands on them. Some women left, bewildered and confused. Some looked almost angry. Others, sensing hope and restoration, kept coming for prayer. Dorothy prayed for the women, then finished up by reading Proverbs 31; the very Bible verse she started with.

For the first time in a long time, Natalie felt a peace about her. She still didn't understand what was happening in her soul, but it didn't matter. She was really, truly learning how to give everything over to God.

CHAPTER 26

"Daddy? Daddy, where are you?"

Benjamin could hear the Leesha's screams and he struggled to find her.

"Daddy, please help me! Daddy, please help!"

The fear and dread increased inside of him. It was a crippling experience that held him captive in that realm of being asleep and being awake. Benjamin, caught in fear, could not find his daughter.

"Leesha," Benjamin yelled in a panic that struck his heart and mind. "Leesha, where are you?"

"Daddy, please help me? Daddy!!"

Leesha's screams turned to tormenting cries. Benjamin felt like he was losing his mind trying to find her.

"Leave me alone!! Don't hurt me!!! DADDY??"

"Leesha, Leesha, where are you?? I'm coming for you, Leesha!"

Was someone with Leesha? Was someone hurting her?

Benjamin ran and ran, but the harder he ran, the harder it was for him to move.

What is going on, here?

Benjamin ran through, what appeared to be, water, mud, fog, dark, fear…everything imaginable.

"Leesha," he kept yelling, but he heard her voice no more.

Then, Benjamin felt a sense of heaviness; so much so that he couldn't breathe. He was not alone, and he knew it. He could feel it…sense it, even. He kept running.

"Leesha??"

NOT PRESENT OR FUTURE...

Benjamin turned and looked, only to see several men holding Leesha by her hair. One of the men had a gun pointed at her head. The men appeared to be dressed like the insurgents that he had fought just years before. But these men were not insurgents. Benjamin could not even recognize them as actual men.

"Benjamin, see what you have done? You murderer! You warmonger! You..."

As they continued speaking, they raised Leesha off the ground as she shouted in pain. Benjamin could not reach her, but as the men went to strike Leesha, Benjamin could only yell from here.

"JESUS, HELP ME!"

The men stopped, looked at Benjamin with evil grins, and then...

"Wake up, Marine!"

It was a sound of intense thunder, if the sound could even be described at all. Benjamin jumped out of bed, breathing heavily and sweating profusely. It took him a second to realize that it was all a dream, but it didn't matter.

"Leesha," he called, just before he started crying.

"Leesha. Leesha. Leesha."

Each time he said her name was quieter than the last.

"Leesha. T.J. Ben Jr."

And then he fell on his knees.

"Natalie."

Benjamin wept bitterly. He could not control it. He did not know what to do or who to talk to. He thought of Brian and Raymond, but he felt guilty talking to them. Plus, what would they understand?

Benjamin did not like the way he felt when he talked to his mother, so that was out of the question. He knew better than to call her. She was another reason that he wanted to go on orders for a while. As if this life made any sense to him right now, Benjamin's mother only complicated his confusion. She had a tendency to do that. And regarding his life -talk about something that made no sense to him. This was not like any experience he had ever gone through.

After all, if he had the chance to explain what was going on, who would believe him?

He was dreaming about events that he had experienced but, in any other way, hadn't happened yet. There was no Natalie, no marriage, or no kids. There was no battle yet. No war. No fighting insurgents. His unit was alive, and they were there. But…

"Jesus, please help me. I am so lost. I…am…so…lost."

The only thing that Benjamin knew was that, whatever dream he just went through, he was not the only one in that room. He felt a presence that was so evil…so dreadful, and that there was no fear that he had ever experienced in his life that could compare to how he felt at that moment. Somehow, he still felt it. It was doubt, accusations, guilt, shame…loathing. It was a heavy burden, and the burden was on him.

I have to leave! I must get away from all of this. I can't take this. Why has my life been so difficult, lately?

After all, this was the second chance he wanted. But, for some reason, it wasn't that easy to forget all the things he had gone through. One would think that a second chance to make the right decision would not be so difficult. But Benjamin had a problem: he carried the baggage of his other life with him, and he knew it.

After he calmed down, Benjamin called Ricky and asked if he could come hang out.

"Sure," Ricky responded. "We just got some beers, and we're chillin' out here at my crib. Come on over."

The thought of having a beer with Ricky did not entice Benjamin, but it was too late to call anyone else for company. This was one of Benjamin's last few nights in Tulsa, so he figured that he could use a break.

Benjamin drove over to Ricky's house, and as he walked into the front door, he noticed some of his other friends were playing a game on the Nintendo.

"Hey, Benjamin! What are you up to? Remember this game? It's Super Techmo Bowl!"

NOT PRESENT OR FUTURE…

Benjamin remembered that game, and remembered that he enjoyed playing it with Ricky. Before Benjamin could respond, Ricky handed him a beer.

"Here ya go, bro. You look like you could use one."

Benjamin took the beer and sat down next to Ricky.

"So how you been, Ben?"

"All right, I guess. Just busy."

"You don't look all right," Ricky commented.

Ben reached up to massage his temples.

"I know, man, it's just been…crazy."

"Well, keep drinkin', man. You're all right here."

Ricky had a look in his eye, like he wanted to say something, but Benjamin just took that opportunity to take a couple of drinks of his beer and check on the boys who were doing something in the other room.

"Hey, Benjamin," came another voice in the group of guys. It was Terrance, another one of Benjamin's friends from school.

"How are you doing?"

"I'm good," Benjamin responded as he shook Terrance's hand.

Ricky approached Benjamin as Benjamin was about to sit down on the couch, next to Terrance.

"You still hanging around that church; what, working with them kids?"

"Yeah, Rickie. I am."

"Working with church kids," Terrance chimed in. "For real?"

"Yeah. I have been a youth sponsor with the church for a while. I like the youth minister there. He does a lot of good things with the kids."

As if there was something funny that he just said, the group of guys all burst out in laughter.

"What's so funny?"

"Nothin' man," Ricky responded. "Here, have another beer."

Benjamin didn't realize that he drank his beer so fast. He looked down at his bottle to find that there was not much left in it. That was a pretty good feat, considering that Benjamin didn't drink.

I don't drink, right?

He couldn't remember. All he knew, at that point, was the taste of the beer became tolerable, and the room began to spin the more he drank.

"Daddy?"

"What was that," Benjamin snapped, looking around the room.

"What was what," Terrence responded, still playing his game.

"Never mind."

Benjamin leaned over and rubbed his temples.

"Daddy?"

Benjamin jumped up from the couch, looking around.

"All right, man, who's playin'?"

"Man, you are trippin'," Ricky grunted.

The others were still laughing at Benjamin, while one of them started rolling a joint on the floor. Benjamin didn't notice anything as he was consumed by this haunting voice. He was paying close attention to his surroundings, and trying to get a hold of himself. After about a minute, he sat back down on the couch as he became overwhelmed with feelings of guilt.

Why do I feel guilty? What am I hearing? What is going on, here? That's sounds like Leesha, but she aint real!

"Daddy!"

"That's it!"

Benjamin jumped up from the couch, only to find that he could not get his bearings.

"Man, what is wrong with you," Ricky snapped. "You got a problem? You bringin' problems up in my place?"

Ricky was not attacking Benjamin, but for some reason, Benjamin lost complete understanding of reality. What Ricky was saying and what Benjamin heard were two different things.

"What is wrong with you, you murderer?"

"I don't know what you are talking about," Benjamin responded, shaking his head.

"Hey, man, I think you need to leave," Terrence ordered as Benjamin stumbled out of the front door. Terrance turned to Ricky in confusion.

"What's wrong with him, Ricky?"

"Man, I don't know. Just leave him alone."

As Benjamin walked out the door, he tried to collect his thoughts but his mind turned to Natalie, and that seemed to spark a whole new set of accusations.

"You left her…"

"No," Benjamin replied.

"You left her many times…"

"No," Benjamin cried.

"You left her many times…adulterer!!"

"No!!"

Benjamin couldn't take it anymore. He fell to his knees, and with his hands over his eyes, he fought the voices that he could not see. For some reason, he started having flashbacks of memories of the mistakes he made in his life. All he felt was an overwhelming sense of guilt and shame.

But that is crazy! I was given a second chance. I am going to do things right, this time!

Right?

If this is a second chance, then why do I feel so guilty? What's the problem?

He brought his hands down and opened his eyes with intensity that would light a fire.

Natalie is not here. I am going to move on. Leesha, TJ. and Ben Jr. are not real. I am not going to feel guilty anymore!

Benjamin became angry. He didn't know why, but it didn't matter. At that moment, whether he understood it or not, whether he was under the influence or not, he reacted in the only way he thought he should. He looked up into the sky and yelled at the top of his lungs, challenging God.

"WHY CAN'T YOU STOP LOVING ME?? WHY DON'T YOU JUST LEAVE ME ALONE, GOD?? WHY???"

All the anger and emotion boiled up to this moment, with the alcohol seeming to act as the fuse to light the explosives inside him. If God would just stop loving him, then maybe Benjamin could go on living the life he wants to live. If God would just stop loving him, then maybe Benjamin would be able to make decisions in his life without feeling guilty. If God would…just…stop…

"I'm tired of feeling guilty! I'm tired of feeling like this! I just want You to leave me alone! Please? Please just leave me alone, God."

Benjamin fell on his knees, again. He was filled with anger, animosity, bitterness, and feelings that he possessed that last night that he and Natalie fought. It was the night before all this began; the night Benjamin told her that he wanted to go back and 'start over'. Benjamin was so caught up in his emotional state that he failed to see the lights coming from the police car that just pulled right up in front of him. Benjamin didn't fight. He didn't cause any disturbances when the police questioned him. He didn't show any resistance, except to God. The police officer placed handcuffs on him after searching him, read him his Miranda rights, and arrested him for public intoxication.

As the police officer placed him in the backseat of the patrol car, Benjamin was too tired and intoxicated to realize that his friends were watching him through the windows of Ricky's house. He wouldn't care even if he had seen them looking. It was a state that he had not been in a while, and though his mind was running, he could not make his thoughts translate to any physical action.

He was consumed in shame and guilt. He thought about Natalie and the kids. He felt guilty that he lied to Natalie about what he remembered. He wanted, so bad, to take advantage of this 'second chance' that he was willing to give up the memory of his three children in order to do so. He was so sure that was what he wanted. He felt that the only thing between him and his freedom, as he saw it, was the memory of his family and, of course, God.

The ride to the station turned out to be a long one. Benjamin started hearing Leesha's voice calling him, again, but the craziness didn't end there. He started having visions: all the moments of fear, moments of anger, and those emotions just seemed to manifest themselves into his reality. But it wasn't until he could see the faces of the men that he served with in Iraq, in 2004, that he really felt a strong sense of melancholy. Those visions and dreams haunted him so dramatically that he went many nights without sleep. It affected him -all of him- and his wife and children saw every bit of his suffering. It was post-traumatic stress disorder to the max, and it had a grip on him. Benjamin was lost in his confusion.

The war hadn't happened, yet. It wasn't 2004; it was 2000. Shouldn't that make it all better? Why am I still haunted by things that haven't happened, yet?? Was it real? Had it happened?

Is this real?? Any of this???

CHAPTER 27

As the engagement ended, Natalie and Carmella walked through some tables where there were Dorothy CDs being sold, along with cool shirts labeled with encouraging Bible verses for women.

"Hey, Natalie, I am going to go look at that stuff to see what I can buy."

"Okay," Natalie responded as she pulled her Bible from her purse. "Take your time. I'm just gonna sit here on these stairs and read my Bible for a bit…until we leave."

"Would you like something from the tables?"

"No, thank you, Carmella."

"Okay, girl! Don't go anywhere!"

Natalie could only giggle at Carmella's comical response. There was something different about Carmella's demeanor, though; something that pushed its' way through her bubbly personality. It was almost like she was trying too hard to remain upbeat. Natalie knew what was on Carmella's mind.

What must Carmella think of me? How will I explain what happened in there?

"Hey," Natalie called as Carmella turned toward the tables.

"Yeah," Carmella responded, turning back around to see Natalie.

"Thank you…for this. Thank you…for…all of this."

"You are welcome, girl!"

Carmella lit up with a smile as she walked back over to Natalie and gave her a hug.

"You are most certainly welcome, girl! Just please don't forget that I am your BFF! You won't forget that, will you?"

NOT PRESENT OR FUTURE...

"Never!!"

After a hug that seemed to last an eternity, Carmella darted for the tables. Natalie watched as Carmella moved through the line of ladies, looking to buy Dorothy's CDs and memorabilia. Natalie looked around and, for a brief moment, she closed her eyes.

Thank you, Lord, she prayed, inside. *Thank you for bringing me here, tonight!*

"And how are you?"

Natalie looked up to see an incredible, unbelievable sight. There was Dorothy, standing right in front of her.

"Uh," Natalie responded as she struggled to come to her feet.

"Oh, sit down, child. I didn't mean to bother ya."

Dorothy had the most beautiful southern-belle accent, and her personality captivated Natalie.

"I'm Dorothy. Dorothy Morris."

Dorothy also possessed a cunning way to make a comical scene of the situation, making Natalie laugh as she tried to respond.

"Yes, Ma'am! You are. My name is Natalie J—uh."

Natalie caught herself, again. She almost gave her married name and stumbled to recover from that.

"Natalie...what? Girl, I knew you looked frazzled, but I have to admit: I have never met anyone who didn't know their last name."

"It's 'Barnes'," Natalie laughed. "Natalie Barnes. It is nice to meet you, Miss Dorothy."

Natalie reached out to shake Dorothy's hand.

"And it is nice to meet you!"

The light in her demeanor made Natalie feel warm and comforted.

"So, child, what is going on with you, tonight?"

"Well...obviously I am here with you."

They both laughed.

"Oh, aren't you funny, child? You are funny. But what I mean is... what is going on with you, tonight?"

For some reason, Natalie began feeling somewhat conflicted inside. Dorothy had Natalie's attention, as she sat down, just a few stairs below Natalie.

"Well, Ma'am, I am not…sure."

Dorothy could see the emotional wall. Natalie was not that difficult to read.

"Child, every time I do one of these events, I always pray that God will show me someone who needs encouragement. For some reason, tonight, I kept noticing you. I noticed you when you raised your hand and when you brought it down. I also noticed your sense of hesitation -when raising your hand- when I asked certain questions."

Now she really had Natalie's attention.

"Questions like, 'Do you love your husband?'"

Natalie felt, in some weird way, like she was being cornered. She didn't know what to say. Her heart started racing, but she didn't know why. She cherished the opportunity to get to talk with Dorothy, as this was clearly a surprise, but she was so afraid that Dorothy could never understand her situation.

"Honestly, Ma'am, I'm not sure you would understand. I'm not sure I understand what is going on in my life right now."

"Let me guess: you woke up one morning and realized that things are way out of control. You feel like you are living a completely different life than you want to, and you feel like you don't even know who you are any more. You have no idea how you got here. Nothing makes sense. What was…is no more. And what shouldn't be…is. Is that about right?"

Um, okay, Natalie thought. *Was this lady reading my mind?*

"Miss Dorothy, I know that you probably hear this a lot, but I actually can't explain what is going on in my life. And you are correct: I am not sure I even understand it myself."

Natalie became emotional as tears began to fill her eyes. But with a slight pause, she tried to gather herself.

"Go on," Dorothy responded.

Natalie tried to think about how she was going to explain it. Then she just let it out the best way she knew how.

"I had a husband and three beautiful children. But my husband and I fought all the time. We fought *all* the time. We became so bitter toward each other, and resented each other. I just got to the point that I felt no love for him."

Natalie paused for a moment to wipe the tears.

"Then, one night we got into it, and he told me that he wanted to go back and just start all over; that I had just wasted his life."

This time, she was so emotional that she could hardly speak.

"He told me that he wished he could go back. He told me that he prayed he could go back. And I wanted to as well. God help me, Miss Dorothy, I wanted to start over. I wanted all that to end— not my kids; not the memories of my kids— but I wanted rid of my husband. I wanted to start over. And now…now I feel like I lost everything."

By this time she was weeping. Dorothy put her hand on Natalie's knee in comfort. Natalie just let it out.

"I had it all, Miss Dorothy. I was married, and I had my children. But I agreed with my husband that I wanted a second chance.

"But…"

Natalie paused and looked at Dorothy.

"But now that I am here, I have realized that having a second chance isn't always what it seems to be. You would think that I would be happy. Everyone wants a chance to start over. But, honestly, how to you unlearn what you have learned? How do you un-love what you loved? How do you miss someone so much that you feel like you had, but you never had?"

Dorothy listened intently as Natalie spoke, and it looked like Natalie was spent.

"How do…you…?"

Natalie couldn't say any more. She just didn't know what else to say. Dorothy remained patient, but interested. She prayed before she responded.

"Child, one of the biggest lies that couples live with is the lie that, if our marriages don't work the first time, that, somehow, we can just get another chance."

Dorothy paused for a moment and looked around the room.

"Look at these women, Natalie."

Natalie wiped her tears and looked up, as Dorothy continued.

"Many women, just like these many women that I have talked to and encouraged over the years, fell into the lie that they could just start over and have another chance if their marriages failed. It happens all the time. 'I married the wrong man,' some would say. 'We were never meant to be together,' others would say. 'We just fell out of love.' 'We were not right for each other.' 'He was not the right person.' On and on, more women told me their stories, and do you know, child..."

Dorothy looked back at Natalie.

"Do you know what they all had in common?"

Natalie shook her head.

"They were all broken. All these women were broken inside. Their hearts were broken. And they all suffered a broken life because of their broken hearts. Some of them had husbands that were abusive, and some had husbands that left them for other women. Some of them had husbands that passed away. And some of them lost their marriages because they, themselves, did something to cause the demise in their own marriages."

Dorothy sighed with a sense of pity, just before continuing.

"Some women -many of them, actually- told me about the times they fell into temptation and were led away from their husbands by another man. They carry that guilt, and it is a tough weight to bear. But no matter what; no matter how they lost their husbands...no matter what, all the women were broken."

Natalie sat there, overwhelmed with the guilt of her own affair. It was just one night, but it didn't matter. She felt so sorrowful and ashamed, even though, technically, she could just chalk that incident off as it never happened because, realistically, it hadn't...yet.

But that didn't stop the shame she felt.

"Now, Natalie, I am not saying that a woman can't have a second chance at marriage. God gives us a second chance...all the time. Many women may need that second chance. But what I am saying is that we are tempted, sometimes, with the lie that all we need is a second chance when God can still work in the lives of the struggling marriages the first time. When a man and a woman, who have struggled in their marriage, just give up, wishing they were able to have a second chance, then it becomes a lie. You carry it with you, child: the emotions, the partnership, the love, the oneness, the kids…everything. You will always carry it with you."

That hurt. Natalie did carry it with her, and she could not escape it. It didn't matter when it happened.

"I have seen women get married to the perfect husband, with the perfect wedding, and have no reason to believe that they wouldn't make it…fall completely apart in divorce. I have seen two people, who I just knew were perfect for each other, end up in divorce. You know, it's those types of situations where you are just scratching your head, trying to figure out what happened."

Dorothy paused.

"And I have seen people get married for the wrong reasons. People who, for whatever reason, should have never gotten married but did. I have seen people who were in abusive relationships, married to godless spouses, and in every other way, these marriages had no logical way to survive…until God got a hold of them and changed them."

Natalie looked up at Dorothy.

"That's the real secret, child. God can save any marriage, no matter how bad it is. If both husband and wife are willing to come together before Him, and repent and commit to serving one another, then the marriage can be saved. That is when you will see God at work."

Natalie couldn't say anything. She was even more convinced that she should fight for Benjamin and for their marriage, whether they had it or not. Every word that came out of Dorothy's mouth turned to gold for Natalie.

"Natalie, I want to tell you something. A woman holds the greatest treasure on earth; the treasure that all men want, and it is ours to give to whomever we choose. And contrary to popular opinion, it has nothing to do with sex."

Dorothy repositioned herself on the steps.

"Inside every woman is the absolute passion, compassion, and love that can only be found in a woman. That is how God made us, Natalie. That is the treasure. It is a beautiful thing, and as women, we seek the attention of the one to whom we desperately want to give that treasure to."

Dorothy paused with a sense of concern.

"And sometimes the attention we seek is from someone who we really should stay away from. We women can be lightheaded at times, relying on our emotions to guide us when we really need to be relying on God."

Natalie agreed with her.

"Think about it this way: what is your relationship with your father like, child?"

"I loved my dad. He was so very good to me. I guess I was a 'daddy's girl'. He would have done anything for me."

"Now, if your earthly father loved you that much, Natalie, that you were his little girl; his 'daddy's girl', how much more do you think your Father in Heaven loves you?"

Dorothy positioned herself again to face Natalie.

"Child, your Heavenly Father loves you so much that when you were born He was crazy about you. Shoot, He made you! You are his daughter, and you are Daddy's little girl to Him just as much as you are to your earthly father. Don't you think He knows what's best for you?"

"Yes."

"Don't you think that, when you are in trouble, or someone tries to hurt you, your Heavenly Father would be so angry that someone would hurt 'His little girl' that He would send a fleet of angels to fight for you?

"I suppose He would, Ms. Dorothy."

"You suppose?"

Natalie tried wiping the tears from her eyes, but now they were flowing faster than she could wipe them.

"Child, what's going on in there?"

"I feel so guilty and so ashamed," Natalie responded, doing all she could do to hold herself together. "Dorothy, I had an affair. It was only one night, but it haunts me every day. It haunted me while I was with my…Ben…"

Natalie paused mid-sentence, and had to catch her breath before she could continue.

"I feel so guilty. I feel haunted. I can't get over it. I am just broken over it. And most of all, I feel like God would not want to give me a second chance at screwing up again."

"Natalie, can I ask you something? Did you ask God to forgive you?"

"Yes. I begged Him to forgive me."

"Did anyone else know about this affair?"

"No, I was so ashamed of what I had done that I never told anyone. The only ones who know about this are God and me."

"God, you…and the great accuser."

"Ma'am," Natalie responded, perplexed.

"Natalie, the reason you are haunted with this is because you are being tormented by the great accuser. He has nothing to do but accuse you, blame you, and constantly tell you that you are never going to be good enough."

Dorothy repositioned herself on the step. The steps were a bit more uncomfortable than she had realized, initially.

"Natalie, while I was fixated on blaming my husband for my bad marriage, I, myself, strayed away. I made one decision, and it affected me for a long time. I prayed for God's forgiveness. I begged for it, as you did. I never felt that He would ever forgive me. I struggled over it more and more. Like you, I thought I could hide it. Sure, God knew, and He forgave me. But I never forgave myself. It affected my marriage and my relationship with my children. I fell into a deep depression. One day, as I was praying, I heard the accusations, again. I called out to Jesus to help me, and then at that moment, something happened. I stood up to that accusing 'snake,' and I responded to him. I said to him, 'I am glad that you know what I did. But God knows it too, and He forgave me. Now get away from me you accusing snake.'"

Dorothy looked right at Natalie.

"What I am saying, Natalie, is that God knows what you have done. He knows what I did. And when I hear the words of that 'serpent' telling me what I've done, I remind him that God knows what

I've done too, and He forgave me. My sins are as far as the east is from the west. Hallelujah!"

Natalie wiped the tears from her eyes as she understood the reality of what Dorothy was communicating to her.

"So you see, child, God's love does not stop because you sin. He loves you through it. It doesn't mean that you don't face the consequences, but you are still forgiven. And that is when the healing truly begins. Through His love for you, God still protects you. You are still His daughter."

Dorothy took a breath, and took Natalie's hand.

"Now, child, it doesn't always happen that way. Sometimes God allows things to happen to us, even when we pray for His divine intervention. But I can assure you that when you are hurt, when His little girls get hurt, He will let his anger be seen, and somebody will feel it."

Natalie chuckled again as Dorothy made that last statement, comically.

"Natalie, your Heavenly Father wants you to trust Him. He wants you to trust him with your secrets. He wants you to trust him with your life. He wants you to trust Him with your marriage. He wants you to trust Him with your future. It is hard for us to do, but knowing that He is our Father, shouldn't we be willing to trust Him when it comes to whom we should marry as well?"

"Yes, Ma'am."

"Yes, Ma'am, indeed!"

Dorothy looked around to see the other women in the room buying souvenirs as they both chuckled again.

"Natalie, let me ask you one more thing. Do you know what scares a man?"

"No, Ma'am," Natalie replied, curious of Dorothy's question.

"I mean: what really haunts a man?"

"No, Ma'am."

"Men are strange and fickle creatures, Natalie. They are charged with so much, and they mostly feel like they have to play their role, alone. Is there something that haunts your husband?"

Natalie was shocked. She began to think that Dorothy had been reading her mind. Dorothy was serious, and Natalie could see it.

"Well," Dorothy pressed.

"There are…were…many things that haunted Benjamin, and many times I felt hopeless to help him."

"So what did you do, child?"

"What do you mean?"

"What did you do for your husband, knowing he was being haunted?"

"Well, I…"

Natalie was stuck. This was turning into an interesting conversation.

"Did you pray for him?"

"Always," Natalie responded.

"Did you love him?"

Again, that was the million-dollar question. Natalie looked down, almost in shame. Dorothy just let her presence be silent, but felt.

"Natalie, there are good men out there and there are bad men out there. I have seen many a woman put to shame, hurt, used, abused…and that is not how women are to be treated. Men have turned away from God and have lost the ability to love their wives. But I will tell you this; if you have a husband that has tried to work with you, pray with you, live with you, and love you, then I say: go and fight for him! Fight for your family! Fight for your future! You, Natalie, take a hold of your marriage and let God save it! Do you understand, child?"

"Yes," Natalie responded, trying to not get any more emotional than she already was.

"And when it gets bad, and you feel like you are drowning, then call out to Jesus! Call out to Him, Natalie, and let Him go through your storm with you. Hold on tight to Jesus! Jesus will either calm the storm, or calm you while you are going through it. Marriages can be powerful storms. Sail those seas with Jesus. Do you understand, child?"

"Yes," Natalie replied, still wiping away the tears.

"Good! Then let's pray, child, so I can go encourage someone else."

Again, Natalie giggled as she held Dorothy's hand. Dorothy prayed for Natalie, then gave her a hug.

"God bless you, child! I will be praying for you."

"Thank you, Dorothy! Thank you for everything!"

Dorothy held her hand, once more, before moving into the crowd. Natalie waited for Carmella to finish shopping, then they both left the building.

CHAPTER 28

Natalie knew what she had to do. She had not felt this focused in a long time. It wasn't just from her time spent talking with Dorothy. It was everything: her memories, her children, her dreams, her… husband.

My husband.

She smiled at the thought of him. She desired him. She loved him. There were no words for the feelings she had. She made her decision: she was going after him. In her heart and soul, she had already made her covenant with Benjamin…whether this time or a time yet coming. He was her husband, and she was his wife. They had experienced it all, already. It was all hers: the arguments, the fights, the struggles. But she also realized the other things that were hers: the warmth of his touch, the way he made her feel, the experience of childbirth, the reality that she was a part of him.

God had made them one. It couldn't be erased; she was going to see to that.

Natalie walked briskly to the car, along with Carmella.

"Natalie, what is going on with you?"

Natalie knew it was coming. She noticed Carmella's demeanor during the event. Natalie contemplated the crazy explanation that she was going to have to give as to why she raised her hand when Dorothy asked about women who weren't loving their husbands.

Somehow, she knew this was coming.

When Carmella approached her car, she unlocked it with her keychain remote, and they both climbed in. Natalie quickly put on her seatbelt, still riding high on the spiritually emotional kite that she was experiencing.

Carmella just sat there, staring at the steering wheel. Natalie could do nothing but look down at the floor board.

"Carmella, thank you for—"

"For what," Carmella interrupted. "I just have one question, Natalie. What was that in there? Are you…married?"

Natalie didn't know how to respond to that.

"Natalie, look at me."

Natalie looked up at Carmella and noticed that Carmella's eyes began to tear up.

"Carmella, I'm sorry, I don't know how to explain…"

"Explain…what…exactly? Explain what? Are you married, or aren't you?"

Natalie looked down at the floorboard, again. She could not understand why Carmella was so emotional. But then she realized: Carmella was her bridesmaid…at her wedding.

But there was no wedding.

Crap! How will I explain this?

"Natalie, did you go off and get married? When did this happen? Was it with Benjamin? Who…what…"

Carmella was becoming more upset. She took a deep breath before she continued.

"I am supposed to be your best friend, Natalie! Would you please tell me what is going on?"

Natalie contemplated her situation. She was really getting tired of trying to explain this, as it still didn't make sense to her. She sat there and prayed while Carmella waited for a response.

"Don't you have anything to say to me?"

Natalie stayed silent, praying about how to respond to her best friend's concerns.

"Okay," Carmella commented, while turning the key to start the car.

"Yes."

"Yes…what?"

Carmella went to put the car in reverse when Natalie replied, again.

NOT PRESENT OR FUTURE...

"Yes."

Natalie reached over and touched Carmella's arm. She was about to do the craziest thing in the world: she was just going to tell Carmella everything, or, at least, she would give it a noble effort.

They sat in the parking lot, talking, as the lot became emptier. Natalie did the best she could to try to explain the whole thing to Carmella, but making it sound like her life was a long dream that she just woke up from. Throughout the conversation, Carmella listened intently, with the occasional generic concluding statement from Natalie.

"Please try not to be upset or think I am crazy."

Natalie talked and talked, and about the time she was finished, all she could think to divulge was the simple truth.

"Carmella, when you asked me if I was married, all I can tell you is that, yes, I am. I made a commitment and a covenant with Benjamin. We have not had a wedding ceremony, and we have not lived as a married couple, yet, but Benjamin is my husband; at least, I hope that he will still be. He is my choice, Carmella, and I must go after him. Please tell me that, in some crazy way, you understand."

Carmella just stared at the steering wheel, clearly not knowing how to process what she heard. She was too tired and confused, at that moment, to try to comprehend anything. But she loved Natalie, and she trusted her. Carmella responded in a manner that only she could.

"Can I still be your maid of honor when the time comes?"

"Absolutely," Natalie laughed, relieved to see this side of her best friend. "I wouldn't have it any other way!"

They sat in the parking lot just a few more minutes, laughing and carrying on, when Carmella made sure that the car was still on. She put the car in 'drive', exited the parking lot, and took off down the road.

"So what are you going to do now, Natalie?"

"I am going to get in my car and drive to Amarillo! I am going to trade my car with my mother's and go after my husband! I figure I can take some stuff to my mother's house, and…"

"Tonight," Carmella interrupted. "You are going to leave… tonight? It's nearly one o'clock in the morning."

It is one in the morning, Natalie thought. *Man, where did the time go?*

Dorothy Morris's speaking event ended about nine, and Natalie and Dorothy visited, in the center for about thirty minutes or so, afterward. Then Natalie and Carmella talked in Carmella's car for a couple of hours.

Wow! Carmella is right. It's late.

Carmella and Natalie were about a mile away from Natalie's apartment complex when Carmella brought up the time, again.

"Natalie, it is just too late. Why don't you just come spend the night? You know Momma loves it when you come over, and at the least, we can talk a little while longer. You can rest before you leave, later on in the morning."

"Well…you know, I think that would be a great idea. I mean, it is late. I am very tired, and we have not hung out in a while. Can't promise I'll stay awake."

"Great," Carmella responded as she drove right past Natalie's apartment complex, and straight to her house.

"Hey…um…I have to stop by and get my night stuff."

"What stuff do you need, girl? I've got tons of 'PJ's' you can borrow, if you need to."

There really wasn't any reason to go by the apartment, so Natalie didn't protest.

"Well, then, let's go!"

While Carmella and Natalie were about five minutes from Carmella's home, Natalie thought that she should have stopped by her apartment to check her answering machine, at least. She kept looking for her cell phone, instinctively, before realizing that they were just coming out, and she didn't have one, yet.

"I also thought I should have gone by my apartment to check my answering machine, Carmella. I thought I might have a message from—"

"Who?"

"You know who," Natalie laughed. "Lately, though, the only messages I've been getting are ones I don't want."

"Really? You mean, like, from Darnell?"

"Yes," Natalie responded in disgust. "He has been harassing me so much, lately. I can't stand it! I was hoping that the one message I did get was from Benjamin."

"Maybe it is…him," Carmella teased with a flirtatious look.

"I should be so lucky."

Natalie knew that Carmella was talking about Benjamin, and the very thought of him made her desperate to want to talk to him even more. She wanted to call him, if only just to hear his voice. As she considered her situation with Darnell, she hesitated, almost in fear. Carmella could see the change in Natalie's demeanor.

"Natalie, what's up? Are you O.K.?"

"I think I need to get away from here. And I mean, fast!"

"Why, what is it? Is it…him?"

"I just have this feeling of fear coming over me when I think about Darnell. We've had our problems, Benjamin and I, but he would never act the way Darnell does."

"I'll help you, girl. By the way, what did you ever see in Darnell?"

"I honestly don't know."

Natalie could not remember why she dated Darnell before Benjamin came back into her life. She could not remember what the attraction was. It was becoming evident to her why she decided to break up with him, though.

But how did I ever get away from Darnell?

She had to think about it.

By this time, Benjamin and I were well engaged. But that was, well, in another time. I left Abilene once I graduated, and never thought about Darnell again. Then, later on, Carmella told me about that incident he was involved in when he assaulted that girl…

As Carmella pulled into her parents' house, Natalie snapped back to reality as she and Carmella got out of the car. As they walked up the driveway to the porch, Carmella put the keys in the door and looked over to Natalie.

"Movie night?"

"Girl, as much as I hate to say it, I am so tired. But we will do it again, sometime soon. I need to get some sleep so I can hit the road to Amarillo, tomorrow."

"Okay," Carmella responded, slightly disappointed.

Natalie went inside the living room and sat down on the couch.

Carmella's mother had already put out the blankets and pillows for Natalie.

"I guess I'll see you in the morning," Carmella sighed as she stood at the hallway entrance.

"Okay. Good night, girl. I'll take a rain check on the movie. I promise! I love ya, girl."

"Love ya too, girl."

Carmella went to her bedroom and closed the door. Natalie sat on the couch, thinking about the day she had. She was so exhausted, and she had a long drive ahead of her, later on that morning.

She caught up in her thoughts about Benjamin. She wanted to call him, but assumed he would be at work, and she had no idea how to get ahold of him while he was at work. She wished that cell phones were more accessible at that moment. Her heart yearning for Benjamin, she slumped into the couch, pulled the covers over her, and quickly fell to sleep.

CHAPTER 29

"Daddy? Daddy, where are you?"

Leesha's voice grew intense with panic the more Benjamin heard it. He tried to ignore it; trying to tell himself that it wasn't real. He wasn't awake, but he wasn't asleep, either.

Or am I?

"Daddy, why did you leave me?"

Benjamin struggled in his rest, tossing and turning. He felt a grip of something that seemed to have him pinned down to the point where he could not move, and could not breathe. Then, there was another voice that entered his presence.

"Jones? Jones, why did you leave us?"

Benjamin could hear the voices, and though they sounded familiar, the feeling that he got when the voices spoke was of sheer terror.

"Jones, why did you leave us? Why did you let us die?"

Benjamin couldn't talk. He couldn't respond. He couldn't escape.

"Wake up, Benjamin! Wake up! Wake up! Please wake up!"

"But you are awake, Benjamin."

Benjamin felt nothing but absolute fear. That voice was not familiar to him. It was not like anything he had ever heard before. In fact, it was an evil voice, one that was accompanied by an overwhelming sense of dread. Benjamin felt like he was in a state of nothingness. He had never experienced anything like this before. He just could not escape it.

"Benjamin, wake up! Wake up!"

"You are awake, Benjamin. You are awake, and you are very afraid. I know what you fear, and I know what grips you."

Benjamin finally realized that this was not anything he had ever experienced. Not all his years of military training could have prepared him for this. He was truly afraid, and he just didn't know what to do.

"I want you to leave me alone!"

"We can't."

This time, it sounded like many voices speaking in unison.

"What do you want from me?"

"You know what we want."

"No, I don't," Benjamin cried.

"Yes, you do."

The voices were scary and deep. They surrounded Benjamin, invading his very presence of being.

"I want you to leave me alone!!"

"It's no use, Benjamin. We aren't going anywhere."

"Go away!"

"We want something from you."

"No! Go away!"

"We will never go away, Benjamin. We will always be here."

"I said, 'leave me alone!'"

"Benjamin, we want something."

Benjamin felt a sense of defeat. He didn't know what else to do.

"What do you want?"

"We want…you."

"No," Benjamin screamed. "You can't have me!"

"Yes, we can. And, yes, we will. We will never stop, Benjamin."

"No! Leave me alone!"

"We have taken stronger men than you, Benjamin. We will get you, too."

"No!"

"You will give us what we want."

"No!"

"We will get what we want from you, Benjamin."

"Go away!!"

NOT PRESENT OR FUTURE...

"You will be next. One way or another, we will get you."

Benjamin panicked, as he was overcome with defeat, despair, pain, sorrow...just about every negative emotion and feeling he could imagine. He had tried to defeat this feeling, on his own, before.

"Calm yourself, Benjamin. What would a Marine do?"

"You think because you are a Marine that you can stop us? We told you: we've taken many before you."

Benjamin looked up and saw something he could not explain. He saw a room with a man sitting alone, in the dark, crying and praying while waving a gun around. There were pictures of soldiers on one wall and an Army poster on the other wall.

"Hey," Benjamin called out. "Hey, are you okay?"

The man acted as if he could not hear Benjamin. He just sat in this room and cried. Benjamin walked up to the man when suddenly the man put the gun to his head and pulled the trigger.

"No!" Benjamin screamed, as the man fell to the floor from the gunshot wound to his head.

"No, no..." Benjamin cried as he shook his head.

Benjamin looked around and saw more and more visions of men and women taking their own lives. They weren't only Marines; there were soldiers, sailors, airmen, some civilians...all war-torn victims. The visions were graphic. Some of them showed family members crying around their lost loved ones while others showed family members lying motionless next to their lost loved ones. It was too much for Benjamin to bear.

"We told you, Benjamin. We got them...all of them. And we will get you, too."

Benjamin was paralyzed in fear at that last statement. In the brief calmness of his mind, Benjamin realized he could not fight this alone. No combat training could ever prepare him for this. There was only one thing Benjamin could do, and he knew it. Surrounded by visions of death and dread, he fell to his knees.

"Jesus, please help..."

"Benjamin, what are you doing? We won't quit."

"Jesus, I call on you! I call on Your Name! Please help me."

"We know where you are, Benjamin. You can't run from us."

"Your Name is a strong and mighty tower, Lord! I will run into it! Jesus, please save me!!"

Benjamin did not know what else to say, as all he could do was call on Jesus.

"Jesus, please…"

"No you don't!"

"Ugghhh!"

Pain shot through his body as Benjamin yelled, jumping from whatever he was laying on. He looked around to find a dark cell with a light on in the hallway. His heart was racing, he was sweating all over, and he was breathing heavily. His soul was overwhelmed by a presence that he could feel, and that made the cell seem even darker.

"Mr. Jones," came a voice near the jail cell door.

Benjamin looked over to see a police officer standing there.

"Mr. Jones, there is someone here to take you home."

"What?"

"You've got a visitor…who's come to take you home."

Benjamin looked up as if to see who would come around the corner.

Maybe it's Ricky.

Honestly, Benjamin didn't know who would be willing to even show up to see him while he was in jail. The officer looked back behind him, then looked back at Benjamin.

"Uh, Mr. Jones, we are not supposed to do this, but since you are leaving, I'll leave the door open. We're not charging you for anything. Just go on home."

Then the officer turned to the person behind the corner.

"Sir, Mr. Jones is in here. Once you guys are done talking, just come get me at the desk and I will let you both out."

Benjamin sat there on the cot, still wondering who it was that came to get him. As he looked down to grab his shoes, he heard the footsteps of this visitor. He looked up to find that it was Brian.

"Brian?"

NOT PRESENT OR FUTURE...

Benjamin stood up, still trying to collect himself. Brian was the last person he expected to see.

"It's okay, Ben. Just relax."

Ben sat down, shaking his head in disbelief as he considered his predicament. He put his hands in his head.

"How are you doin', brother," Brian asked, sitting down on the cot next to Benjamin.

Benjamin didn't know what to say. He was still struggling, emotionally, from his dream. He tried to catch his breath and shake off the fear that seemed to overtake him.

"Brian, I don't know what to say. I've…I've really screwed up this time."

Benjamin became emotional.

"I am so sorry, man…"

Brian just sat there and listened, displaying his patient manner, as Benjamin sighed while trying to collect himself.

It didn't take. Benjamin lost it.

"I just don't know what is going on with me, Brian. I am so confused. I can't explain what is going on. If I try to do so, you will only think I'm crazy. I…I…"

Benjamin stopped as he didn't know how to communicate what was going on in his mind.

"I feel like I am being haunted. I feel like I can't escape these feelings that I can't explain. I…I…."

Benjamin looked up at Brian and said the only thing he knew to say to him.

"Brian, will you forgive me?"

Benjamin became emotional, again.

"Please, Brian? Please forgive me for the way I acted?"

"I do forgive you, Benjamin, but it's not necessary. You really didn't do anything wrong."

Brian sighed as he contemplated his next statement.

"Ben, I am not sure what has been going on with you. You have seemed a bit different since you came home from the Marines. But lately, especially after the Chik-filet incident, you just seem to really be struggling."

Brian's voice was patient and calming, and though Benjamin appreciated it, he still held his head low in shame.

"Benjamin, I have to tell you something. The other day, Samantha and her parents were in my office, and while they were there, we asked Samantha several questions about what happened the other night at the Chik-filet. I want to tell you what she said."

Brian paused for a moment to reposition himself on the cot.

"Benjamin, we asked Samantha why she did not leave with the other kids; why she stayed in the restaurant, knowing how dangerous it was for her. Do you know what she said?"

Benjamin looked up at him.

"She said that she stayed because she was praying for you the whole time, and she felt like she needed to stay there, with you."

Benjamin shook his head.

"We then asked her if she was afraid, and she said that she was not afraid because she knew that you were going to protect her. Samantha believed that God put you there to protect her. That is what she told us."

Benjamin cried, even more, as Brian continued.

"Samantha was telling us all about what she saw, and how she perceived what happened. She said that, while you were fighting that gunman, she could have sworn that she saw flashes of things around you, fighting you and getting mad at you. She said the more she saw, the harder she prayed for you. She also described how, when the gunman looked at her, she saw your face and noticed the fear you had on your face. She said that she prayed even harder at that moment."

Benjamin could hardly control his tears.

"And when we asked her about why she told you to stop, she said that she yelled at you because the look you had in your eyes when you were hitting the gunman while he was on the ground was different than the look you had in your eyes when you were trying to get him down. Samantha said that she thought she was losing you, and she wanted you to stay with her. We didn't understand what she was telling us, at first, until she explained it, further."

Brian paused again, taking a deep breath.

"Benjamin, I want to be sure that you understand what I am saying. Samantha saw you fighting that gunman, and she knew you were protecting her, but she got to a point to where she did not recognize you. She prayed that God would help you overcome the gunman, and then she prayed that God would keep you from losing yourself. That is absolutely incredible, as it is profound, coming from a twelve-year-old little girl."

Benjamin wiped his eyes.

"A twelve-year-old little girl…who absolutely adores you," Brian continued as he leaned in to get a little closer to Benjamin. "What is even more spectacular about Samantha is not what she said, Benjamin, it is what she didn't say. She didn't say that you were a monster. She didn't say that she was afraid of you. In fact, she calls you 'God's Marine'."

"What?"

Benjamin looked up at Brian, perplexed.

"Yeah, that's what Samantha calls you now: 'God's Marine'."

Benjamin smiled a little, while running his fingers through his hair. Brian sat up, straightening his back a little, took another deep breath, and continued.

"Benjamin, I need to tell you something. You are a great youth sponsor. The kids love you so much, and they appreciate the passion and the time that you invest in their lives. They all love you, Benjamin: the football players, the basketball players, the baseball players, the Bible bowlers— all of them. They don't care what color your skin is. They don't care what you have done in your life. They DO care that you love them enough to fight for them, as you did the other night."

Brian paused.

"They connect with you. You are young enough to reach them, but old enough to gain their trust and their respect. Raymond loves having you as a sponsor because of your commitment to him. He needs you. You have really become his right-hand man…in so many ways. I would think that has become very evident. I can't tell you how much we, as a church, have really enjoyed having you there.

And I know many families who are more than grateful that you have been there."

Brian took a breath.

"Benjamin, you have value, here, at the church. You have value in this world. I just wish I knew what it was that was holding you down; what it was that troubles you. I have been praying for you for a while, and I know that God is trying to communicate something to me about you, but I can't figure it out."

Then it came; the question that Benjamin was afraid to be asked.

"Ben, what is going on in your life?"

What could Benjamin say? He was married with kids. He had a house and a good job. He got into a fight with his wife and told her that he was so disappointed in his relationship that he wanted to start completely over. He told her that if he had another chance, he never would have asked her to marry him. He had even asked God to give him another chance and let him start over. Then Benjamin wakes up the next morning, only to find that it is fifteen years earlier and Benjamin is back in his old apartment, not married, at a time that would have been about one month after they would have become engaged!

Really? Is that I'm going to say to Brian?

"Brian, I don't know what to say. I don't know how to tell you what is going on because it is so crazy that you really, really would not get it. I just…I just…"

Benjamin paused, trying not to become emotional.

"I just feel so broken inside."

Benjamin shook his head, and even started to laugh. He calmed down and sighed again, before he continued.

"Brian, it's like, being angry at someone who is not there, or wanting to hold someone who was there, and then is no longer there."

Benjamin paused.

"That sounded crazy, I know. But it's also like trying to live a life that is a lie, only the truth is it does not exist, yet. It's like I am haunted by things that are not real while trying to figure out what is real."

Again, Benjamin cracked up in a laugh. He really did not know how to explain this.

"And most importantly, Brian, I asked for this. I wanted another chance, and I got it. And now that I got it, I can't shake the memories. I can't shake the feelings. I can't…I can't shake the feeling that this life I have is the lie, and the truth is somewhere out there."

Benjamin shook his head, again and looked over at Brian, who possessed a puzzling look on his face.

"It's crazy, Brian. I told you it was."

Brian did not know what to say, as he could not understand what Benjamin was going through. How could he? Brian was a chaplain in the Navy but never had to deploy to any combat zones. Benjamin was gone for a while in the Marines, then came home, helped with the youth group for about eight months, then started acting a little strange for, what Brian understood was, no apparent reason.

Brian prayed for wisdom in his response.

"Benjamin, I heard of an ancient oriental proverb that I just absolutely love. It says that, 'one usually finds his destiny on the road he takes to avoid it.'"

He looked at Benjamin.

"I don't know what you are running from, but it is apparent that, whatever it is, you seem to be running in the wrong direction. I also wonder if whatever you are going through is pushing you to take orders back into the Marines."

Brian searched for the best words he could to continue.

"Now, you are not doing anything wrong, and your love for God is very evident -as is your faith- but you have something you need to do, and I am not sure that you could do it, here. But if it is here and this is where you are supposed to be, then I encourage you to keep working with Raymond and the kids. Your presence in the youth group is a blessing. If it is in Los Angeles with the Marines, then we would miss you, but so be it. But if there is something else you need to do, then by all means, go do it. I will pray for you every step of the way."

Benjamin realized that Brian said all he could, not knowing the feelings, emotions, and memories that he had bottled-up inside.

"Thank you, Brian," Benjamin responded. "Thank you for not being mad at me. I was ready to take the responsibility for actions, tonight."

"I just have one question, Ben: did you really tell God to stop loving you?"

"Oh, crap," Benjamin responded, putting his hands over his face.

"Because I gotta tell ya, brother: that was the boldest, craziest thing I have ever heard."

Brian stood up, giggling in amazement.

"Like I said, I really screwed up, Brian. Man, I really screwed up. I have been so angry about so many things…for so long, and I guess I get tired of feeling like I have to live for God. Sometimes I just want to do what I want to do, and it seems much easier to do that if you think that God doesn't love you. I guess that is the only way I can explain it."

Brian sat there, almost shocked at what he heard, but appreciative of Benjamin's honesty. The reality was that many people have been there.

"Benjamin, do you recall the Bible verse from Romans 8:38? It says, 'For I am convinced that neither death nor life, neither angels nor demons, neither the present nor the future, nor any powers, neither height nor depth, nor anything else in all creation, will be able to separate us from the love of God that is in Christ Jesus our Lord.' Benjamin that means that nothing can separate you from God's love; not even time. When you have Jesus, you have God's love. When you feel alone, God loves you. When you feel ashamed, God loves you. When you feel…broken, God loves you. I just don't want you to ever forget that, okay?"

Benjamin shook his head in agreement. Brian took this moment to try to uplift Benjamin's spirit.

"I guess it's a good thing God can't stop loving us, isn't it, 'Marine'?"

Brian smirked, trying to lighten the mood.

"Hey, there is one last thing, Ben. You said you felt 'broken.' In the future, when you feel that way, just look up Isaiah 53: 5–6. Read that, Benjamin. That verse is my power verse. You can make it yours, too. It is, perhaps, one of the most powerful verses in the Bible."

"What does it say?"

"Look it up, brother."

"I will," Benjamin replied.

"Now come on, 'Marine'. It's late. Let me give you a ride home."

Benjamin grabbed his jacket, smiling, as he walked out of the cold cell.

"I mean, isn't that what sailors do? We give you guys rides everywhere?"

They both laughed as they walked down the hall and out of the police station. Brian and Benjamin talked a little more on their way to Benjamin's house. Their conversation ended as Brian pulled up to the driveway. It would be another dark and lonely night for Benjamin, and before he got out of the car, Brian asked if he could pray for Benjamin. They prayed, and Benjamin exited the car.

"Thank you, Brian, for everything."

"You're welcome, brother."

Benjamin shut the car door and started walking away. Brian rolled down the passenger's side window to get Benjamin's attention.

"Hey, where's your pick-up?"

"Oh, man!!"

"Don't worry about it," Brian laughed. "I'll come by, tomorrow, before church, and take you to it."

"You don't have to do that, Brian, but thank you!"

"Well, just remember this, Benjamin: whatever happens out there; wherever you're going, you will stay safe, right?"

"I sure will, Brian," Benjamin responded, smiling back at Brian.

"Good! I'll see you in, about, eight hours," Brian joked.

Benjamin caught that. It was very late.

"Okay, Brian, I'll see you, soon," Benjamin laughed.

Brian took off as Benjamin walked to the house. As Benjamin unlocked the door, he felt alone. He made the decision to go to Los Angeles, and to deploy wherever the Marines were headed to, but he began to feel uncomfortable about it. It didn't matter, as far as he was concerned. He was leaving, and he was to pick up his orders, in just two days, before catching his flight to California.

He went through his bags to make sure that he had everything packed, and sat down on the couch. He was completely exhausted, as it had been long night. It was already 1:30. He felt guilty as he realized that Brian probably got out of bed to come get him out of jail.

It was a good thing I wasn't charged with anything.

The officer's just let him sleep it off. When thinking about that, Benjamin giggled. He really hadn't had that much to drink, had he? It didn't take much considering that he never, really, drank. He was very fortunate that this incident wasn't significant enough to interfere with his orders.

"That could have turned out a whole lot worse. Thank you, Lord."

As he sat there, contemplating on going to sleep, he couldn't help but think about the dreams he kept having about the kids. Also, for some reason, he really missed Natalie. He had to fight off the emotional longing that he had for her. He tried, for the past couple of weeks, to realize his blessing of getting another chance, only to be haunted by what he didn't have. He could not unlearn what he had learned. He could not just disregard all the memories. But he had a difficult time accepting that they were no longer real.

Were they? Ugh! I'm still going crazy thinking about this!

He needed some sleep. As he got up to go to bed, he glanced down at his phone. He felt this demanding need to call Natalie. But, if he did, what would he say? He lied to her. He has been lying to her this whole time.

He did remember everything. He did feel everything. He did miss the kids. He missed Natalie.

But, honestly, what does it matter now?

Still, he couldn't help but to think about her. It was early in the morning. Surely she would think him crazy for calling her.

This went on for about ten minutes before he decided that he could not just leave without saying good-bye. He felt he owed her that much. He picked up the phone and dialed her number, shaking his head.

"Please don't be mad? Please don't be mad? Please don't be mad?"

NOT PRESENT OR FUTURE...

The phone rang and rang, and the answering machine picked up.

"'Hi, this is Natalie. You know what to do.' Beeep."

She didn't answer. What do I say?

"Uh, Natalie, um, it's Benjamin. Hey, uh, I'm headed out, tomorrow, for Los Angeles, and um…well, I just wanted you to know that I was thinking about you. I didn't want to leave without saying good-bye. I'll keep in touch, okay? If you would like, I could give you my add—"

Beeep.

And just like that, it was over. Benjamin sighed.

It was probably for the best. She must hate me by now. Why shouldn't she? I got what I wanted: a fresh start.

Benjamin's heart sank. He had a lump in his throat. He straightened up and tried to pull himself together.

It doesn't matter anymore. I made my decision to go on orders. I am good at that: sternly making decisions for God and country.

Maybe that's part of the problem.

Benjamin set his alarm, climbed into bed, and went to sleep.

CHAPTER 30

The sun came up just as quickly as it went down. Natalie struggled to open her eyes as the sun came through the living room window. As tired as she was, she quickly jumped up and looked at the clock on the mantle above the fireplace.

7:28. Okay, I have to get up! Gotta wake up! Gotta get to Mom's!

She couldn't help but smile, inside, at the thought of seeing Benjamin again. However, the road to Tulsa went through Amarillo, and she needed to get moving. While thinking about Benjamin, Natalie's feelings of joy became quickly overshadowed with doubt.

Will he listen to me? Will he even give me a chance?

Their last meeting didn't go too well as Benjamin didn't act like he wanted anything to do with her. But she couldn't disregard their old life together. He tried to play it off as if he didn't remember it, but she knew him, and she could tell when he is hiding something.

After taking a shower and getting dressed, she grabbed her purse and went to Carmella's bedroom door. She knocked on it and opened it, slowly.

"Carmella I'm headed out, girl. Please pray for me as I make my trip to Amarillo…then to Tulsa."

"What time is it," Carmella asked, barely awake.

"It's about 7:45. I'll see you as soon as I get back!"

Briefly, Natalie thought about how much she appreciated the friendship that she had with Carmella. She felt that she needed to let Carmella know just how much she was appreciated. Just before Natalie left the room, she reached back through Carmella's bedroom door and gave her a whisper.

NOT PRESENT OR FUTURE...

"Carmella, thank you for everything! I could not have been able to get through this without you."

"You're welcome, girl. You just go do what you have to do. Call me if you need me. I'll be praying for you."

Natalie smiled and shut the door, quietly, trying not to wake Carmella's parents. She briskly walked to the front door, opened it, and walked outside. She turned to the driveway, looking for her car, before she realized that she didn't drive herself to Carmella's home.

Oh, no! What should I do? I can't drag Carmella out of bed just to give me a ride back to my apartment!

Natalie's apartment was five miles away, and it would be an interesting walk. It was a beautiful October morning, but still, Natalie was ready to get on the road. She thought about it for a second, turned and looked back at Carmella's house, then made her decision. It might take her about an hour or so, but she was going to walk it. As she started toward the sidewalk, the garage door opened. Natalie was stunned.

"Mr. Theodore?"

"Oh hey, Natalie! What are you doing up so early? I hope I didn't wake you."

"Oh no, Sir," she replied. "I was trying not to wake you."

She thought about it for a second and didn't recall hearing any noise from Carmella's parents' bedroom.

"What are you doing up so early, Mr. Theodore? Is it church time, already?"

"I am not going to church today. I've got a golf game at the Diamondback. T-off is at 8:30. Don't want to be late."

She then noticed he was in his plaid golfing shorts and his favorite collared shirt. He walked over and grabbed his clubs and placed them in the trunk of his car.

Natalie smiled. She loved Carmella's parents. They were always so good to her. Then she realized she hadn't told him why she was up and around.

"Mr. Theodore, I have to hit the road today, to Amarillo, to see my mom, and then I am heading to Tulsa. I got up early so I could leave, but I realized I didn't bring my car as I rode home with Carmella last night. And, well…"

She paused.

"Well, you better hop in," Theodore interrupted. "I'll run ya home."

"Thank you so much, Sir," she replied, thanking God for Theodore and his golf game.

While they were driving toward the apartment, Theodore broke the silence with the claims of how excited he was about his golf outings. Normally he played on Saturdays. But for some reason, his golf buddies were only able to get a T-time, this early in the morning, today.

"So what are you headed to Tulsa for? Is it that 'Marine' you're after?"

"Now, Mr. Theodore, how did you know about that?"

"Carmella told us what has been going on with you, and we've been prayin' for you at church. We've been prayin' that God will show you what He wants for you. Carmella has been keeping us updated."

Natalie felt so loved, and she felt more at peace every second. She really did appreciate Carmella, her parents, and the way they made her feel.

"Well, Sir, I do so much appreciate it. If you don't mind, I may need more prayers. I've realized -all this time- what I have been missing. I just hope that my 'Marine' realizes it, too."

"Is he a Godly man?"

"Yes, he is."

"Do you love him?"

She lit up at the thought of that question.

"Yes I do!"

Then Theodore asked the most peculiar question.

"Do you see yourself with him in twenty years, and with a family? Is he the one that you can't imagine growing old, without?"

That question caught Natalie by surprise, but in a good way. She burst in excitement and anticipation at the thought of his inquiries. The reality was…she had seen herself with Benjamin, and a family.

"Yes, Sir, I do!"

"Then go get him! We will be praying for you that God will be with you both, regardless of what happens."

Theodore pulled into the parking lot of Natalie's apartment, and as he turned toward her apartment building, he nearly had to slam on his breaks as a yellow Mustang sped in front of him, cutting him off, as it was leaving the parking lot. Natalie looked to see two guys in the front seat, but didn't recognize them.

"That was crazy," she stated, as they drove into the parking lot.

"Yes, it was. Is this your car?"

He pulled right up to her Chevy Lumina. She got out of the car and thanked Theodore for the ride. Theodore got her attention before she shut the door.

"Natalie?"

"Yes," she answered, looking back into the car.

"Do you remember the verse from 1 Corinthians 13:4? 'Love is patient and kind; it does not envy or boast; it is not arrogant or rude. It rejoices in the truth. It forgives all things, bears all things and hopes all things'?"

"Yes, Sir," Natalie responded, smiling.

"Don't ever forget that; not ever. So many people focus on trying to find the right person that they forget to be the right person. You go 'be' the right person, okay?"

"Yes, Sir!"

"God bless ya, Natalie! Be safe on the road."

Theodore drove off as Natalie watched in admiration.

What a wonderful man he is! He rarely engaged in deep discussion, but when he does, I'd better listen.

Natalie ran into her apartment and quickly grabbed as many boxes as she could to load into her car. She took little knickknacks that she had —blankets, books, clothes, and other small items— and stuffed them in the smaller cracks and crevices between the boxes. The only things she had left in the apartment were necessary toiletries, her bed, a set of sheets, a blanket, a pillow, some dishes, a few pots and pans, and her nightstand alongside her bed, supporting her phone and answering machine. She looked over and noticed two messages on her answering machine, but she decided not to check them as she assumed they would be from Darnell. She took a look around her apartment, and with a sigh of some type of relief, she shut the door, got in her car and left for Amarillo.

Though it was a four-hour trip, Natalie felt like the drive went quickly. Before she knew it, she was at her mother's house. Natalie parked in her mother's driveway, ran in to the house, and gave her mother a huge hug. She told her mother everything that happened over the week; clearly in much more detail than their conversations over the phone. Natalie told Florance about Dorothy and how awesome she was. Most importantly, she told Florance about her resolve to seek a relationship with Benjamin.

"Wow, honey! Sounds like a lot happened this past week."

"It has, Mom! And I am going to Tulsa to see Benjamin. I need to see him again. I want to try to work this relationship."

Natalie took a deep breath and her face lit up.

"I love him, Mom!"

"Is that so?"

"Yes, Mom, it is. And I have to go and tell him how I feel."

"Okay, well then, what are you still doing here?"

"Mom, I wanted to see you first. Plus, I came by to drop some stuff off. Regardless of what happens, I want to be here with you as long as I can."

"Honey, I've been meaning to talk to you about that. I am very glad to have you back in Amarillo. God knows I love having you here with me, but I want you to understand that I want you to be happy. I don't want you to hold so tight on to me that you have a hard time moving on with your life."

"Mom, please let me stop you there," Natalie interrupted. "I can't begin to tell you what type of month I have had. If I seem to be clingy to you, it is because I am, and I can't tell you why. Quite honestly, I don't know…why. But I want to cherish every moment that I have with you. There will come a time, Mom, that I will no longer have you in my life. And I can tell you that I absolutely dread that thought. Mom, I…"

Natalie paused, and Florance took that opportunity to respond.

"Natalie, honey, whenever God takes me, He takes me. That time will come for me as it will come for all of us. I don't know when that is, but whenever that is, you will know where I will be. Please don't be so afraid to let go of me that you forget to live, Natalie? I will always love you, and I will always be with you, no matter where I am. And at the time that God does take me, I want you to look at it this way: I only went to help Jesus prepare your room for you for when you come. Remember, Natalie, Jesus said,

'You believe in my Father, believe also in Me. In my Father's house there are many rooms. If it were not so, I would have told you. I tell you now that I go to prepare a place for you that where I am there you will also be.'"

Florance had Natalie's attention.

"You see, honey, you don't have to be afraid of death. You don't have to ever be afraid of losing me, whenever that time comes. Because when it does, I will not be dead. In fact, I will most certainly be alive. And like I said, I will be helping Jesus prepare your room for you."

Natalie got up and hugged her mother, very tightly.

"Thank you, Mom! Thank you so much. I love you!"

"I love you too, honey. Now let's get your car unloaded, your room prepared, and you rested up for your trip, tomorrow. There's a man in Tulsa that you need to go and kidnap!"

Natalie laughed as they got up from the couch. They began to clean, rearrange furniture, and unload boxes. They listened to Florance's favorite gospel music, which had Natalie dancing and praying; meditating on the words she heard, as well as the reality of God's grace. There was only one thing left.

Benjamin.

"Please, Lord," Natalie prayed. "Please save what only You can?"

CHAPTER 31

Man that was quick, he thought, stumbling out of bed.

It sure didn't take long for Benjamin's alarm to go off. It was a good thing that it did when it did, though. He still could not escape his dreams.

Benjamin got up, showered, shaved, grabbed his gear, and loaded it into his pick-up. He then walked over to Hope's house and put the keys in the mailbox, along with a letter. He had locked up his place, for the last time, for a while.

It's a good thing that Hope is still allowing me to pay rent…just to keep my stuff, here.

Benjamin got back into the pick-up and took off to the reserve center. When he arrived at the center, he walked into the door and approached the front desk, where he saw Lance Corporal McDaniels pull a file from a drawer. She, then, handed him his orders and his military file.

"Here you go, Sarge! You're just about set."

"Thank you, Lance Corporal!"

"Hey, Sergeant," came a voice from behind the desk. It was Corporal Bates, and he was holding a folder.

"You are scheduled to fly out of Tulsa International Airport at 1300. You will fly into Dallas Love Field, catch a flight to Phoenix, and then to Los Angeles. Here are your tickets."

"Really? I thought I had a direct flight to Phoenix."

"I'm not sure what happened, Sargent. This was the itinerary we were given for you."

"Okay, no problem," Benjamin responded.

NOT PRESENT OR FUTURE...

Benjamin stepped behind the desk to finish up some other administrative paperwork. After about thirty minutes, he had signed all the papers he needed to, and he was done. He grabbed his paperwork and looked at the Marines behind the counter.

"Thank you guys for helping me. I appreciate it. I'll see you all when I get back."

"Hoorah, Sergeant!"

"Hoorah!"

As he was leaving the office, there came another voice coming from down the hall.

"Sergeant Jones, we have your commissioning packet here. What do you want us to do with it while you are gone?"

It was Private Sissler, and he was holding a file with some interview appraisals, evaluations, and other forms.

"My...commissioning package?"

"Yeah, Sarge, we got the letters you needed. Your package is complete."

Benjamin almost forgot about his commissioning package. With everything going on, he hadn't put much thought into trying to become an officer.

"Wow! Um, I am not sure. What happens now?"

"Well," Lance Corporal McDaniels replied, listening in from behind the desk. "It will go up before the board. If you are selected, we will notify you, and we will go from there. You may even have the option to come home early from your orders to go to OU on a commissioning scholarship program."

"Wow!"

Benjamin was shocked. This was a bit overwhelming.

I had made it before. But would it happen, this time? Is this what I want?

"Thank you, Lance Corporal. I will wait to see what happens. Please submit this on to the board."

"We'll do, Sergeant. Hey, God bless, and be safe out there."

"You got it!"

Benjamin got to his pick-up and drove to Owasso to drop it off with Brian. Brian still planned to give Benjamin a ride to the airport, and Benjamin was grateful. But on his way to Owasso, Benjamin couldn't help but to feel a bit unsure about his orders. He began to feel uneasy, but he didn't know why. He dismissed it as the willies and pressed on.

Natalie got up, early, and jumped in the shower. Florance had breakfast all ready for Natalie; cooked and setting on the table. As Natalie finished her breakfast, she grabbed her purse, went over to kiss her mother on the cheek, and headed for the door.

"Bye, Mom, I'm headed to Tulsa."

"Now just one minute, young lady!"

Natalie looked at her mother, perplexed. Florance walked up to Natalie, gave her a huge hug, and handed her the keys to her car.

"Thank you, Mom! Thank you, so much!"

"Be careful, darling, and go get 'em!"

Natalie ran out the door and to her mother's car. She started it up, and noticing it was already full of gas, she hit the road to Tulsa. Highway 40 would be a straight, fast shot to Oklahoma City, and then the fast-paced Turner Turnpike to Tulsa would give Natalie the chance to speed even more.

There was no stopping her now. She drove as fast as she could get away with. She stopped only when she needed a break, especially to get some coffee. During her drive, Natalie meditated and prayed for Benjamin, for herself, and, most importantly, for their future. She was excited and scared…all at the same time. She had no idea how he would respond when he saw her, but she was determined to get to him.

This is crazy! I can't believe I am making this drive, again! Lord, please don't let this be too crazy. I love him! I want to be the right woman for him. Please, Lord, give me one more chance with him?

While Natalie meditated, she considered everything that they had gone through, together. She cringed when she thought of the fight they had that night before all the 'weirdness' happened.

Ugh! I can't believe this! I wanted another chance without him, and now I am begging for another one with him. Oh, the irony of it all!

She could only smirk at the situation. But reminiscing about him came with some personal baggage. She could not help feeling guilty for her part in this. She was still stuck on trying to hold on to what she knew was real.

It wasn't a dream. It wasn't a fantasy. I had a family. I had Benjamin. But how can I get that back? Maybe I can't get it back. But maybe, just maybe, I can do better, this time.

After driving about four hours, she was coming off of the Turner Turnpike, right into Tulsa. She thought about the quickest way to get to Benjamin's rent house off Highway 75, North of Tulsa. She drove through downtown and jumped on the Highway 75 on-ramp, headed toward Bartlesville. She looked down at the clock in her car. It was 12:14, just after noon. She was almost there.

Will he be there? Would he be at work? Asleep? I can't remember his work schedule; only that he worked nights. Surely, he would be home, sleeping. But, was he off last night, or did he work? I just can't remember.

That last ten minutes went by so slowly, but she finally made it to the 86th Street North ramp, just between Sperry and Owasso. She turned left, off the ramp, crossed the overpass, and turned into the neighborhood of his home. She parked her car, exited, and walked to his house.

Oh, no! Where is his pick-up?

Natalie walked to the door and knocked.

"Benjamin, are you here?"

There was no answer. All Natalie could hear was the ambience around her.

Where could he be? Maybe last night was his night off, and he was just out running errands. Maybe he was at a funeral. Or, maybe he was at his mother's house.

She could go over there, but his mother didn't like her, much. She was the source of many of their problems. Natalie contemplated it for a minute, then decided that she was going to go ahead and go see his mother. As she turned from the door, heading back to her car, she saw a lady walking toward her.

"Can I help you?"

"Hi, I'm Natalie. I am just looking for Benjamin."

"Oh, I am sorry. Benjamin just left this morning. He went to Los Angeles to work with the Marines. He will be gone for, at least, nine months or so."

"What? This morning?"

Natalie was in shock.

"Yes. I am so sorry."

Natalie stood there, stunned.

This can't be happening! This can't be really happening! What do I do, now?

"Are you his…girlfriend? He never mentioned anyone might come looking for him."

"I…I was hoping to be that, and more."

"Well, I am holding the house for him while he is gone. He told me that he would have a phone number for me to contact him when he got to where he was going. Unfortunately the only way I could get a hold of him, now, is through the reserve center."

The reserve center? That's it! If he left this morning, maybe he would still be there.

"Thank you, Ma'am," Natalie replied. "I have to go."

"You're welcome. By the way, my name is Hope. I'm pleased to meet you. I hope you find him before he leaves."

Natalie shook her hand.

"Thanks again, Miss Hope. God bless! Gotta run."

Natalie ran to the car, jumped in, started it up and took off. The reserve center was in Broken Arrow, about thirty minutes away from her current position.

Hurry, Natalie!! I have to hurry!

CHAPTER 32

As Benjamin arrived at Brian's house, he pulled into the driveway, exited the pick-up, and grabbed his bag from the back seat. Brian was on the porch waiting for him.

"Hey, Marine," Brian teased.

"Hey, yourself, Sailor."

"You ready to go?"

"Yep."

Janet came out of the house as Brian got up out of his porch swing.

"Hey, Ben," Janet greeted. "I gotcha something."

Benjamin sat his bag down by Brian's car, which was right next to where Benjamin parked his pick-up. He walked over to the porch and took the bag, looking inside it.

"Nice!"

Benjamin's goodie bag was full of banana-twin cakes, candy, a deck of cards, and some other little trinkets. At the bottom of the bag, there was a Hallmark envelope sitting on, what looked like, a brown T-shirt.

"It's from Samantha," Janet commented. "She thought you may need something for the trip,"

"Samantha?"

"Yeah," Brian responded. "She wanted to say 'good-bye', but her parents thought this would be a sufficient going-away present in her absence."

"Thank you," Benjamin replied, giving Janet a hug. "And please thank them for me?"

"You be safe out there," Janet responded. "And come back to us, soon."

"I will, Janet."

Benjamin walked over to Brian's car, put his bags in the back seat, and then climbed into the passenger's seat. Brian kissed Janet, then got into the car.

"You ready, brother?"

"As ready as I'm ever gonna be," Benjamin replied.

"Let's go then."

Brian started the car, pulled out of his driveway, and off they went. Benjamin was quiet. He couldn't help but feel low and melancholy. He didn't know why. He looked away from Brian as they drove, hoping that, whatever was wrong with him, Brian wouldn't see it. It didn't work. Brian could read Benjamin like a book, even though he had been trying to figure Benjamin out for the past couple of weeks.

That became a challenge.

"I'll take your pick-up and put it into a storage lot," Brian commented, trying to start some type of conversation. "We will keep an eye on it for you."

"Well, okay. I figured you would just give it to someone who needs it. The title is in the glove compartment, and I signed it over to you."

"Well, thank you, Ben. But, to be honest, I would prefer giving it back to you when you return."

"Okay. I appreciate what you are doing for me."

That was all Benjamin could muster, for some reason. He felt so awkward. This was Brian, and he always felt that he could talk to Brian. But this time, the issues were too surreal to Benjamin.

"So you got our number, right?"

"Yeah, I got it, Brian."

There was no traffic on Highway 169, and they were coming up on 244, about three minutes away from the airport. Brian couldn't take the silence any more.

"So are you all right, Benjamin?"

"Yeah, I think so."

NOT PRESENT OR FUTURE...

There was just enough silence to make Brian think he had to say something else when Benjamin spoke again.

"I can't help but to think about William, Brian. I just know that…"

Benjamin paused, shaking his head.

"I just feel that he could have been saved, somehow."

"I know, brother. I tried, so many times, to witness to him. I just could not break through to him."

But I did break through, Benjamin thought. *I witnessed to William, and we became great friends. William got saved, joined the church, married Julie, and they had Paige. Our families were close. But, again, that was a different life. Ugh!! I just can't wrap my head around this!!*

Benjamin knew what was…and there is nothing he could do to change it. All he could do was just run away.

Is that what I'm doing: running away?

"I just hope that Julie and their daughter are going to be okay," Benjamin continued.

"Julie. You mean, Julie Wagnor?"

"Yeah, why?"

Brian was silent, but he looked like he had something on his mind.

"Brian, why do you ask?"

"Ben, I am not sure how to say this, but…"

Brian paused, shaking his head.

"Julie had an abortion."

"What??"

Paige! Not Paige! Was it Paige? What happened?

Benjamin's heart was struck, again. He could not believe what he was hearing. He knew he hadn't seen Julie in a while, and he heard people talking about her. The past couple of weeks had been so confusing that he almost forgot about her. Brian didn't seem to be finished with this conversation.

"Well, first off, what did you mean when you said, 'Julie and their daughter'?"

Crap! Brian didn't know. No one knew!

"Um, well, the baby was William's," Benjamin replied, cautiously.

"What?? What do you mean, 'William's.' And how do you know that?"

Brian was clearly floored.

Great, Benjamin! How do you explain this one?

"Because he confided in me, like a while back," Benjamin sighed.

A while back? It wasn't a while back. It was in a different life!

"Okay, hold on!"

Brian was clearly perplexed. He pulled the car over to the side of the road, just before they came upon the airport exit on Highway 11. Brian looked at Benjamin with confusion all over his face. He was stunned.

"So, Benjamin, what makes you think that the baby was William's? You do know about William, right?"

Yes, I know all about William. I know all about Julie.

Why?

Because Julie was in love with William, but William struggled with feelings of homosexuality. Julie's parents went to the church, but Julie strayed away after she graduated high school. She knew William through the youth group at the church. They were both two years behind me in school, and while I served in the Marine Corps, both Julie and William tried their luck at college. Julie dropped out when she began hanging with the wrong crowd, and William reached out to her. Julie was happy that William showed interest in her but did not know about William's secret.

William loved Julie, but still struggled with his feelings of homosexuality, so he left the church because he could not understand why -what William believed- God would make him that way. Julie chased William for a relationship, and though they dated, William kept his emotional distance. In the midst of all that, Julie became pregnant. William could not handle the fact that he loved Julie, but was still confused about himself. When Julie told William she was pregnant -and that she loved him- William became even more confused, and refused to talk to Julie out of shame.

Julie, then feeling overwhelmed with her own guilt, started hanging out with the wrong crowd, again. But Natalie caught Julie at a gas station, one night, and invited Julie to go to a women's devotional night at the church, in which Julie accepted. Julie confided in Natalie, who then told me what was going on. I went to William and earned his trust, enough, that William confided in me. Then, I invited William back to church and encouraged him to communicate with Julie, again. Natalie and I prayed for, encouraged, and witnessed to Julie and William; and both Julie and William gave their lives to Christ. Through time, they got married and began raising a family. William even graduated college at OU Tulsa. God blessed William with a good job and a good marriage. Both families grew together.

That is exactly how it happened.

Or did it?

No, it didn't!

Benjamin's mind raced as he tried to recall the manner in which he and Natalie witnessed to William and Julie. Brian sat there, waiting for Benjamin to respond to his question.

"I knew about William, Brian. I knew a lot about him."

Benjamin tried to be cautious. He didn't know what to say without divulging too much information while trying to explain how he knew everything.

It really doesn't make any difference now, does it?

"Julie loved William," Benjamin continued. "And even though William was confused about many things, I think that, in many ways, he loved Julie."

Benjamin was trying. He sighed as he continued.

"They confided in each other, and I guess one thing led to another, and she got pregnant."

Brian still looked floored.

"I am not exactly sure what happened between the two, but…"

Benjamin didn't know what else to say. He didn't even know how he felt about all of it.

Why did William commit suicide? Why did Julie get an abortion? Did she find out about him and freak out? Did he find out about the baby and become overwhelmed with the thought of struggling with his confusion, as well as becoming a father? Did he find out about Julie's abortion and lose it?

It all overwhelmed Benjamin, and he couldn't take it.

This was not supposed to happen! In fact, this is not what happened!

"I don't know what else to say, Brian. I just think it is time for me to go."

"All right, Benjamin. Yeah, we gotta get you to the airport."

Brian obviously had more questions, but gave in to the fact that Benjamin had to catch his plane. As they drove up to the drop-off area, Benjamin exited the car and grabbed his bag from the back seat. Brian got out and gave Benjamin a hug.

"You be safe, brother. God bless you."

"You too, Brian. Thank you for the ride."

Brian went to get into the car, and looked back at Benjamin.

"See you when you get back."

"Yeah, see ya then," Benjamin replied as he walked through the doors to the baggage area.

Natalie was so caught up in the shock of what Hope just told her that it didn't register, until just then, what Hope said about how long Benjamin would be gone.

Nine months? Nine months?? What is he doing?

She drove as fast as she could get away with. When she reached Highway 51, she drove east, again, as fast as she could. She came upon the ramp and saw the reserve center to her right. Her heart raced as she turned off the ramp and then right onto 71st Street.

Lord, I'm almost there! Please let him be there??

She drove into the parking lot, parked her car, and looked around. She wondered why she didn't see his pick-up, and feared the worst. She exited the car and ran to the door of the Marine Corps side of the reserve center. She went inside the building and walked straight to the counter, where she saw a female Marine who just happened to look up to see Natalie approaching.

"Ma'am, can I help you? Do you have an I.D.?"

NOT PRESENT OR FUTURE...

"My name is Natalie J—uh, Barnes."
I almost did it again!
"I am looking for Benjamin Jones."
She stuttered, trying to remember what rank he was.

"Sgt. Jones left for Los Angeles this morning. He came and got his orders and his tickets, and then he left. He should be on his way to Dallas, by now, for his changeover to Phoenix."

Natalie was stunned even more. She felt like her heart had been crushed.

"Do you have a number for him, or where he is going? Do you have any way I can get a hold of him?"

"Sure, but do you mind if we ask who you are? Sgt. Jones made no mention of having a girlfriend."

"I am, uh, I just really care about him."

She didn't know what to say. She lowered her voice enough that only the corporal could hear her.

"We got into a fight a while back, and I just didn't want him to leave without saying 'good-bye'."

The female Marine turned and spoke to another Marine working behind her.

"Private Sissler, see if you can't locate that number for the fifteenth MEU admin office."

"Fifteenth MEU," Natalie asked.

"Yes, Ma'am, out of Camp Pendleton. That's where Sgt. Jones is headed."

Natalie's heart sank even more.

Not the Fifteenth MEU! They lost so many Marines in Iraq and Afghanistan.

She could not believe it.

"Do you know what he is going to be doing," Natalie asked, trying not to become emotional.

At that moment, all the Marines in the office stopped what they were doing and looked at Natalie.

"He took a year of orders, Ma'am. He is going to do some counterterrorism stuff."

"A year? I heard it was just nine months."

"Well, the original orders were for nine months, but Sgt. Jones stated he would push for a full year."

Natalie could not believe it. It was like a knife was stuck in her heart, being pushed in even further, with every word she heard. Natalie could not concentrate to what anybody was saying, any more. She was still dealing with the shock of the situation.

"It was funny, though. He kept going on about Afghanistan."

"What do you mean?"

Natalie snapped back to reality. That comment caught her off guard.

"He just kept making comments about how he believed we were gonna wind up there. It was almost like he knew something the rest of us didn't."

Natalie's heart could not sink any lower.

I know exactly what you're doing, Benjamin. You are going to prepare to fight an enemy that's not the enemy, yet. You are going to try to save the lives of as many Marines as you can; Marines that you served with, and lost. You are honorable like that.

You... my husband.

I realize that it was that sense of duty and honor, something that I had always hated -so much- about you, was the one thing I truly admire about you, now.

Only, now, I can't tell you that.

Natalie was stunned. She couldn't breathe. She couldn't move. She couldn't do anything. She just stood there.

"Ma'am, I have the number to an administration department aide for the Fifteenth in Camp Pendleton here for you."

Private Sissler handed Natalie a note with a number on it.

"I don't know when they will be available to give you any information on him when he arrives, but it is all we have right now. They should be able to help you get a message to him."

"Thank you," Natalie replied as she took the note. "Thank you for your help."

Just then, Natalie thought about Ben's commissioning package, and she inquired about it.

"Would you happen to know about Sgt. Jones's commission package?"

She knew that that was the one thing Benjamin was so proud of back when they were dating, and she thought she would inquire about it.

"Well, I am not sure what I can tell you, Ma'am, but..."

He paused, as he could tell that Natalie was emotional, but he still didn't completely understand her relationship with Benjamin.

"His commissioning package will go through the normal procedures, and if he gets accepted, we will contact him. I am not really sure much more I can tell you."

"Okay, thank you."

Just then, Natalie heard another voice coming from inside an office to her right.

"Private Sissler.".

"Yes, Corporal."

"The reserve center commanding officer is calling for a meeting in the conference room, and the I&I wants us to be there. Looks like we may have a severe weather situation this evening and the C.O. wants to communicate his instructions. There is a massive storm system that will be moving in late tonight from Texas. The meeting is in five. We will have more information then."

"Okay, Corporal. I will be right there."

He then looked back at Natalie.

"I'm sorry, Ma'am, I have to go."

"It's okay. I understand," Natalie responded.

"Will you be okay, Ma'am?"

"Yes, thank you for your help."

Natalie walked out of the reserve center and to her car, fighting the urge to cry. She sat in her car and remained in the parking lot. She did not know what to do or where to go. Everything was so upside down. She tried to find some reason for this; some way to make sense of it.

Could I still talk to Benjamin? Could I still get a hold of him?

CHAPTER 33

Benjamin was overwhelmed with depression. Considering everything that was happening, he felt alone. He didn't quite imagine it like this.

Is this really what I want? Are these orders really what I want? Wait, wait…focus! I have to focus. I am going on a mission to protect fellow Marines. I have to focus.

He checked in his luggage and confirmed his flight time.

"Sir, your flight should be boarding in about thirty minutes," the attendant confirmed. "Proceed to gate 32. You will meet your next plane at Dallas Love, then to Phoenix, with Los Angeles your final destination. Is that correct?"

"Yes, Ma'am," Benjamin replied as she gave him his tickets. He became lost, for a second, standing there in a trance.

"Are…you okay, Sir?"

"Yes, Ma'am," he replied, snapping back to reality.

"You have a good day, Sir!"

"You too."

Benjamin walked toward the gate, feeling like a zombie. He did not understand what was happening to him. He just had no life in him.

Just keep going, he thought. *This should pass soon.*
Or will it?

When he got to the gate, he took a seat and waited. He thought about everything as he realized the reality of his current situation.

There was no William.
There was no Julie.
There was no Leesha.

NOT PRESENT OR FUTURE...

There was no T. J.
There was no Ben Jr.
There was no...Natalie.

He put his head in his hands and desperately tried to grasp this reality he was in. He got caught in his own thoughtful struggle, so long, that he lost track of time.

"Good morning, ladies and gentlemen, we are now ready to begin boarding the plane for the 1120 flight to Dallas Love. Please have your tickets ready, and we will be boarding, shortly."

Benjamin quickly regained himself, again, and grabbed his bag with his ticket. He stood up to get in line, which seemed to move quickly. Once inside the plane, he took his seat and began to drift away. He was very tired as he had a long night. As if being in jail, the night before, was not enough, he had a hard time sleeping.

He drifted so fast that he did not even hear the flight details and instructions from the flight attendant. Once the plane backed away from the gate, he was out.

After a couple of minutes, Natalie started the car and drove out of the parking lot. She turned west on 71st Street and drove a mile to a QuikTrip gas station, pulling into it to get gas. Looking in her wallet, she realized that she only had $24.00. It might have been just enough to get her home.

She went inside to pay for the gas when she ran into a girl that looked so familiar to her. The girl was a beautiful Caucasian girl, who looked as if she bleached her hair.

She looked very tired and run down.

The girl saw Natalie but kept moving, leaving the store.

Who is this girl? I know I've seen her before.

Then it hit her.

It's Julie!

Natalie piped up enough to go talk to her.

"Julie! Julie, how are you?"

Julie looked back just before she got into a jeep with a man that Natalie didn't recognize.

"Do I know you?"

"It's me, Natalie. Natalie Barnes. I am Benjamin's friend. He goes to church with you. How are you?"

"Lady, I don't know you. And I have not gone to that church in a long time. I am done with that."

Julie was very cold and distant.

"Well, I have seen you around. I just wanted to say 'hi' and see how you were doing."

Natalie backed off a bit, and Julie's demeanor seemed to be easing a little.

"Well, see ya," Julie responded, showing little interest in Natalie.

"Hey, when are you due?"

"What?"

"Your baby. When are you due? Do you know if it is a boy or a girl?"

Natalie knew what it was but tried to keep the discussion as innocent as she could. Julie's demeanor changed. She went from uncomfortable to almost aggressive.

"Who told you about that?"

Natalie didn't know what to say because, in reality, it was Julie who told her. Natalie tried to think something up, quick.

"I am so sorry, Julie. I heard about it in a prayer chain. I didn't mean to pry."

"Nobody knows about that, so don't you say a word. And I don't know about no prayer chain either."

"I am so sorry, Julie. I didn't mean to…"

"I have to go," Julie interrupted as she walked toward the passenger's side of the jeep. The driver seemed to be just as uncomfortable with Natalie's presence. Natalie's heart went out to Julie, but didn't know what else to say to her, under the circumstances.

"Take care of yourself, and your baby."

"There ain't no baby! Not anymore."

"What? No! Paige…"

"Who the hell is Paige?"

NOT PRESENT OR FUTURE...

Natalie was floored and speechless. She could hardly breathe.

"I gotta go. Please stay away from me!"

Julie climbed into the jeep. They backed out of the parking lot and spun off.

Julie did it! She aborted her baby! She aborted Paige! Not Paige!

Paige and Leesha were best of friends. They grew up together. Paige was just about a year older than Leesha, and she was a huge part of Natalie's heart. The thought of what Julie did overwhelmed her. Natalie witnessed to Julie and encouraged her when Julie confided in Natalie about her pregnancy, and about her love for William.

It was Natalie who talked Julie out of aborting her baby.

But that didn't happen this time.

Natalie felt sick. She struggled to get back over to the gas pump. It was all she could do to maintain any sense of awareness she had. She felt like she had been hit by a truck, over and over, and this was the event that just set her off. After she pumped her gas, she pulled out of the QuikTrip and drove to a local park where she parked her car so she could try to get a grip on herself. She was shaking all over, and she started to pray.

"God! God, where are You? Why, God? Why did this happen? You know this is not what happened. You know that this is not real. What is going on here? Where are you?"

Natalie lost it.

She sat there, crying uncontrollably. So many thoughts and emotions were running through her head. This was like a nightmare that she could not wake up from. From where she sat, the reality of the situation was simple: there was no more Benjamin, no more Leesha, no more T. J., and no more Ben Jr.

Julie aborted Paige. They were both lost. These thoughts overwhelmed her. She could not take it anymore.

After crying for a while, she started the car, drove out of the parking lot to the highway, and began her long, lonely trip back to Abilene. It was a drive she loathed. She had to face the reality of trying to figure out things from here. She thought about Dorothy and their talk. Natalie was so confident that God would work this out.

Why was this happening? Is it really too late?

Everything changed. This was not the way it was supposed to be. Natalie's whole world was turned upside down. Now, after all the fighting, arguments, and drama she went through with Benjamin, she began to realize that Dorothy was right: the idea of starting over was nothing but a lie.

CHAPTER 34

Bombs were exploding. Marines were running all around, responding to the attack with gunfire. There was chaos everywhere.

"Corporal Johnson, get over here and lay down cover fire! We're getting killed here!"

Benjamin ran to a mound of broken walls, to his left, to provide cover fire.

"Shoot! Shoot! Corporal…shoot!!"

Benjamin could see nothing.

"SHOOT! SHOOT!"

The Marine in front of him yelled for Benjamin to keep shooting, but Benjamin couldn't see anything in front of him.

"I don't see anything," Benjamin yelled back.

"Just shoot!"

"Okay," Benjamin yelled, firing his gun at different directions in front of him. He couldn't see anything but smoke and sand.

"Keep shooting!"

Benjamin kept firing. Up, down, left, right…it didn't matter. Overhead, he heard a helicopter, flying, that seemed to make a turn toward a landing pad just about two hundred feet from Benjamin's position.

"Protect the chopper!"

"Okay!!"

Benjamin still kept firing, even though he had no idea what he was firing at. The more he fired, the more explosions occurred. Men, women and children were screaming all around him. Benjamin looked around, trying to figure out what was happening. Just then, an explosion came from the helicopter. Benjamin looked up as it was coming down. It crashed into a building located right next to the landing pad.

"Marines are in that chopper! We have to go get them!"

"Okay," Ben yelled as he followed the Marine around, a gauntlet of fire, toward the chopper.

They moved here and there, dodging bullets and shrapnel. From the looks of it, they had to cover about 175 feet to get to the chopper, but the fighting got worse as they went forward. Benjamin was so caught up in the fight that he didn't even get a chance to see the Marine who was giving him the orders. At this moment, he didn't care. He had to get to the helicopter.

As they came to an opening through a destroyed wall in a building, they noticed that the helicopter was just across the street in front of them. Shots were being fired into the helicopter, and Benjamin began to lose it, covering his ears. He could not take it much longer.

Focus, Ben! Focus!

"Okay, Marines, let's go!"

Benjamin followed the other Marines out into the street, crouching as low as they could while dodging bullets. About halfway through the street, the Marine in front of him fell to the ground. Benjamin ran to him and grabbed him, pulling him as hard as he could toward a protective barrier of rubble, not too far from the helicopter.

"Hey," Benjamin yelled. "I got you! I got you!"

Benjamin reached the barrier, trying hard to make sense of all the violence and chaos around him. He pulled the Marine through a wall, inside a hole of the building, next to the helicopter. Benjamin sat his weapon down and pulled the Marine close to him to see who it was, and froze with fear. It was Sgt. Jason 'Mac' McCready, a Marine who died while serving with Benjamin during his initial deployment.

"MAC! MAC!"

Mac was unresponsive.

"No, not again!"

Benjamin tried to find the wound and plug it, taking off Mac's gear.

"Mac, hang in there!"

The violence did not stop. Screams, explosions, shots fired —all of that filled the air. Benjamin felt claustrophobic. He felt like all the violence was headed his way, and he could do nothing about it. It was an unsinkable feeling of loathing and fear, but he kept moving. He tried to get the bulletproof vest off Mac, but the more he tried, the harder it seemed to get Mac's gear off. Benjamin became frustrated as Mac was not breathing. Just then, Mac's eyes opened. He looked at Benjamin, and he spoke.

"Corporal, why did you leave us? Why?"

"What? I didn't leave you."

"You left us to die. We are all dead."

"No! That's not true!"

Mac's eyes began to grow dark and cold, and Benjamin was consumed in fear. He could feel it, but he couldn't understand it.

"Daddy!"

Benjamin looked up.

Where did that come from?

"Daddy, help us!"

That is T. J.'s voice!

"T. J., where are you?"

Somehow, throughout all the noise, explosions, and screams, Benjamin could hear T. J.

"Daddy, help us!"

What? That was Leesha!

"Leesha, where are you?"

Benjamin grabbed his weapon and headed out into the chaos.

"Where are you, Leesha? I'm coming!"

"Benjamin?"

Benjamin froze. The chaos of war surrounded him. Fear still gripped him. But that was not the kids. It was Natalie.

"Benjamin, help us!"

This isn't real! This isn't real!

"Benjamin??"

She kept calling his name over and over, and the calls were coming from the helicopter. Benjamin looked over at the helicopter and realized it was right in front of him. All of a sudden, the noises stopped. All the voices… stopped. Benjamin rushed to the helicopter as there was, now, fire all around it. Men in Middle Eastern clothes ran past him; some here and some there. He could not look at them as, for some reason, he was afraid of them. He could not explain it. Fear crippled him, but he kept his focused on the helicopter.

As he arrived on the scene of the crash, he ran to the pilot's door. There was no one there. He didn't see anyone in the copilot's seat, either. He maneuvered his way to the side door and opened it.

Nothing.

What is going on here? Where is everyone?

He looked around for Leesha, T. J., and Natalie. He was confused, and still crippled in fear. He turned away from the door when he felt a hand grab him, crushing his rib, as he heard the most dreadful sound ever, shooting through his soul.

"BENJAMIN!"

Benjamin woke up with a jolt and found himself on the plane. He was sweating, profusely, his heart rate was raised, and he was breathing heavily.

"Sir?"

Benjamin looked up at the flight attendant who was trying to get his attention.

"Are you okay?"

Catching his breath and trying to overcome this unexplainable pain on his side, he responded as best he could.

"Yes…yes, Ma'am."

"Would you please pull your seat upright? We are about to land."

"Yes, Ma'am."

"Thank you, Sir."

The flight attendant made her final trip up and down the aisle, getting the last of the trash. She, then, took her seat, and the plane made its approach. She got onto the intercom and proceeded to give the gates for the connecting flights. Benjamin listened for the flight to Phoenix. It was gate 14. Then came her final statement:

"Ladies and gentlemen, we are expecting some rough weather coming in from the west within the next couple of hours. Be sure you check in with your gate for any potential changes to your flight. Thank you for flying with us and have a nice day."

The plane landed, and taxied to the gate. Benjamin grabbed his carry-on bag, got off the plane, and immediately proceeded to the restroom. He splashed some water on his face and tried to calm himself down. He was still a little shaken up from his dream.

Man that was crazy! For such a short flight, I was in deep.

He couldn't help but think about Natalie and the kids. He was so confused, and started feeling really uncomfortable, inside. He began to shake, physically. He had no idea what was going on. He did not feel comfortable.

In fact, he felt so wrong.

I gotta keep going; gotta stay focused!

As he grabbed a paper towel to wipe his hands and face, Benjamin looked down into the bag that Samantha gave him and he reached inside it, pulling out the brown T-shirt. He noticed a Bible verse on the back of the shirt, and he decided to step inside a handicapped stall to put the shirt on. Coming out of the stall, he looked at himself in the mirror. On the front of the shirt, there was an emblem, just over the heart. The emblem was a Marine Corps emblem with a larger cross just behind it. Above the emblem was written the term 'God's', and just below the emblem was written, 'Marine'. The verse on the back of the shirt was taken from Psalm 144:1,

"Praise be to the Lord my God, who trains my hands for war; my fingers for battle."

Looking at the shirt, Benjamin felt so unworthy to wear it, no matter how much he appreciated it. Sighing in desperation, he tried so hard to see himself the way Samantha saw him. It was hard for him, feeling broken as he did. He was turning back toward the stall to take it off when he heard a call over the intercom that got his attention.

"Ladies and gentlemen, there is a change in the flight to Phoenix. If your destination is Phoenix, please stand by for further instructions."

Benjamin grabbed his bags and left the restroom, proceeding to gate 14. He sat down, waiting for the flight instructions. His mind was still rolling, and he was struggling to maintain himself, emotionally.

Natalie. Natalie.

That is all he thought about. His heart raced even harder. He could not shake this feeling.

What was going on with me?

He began to pray, and while he was praying, he remembered what Brian said about the power verse.

What was that verse? Oh, yeah: Isaiah 53: 5-6.

Benjamin grabbed his Bible from his bag, opened it up, and went right to that verse, where he read it with eager anticipation.

"He was wounded for our transgressions; he was bruised for our iniquities: the chastisement of our peace was upon him; and by his stripes we are healed."

Benjamin held the Bible to his chest and prayed even harder. He wanted to be healed. But he was so broken.

Could God really heal me? Would God heal me?

And then it hit him like a bolt of lightning.

Why didn't I ask this question, before? Could God have healed me and Natalie? Did it matter now?

He couldn't stop thinking about her.

Time passed slowly, but it still passed. The plane was there, but they weren't boarding. It was getting later. Ten minutes…twenty minutes…thirty minutes. Prospective passengers were getting anxious, as was he. A flight attendant came up to the desk.

Finally!

"Ladies and gentlemen, we apologize for the delay. We regret to inform you that, due to the weather…"

CHAPTER 35

Arriving in Abilene, just minutes from her apartment, Natalie fought to hold back the remaining tears she could physically muster. She could not understand anything that happened over the last month. She thought about the kids, her husband, her friends, and her old life.

Was it even real? Was it real? Any of it?

At that last thought, she lost it again. She didn't even know how she was keeping the car on the road. It was getting dark outside as storm clouds were rolling in, and she was so ready to just get out of the car.

God, what is going on here? Where is my life? Where are my kids? Where are you?

Natalie had to pull over at a local gas station to put gas in the car, using what little bit of money she had left. Once she was done with the gas, she decided to call her mother from a pay phone.

"Mom, I tried. I am so tired. All I want to do is sleep."

"Everything's going to be O.K., honey. I know everything will work out, you'll see."

Florance tried to encourage to Natalie, but Natalie was too emotionally spent. Natalie told her mother that she would rest up, then pack up the car and drive to Amarillo the next day. Once Natalie hung up the phone, she got back in the car, started it up, and left for the apartment complex.

Physically exhausted and completely emotionally drained, Natalie turned into the parking lot of her apartment complex and pulled into a parking spot. She didn't move. She couldn't breathe.

She just sat there. Seconds turned into minutes, which seemed to turn into hours. She knew that everything in her life at that moment was wrong. She was constantly bombarded with thoughts of her past, thoughts of events she would rather forget: sins committed, pride displayed, arguments started—and those were the easy memories to bear. She was overcome with guilt and shame. She felt, in some way, like she was being attacked.

Literally.

There was no husband, no kids…and at the thought of that, her feelings had erupted in such that she experienced a complete and total sense of depression and loathing.

Was it dread? What was it? What is this that I am feeling?

It was unlike anything she had ever experienced before. There was nothing left: no accusation, no fighting, no arguing…and no sense of fulfillment, ironically. She had literally lost everything before she even got it.

But how is that even possible?

It didn't matter to her. As far as Natalie was concerned, Benjamin, in one way or another, was her husband; her best friend. That idea, true or not, made her heart feel so empty, given the situation. Her thoughts crossed every plain of understanding and memory she had. She thought of her mother, and how she had her mother back. She was grateful for that. She was grateful to have another chance to hug her mother's neck when she saw her.

Had this been another chance at life…really? It sure didn't feel like it. It doesn't matter, now. I can no longer think about this. I can no longer think…at all.

She opened the car door, and with every ounce of energy she had, she got out and began walking toward her apartment door. The wind picked up, and it started raining. It was really dark now, and lightning flashed in the distance. Natalie was so tired, and the thought of that pillow seemed real good at the moment.

Get some sleep. I just need some sleep.

She got to the door, put her key in the lock, and just as she was turning, she started to pray.

"Lord, please be with my hus—"

NOT PRESENT OR FUTURE...

BAM!

Her head slammed against the door as it opened, and she hit the floor. She was disoriented, lying on the ground, looking around and trying to figure out what happened. Just before she could get her bearings, she looked up to see Darnell standing over her.

"Oh my God! No! Darnell!!"

Fear came over her as he grabbed her by the shirt and yanked her up.

"Where have you been, girl?? Who have you been with??"

"Nobody," she answered, frantically, trying not to lose her balance. She could smell alcohol on his breath.

"I was with nobody, I just—"

"Just what?" Darnell interrupted. Getting in her face and putting his finger nearly in her eye he yelled, again.

"JUST WHAT??"

She couldn't back up fast enough, knocking over the lamp near the dresser.

"I told you that you were mine! Who do you think you are? You do what I say, woman!"

"Hey, Darnell," came a voice from another man coming through the door right behind him. "I think she's been messin' around on you."

"Yeah, Darnell," responded the voice of another man. She did not recognize either one of the other two.

"What are you gonna do about that, Darnell? Sounds like she needs to be taught a lesson."

"I think you are right, Reggie," Darnell replied. "Apparently she don't know who she belongs to."

"I don't belong to you, Darnell," Natalie responded, trying to muster up whatever courage she had.

"What??"

Darnell responded with a sense of fierce intimidation.

"I told you, woman, you are mine!!"

"No, Darnell—"

Slap!

She shut her eyes just quickly enough to escape an open contact from the slap she felt across her face. She hit the bed and caught herself from rolling over. Darnell grabbed her, again, by her throat and threw her against the wall. He put his finger in her face again, yelling at her.

"I'm gonna ask you again, woman, who were you with? I'm gonna kill 'em! I told you…"

She tried to slide away, but he forcefully grabbed her side, putting pressure on her rib cage, and slamming her body back into the wall as she groaned in pain.

"You belong to me!"

"No, Darnell," she continued, overwhelmed with pain and tears rolling down her cheeks. "I am not yours!"

She tried to be courageous, knowing there was nothing else for her to do. Would she scream? Who would hear her? Would she try to escape? Where would she go? She had no strength left.

Wham!

She was thrust upon the floor from the blunt shock of the back of Darnell's hand hitting her head. The hit came with such force that she felt her head slam against the wall on the corner. She was caught between the realm of consciousness and complete disorientation. Darnell was strong, as he was ferocious and abusive. It was only going to get worse.

"Hey, Darnell," Reggie continued. "Look at this. Look at this phone number on this paper."

Darnell reached over the bed where Reggie handed him the piece of paper. Then he looked at her with dark eyes.

"Who is this?"

Natalie couldn't talk. She couldn't move. Her nose started to bleed.

"Who is this, you filthy trash?"

She slowly positioned herself a little more off the floor and against the wall, but still not on her feet.

"He…is…."

She tried to respond as tears flowed as she stared at the paper. She began to weep, mercilessly. She couldn't keep it in when she thought about the man that would have been -should have been- her husband. She felt shame, pain, and a sense of dread. Her soul felt like it was being attacked from every direction. Accusations seemed to fill her mind, as Darnell continued his interrogation.

"Is that right," Darnell responded, tormenting her.

"Donny," Darnell continued as he turned and looked at his other friend. "Why don't you look around to see what else you can find in here? Seems like she has been playin' me."

Donny was a rough-looking Caucasian guy about five feet eleven inches tall, tattoos over his arms, and weird piercings of skulls on his ears. He looked just as intimidating as Darnell and Reggie.

"All right, Darnell. But it sounds like you need to teach this girl a lesson. I know what I'd do if I were you."

Darnell bent down to get within just a few inches from her face and began scoffing.

"So who is he? Is he cute? Is he as strong as me?"

Darnell grabbed her chin, forcefully turning it to face him.

"Who is he??"

"Yeah, who is he," Reggie responded, adding to her torment.

Donny continued looking through the apartment. He walked over to the other side of the bed to where the answering machine was.

"Hey, Darnell, there are a couple of messages on this machine. Maybe one of them is him."

Donny pushed the play button. The first message was from Darnell.

That was no surprise.

The second came right up.

"Message 2: 'Uh, Natalie, um, it's Benjamin. Hey, uh, I'm headed out tomorrow, for Los Angeles, and, um…well, I just wanted you to know that I was thinking about you. I didn't want to leave without saying good-bye. I'll keep in touch, okay. If you would like, I could give you my add—' Beep End of message. There are no more messages."

"So there he is. Benjamin. That's who you have been cheatin' on me with, huh?"

Natalie couldn't look at Darnell, but she didn't have to. The look on her face when she heard Benjamin's voice said everything. She was done for.

Donny walked over to a radio near a box full of pans.

"Hey, check out this radio."

Donny turned it on, and the song that was playing put her in more tears.

"Still in this life, there's so much to learn. Barriers to cross; there's bridges to be burned. And where the Lion walks, I will not be afraid. My feet may touch the earth, but my heart is swept away!"

It was 'Sacred Hideaway' from the Christian group '4 Him'. Of all the songs that could be on, of all the music that could be playing, it was this one; one of her favorites.

Where the Lion walks? Lord, please walk with me? Please help me? Please save me?

"What's that music? Never heard that before," Darnell remarked. "What station is that?"

"I think it's Christian music or something like that," Reggie replied. "Heard that song a while back at my ma's church."

"Christian music," Darnell scoffed. "Girl, you listenin' to Christian music? What? You think that God loves you or something? Is that right?"

Natalie turned her head in tears.

"Answer me when I talk to you, girl!!"

Darnell's advances were unbearable and threatening. He grabbed her face.

"You think God loves you?"

She whispered something, but it barely came out.

"WHAT??"

"I hope so."

Does God love me? Does He? He's not here, is He? I feel so alone.

Natalie's mind raced as she thought more about God.

God, you always told me that You would be there for me. Jesus, where are you? Do I deserve this? Is this why I am going through this? Is this why Darnell's here? God, can you hear me? God, please hear me? Lord, please hear me? Father, I beg You…please hear me??

"You think God is gonna save you," Darnell asked, still tormenting Natalie. "Whatchu think?"

"God ain't gonna save her. God don't care nothing for that no-good cheater you got there, Darnell," Reggie exclaimed as he and Donny were still rummaging through the apartment.

"Oh that's right, I can't forget about that," Darnell responded. "You've been messin' around on me. I need to handle this. How do you think I should handle this?"

He mocked Natalie, while turning to the other two.

"What do ya'll think?"

"I done told you what I would do," Donnie responded, this time with a vindictive look in his eye. Donnie, then, took off his belt.

"Here, Darnell. You need to handle this."

Natalie glanced up enough to see Darnell take the belt.

"Yeah, girl," Darnell scoffed. "You need to be taught a lesson, and since we know that God ain't gonna protect you, then you will know who you belong to."

Natalie turned her head, facing the wall again. And as Darnell reached to grab her arm, she began to pray.

"Jesus, please forgive me. Please be with…"

She dropped her head in pain as Darnell yanked her up off the floor with his left arm while raising his right arm, holding the belt to hit her. She closed her eyes and, in her mind, gave herself to God.

Jesus, Just Jesus…

Thump. Thump. Thump.

"Natalie?"

The voice came from outside the door. It was Carmella.

"Natalie, are you in there?"

"Who is that," Darnell snapped. "Check that, Reggie!"

Reggie looked at the peephole.

"It's some girl, Darnell."

"Get rid of her," Darnell demanded.

Reggie opened the door.

"Get lost, girl!"

"Who are you? Where's Natalie?"

"Natalie ain't here, and I told you to leave!"

Reggie got in Carmella's face, but Carmella slipped by him and entered the apartment. She saw Donnie in the kitchen and Darnell over by the bed staring at her angrily.

"Who are you, and where's Nat—"

Carmella choked, midsentence, when she saw Natalie on the floor by the bed.

"NATALIE!"

Donnie grabbed her from behind, but Carmella fought him off. She was going to do everything she could to get to Natalie.

"Get off me, you freak!! Natalie!!"

"Man, I told you to get rid of her," Darnell yelled at Donnie.

Natalie could hear Carmella but was too afraid to look up. She was bleeding from her nose, her jaw hurt, and she felt very disoriented. For the moment, she welcomed the disturbance from the abuse she was taking from Darnell. But now, Carmella was in danger.

Reggie rushed over to help Donnie with Carmella, but Carmella was giving both of them a run for their money.

"Natalie," Carmella kept yelling. "You leave her alone!"

"Shut up," Darnell yelled. "Get her out of here!!"

Reggie pushed Carmella down and stood over her, trying to overpower her.

"God, please help her," Carmella prayed. "Please help us?"

Darnell wasn't done. He turned to look back at Natalie, the belt still in his hand.

"God, please…" Carmella prayed, before she yelled at Darnell. "You leave her alone!"

Carmella was fighting with everything she had to break the grasp of the two men trying to force her from the apartment.

"It's too late," Natalie whispered. "Jesus, I am so sorry. Benjamin, I am so sorry. Please forgive me."

Natalie began to hear whispers of accusations and torment. She heard it all this time, but it was very clear now.

"Sinner…worthless…adulteress!"

NOT PRESENT OR FUTURE...

Tears flowed, heavily, as Natalie realized her predicament. Darnell reached down and grabbed her pants leg, pulling her away from the wall. He then grabbed her hair back, staring into her face.

"I told you, God don't care about you. It's just you and me now…"

As he raised the belt, Natalie looked down, preparing for the blow, when unexplainably, she could hear, in her mind, Dorothy's voice.

Child, remember, you are not only your father's daughter, you are the Father's daughter. Nobody hurts his little girl and gets away with it.

Whap! Thump! Crash!

Lighting flashed and a loud sound of thunder crashed so loudly that it felt like it was right on top of Natalie's apartment building. Electricity went in and out as the ground shook. The lights flickered, quickly. It was so loud and quick, and in a split second, it was like a loud voice shot through the apartment, as if only one person there could hear it.

"WAKE UP, MARINE!"

The lights came back on, and Darnell found himself falling back to the floor after a blunt force struck his face.

"KEEP YOUR HANDS OFF OF MY WIFE!!"

Natalie fell to the floor only to realize that it wasn't from force. She didn't feel anything more. She was confused by that voice.

That voice. That voice! Who was that familiar voice?

She looked up to see what, at that moment, was the most beautiful, powerful, and emotional man she had seen in a long time. There he was, standing between her and the pain; between her and the abuse; between her and the evil.

Could it be?

It was!

Benjamin!

She couldn't believe it, and didn't know what to think. She didn't care. There he was.

Her man!

Her Marine!

Her strong Marine!

And he was ready for war.

Reggie lunged at Benjamin, and with a response only seen in karate movies, Benjamin moved, perfectly, to avoid a hit and with quick Jujitsu-like moves and threw Reggie into the wall.

Amazingly, Natalie started experiencing something different; something powerful with every strike that Benjamin gave in her defense. She was alert, and her dread faded away to a feeling of relief.

Donnie came up behind Benjamin and threw a punch at his head. In a flash, as if Benjamin knew where it was coming from, he ducked and responded with a quick strike to the face, throat, and then back to the face. He then threw Donny into the wall near the door. Carmella got out of the way; trying not to get in the middle of the scuffle as she could not believe what she was seeing. Darnell scrambled to his feet, and gaining his balance, he lunged for Benjamin, trying to wrestle him to the ground. Benjamin quickly got down, maneuvered his arms around Darnell's arms, broke loose of Darnell's grip, and, using Darnell's weight, spun Darnell around and into the dresser, head first.

Lightning continued to flash, and thunder sounded all around them, loud and clear. Darnell, Reggie, and Donnie each continued their assault on Benjamin, however weaker they seemed in their aggressiveness. Natalie looked up at Benjamin, and her fear turned from her receiving injuries to the potential injuries that Benjamin would incur from Darnell and his two thugs.

But Benjamin wasn't there to get hurt. That was clear.

They charged Benjamin again, and he fought them off as hard as he could, keeping himself between them and Natalie. Reggie picked up a chair and threw it at Benjamin. Benjamin ducked, and the chair hit the wall. Benjamin moved toward Reggie, and he pulled out a knife. That mere barrier did not stop Benjamin as he slapped the knife out of Reggie's hand, and onto the floor. Just then, Donny was able to sneak behind Benjamin and grab his legs, causing Benjamin to hit the floor.

"Hold that punk," Darnell yelled.

Donnie grabbed a stone skillet off the stove and walked over to Benjamin. Natalie, watching this fight turn in a different direction, became afraid for Benjamin. *They are going to hurt him.*

They were going to kill him.

Benjamin was nowhere near being done. When Benjamin saw Donnie grab the skillet, he leaned over and punched Reggie, got one leg loose from Reggie's hold, and kicked Reggie square in the face. Reggie sat up holding his nose as blood poured from his nose and mouth. He was done.

Benjamin stood up only to meet a punch from Darnell's fist. Darnell landed a lucky punch, which caused Benjamin to fly back onto the bed, rolling onto the floor, and landing right in front of Natalie. She looked at him, as if to communicate concern for him. She touched Benjamin's hand with hers.

That was all it took.

It's time to end this once and for all.

Darnell jumped over the bed and lunged for Benjamin. As if Benjamin had a burst of strength, he caught Darnell's throat and stood up. Looking deep into Darnell's face, Benjamin pushed Darnell away from Natalie and toward the door. Donnie maneuvered toward Benjamin and swung the skillet toward Benjamin. Benjamin ducked, perfectly, to where the direction of the skillet flew right into Darnell's face.

Benjamin got his grip on Darnell, again, and threw him out of the apartment, and onto his car, breaking the passenger's side window with his head. Benjamin, then, turned around and went straight for Donnie. Donnie pulled out a pistol, but before he could even point it, Benjamin grabbed the pistol, spun it around in Donnie's arm, bending Donnie's wrist, and breaking it. Donnie fell back in pain as Benjamin took the gun, released the magazine, and emptied the chamber. He then threw the gun down, went over to Donnie, picked him up by his throat, and carried him to the door. He then threw Donnie onto the ground. Benjamin looked over at Darnell, trying to control his anger.

"Do not ever come anywhere near my wife again, or I'll…"

Benjamin wanted to kill them, and he was shaking, but he had to keep control of himself.

"I didn't know she was married, man," Darnell responded.

"Yeah; we have been married for fifteen years. Pretty crazy, isn't it, fool?"

Benjamin shut the door and went over to Natalie, who was still on the floor. He looked over to Carmella.

"Are you okay?"

"Yes."

Carmella was so relieved as she began to pray.

"Thank you, God! Thank you, so much!"

Benjamin knelt down and looked at Natalie. He studied her. He felt so much love for her, but he also felt guilty.

She just sat there in tears.

"Natalie, are you okay? They won't hurt you anymore. I promise!"

Natalie couldn't say anything. She just looked at Benjamin with thankfulness and love.

"Natalie, I just…I don't…I—"

"You are here," Natalie interrupted. "You…are here."

She lost it again, crying and touching his face.

"Natalie, I am so sorry."

He began to get emotional, trying to talk to her.

"I am so very sorry. I lied to you. I do miss the kids. I do remember them. I…"

Benjamin couldn't finish his statement. Natalie still could not believe it. She had been so angry with Benjamin for so long. She hated him, felt no love for him at times, and loathed being around him. But for some reason now…

Now.

Now, she felt closer to him than she ever had.

Say it, she thought. *Please say it? Tell him how you feel!*

"Natalie, I tried to live my life without you. I thought I wanted another chance at a different life. I thought I wanted to do things over. I thought that is what I wanted. I am so sorry that I tried that. I can't…"

He paused, as he began to weep.

"I can't do it. I just can't. I love you, Natalie. I love you! I am sorry for the husband I had been."

There was no denying their life together before this confusing time. She knew it was real, and so was he.

But was he too late?

"You fought for me? You came back for me? Why, Benjamin, why? Why did you come back for me?"

"Because, you are my wife."

He said it!

He really said it!

She continued to cry as she grabbed Benjamin and held him. She would not let go. It didn't matter what life they were in: the one in the past or the one in the present. Benjamin said it. It was a proclamation.

I am his wife, she thought. *I am his wife! I am...his!*

"I love you too, Benjamin! I am so sorry. I have been a terrible wife. I have made so many mistakes. I have been miserable. I have been selfish. I have been unworthy."

She continued to cry.

"I have been—"

"Flawless," Benjamin interrupted. "You are flawless. God gave you to me, and He made you flawless. You are not perfect, but you are perfect for me."

Benjamin looked deep into her eyes, her face...her soul.

"Natalie, you are my mate, my lover, and my best friend. Would you please, please, be my wife again?"

Natalie said nothing, but she lit up. She felt no pain, no fear... no shame. She was, in every way, Benjamin's bride.

They just sat there and held each other, crying and praying, and though Carmella was there, they were alone; alone in the room, while the rain was pouring outside. They could hear sirens in the background and a knock at the door, but all the ambience in the background could not tear them away from each other. Yes, they were alone, the two of them becoming one, once again.

They were alone, but this time, they were not only alone.

Thank God, Almighty! We were no longer alone!

CHAPTER 36

Benjamin's breathing was heavy and deep. He was warm, wrapped up in a blanket and stretched out on the couch. He opened his eyes and sat up, looking around at an environment resembling one that he was familiar with.

Benjamin was in a different room. It was familiar, but different.

Did I fall asleep at Natalie's apartment? This certainly did not look like Natalie's apartment.

He stood up and looked around. He could hear the faint sound of activity coming from a room upstairs. After waking up, a little more, he quickly realized where he was, and his hopes rose with every second. Benjamin walked to the stairs and slowly began the climb. When he reached the top of the stairs, he headed toward the door of the master bedroom. He was so focused on the doors that he did not notice a little pair of eyes peeking at him from behind a half-opened door on the other side of the hall. Benjamin opened the doors to the master bedroom and entered the room. The room was dark enough from the curtains being shut, but light enough to notice a figure lying in the bed. Benjamin approached the bed, cautiously, wondering if this was all real, and trying to convince himself that it was. He sat down on the bed and stared at the figure under the covers.

It was Natalie, and she opened her eyes to see Benjamin sitting at her side.

"Benjamin?"

"Hey, Natalie. Are…are you…"

Natalie reached her hand up and felt his face. She studied his eyes, his facial features, his gray hairs on the side of this head. It was an older Benjamin, but it was Benjamin. She sat up, wrapped her arms around him, and held on tight. Assuming that the other remembered everything –and that it wasn't just a dream- they just held, tight, to each other.

"Hey, you," she responded, not letting go.

They just held each other for what seemed to be hours, and then it came.

Knock, knock, knock.

"Dad," came a voice from the other side of the door. "Dad, are you and Mom awake?"

The bedroom door opened, and a little figure entered into the room, looking cautiously at Benjamin.

Dad? Dad? Dad! T. J.!

Benjamin jumped up out of bed and got down on his knees in front of T. J., looking at him in disbelief.

"T. J.!"

Is this a dream? It can't be!!

"T. J.," came Natalie's voice from the bed, clearly confused.

Ben turned to her and looked at her.

"Natalie. I don't think we are dreaming, again."

Natalie sat up in bed and pulled the covers to her face, shaking her head and looking around the room. She so desperately wanted to believe what she was seeing. She looked at her arms, her closet, her dresser, Benjamin, then T. J.

"Benjamin, are you sure?"

Natalie became emotional. Benjamin walked over to her side of the bed and sat down in front of her. He looked at her, studying her and examining her beauty.

"I don't know, but you will never be more beautiful than you are now, Natalie. I love you!"

Acting in impulse, she felt her own face. There were no bruises from the assault, and no pain or evidence of being struck by Darnell's hand. While Ben sat there looking at her, she leaned over to her nightstand and grabbed a small mirror. She saw her face. It was her; not her younger self, but the 'Natalie' that she once was.

"Benjamin, could it be? Are we…"

"Mommy," T. J. called as he walked over to her side of the bed. "Hi, Mommy."

Natalie did not know what to think. She couldn't believe her eyes. There was Benjamin, and there was T. J.

"I believe we are home, right where we need to be," Benjamin responded.

Natalie hugged Benjamin tight, again, and did not let go. T. J. walked back over to the door, only to find a taller figure standing there.

"Um, Dad?"

Benjamin looked up at Leesha, standing at the door with her NOAH soccer uniform on.

"Leesha…"

Benjamin paused. He did not know what else to say. Leesha was cautious and reserved. Her face was flushed, and she looked tired.

"I'm gonna be late for my game, Dad,"

"Oh," Benjamin looked at the clock, then looked at Leesha.

"It's okay. I don't want to bother you guys."

Leesha turned and left the room in a hurry.

"Leesha, wait!"

Benjamin followed her out of the room. Natalie was right behind him, looking to go get Ben Jr. from his bed. Leesha made it to her door and grabbed the handle as Benjamin called for her again.

"Leesha—"

"I can't do this anymore, Dad."

She turned and looked at Benjamin with tears in her eyes. Benjamin and Natalie paused.

"Did you hear me, Dad? I said, 'I can't DO this anymore!!"

Benjamin became emotional

"I'm sorry, and I love you guys -both of you- but I just can't do this anymore. I'm tired of the fighting, okay?"

Benjamin looked down, and Natalie put her hands over her face to catch her tears.

"Please tell me you hear me, Dad?"

"I do hear you, Leesha," Benjamin responded as he stepped closer to Leesha.

"And there is something that I need to say to all three of you."

Natalie walked into the other bedroom to get Ben Jr. When she came back, she had Ben Jr. in her arms and T. J. at her side, wrapped around her leg. Benjamin knelt down in front of Leesha. He tried to be as strong as he could, but if there was ever anyone who could bring him to his knees, it was Leesha.

"Leesha, you, T. J. and little Ben need to know that I am so very sorry. I am I sorry for all the things I said to your mother. I am sorry for all the fights. I am so sorry for the way I have been acting the last couple of, well, for a long time."

Benjamin paused and looked at Natalie, who was in tears, but smiling back at him.

"I'm sorry too, Leesha," Natalie chimed in. "I have not been the wife to your father -and the mother- that you deserve. I have been selfish, nagging, and I have no excuse."

She looked at Benjamin.

"Your father and I spent some time together…uh…last night…"

She was dumbfounded, trying to think about how she was going to explain what she and Benjamin went through. In her mind, it seemed like some kind of crazy 'Chronicles of Narnia' adventure.

"And we were able to work some things out," Benjamin interrupted, cautiously. "But you need to know that I love your mother with all I have. And we both love you very much. We love you and your two brothers. We have no excuse for our actions."

Benjamin thought a little more about what he was going to say next.

"And, Leesha, I have been thinking, and I have decided to go talk to somebody about my dreams and about some of the problems I have been having."

He looked back down to the floor, hoping that he was breaking through to her.

"You mean, from your time in Iraq and Afghanistan?"

Benjamin looked up at here, somewhat relieved.

"Yes," Benjamin responded, getting closer to Leesha, and grabbing her hand.

"Yes, because of that. I know that my actions have left many questions for you. I am going to talk to someone that, maybe, can help me. What would you think about that?"

Leesha wiped the tears from her eyes. She clearly looked cautious, but in all aspects, she wanted to believe her father.

"I like that idea, Dad, but it might take some time for me, okay? This just doesn't seem very real to me right now."

"Oh, believe me, honey, your mother and I know exactly what you mean. I want to thank you for trying. I will take any opportunity I can get to prove to you that I want to change, okay?"

"Okay, Dad."

Benjamin stood up and gave her a hug.

"Now let's get ready to go play some soccer."

All Natalie could do was look at her husband and her daughter, and thank God for this other chance. As Benjamin released Leesha from her hug, he and Natalie got the two boys ready for the game, then they got ready, themselves. They grabbed their soccer gear, along with some snacks, and loaded up the car. After everything was loaded, they backed out of the driveway, then took off down the street.

As they were driving, Natalie kept looking at Benjamin, smiling with contentment and shining with desire for him. Benjamin noticed her stare and smiled back at her.

"Are you okay," he asked.

"Oh, absolutely! In fact, I was just sitting here thinking that you and I might need a little rendezvous, tonight. It's been a while since we have had a date like that."

"I like that idea," Benjamin responded as he took her hand and kissed it.

"There is just one thing that I don't get," Natalie continued. "Not that it matters now, but you flew out of Tulsa. You were on your way to Los Angeles. How did you wind up at my apartment?"

Natalie was speaking soft enough to where the kids couldn't hear her. Leesha was comfortably in the back seat listening to her iPad.

"Well, after Brian dropped me off at the airport, I started really struggling with thoughts of you and the kids. I fell asleep on the plane, only to be subjected to more terrible nightmares. When the plane landed at Dallas Love Field, I began to feel very uncomfortable, but I can't explain it. I started shaking, uncontrollably, and I had to get a hold of myself."

He then looked at Natalie.

"I could not stop thinking of you. I just couldn't stop. And when I went to the next gate, we waited to board our plane to Phoenix and the flight attendant said that, due to the weather, the people going to Phoenix would have to travel through Denver. It was like, at that moment, I knew I couldn't go any further; like a sign or something. I just got up, went to an Enterprise agent, and rented a car. I just felt I had to get to you, somehow."

Natalie couldn't believe it. All she could do was look at Benjamin.

"But your orders; you had to check in to Pendleton. Weren't you taking a risk?"

"I didn't care at that point. I guess I just felt that, at that moment, my real duty was to you."

Wow!

Natalie was shocked. She knew that Benjamin loved her, but she always felt that he loved the Marines more. She didn't know what to say. Something had changed in Benjamin. She was glowing with pride.

After contemplating what he said for a couple of minutes, she realized how much he really did love her. As Natalie felt a sense of peace, she grabbed his right hand as it was resting on the middle console, holding it tight.

"Well, I'm glad you remembered where I lived."

"Actually, I didn't," Benjamin replied. "I had to stop at a local gas station to call your mother. She gave me your address, but then I had to ask the attendant there at the station for directions. That is why I was so late."

"You called my mom?"

"I did. I didn't know what else to do. Believe me, it was…it was kind of weird."

Benjamin paused for a second. In his mind, it was strange talking to Florance after she had passed away. He wanted to be careful how he communicated that to Natalie, in order not to hurt her or dig up old memories.

"I was just glad that I remembered her number. For some reason, I remembered it at the right time."

Natalie was impressed that he did all of that to get to her.

"Thank you, Benjamin. Thank you so much!"

"You are most certainly welcome!"

About that time, they pulled into the parking lot of the field that Leesha was playing at and they got out of the car, unloading their necessities. Natalie grabbed the stroller for Ben Jr., and Benjamin grabbed the soccer gear. As they all started walking toward the field, they heard a voice coming from a few cars away in the lot.

"Hey, Leesha!"

They all looked over to see who it was, and Natalie froze.

"Paige!!"

Natalie left the stroller and ran over to her. Natalie looked at her face and tried to hold back the tears. It was Paige…beautiful Paige. Natalie had to catch herself as Paige was surprised at Natalie's actions.

"Ummm…" Paige was confused, looking over at Leesha.

"Nuh-uh, girl! You're on your own," Leesha responded.

Just before Natalie could respond to Paige, she looked over to see another familiar face; one that she was very glad to see.

"Natalie, what is going on? Are you okay?"

"Julie," Natalie responded, trying to keep her composure. "Look at you, you're…you're…"

Natalie could not speak. The sight of Julie, as she was, made Natalie's heart jump.

"Natalie, what's wrong?"

"Everything's fine," Natalie responded as she wiped away a tear, trying to pull herself together. "Everything's just fine."

Julie looked confused, but Natalie was just so very glad to see her. Natalie looked over at Benjamin as he was putting the soccer gear and the chairs down on the ground. He caught her eye, smiled at her, and blew her a kiss. Natalie smiled, looked back at Julie, and grabbed her hand, firmly.

"Everything's perfect. Let's go watch our girls, and maybe I'll tell you all about it later."

Just then, William came from around their car with a handful of folding chairs of their own. Benjamin was never so happy to see him than he was at that moment.

"Hey, Ben. Do you think we got a chance against Skiatook, today?"

"Who knows," Benjamin replied, trying not to stare at William. Deep inside, Benjamin was very thankful he was there.

"One thing I've really learned, lately, is that with God, all things are possible."

William liked that answer. They both continued to talk as they walked toward the stadium. Natalie grabbed a diaper bag that Julie was trying to juggle with all the other stuff in her arms. They both walked over to their seating places, and the coach was giving the final game instructions to the girls. Benjamin helped the coach gather the girls as they prepared their final 'hoorah' before starting their warm-ups. The field intercom system came on just in time for the pregame warm-up.

"Ladies and gentlemen, welcome to the first game of the season between the Skiatook Lady Bulldogs and the Lady Jaguars of the Northern Oklahoma Association for Homeschoolers."

Several people clapped and cheered as the stadium watched the two teams warm up and get their final practice kicks in. Benjamin took a huge breath of anticipation and thankfulness as he watched Leesha take the field with Paige and the rest of the team. He looked over to Natalie and caught her eye. She blew him a kiss, and he met her kiss with a big smile.

"I love you," she spoke quietly to him, but her moving lips were enough for him to catch her message.

"I love you too," he responded.

The coach blew the whistle for final preparations. Benjamin walked with the coach to round up the girls for the final pregame motivational speech. Natalie watched as Leesha stretched, leaning on Paige. The two laughed together as they continued their warm-ups. T. J. was talking to another girl he knew, and Benjamin Jr. sat patiently and quietly in his stroller. Julie sat with William as the two flirted with each other, kissing each other gently.

Natalie thought about her mother, and how she was no longer with her. As hard as that thought was, Natalie was appreciative to be able to hug her again. She realized for, a moment, that she wasn't able to say 'good-bye' to her, again. But for some reason, that was okay. Her mother was with God, and Natalie had another chance with her, not in any way that she understood it, but…

Natalie was going to call Carmella and soon as she could. She never really realized how special Carmella really was to her. It took this experience for Natalie to understand that blessing, as well.

Most importantly, Natalie was given a second chance at her first marriage. She was content and had a new sense of love, desire, and compassion for Benjamin. There would always be problems. There would always be difficulties. But most importantly, there would always be…

Jesus.

Finally, Natalie was complete. It appeared that Ben was, too. They finally found each other.

"Thank you, Jesus," Natalie prayed, silently. "You have me right where You want me."